People in Love

CLAIRE DAVERLEY

MICHAEL JOSEPH
PENGUIN
Est. 1935

PENGUIN MICHAEL JOSEPH

UK | USA | Canada | Ireland | Australia
India | New Zealand | South Africa

Penguin Michael Joseph is part of the Penguin Random House group of companies
whose addresses can be found at global.penguinrandomhouse.com

Penguin Random House UK,
One Embassy Gardens, 8 Viaduct Gardens, London SW11 7BW

penguin.co.uk

First published 2026
003

Typeset by Six Red Marbles UK, Thetford, Norfolk
Printed and bound in Great Britain by Clays Ltd, Elcograf S.p.A.

The authorized representative in the EEA is Penguin Random House Ireland,
Morrison Chambers, 32 Nassau Street, Dublin D02 YH68

A CIP catalogue record for this book is available from the British Library

HARDBACK ISBN: 978–0–241–61459–4
TRADE PAPERBACK ISBN: 978–0–241–61460–0

People in Love

Praise For Claire Daverley

'Tender and compelling. *People in Love* is a wistful love story that grapples with the conflict between reality and idealism' Alice Winn, *Sunday Times* bestselling author of *In Memoriam*

'Claire Daverley's love stories are heartfelt, full of warmth and show the everyday intimacies that make a life' Florence Knapp, *Sunday Times* bestselling author of *The Names*

'*People in Love* is pure heartache, pure poetry, pure, brilliant moonbeam Claire Daverley. The revelations in this novel glow like opals: fiery, clear, milky, the way life is. I couldn't wait to see what would happen, even though I never wanted it to end' Catherine Newman, *New York Times* bestselling author of *Wreck*

'Yet more beautiful, lyrical, sledgehammer-to-the-heart writing. A tender and nuanced novel that you will steal away hours to read, called back by its cast of gloriously warm and flawed characters, and the ramifications of how they try to love one another' Lottie Hazell, author of *Piglet*

'*People in Love* is magnificent. Daverley writes with wisdom, kindness and humour about the glory and pain of love in all its forms' Emma Knight, *New York Times* bestselling author of *The Life Cycle of the Common Octopus*

'Quietly devastating, entirely beautiful, bruising and hopeful. In a world of compromise, Claire Daverley has created a perfect thing. *Talking at Night* takes its place amongst my all-time favourites. I implore you to read it. I'll never forget it' Chris Whitaker, *Sunday Times* bestselling author of *All the Colours of the Dark*

'A beautifully observed, tender love story with characters you really care about . . . a bit like *Normal People*. I devoured it' *Sunday Times* bestselling author Jojo Moyes

'Tender and true, this is a stunning debut with lyrical and emotional writing that reminded me at times of Sally Rooney' *Good Housekeeping*

'The story of Will and Rosie is a classic love story in every sense, and yet, in Claire Daverley's hands, it felt entirely new' Mary Beth Keane, *New York Times* bestselling author of *Ask Again, Yes*

'I absolutely adored *Talking at Night* – it should be on everyone's must-read list. Beautiful, poignant and heart-wrenching' Carley Fortune, *New York Times* bestselling author of *Our Perfect Storm*

ABOUT THE AUTHOR

Claire Daverley was born in 1991 and has been writing stories ever since she was six years old. After graduating with a degree in Fine Art from The University of Oxford, she began a career in publishing, writing about books by day but penning her own by night. Her debut novel, *Talking at Night*, has sold in over twenty languages to date, was nominated in the Debut of the Year category at the Nibbies and shortlisted for the Nota Bene prize. *People in Love* is her second novel. She lives in Scotland with her husband and spaniel.

For my mum and dad,
best friends who got married

Be patient toward all that is unsolved in your heart and try to love the questions themselves . . . Do not now seek the answers, which cannot be given you because you would not be able to live them. And the point is, to live everything. Live the questions now.

Rainer Maria Rilke

one

Nora is on the train home when Bren emails her, after months of nothing. It is the same day that Robin has asked her to marry him, and she is still dazed, and full of celebratory butter cake, and feelings she cannot quite name. Sugar down her top. Sun already set, because it is winter; dark even before she leaves work.

It is normal to go for such stretches without hearing from him. Why today, though. Why now. LIFE CHANGED, says the subject line, and Nora stares at it for a full minute before she opens the email. Train swaying from side to side as she reads.

His entire message is just a short paragraph. Something to write home about, he opens with; she can hear his voice in her head, see his freckled hands as he taps out the words. He's found a chocolate bar in New Zealand that's changed everything. Whittaker's, it's called, the Coconut Block. Big news, is she writing this down, he can't have her moving through the world for another moment without tasting it. Then he tells her about the spare room he's renting, the silhouette of the mountains in the morning, the colour of the water in the lake. He doesn't actually describe these things, because he is no poet, pretends there is no sentimentality about him. But Nora reads between the lines, as always. Glimpses the lyricism that she knows is there.

He signs off with his name, a single kiss, and Nora reads it three times while the train passes through stations that are not hers. Heartbeat slow, almost stalled.

Bren, she types back, before congratulating him on the chocolate. While she appreciates his insistence that she try some, an online search shows you can't buy it here in England, oh well, there will always be Cadburys. She keeps her message light, as ever. Does not say the things she wants to, does not ask the questions that hang in her heart like dark fruit whenever they exchange messages like this, which is not often, but often enough, before things go quiet again.

She finishes her reply just as the train slows into her stop. She mentions her mother, and his mother, as fellow commuters file for the door. Tells him about the workshop she's running next week. Tells him, too, about the storm, the train disruption, how three people have died due to the winds and the falling trees.

I don't know why we give storms names now, Nora types. That Alwen is too charming a name, surely, for something that has killed people in their own back gardens, or while they walked their dogs in the park. Living out ordinary days, until they're the opposite. Something you'd never see coming.

She does not tell him, in this email, that Robin has proposed to her.

Or, by extension, that she has said yes.

Three times, in fact. Yes, yes, yes.

–

Off the train, she climbs the stairs with the dozens of others alighting for home; jostled by damp coats and umbrellas as they cross the bridge to the ticket barriers. Into the night air, wet pavements but no rain, making her way across the car park to the small supermarket on the corner. Taking a wire basket, wandering the aisles as she muses on what to have for dinner. Has to be Robin's favourite, surely, after a day like today. Tomatoes firm in her hand, block of extra mature Cheddar. Expensive chocolate she'd usually only buy at Christmas. Hot coffee from the machine, too, which she hands to Joe on her way out, the man with the Staffie who sits by the sliding doors on a tattered blanket. Who always gives her a smile, says thanks love, with such familiarity it makes her kind of sad, because coffees change nothing, ongoing kindness seems to do nothing, except it's not nothing, her mother would argue, it's something. And the world is built on small somethings.

Her fingertips brush Joe's as she passes him the paper cup, and he says you take care now, and she says yes, you too. Lingers, scratches the soft head of his Staffie. Wanting to tell Joe – or anyone – her news. Wanting to say, my partner proposed to me today. Crazy, right. Except it's not really, seeing as we've been together for nine years, lived together for seven. Long enough that she'd not expected any huge surprises, only small ones, like the text he'd sent her, earlier that day.

Big news, Robin's message had said, at noon, interrupting her review of the spring events calendar, her tea half drunk on the desk. I'm on lunch and in the vicinity. And so she met him at the deli, the one they always liked to go to when they were both in London; would order bagels, one poppy seed, one everything, to share. He was already in the queue when she arrived. A head taller than everyone else, his dark hair hidden beneath the hat she'd knitted him to stave off the January chill. Long coat, smart shoes, because he was working for a new client that month. Or perhaps he'd dressed for the occasion. For her.

Nora thinks about this as she climbs the steady hill behind

the supermarket. Silver light from the street lamps, shopping bag heavy in her hand. How they'd found a bench by the water, looked out at the boats and buildings as people walked by, on their phones, looking at their feet. Just her and the man she shared her home with, shampoo bottles and tea bags and a corner sofa they'd picked out with the care normally reserved for children's names. Silent chewing between conversation. Crumbs on their coats, brushed from their knees.

And then it happened. He'd said he had to get back to his shoot, so he stood to hug Nora goodbye and she'd put her hands in his pockets because she was cold, and her hands brushed against something so she pulled it out and looked down at this small black leather box, and her heart swelled and her stomach plunged, like she'd fallen off something tall.

She feels that in her, now. As if it's happening all over again as she crests the station hill and turns down an alleyway. The way everything had slowed. Strangers, passing, by the river. White noise of cars, an overground train.

And she'd flipped the box open – because he didn't say she couldn't – and there was a ring, even though they'd always said there wouldn't be, that they didn't need one or agree with it necessarily, the cost and the pomp and the paperwork. But there it was. Untraditional and asymmetrical, like her eyes, an emerald stone set in gold, and she looked up at Robin and he seemed hesitant, as if he wasn't sure she was going to like it, and before he could say anything or even ask the question she had said yes, three times, and she did not think of Bren as she said it. Just as she won't think of him when anyone asks for the proposal story, which, presumably, people will.

She turns now into her street, to the large house split into two-bedroom flats. Robin is not home yet; their lower-ground flat still in darkness as Nora lets herself in, slips off her shoes, flicks the lights on. Her own shadow passing the frames on the walls as she heads for the kitchen. Heating on, windows steamed up as she boils water, slices tomatoes. A little music at first, but her thoughts are loud enough, so she's turning it off just as her fiancé – weird, wondrous – is through the door, saying sorry, sorry, there was this one shot we couldn't quite get, ah, something smells great, as he crosses the kitchen, hands on her waist. Kissing her. All other thoughts, loud or otherwise, melting away.

What a day, Robin says, his forehead on hers.

It's about to get better, she says. I'm making pomodoro.

And Robin does an actual little dance right there in the kitchen, says can he do anything, no, a quick shower then, he'll be back, and Nora nods, keeps cooking. Scatters fresh basil like confetti once he returns, and they have spaghetti then sex, in that order. Pasta simmered and devoured, richly red and flecked onto the table as they twirl their forks and relive what has happened. Bowls abandoned without washing up, slow, full-tummied move to the sofa after they've eaten. Too full for such a thing really, laughing, soft mouths, light breath. Heavy, dense warmth as he lies on top of her afterwards, her hands trailing along his back. Small crater of a scar above his coccyx.

Getting married, Robin says, as they break off the good chocolate with their fingers, later, in bed. Yes, says Nora, as she leaves the cocoa on the back of her tongue, not Whittaker's Coconut Block, but delicious, all the same.

Who'd have thought.

–

Not *me*, says Shay, the next morning at the art café. It is a Thursday, and they start early on Thursdays; host a morning qigong class before they open to the public and serve breakfast. I was thinking about it last night, Shay tells her, as she raises the blinds, grey light touching the objects on the shelves. Ceramics, dried flowers. Bronze writing implements that nobody ever buys but look alluring, all the same; Nora harbours a secret desire for the sashiko needles, gold plated and imported from Hiroshima.

No? Nora says, as she flicks on the coffee machine. Engagement ring gleaming as she does it, a strange new weight on her finger.

It shouldn't be a surprise, Shay says, but it is *because* you've been together so long. I figured you'd have done it, by now, if you were going to. And Robin's like, kind of old now.

Nora laughs, knowing that Shay would say that to his face, if he were here, which somehow makes it okay.

Is thirty-seven old?

Old enough that I figured that ship had sailed for him, Shay says. For you, too. All the hen parties we host, here? All the wedding invites you make? And you've always said you're not the least bit interested.

And I'm not, really, Nora says. She takes a duster to the shelf and sweeps around the ceramics, careful not to nudge them out of place. But I felt something, when he asked me. Out of nowhere, it just felt . . . right.

She turns on the spotlights, then, and the pot plants throw shadows around the room.

I had that with Horace, Shay says. All those years insisting I was a cat person, and then there he was, with his spindly legs and his slobbering chops and I was the proud owner of the Greatest Dane in all the land, buying squeaky toys and butternut boxes and a mattress bigger than mine.

I remember.

So soon you'll be floating down an aisle in a frothy white

dress, Shay says. Throwing tantrums about seating plans and lobbing a bouquet at me, your last single friend –

None of that, says Nora, but Shay says just you wait! Everyone *says* they want something casual and then gets swept up in diamond shoes and hand-embroidered napkins and salmon babies on crumpets.

Blinis, you mean.

So you *were* thinking about hand-embroidered napkins?

That's hardly off brand, for me, Nora says, just as the door dings open and the qigong master, Colleen, walks in, stamping the slush from her boots.

What's off brand? she asks, and Nora offers her a cappuccino; Colleen says she's a gem.

She *has* a gem, Shay declares. On her finger.

Thanks for sharing, Shay, Nora says as she pours milk into a jug, and Shay says well *you* wouldn't have said anything, and Colleen looks like she's not following, so Shay points at her own bare finger and then at Nora, who is hiding behind the coffee bar. Glint of gold, as she raises the steamer wand; a gasp, then, from Colleen.

No, she says.

Yes, says Shay. Colleen claps her hands, her leather gloves making a light smacking sound before she strides across the room, pulling Nora into an embrace.

To Robin? she says, and Nora blushes, both thrilled and embarrassed to be rammed against Colleen's breast pocket, as Shay laughs, says come on, who else?

–

Quite the normal Thursday ensues. Coffee-making, a calligraphy class. Nora sells a Jesmonite vase and some soy candles and a bouquet of dried flowers that cost more than the flowers she won't be having at her wedding. None of that, she repeats, to Shay. No white dress, no chair covers or family drama. And then it rolls round to half five, and she knows the actual drama she'll have to deal with is imminent. Robin is shooting on location, won't be back for dinner, and she has to face her mother sooner or later.

Good luck, Shay says, as she pulls on her hat and gloves, just as Robin texts her the exact same thing. Thanks, Nora says. I'll need it.

Outside, there are still Christmas lights strung above the traffic despite the fact that it's the end of January. She dawdles the short distance to the train station, buys a different ticket to usual and gets on a different train. Puts her headphones in, chews her thumbnail as she watches the lights of London melting into suburbia, going over what it is that she'll say. Then half an hour has passed and she's off the train, over the bridge, past the pub she used to get served in, underage. Flash of the time she sat so close to Bren his thigh was wedged against hers. Smell of stale smoke in the upholstery. Bag of crisps shared, salt on the film of the open packet, their friends, his friends really, laughing and joking. Salt-vinegar of their breath as they all talked until closing, the two of them alone, still talking, on the last bus home.

This same bus, right here. She sits in her preferred seat at the back and watches as the kebab shops and traffic lights give way to a mass of fields and night sky, a place with no street lights, cottage windows glowing gold. And then there is the duck pond and the village hall, the cottages she knows by name. Nora wants to stay sitting on the bus, loop back into town. But instead she thanks the driver, steps off and heads across the grass, barely acknowledging the memories that rise as she passes the swing set on the green. Summers spent scuffing their shoes on the tarmac, too grown up, then, for swinging back and forth. Watching the sunsets and the house martins. Stretching out the hours before Josie would call Bren inside, and she herself would go back to Freya, because there was no point sitting there without him.

Edge of the green, now, where there are two semi-detached cottages standing separate from the others. Shared gravel driveway, hanging baskets. Both living room windows with their curtains drawn, pink-patterned on the left, velvet on the right. Shadow of Jon in the driveway with his buckets and rags, there she is, he'd say, as she crunches past the two parked cars. Dirt and grime visible now on both bonnets in the moonlight, because he was the only one who ever cleaned them.

At the door, she lets out a long, steadying breath. Then pushes open the unlocked porch, so that her mother calls out, Josie?

It's me, Nora says, as she steps over the gardening magazines piled on the floor.

Darl! her mother cries when Nora enters the kitchen. The oven is on, the fan whirring, and the usual jam jars are everywhere, filled with pulses or pebbles, spider plants sprawling from the shelves. A lucky cat waves on the window sill as Freya glances round from her place by the sink, dressed in a carmine tracksuit, her hair tied up with a head scarf. Just you?

Robin's on location, tonight.

And to what do I owe this impromptu visit?

Oh, you know, Nora says, her heart pounding in her throat. Boredom.

Touching, Freya says. Make yourself useful then, will you? Good haul today. I nabbed some velvet shanks, would you believe! Winter chanterelles, too, and some other interesting specimens that I can't quite identify . . . could be delicious, cooked in a bit of garlic butter, *or* they could temporarily blind the poor sod who decides to eat them.

Risky, Nora says.

Worth it, I reckon, Freya says, as she holds one up to the light. They'll go nicely with dinner, if they're safe.

Oh yeah? What's cooking?

Turkey dinosaurs, her mother says, which makes Nora snort and say wow, what a throwback.

That's the second time I've heard that term this week, Freya says. Romi says it's something we should do at the hospice. Throwback Thursdays, or some such nonsense. Remind the residents of the *good times*.

What's wrong with that?

What's *wrong* is all they bloody do is sit in their beds and throw back! They're dying, for Pete's sake. Lying there just *waiting* for death. We don't need a day marked for throwing back to the good times; we should make this day, this very moment, a *good time*.

They both reach for the same mushroom, fingers touching; her mother's scratched from foraging, Nora's calloused from her sewing.

Seize the moment, Freya goes on, as Nora chooses another. Let them live, because lord knows people don't, before they realise they won't be able to. Eat the cake. Drink the champers. Fart long and recklessly between the bed sheets, which some of them do, mind.

Nora knows this is funny; knows she should laugh. Instead she scrubs harder at her mushroom so that it comes apart in her hand, splits the soft cap from the stalk.

On that, Nora says.

Farting between the bed sheets?

No, she says, and she does laugh at that, a little; Freya too, the sound fluttering, like a shuffle of papers. I, uh. Have something to tell you.

Freya doesn't look at her; keeps scouring. Nora takes a

breath, but then her mother cuts across her, says she's sensing that this is a moment for the greenhouse.

No, it's not, Nora says. It's fine.

Don't fight it, darl. Sanctuary awaits.

Freya, I –

Your wellies are where you left them. Let's go and be with the tomatoes.

I don't need to be with the tomatoes! Nora says, but Freya is already out of the kitchen, pulling on her gardening shoes in the utility room and wrenching the door open. It's ruddy freezing, she calls out. Grab your coat!

Nora looks at herself in the dark glass of thc kitchen window and sighs. Her mother had always insisted on having emotional conversations somewhere grounding – somewhere you could step outside of yourself, be at one with the earth. Feel your emotions, yes, but only somewhere sealed off, and appropriate. So she shrugs on her coat and follows her out, pulling on her once-fuchsia, never-before-cleaned wellington boots. The oak tree looms at the end of the garden, fanned black against the night. The river flowing beyond it, silent and unseen. Stars out, now. Rain threatening.

Nora braces herself, ducks into the greenhouse – which is heated, through the winter – and Freya slides the door shut.

Now, she says, taking her hands. Close your eyes, daughter of mine, and breathe with me. In through the nose, out through the nose, that's it. And again. Now, isn't that better?

Nora knows it is best to go with it. Keeps her clammy hands in her mother's rough ones, breathes as she is told to. The sodium lamps are off. The greenhouse smells verdant, a little damp. The tomato plants are –

Frey, Nora says. What's wrong with your tomatoes?

You're supposed to have your eyes closed!

But they look –

Like a Kandinsky painting, I thought? But don't be taken in by aesthetics, Nora. It's Spotted Wilt. A killer, if you don't step on it post-haste.

So have you –

Nora, her mother says, an edge to her voice now. The tomatoes are fine. I am fine. Are you not fine? Because I'm sensing something's off.

Light filters through the greenhouse from the back door, everything dim and shadowy, like a high-grain photograph. Nora looks at her mother, dirt streaked on her brow; her vegetables all around them, hanging like baubles in the silver-gold light.

I'm engaged, Nora tells her, her hands still clasped tight in her mother's.

Freya stares at her.

Robin asked me to marry him yesterday, Nora says. And I said yes.

There is a moment where neither of them moves, her words landing like the rain tapping, now, on the glass roof. Then Freya lets go of Nora's hands, steps back and yanks on a chain so that a bulb douses them in light. She turns, then, picks up some small secateurs and starts snipping at leaves; the ones with the deadly disease, Nora assumes.

So what d'you think, Nora says, watching her mother's elbows, hearing the snap of stems as she works.

Clearly, Freya says, it doesn't matter what I think.

Don't do this, Nora says.

Do what? Respond when you've asked me a question?

I know how you feel about marriage, Nora says, but I –

Are seemingly *quite* happy to squeeze yourself into the outdated box of wifedom, yes! Wear virginal white, vow to obey him, be bound to him forevermore because that's what capitalism – nay, our white male *governments* – demand of us all?

I love him, Freya. He loves me.

And isn't that enough? Why marry him at all? I thought you didn't *want* to get married.

You didn't want me to get married, Nora muses, but does not say. Thinking back to the fairy tales she was never read, as a child. How she was lectured on women's rights when most girls were watching *Cinderella* or *Snow White*, which was *not fair*, she'd shout, stamping up the stairs. What's not fair, Freya would shout after her, is that unavoidable something called the patriarchy!

But there are other memories too, Nora knows, from this greenhouse, and their cottage, behind it. The paintings she'd made, with her mother's encouragement. Not allowing her a phone, in case she got brain cancer, which meant she spent her adolescence outside or making things, instead of scrolling on a screen. The women-only meditation groups and book clubs that had, in turn, inspired her own events programme at the art café she set up with Shay, and something softens inside of her, at the thought. At the stubborn movements of her mother's hands, not even two decades older than hers; after Freya fell pregnant at sixteen, and left home; left her Catholic parents, and everything she'd known, just so she could keep her. Give Nora a life.

I guess I just . . . changed my mind, Nora says, gently. There is another long silence, and her mother lets out a humph.

Did you just *humph*, Nora says. A pause, more snipping. But then her mother breathes through her nose; half laughter, half snort, but before she can respond, more light floods forward from next door; Josie's back door opening, the gate connecting their gardens swinging backwards.

Freya! Josie calls out, her voice carrying across the night air. Freya, how're the tomato plants?

Fine, Jose, Freya says. Just fine, with a bit of pruning, like I told you.

I've been reading up about it, Josie says, who is a soft shadow now through the mottled walls, the glass thick with algae. Apparently the best thing to do is remove all of the infected plants. *All* of them, not just the leaves.

I do know this, Josephine.

Well I saw your greenhouse light on and thought I best come and tell you. I've got the web page up on my phone; I could read it out to you, if you like. There's a whole *Gardeners' World* page on it. It's ever so good. Ever so informative.

Freya doesn't respond; carries on snipping.

Hi, Josie, Nora pipes up, and there is a startled pause.

Nora? Sweetheart!

We were having a greenhouse moment, Freya says, and there is a beat of silent panic before Josie asks why, what's wrong?

Nothing's wrong, says Nora.

I beg to differ, Freya says.

Robin's asked me to marry him, Nora says, to another startled beat, but then Josie lets out a coo, like a collared dove.

Oh, *Nora*! That's wonderful!

And *that's* a normal reaction, Nora says to Freya, as her mother's friend hurries round to the greenhouse door. Nora slides it back to see her smiling face, her slender frame draped in a shawl. Mist of rain above her.

I'm so happy, Josie tells her, clasping Nora's wrists as though she truly means it, in spite of everything. In spite of her husband dying so suddenly, more than a decade ago. Her only son leaving, never to return. Pills she has to take, daily, lined up on her window sill, a cocktail of drugs she will never stop needing that keep her confined to the house, keep her from becoming fixated on abnormal things, keep her life small and solitary and contained. And yet she is overflowing, it seems, with this moment, this joy that is not even hers, beaming at Nora as if she's her own daughter, as if this is her own wonderful news, and Nora swallows all the feeling this stirs up in her as she says me too, Josie. Me too.

–

Well, Freya says, back in the kitchen. I suppose it's an excuse to wear a giant hat.

Josie is taking down three glasses from a shelf, and Nora is putting the now-clean mushrooms into a Tupperware. You do rock a hat, Nora says.

Don't butter me up, Freya says, and when Josie looks confused, Nora explains that her feminist free spirit might as well be dead, now she's engaged. Freya snorts, but when Josie still looks nonplussed, she says, *marriage*, Josephine! It's just not for me.

Something burns, briefly, in Nora's stomach; at how her mother can say this to Josie, of all people. But Josie doesn't react, as if she's barely noticed. Nora often wonders if this is how they've remained such good friends; Freya, able to say what she wants, unfiltered, and Josie, so often oblivious, letting it slide.

So did he get down on one knee, Josie asks Nora, handing her a water glass.

No, Nora says. We were outside, by the river. On our lunch break.

How *love*ly. Jon proposed to me outside, did I ever tell you that? Up a hill, somewhere.

More burning, then, a twist in her gut. Nora puts down her glass and turns around, pulls out knives and forks just as Freya opens the oven door, steam expelling in a cloud. Hot tray slid outwards, hiding her face. But the moment passes.

Josie is talking about garden birds, now. Nora's news has been acknowledged and left behind, just like anything else in Josie's world, and rather than disappointing, this feels like a relief. Because it's no big deal, like Freya might make it out to be. People get married all the time; it requires no justification to herself, or to her mother, or to old friends she's not seen in years.

I put out the Niger seed, Josie is saying, and would you believe it, the goldfinch came back. All five of them. D'you know they're called a charm, when they're in a group?

Really, Nora says, though Josie's told her this countless times.

I've not seen the bullfinch for a while, though. And I do worry about him. When it's been this long.

Nora hears this, and doesn't respond as she lays down three sets of cutlery at the table.

Oh, I won't be staying, pet, Josie says, but Freya demands that she join them, come on. But I already had my soup, at six, Josie says, as though that settles it.

Wait, Nora says, catching sight of the tray on the side. I thought you were joking about the turkey dinosaurs?

Why would I joke about such a delicacy? Freya says, dislodging a stegosaurus with her spatula.

Aren't you a vegan, these days?

I am! And as part of a varied diet of self-care and plant-based intentions, they're a once-in-a-blue-moon treat. Plus tonight is the Wolf Moon, which counts. I might even add the mushrooms to the side salad.

The mushrooms that could end up blinding us?

I thought they'd add a certain beige thrill, yes.

I think, Josie says, with a sip of her water, that's my cue to leave.

Freya says suit yourself; waves her off. Nora waits, then follows her without a word. Through the hallway, then porch, saying her name in the driveway. Nora! Josie says, turning from her own front door. You'll catch your death!

It's okay, Nora says. I just wanted to . . .

The moon hangs above them, shining behind the branches of the birch on their shared lawn. Josie watches her, the orb reflected in her eyes.

It's great that Robin's proposed, Nora tells her. Obviously.

Really lovely, Josie agrees, and Nora nods, says yes, but she'd really like her not to say anything to Bren, yet, until she can tell him herself, although she does not say this last part, because it is a stupid, unexplainable thing to want to say; and also because it's a lie, seeing as she'd had the chance to tell Bren, just recently, over email, and she hadn't.

Josie, though, is still watching her. The rain has stopped, now, the night fresh and cold. Frost due on the ground by morning.

Do you think, Nora says, instead, her heart slow. Do you think Freya will be okay with it, once it's all – sunk in?

Josie's cottage door stands half open, her hand on the frame; wedding ring agleam on her left knuckle, as she studies Nora's face.

Yes, pet, Josie says. It might just be . . . a surprise, at first.

No wind, or noise. Shadow of the swing set behind them on the green.

But if you're happy, Josie says, then that's all that will matter, in the end.

She takes her hand off the door and rests it on Nora's arm. Just lightly. Like a moth landing there.

Have you heard from him lately, she asks, and Nora's heart does not stop, at the question, but keeps beating, slow, slow, slow.

No, she says, but then, well, yes, but just over email. Have you?

A sigh from Josie, small and sad in the moonlight. Shake of her head.

I'm sure you will soon, Nora says. He's just moved into a new place, in New Zealand, he said. He's probably just settling in.

Your dinner will be getting cold, pet, Josie says. Send Robin my love, won't you?

And Nora nods; waits for Josie to step inside and close her door against the dark, then returns to her mother's cottage, something sinking in her, or perhaps thawing. Wondering if it could somehow be both.

two

We should have a party, Robin says.

A party, Nora repeats, from her place by the hob. She is frying onion, steaming up the windows as the rain falls outdoors. First week of February, now, and the frost is long gone; more rain, again, near relentless. Higher winds.

Isn't a wedding a party in itself? she asks as she adds more oil, turns up the heat. Robin calls her a joy thief. She calls him a joy addict.

Shared smiles, then. Cooking smells.

All I'm thinking is a wedding's expensive, Robin says. And takes years to plan.

Does it have to?

Well, I suppose not. But we could have a warm-up act, first. Celebrate this moment, right now. Carpe diem!

You're very spontaneous these days, Nora says, and he says he knows, it's his middle name. Or at least, he wishes it was. It's far more inspiring than Brian.

Nora laughs. Tips a packet of spring greens into the wok.

I think it'd be great, Robin goes on. We could host it here, keep it simple.

He pulls his notebook out from his back pocket; a folded leather journal he carries everywhere. Engagement party, he narrates, elongating the vowels as he says it, and writes the words. First up, he says, the guest list.

Nora adds water chestnuts to the pan, starts mixing soy sauce with sesame oil as Robin reels off the names of their friends. Old colleagues. Art school peers they've kept in touch with. Shay, Jin. Henry who runs the bakery down the road. And family, he says. All of mine, and Freya and Josie, of course.

I doubt they'll come, Nora says.

We should invite them, all the same, he says.

More lines in his notebook, muted agreement in Nora's throat. The wind outside flecking rain at the window. Ginger paste added, one teaspoon, when Robin says oh, hey, what about Bren?

The oil spits; stings Nora's skin.

What, she says, as if she hasn't heard the question.

Would you want to invite Bren?

Um, Nora says, as the sauce continues to spit; she turns down the heat. I don't even know where he is right now, she says, and then wonders why she is saying this, when she does. Maybe New Zealand, actually. Which is a bit of a way to come, I reckon, for prosecco and pizza.

Robin, who is still scrawling in his notebook, looks up. Pizza?

I was thinking Alessandro's, she says.

Yes, Nora, Robin says. *That's* why I'm marrying you.

She smiles, again. The flame on the hob still too high.

Prosecco, though? Robin asks.

Isn't that what people drink at engagement parties?

I think they drink whatever they want to drink.

Rum cocktails, then, Nora says. And red wine.

And olives! Robin says. The really good ones in the green can.

Don't they cost the earth?

You only get engaged once, Nora, he says. Twice, max, he

adds, which was a joke she saw coming, but she laughs all the same. Ignores the fridge magnets that Bren has sent her over the years, as she opens the door for the beansprouts. They're the one thing she can rely on him for; magnetic reminders that he still exists, after they'd once shared a bedroom wall, a school bus, long, lazy summers dangling their feet in the river. All that reduced to an ad hoc parcel in the post, the occasional glitching video call, are you there? I've lost you. When did I lose you? Things she's asked herself, privately, away from a screen, as well. When she's staring out the train window after a long day at work. Or if Robin's working late so she's taking a bath, staring at the flicker of a scented candle and thinking about things she tries not to. As she reaches, now, for a bell pepper, redder than Bren's hair, as Robin goes on listing the other people who are still present in their lives; Jemima, Gaya and Jack.

–

Robin wants an engagement party, she texts Shay later that night. She's sitting at her craft table, littered with fabric swatches and calligraphy pens. Threads in black and cream and taupe, wound into an old shortbread tin.

It begins! Shay replies, after three waving dots. Are you hiring a hall, wearing a diamanté dress and coming up with a pun-worthy hashtag?

Three middle finger emojis from Nora. Laughing emoji from Shay.

We're just hosting it here, Nora explains. I'm making the invitation right now; photo, then, of her desk, the blank page. Are you free, she asks, the last Saturday in Feb?

If I can bring a date, Shay says.

Horace won't fit in our flat.

Then I'll need to think about it, Shay says. More laughing emojis, then. Course, she says. Any excuse to spend some time with your barmy mother.

Hey, Nora texts back. She doesn't like being called mother.

Jokes, and deliberate lightness; warmth, in Nora's gut, alongside that tight twist, again, as if someone's wringing out her abdomen.

She puts her phone down and pulls a sheaf of paper towards her. Grabs a fine line pencil and writes something in elegant, looping font. Nora and Robin, she writes. Sitting in a tree. She draws some little trees, along the bottom, but no. Not right. New sheet of paper.

Nora and Robin, she tries again: PARTY PEOPLE.

But that's not them, either; it's undermining this thing they have planted, in a way that feels wrong to her, now. Years they'd spent, saying they did not care for marriage or weddings or being husband and wife – but now it is a choice they've made, and something to be sincere about.

Nora and Robin, she writes, are engaged.

There.

She outlines it in ink, chooses her darkest blue, the colour of late nights and deep waters. Once satisfied, she writes a smaller sentence: *there will be pizza*, above the date: a Saturday night three weeks from now, the address of their flat beneath. Then she takes it across the hall and hands it to Robin who looks up from his own work and says it looks stellar, that *she's* stellar, his star. He turns it into a digital file on his laptop and the next day Nora sends it to all of their friends and her mother and Josie and even, in a moment of wild, hot abandon, to Bren, in an email she is fairly certain he will not read for months. And then she returns to her day.

–

A fortnight, then, of planning. Prepping, ordering pizzas for forty people, is that too much garlic bread, *is* there such a thing as too much garlic bread? Valentine's love hearts and teddies and roses in the windows as she walks to work; a candle-making workshop at the café, coffees made, spilled, mopped up, a drawing exhibition with Shay, one evening.

Another night spent with her mother when Robin is out late with work.

Braised chickpeas for dinner, passing comment about how she won't be coming to the party, you don't mind, do you darl, in case something happens next door, because Josie won't come, can't leave the house, as we all know, best not. And Nora nods with the chickpeas mushed in her mouth and says sure, even though Freya goes to work at the hospice every day – some nights, even, when she's working the late shift – and Josie is just fine, which *actually* means Freya doesn't want to mark her engagement, and that's fine, too, but still Nora feels something small and sharp lodged inside her, like the grit that got stuck under her palm when she fell off her bike, once, in the driveway. Feels it, still, as she gets into her childhood bed that night, the wall still plastered with art postcards, Rothko, Kahlo and Sheila Hicks, *colour is in my blood*.

A dreamcatcher, in the window.

And her final thought, before she drifts off, is of knocking on the wall to see if Bren would knock back, and when she wakes for a moment she is sixteen and her first thought is to wonder if he's awake, too, on the other side. But then she is actually awake and thirty-one years old, and Robin has messaged her, overnight. Said he's home. Said he misses her. Said can she pick up some ginger ale, for the cocktails, on her way home?

Sure, she says. Dresses for work, checks her emails on the train.

Still no reply from Bren.

–

A week later, and she's wearing a satin dress and embroidered waistcoat. Something she'd made at art school as a wannabe textile artist, darned with abstract shapes and large pockets. Applies eyeliner, though she rarely wears make-up, blusher not needed, when she's naturally rosy-cheeked. Some occasions call for a little effort, though, and agreeing to marry your partner of nine years, she thinks, is one of them.

Nora has decorated the flat with fairy lights. Robin has made a playlist. They have revised the pizza order three times and she's panic-bought more crisps and made an installation of Polaroid photographs; memories, captured, with all of the friends who have RSVP'd for tonight – a surprisingly large number – pegged onto a stretch of string in the living room, for people to take home after the party.

WEDDING CHEESE, Shay said, when Nora had mentioned the idea. This is a strong Cheddar, on the cheese scale. I'll let you know when you reach ripe levels of Camembert.

But Nora didn't mind. Has always been partial to a cheeseboard.

It looks marvellous, Robin says now, wrapping his hands around Nora's waist from behind and resting his chin on her shoulder. It is an hour before the party starts and he has shaved and smells good, of oakmoss and sandalwood, the cold night air, where he's had the bathroom window open. They straighten cushions, drape more lights, have to stop themselves eating all the olives, and then the doorbell chimes an hour early.

Who on earth, Nora says.

Probably my cousin Pete, says Robin. Never been to a party in his life.

That's so sad, Nora says.

You'll feel less sad when you meet him, Robin says, but when he opens the door it is Freya, laden with cotton tote bags. I'm not staying, she says. I've just brought some essentials, for the Bloody Marys.

The Bloody Marys? Robin says, following her into the kitchen as she rustles past him in the hallway.

You can't have a party without Bloody Marys, she says, unpacking her home-grown tomatoes onto the kitchen side. Remember to add more Tabasco than you think, she says over her shoulder, like I showed you. Don't skimp.

Stay for one, won't you, Freya? Robin says, but she waves her hands and says she has to get back, she's making a beetroot stew, said she'd have Josie over, for tea. She sends her love, and some shortbread, by the way; Robin says score.

Her mother has high spots of pink on her cheeks, just like Nora, as she hands over the box. Then she bundles her emptied bags into the pocket of her wax jacket and troops back to the front door, says well now, have a good night, but before she can leave Nora says her name, catches her hand in her own.

Thank you, she says to her mother.

Tabasco, Freya says, squeezing her hand. And then she's gone, and Nora turns to Robin who shrugs, says she's unpredictable, we'll give her that. He turns up the music while Nora blends the tomatoes in the kitchen, a pre-party drink for the two of them, and he kisses her after a single sip, spice on their lips, long and slow and tingling, when the doorbell rings once more and then there are people in their living room.

–

Robbbbiiiiiin, again, and again. His friends, his family. Mutual friends, too. High fives, brief hugs, she's finally making an honest man of him, all the things she knew were coming but has nothing to say to, and as the flat fills up she is more and more aware that her own people are missing. Jon, dead: Josie, housebound: Freya, disapproving. Her own grandparents and father unaware of her existence, even, not that this bothers her, just comes up, like this, when she least expects it; and her oldest friend, her *best* friend she thinks, still – stupid, really – silent over email, despite the invite, but then Shay arrives with a bottle of red and a fiery-peach flower crown. There! she says, adjusting it on Nora's head. You're not a proper bride-to-be unless you're wearing ranunculus. And before you say it, this is like, really mild on the cheese scale.

Is it ranunculus or ranunculi, Nora asks, tilting one of the stems out of her eyes, and Shay says who cares, you look hot, in a sort of whimsical, fairy queen kind of way. Like what's-her-name.

Titania?

No, the one with the rabbit heart. Frozen in the headlights.

You mean Florence?

I have no idea, Shay says, but real talk, Nora, *when* is the pizza getting here? I'm starved. And I'll be taking leftovers for Horace, by the way, who is distraught that he's not here. I left him gazing out of the window, pining, and I plan to get wildly pissed to block out the pain.

Be my guest, Nora says, gesturing to the drinks table.

People pour in and mingle. Graze on the crisps, fawn over the snacks that Nora prepared herself. Olives with anchovies and green chillies; tomato and onion crostini cracked with black pepper. Wine, full-bodied and dusky, one glass, two, another bottle opened then another, it's only half seven and she's four drinks in. Dancing, too, because they'd pushed back the furniture. Shots! someone suggests, because they're in their thirties and clawing back at their youth and it is loud and warm despite the cold outside and there are a lot of hugs and cheek kisses and Nora needs some air after too many drinks, face hot and flushed, her heart full and somewhat panicky. She's always been a lightweight.

In the bathroom she splashes water on her face, swears when it smears her eyeliner. Walls spinning, realising how drunk she is now she's alone. Shower head dripping. Hand towel rough on her palms, Josie's towels are always so soft, she uses an entire bottle of fabric softener per wash, Freya berates her for it, think of the *environment*, Jose, all those chemicals in the seas, but my towels aren't going in the sea, are they, Josie says, Freya's head, then, in her hands. Nora's own hands dry, now, as she stares at herself in the mirror. Emotions high, tonight, and happy, yes, but with a melancholy for what was, because a new chapter means the current chapter is ending, and she sort of doesn't want it to. She's just tired, though, probably. Just hungry.

Glance at her watch, then, because the pizza is due any minute. And then right on time the doorbell rings, she says yesssss, under her breath: laughing to herself as she escapes the bathroom, because she's thirty-one and excited about dinner. There are people singing in the living room, a drink spilled, dark and wet on the carpet as she unlatches the front door and swings it open and there, on her doorstep, is someone who is not delivering pizza.

She stares at him. At his flare of red hair.

At his pale skin and green eyes.

And he smiles, a little. Like he always has; shy, almost, like he's unwilling to show his teeth; like he is figuring things out, first, waiting to see how things might go.

Bren, Nora says. Still staring.

Hey, Nora, he says, and time, for one long, immobile scene, stops, as if with the flick of a switch.

–

He looks the same. Except he doesn't. His face is thinner, his cheekbones stretching the skin as though he needs a good meal, like he's been up before dawn for years, or is jet-lagged, or hungover, or both. White T-shirt, cargo trousers low on his hips. Muscles on his arms, defined but not with weightlifting or gym visits, not as though he makes the effort. He never had to make the effort, with anything.

There is a small gold hoop in his left ear.

A stain, like suncream, on his neckline.

And his hair is as red as she remembers. The colour of mandarins. Shorter than it used to be, when he used to sculpt it with his hands, checking it in shop windows or car wing mirrors as they passed, withstood her gentle mockery about that, didn't care.

Bren Ferguson.

The boy who walked out on her, and their plans, and his mother. The boy who is no longer a boy, but a man, and she, a woman, with *new* plans, her own life, but she feels it all behind her, for that one stilled, suspended moment – a party with music Robin had chosen, snacks she had prepared, friends celebrating a choice they had made – and all of it feels like a vague sort of nothing as she steps out of the flat and closes the door behind her and leans her body against it and says his name, again, her heart rushing, now, after the initial freeze, everything kicked back into full speed.

–

Bren, she says.

You already said that, he tells her.

What are you doing here?

Street lights behind them, orange like his hair. Dark shadow of trees on the other side of the street. Nora squints at him, wishing she was sober, and Bren grins, properly this time, that crooked break of a smile that moves something in her, a slow, upward sensation, like a trap door lifting.

You invited me, didn't you?

I didn't think you'd actually . . . come, Nora says.

Well, surprise, Bren says, and he lifts one shoulder in a shrug, the way he used to when they were teenagers, and the familiarity of that gesture does something to her; the shock of having him here, in front of her, melts away. She begins to feel other things. Elation, and disbelief: two things at once, hot despite the cold February air.

I can't believe you're here, she says.

Same, Bren says, and he's still grinning. They stand opposite one another for a second longer but then he steps forward to touch her, hug her, maybe, and Nora knows she should do the same but she's feeling too much and so ends up holding out her hand to stop him, which instead turns the whole thing into an awkward, half-missed high five. They sort of clasp hands and knock shoulders before she steps back, sorry, him too, sorry, someone singing loudly from the living room where Robin must be. *Robin*, she thinks, likely wondering where she is – and she is going to turn away when Bren says her name.

Steps closer again.

So close now, that if she were to inhale, she would be able to smell him; the suncream, the sweat and sleeplessness from the plane. He reaches a hand towards her, says it's okay, which he's probably saying because she feels like crying, or is crying, maybe, she's trying not to.

She looks at his hand, reached out towards her, like that. Doesn't take it in her own.

And then a car mounts the kerb and the pizza is here, and Bren turns at the sound of the engine, drops his arm. Both of them standing there as the guy gets out in his branded polo shirt and baseball cap. Says Robin's name, which sees her pulse skitter with alarm, or guilt, but he was simply the one who placed the order, so she says yes, and the guy opens the car boot and begins to ferry pizza boxes down the garden path, and Bren moves forward to help. So Nora opens the front door, says in there, please, the door to the right, and the pizza is carried in, towers of it, and she hears people cheer when it enters the living room, and in all the chaos and excitement and after paying the delivery guy and taking a breath she is back inside with the fug and the noise of the party, and Bren is there, too. Already eating pizza with her friends, Robin's friends. And somehow they've sidestepped their chance for a proper hello, the need for introductions, and there is no moment of truth or understanding, after all the years she had pictured seeing him again; there is simply garlic bread, an array of dips in plastic pots, and someone turning up the music and announcing that *now*, people, it's a party.

–

Why do you look like you've never seen a pizza before, Shay asks her, as they stand by the living room door.

What, Nora says, as she watches Bren lift the cap off a beer. Robin, feet from him, with his hand on someone's shoulder, laughing his great Robin laugh, his shirt black and gold like the song that's playing.

What's up with you, Shay asks.

More friends, then, in front of them, eating pizza, asking

to see her ring. Wow, Nora, it even looks like you, then Robin is there with a slice in his hand just for her. Saying he saw she was pizza-less, and that was just wrong. Arm around her waist, kiss on her temple. Marry her already, someone says, and he guffaws, says shall we?

Robin, Nora says.

Yeah?

There's –

But then his brother is tugging him onto the makeshift dance floor and Robin is calling back to her, come dance, Nora, and she says she'll just – points at her pizza – the introduction dried in her throat. Bren is talking to some of her art school friends, now. Back turned, his neck bronzed with sun, trailed in a black twine necklace like the one she gave him for his birthday, years ago. Surely not the same one.

Who's the guy, Shay asks her, handing her a glass of wine. Nora takes a mouthful, swallows, says who?

The one you're pretending not to look at?

More wine, to hide the red in her cheeks.

No one, she says, when she lowers her glass. Just my old neighbour, Bren.

Shay's own lips are stained red with wine, her teeth mauve, like her hair.

The one who travels, and does nothing?

It's not *nothing*, Nora says. He works in outdoor centres and stuff.

You didn't say he was coming!

I didn't know.

Hair brushed behind her ear. The rest of her pizza eaten, steadying, the warm dough, salt of the soft melted cheese. So why don't you go say hi, Shay says, and Nora nods, says she should. She will.

Doesn't move.

Shay frowns, puts down her wine glass. Says come on, and grabs her elbow.

No, Nora says, Shay, I don't – but instead of dragging her towards Bren, Shay steers her out of the room, past friends talking in the hall, past the bathroom where there is a short queue of people waiting; out through the kitchen into the bricked backyard. Two people smoking by the gate. The stars are out, the night fresh. Feels cool on Nora's too-warm skin.

Talk to me, Shay says.

There's nothing to talk about, Nora says, tweaking a flower that's flopped into her face.

I know you better than you think, Shay says, and I can tell you have something going on in that quiet heart of yours.

How can a heart be quiet?

See! You're deflecting! And you look like you're going to cry and you can't do that at your own engagement party, Nora. It's too tragic.

The moon shines above them, half concealed by the rooftop. Steady drip of prior rain from the clogged gutters as Nora folds her arms, music carrying through the closed back door. *Chelsea Dagger*, rowdy, hollering.

I just didn't expect to see him, Nora says. Bren, I mean.

And that matters because . . .?

Nora exhales, her breath silver on the air. It doesn't, she says. You're right. It's been a while, that's all. I'm just . . . thrown.

Shay regards her.

Does he hold a candle for you, she says, and if Nora was still drinking her wine she'd spit it out, droplets spraying, ludicrous, laughable. Instead, glad of the darkness in the yard as her cheeks glow afresh, she says no! No. He was – is – my best friend. Aside from you.

Good save.

Our mothers are close, Nora says. We're still. You know.

Shay waits.

In touch, Nora says, with a shrug. She can see people drifting into the kitchen through the glass of the back door, looking for more crisps or wine.

I should, she says, nodding inside. But you're right, Shay. We're friends. It's a nice, normal thing that he's here. I should go and talk to him.

She is still looking at the back door, at the square of gold light through the glass. At the people she knows. The people she expected to see.

No candles here, she says, and Shay nods. Says cool.

Back inside, they get caught talking to more friends, but eventually she's in the lounge again, only to see Bren in the corner with one of Robin's cousins. Her arm on his. Him, saying something into her ear. And so instead of going to talk, Nora goes to Robin, who is waving at her from the dance floor, shirt unbuttoned now as he jives to *Night Fever*. Pulling her towards him, twirling her under his arm, everyone cheering, looking at the two of them.

Almost everyone.

Her heartbeat high.

—

Midnight comes, and most people have left. Robin got pleasantly drunk and is asleep on the sofa, danced out and wearing only one shoe. Stragglers kiss the top of his head as they filter out and Nora says goodbye to them at the door, more hugs, more congrats. Shushing them as they make noise down the street, worried about the neighbours, though most of them, in all fairness, had been at the party. Robin's doing. That ability he has, to befriend pretty much anyone. And then she closes the door and is left alone in the hall. Soft lamplight from the living room, as she leans her head against the wood. Breathes out.

Bren must have left at some point, while she was dancing or mingling, wondering how to play this and not looking his way.

She can't believe he did that, she thinks.

Can't believe she let him.

But she latches the door, straightens her waistcoat. In the living room Robin is snoring lightly and she picks up a few dropped olives off the carpet, gathers empty glasses to take to the kitchen. Down the hall, through the doorway, when her heart stops.

Because he did not leave.

He is there, standing in her kitchen with his back to her. Tanned neckline, laced-up boots. Opening a drawer before closing it, then rolling open another.

Looking for something? she says, and at her voice, Bren pauses. Slides the drawer shut, turns around.

I was just, he says.

Snooping?

She puts the glasses down and Bren clears his throat. A noise that Nora has heard only over the phone, or on a lagging video call, for so long. Something simmers inside of her, like olive oil left on a low heat.

She looks at him looking at her. Sees the pendant around his neck.

Shall we start over, Bren says, and there's a lightness in his voice.

Start over, she repeats.

Tonight, she wonders, or back twelve years.

From across the room, he half shrugs again with just the one shoulder, easy-going, nonchalant. Waiting for her to go first. Standing there with the shadows beneath his eyes, the magnets he'd sent her scattered behind him on the fridge door. Same smile. Same freckles on his neck. As if, like she'd said earlier to Shay in the yard, this is entirely normal.

I know I invited you, Nora says, but you didn't *reply*. You didn't say anything.

Just like you didn't, Bren shoots back. No heads-up that you were getting married. Just a jpeg file, attached to an email.

Colour travelling up her throat, at that.

Midnight black outside the kitchen window.

Which is fine, Bren says. Obviously.

He shrugs again, with two shoulders now, and looks so unconcerned that Nora wonders if she should be, too.

I wasn't being accusatory, she says, attempting a lightness of her own. I'm just confused, that's all. Did you come back just for . . . I mean . . .

She rubs her arm, wishing she hadn't drunk so much at the start of the night; wishing she didn't feel so tongue-tied in his presence. Wishing she could pin this feeling, this slow-motion bass of her heartbeat, solely on too much alcohol.

Of course, Bren says. This is you, Nora. And this is a . . . big deal.

A bigger deal than your dad's funeral? she says, but as soon as she does, she wishes she hadn't, because something changes in his face. That ease of him dropping, like a curtain. Shutters brought down, locked up for the night.

I didn't mean, she begins, but he says no, he gets it. He . . . thought it would be a nice thing, showing up like this. But clearly he's read this all wrong.

No, she says. It's –

I'm gonna go, he says, and he walks out the kitchen so she's left looking at the empty wine glasses and the fridge magnets, the space where he had just been standing, thinking no, this isn't right. She has pictured their reunion many times over the years, and this is not it. This is not how it's supposed to go.

Bren, she says, as she follows him down the hall, music still playing, her fiancé, she assumes, still sleeping. This is stupid. You came all this way.

And you're right, Bren says. It was stupid.

It wasn't, Nora says, a note of urgency in her voice as he tries to unlatch the front door. It was just – unsettling! You didn't talk to me, all night.

You didn't talk to me, either.

So you didn't talk because I didn't talk?

I flew across the world to be here, Nora.

So shouldn't crossing the room be the easy part?

She is forcing humour into her words now; pleading with him, to see, come on, isn't this funny?

But Bren releases the latch, says he's jet-lagged, and she's, you know. Got a life, here. He shouldn't have sprung this on her.

No, you shouldn't've, Nora says, but it doesn't mean I want you to leave. I just – she holds up her palms – would've liked some notice, Bren, that's all. I printed Polaroids of everyone. I didn't print you a Polaroid.

I don't care about the Polaroids, Nora, Bren says.

Where are you staying? she asks, slightly desperate, now, as he opens the front door. He's left his expedition rucksack – the one he'd owned as a teenager, would pack for hiking weekends with his dad – propped against the wall of the flat. He lifts it onto his back, the street deserted, now. All of her other friends long gone.

I'll figure it out, Bren says. A hostel, maybe.

There aren't any hostels in suburban Hertfordshire, Nora tells him, and before she knows she will offer, she says stay here. We can have breakfast, in the morning. We can talk, properly, you can meet –

But it is her turn to falter as Bren clips his bag straps around his waist, still not looking at her. Sorry, Nora, he says, and he truly sounds it. Sorry I messed up.

And does he mean now, or does he mean then, and it is like a needle being pushed through her heart as he turns to walk down the path.

Bren, she says, a wild note in her voice, and to her surprise, he turns. Eyes on hers again, that nothingness – so practised, so calm – in his face.

Is that it, she asks him.

He stands there, looking at her. Weeds pushing through the concrete at his feet. Overgrown grass, cars mounted on the kerb. No one awake. No one watching.

And he unclips his bag and drops it to the ground and moves forward and kisses her, right there, on the night of her engagement party, with her fiancé – her good, generous, desirable fiancé – asleep inside, just feet from them. And he tastes how she'd always expected, of strawberries, and summer, and her hands go to his hair and it is thick and coarse and she tugs on it as he lifts her, moves her backwards so that she's up against the outside wall, takes her feet, just slightly, off the floor, and his chest is so firm and so solid against her own and nobody has ever picked her up like this before, like she weighs nothing, and she wraps her legs around his hips and she is not thinking about how he left, how she stayed, how they never were, she is only thinking of now, of this, of the touch and the heat of him, but of course, none of this happens. Of course it goes through her mind but this is Bren, and her, and they are polite and awkward and never face their true feelings, could never be so remotely bold or morally questionable, haven't seen one another in twelve years, haven't touched each other since the week he left, and flashes of thoughts, like this, hot and burning, are all that she has: all that there will ever be, between them.

So no. This does not happen.

Cars parked, stars out.

No movement, towards her, from her oldest friend.

He simply clips his other rucksack strap into place, the one across his chest. That firm, solid chest she has not touched.

Night, Nora, he says, ignoring her question. Congratulations, by the way.

And then he leaves her. Again.

three

You wake, your head heavy as an anvil. Dry mouth, full heart. Please, Nora, you say, from your side of the bed. Legs tangled, warm as toast. Don't ever let me drink again.

You just need caffeine, she says into the pillow, and you deduce that this means *she* needs caffeine, so you drag yourself to the kitchen to make coffee and the actual toast, take it back to her to eat in bed; Sunday morning prerogative. Soft light through the window on the duvet. What a great night, you say. Stupendous. Something niggling at you, though: did you lose your own shoe?

It's in the bathtub, for some reason, Nora says.

You laugh at this, and she does too, but only a little. Like her mind is elsewhere. You kiss her bare shoulder, leave a smear of butter on her skin from your mouth.

Tell you what, you say. Having everyone there, last night?

Almost everyone, says Nora.

Having everyone except your stubborn feminist of a mother there last night, you say, got me pretty jazzed for the actual wedding.

You don't tell her you've been jazzed about the idea of it, for years; don't tell her you've often thought about what your wedding day might look like, even when you'd agreed you wouldn't have one. Fleeting thoughts, over the past decade, like how it might feel to win the London Photography Prize. How you'd fare in old age, or with fatherhood. Just musings. Pictures in your head.

Yeah? Nora says, as she props herself up to eat her toast. Crunch of her teeth, crumbs on the sheets.

Yeah, you say. You had any thoughts?

Not really, she says, dabbing at the fallen crumbs with her finger. Have you? And you say a few, actually, and take your notebook from beside the bed and flip to the notes you've been making since she said yes, by the river that lunchtime, yes yes yes.

Oh, she says, a note of surprise, on seeing your black biro scrawls. Wow.

Nothing major, you say. Just brainstorming locations and stuff. I've been to some real stunners with work, over the years.

She nods, her hair mussed from sleep. I figured we'd just do it locally, she says, as she brushes it behind her ears.

And we can, you say. I just don't know of anywhere around here, really. Unless we look into, I don't know, a room above a pub or something. But that doesn't seem special enough. Or very *us*.

A gallery could be cool, Nora says, as she sweeps yet more crumbs off the duvet. Like I say, I've not really thought about it. But I guess something . . . different, would be nice. Intimate.

Different and intimate, you write in your notebook, before saying okay, that is a *wildly* unclear brief, but you accept the challenge. She smiles at you, then, that soft Nora smile. Slight gap in her front teeth, speck of burnt toast on her chin.

Affordable, she clarifies. And handmade.

Got it, you say, as she puts the plate down on her bedside table. Interesting you say that, you tell her, because I was talking to Clara and TJ last night, and her cousin bashed out this glorious day in under three months, apparently, all because they were willing to move on a cancellation. They said it was the most relaxed wedding they'd ever been to. Tenth of the price, too.

Nora nods again. Sips her coffee. You do the same, enjoying the dark roast, hint of blackberry; just the right amount of milk. Then she sighs. Her skin radiating heat, like it does in the night when you wake, sometimes, and she's twitching in dreams.

Bren came last night, she says.

A moment of quiet, post-toast, the rush of a distant train.

Bren, you repeat. As in, fridge magnet Bren?

Yes.

What! Nora! Why didn't you introduce us?

She drinks more coffee, then shrugs as though she is sad; her shrugs have emotions, you have learned.

I don't know, she says, and you can tell it's the truth. I was so thrown, she admits. And kind of drunk. And there were so many people around, and we didn't talk much, and then when we could've said hi, you were passed out on the sofa. Wearing only one shoe.

Oh gawd, and she says it's fine, rubs your arm, vaguely, with sympathy. Looking at the bedroom wall now.

You could've woken me, you say, and she says sorry, yeah.

He's come home, then?

I guess, she says, pressing her coffee mug to her cheek. I don't know how long for, though.

You didn't ask?

It didn't come up. He just sort of . . . ate pizza, and talked to people.

I guess that's what you do at parties, you say, and she makes a noise of agreement, though you're not sure she actually does. More coffee, swallowed. Mug put down on the toast plate as she gets out of bed, pulls on a sweat-shirt she'd left hanging on the radiator, for warmth.

It's just so *Bren*, she says, with her head beneath the fabric.

What is? Turning up at engagement parties?

She emerges without answering, picks up her hairbrush and tugs it through her hair.

He flew all the way from Queenstown to come to our party, she says, when he's not been home for twelve years. Didn't even come back for his mum's sixtieth.

But you're close, you remind her, you've always said so. Far closer than he is to his mum.

Yeah, she says again; all these yeahs, and no certainty in her voice. Keeps brushing. A car drives past the window, drone of the engine fading into the Sunday morning quiet.

*May*be, you venture, he just wanted to surprise you?

He did say that, she admits, swapping the brush for a scrunchie and gathering her hair into a bun. She's next to the Sophie Derrick painting you bought her for her thirtieth birthday, and there is a moment where you realise you will always get to see her like this, in the mornings, beside that painting, strands of hair by her face, bed-creases on her skin. And it is so familiar but almost profound, in that familiarity. Like the painting itself. Because to take home a piece of art, your grandfather once told you, you have to *really* love it, Robin: you have to want to keep it around, forever. Want to be with it, every damn day.

Well I'd have liked to have met him, you tell her.

Yeah?

Yeah! I'd have thanked him for all of the magnetised objects he's sent us over the years, you say, stretching your arms above your head. Without him, there'd be nowhere to stick our shopping lists or takeaway menus. No outlet for our undying love of pineapples wearing sunglasses.

It's a pie wearing the sunglasses, Nora says.

And where would we be without our pie that looks like a pineapple?

She turns to you, hair up, sweatshirt over her pyjama bottoms. Feet bare, blush of colour in her face. Love, you are sure, in her two-tone eyes.

Right here, she says. Probably.

Right answer, you say, swinging your legs out of bed now too, to start cleaning up from the night before. Speakers on, music playing, you love this song, you call to Nora who is still in the bedroom, I *love* this song! Humming because you don't really know the words, something about clear minds and best things and coming a long way as her phone begins to ring. You hear Josie's ringtone and Nora's voice, the lilt and fall of it through the baritone and trumpets; so jubilant, this track, definitely one for the wedding playlist, you'll write that down, when you're done, Nora's voice carrying through the open door saying I know, I know, Josie. Don't thank me, I did nothing.

four

Bren wakes in his old single bed and takes a long, slow-motion moment to remember where he is. Textured wallpaper. Floral smell.

Home. Actual home.

Teenage bedspread, hockey trophies, radiators-on-all-year-round home in the middle of an English village in Hertfordshire, county of opportunity, whatever that means; dehydrated, jet-lagged, several beers and two surprise greetings down.

He breathes out. Rubs his eyes with one hand. Looks at the old posters stuck to his wall of places that, oddly, he still hasn't been. Mount Fuji, Lake Louise, the Teotihuacán Pyramids. Clichés he never actually got around to visiting because he got caught up living and working in normal places, because living and working, it turns out, are two things you need to do wherever you are. Doing abnormal things, sometimes, sure, as a part of his poorly paid, richly rewarding day job. Kayaking through gorges or abseiling down rock faces. Coaching someone to jump from a canyon into the pool below, it is canyoning, after all, they did pay to do it, they can turn around and go back if they want but that's not such a good story, is it, fear just means you're alive, and do you want to live, *really live*, or do you want to get back in the minibus with dry feet because we can, if you want to, but I don't reckon that is what you want, is it, so let's do this. Screams, then, from fully grown men as they jump or soar or reach the summit. So much of that, in his line of work. Tears, too, and elation. Pulling pints, as well, between the more seasonal work, doing whatever he needed to make rent and buy his next plane ticket. Settling for months, even years at a time, before going again, because he could. Because he wanted to. Because there was nothing to stay for.

And now here he is, back in his childhood bedroom, looking again at these posters. Surprised to be here. Surprised, too, that the Blu-tack has held firm.

There are muffled noises from downstairs; it's less surprising that he is attuned to his mother's movements, still, to the layout of this house. Fridge door opened, whoosh of gas for the frying pan. Everything else, though, is silent, as it so often was in this cramped cottage in the middle of nowhere. Surrounded by farmers' fields, so much mud and grass, miles from town, from school, from his friends.

Most of them, anyway.

Bren rolls over, then, faces Nora's old room on the other side of the wall. Thinks about the moment she saw it was him on her doorstep last night. The shock on her face, which didn't fade; didn't turn to surprise, or delight. Something else, too, he thinks, like sadness. Which troubled him more than he'd let on. Meant he didn't know how to approach her, afterwards; couldn't forgive her, either, when she herself couldn't seem to move past it even when he stayed behind, was looking for a sponge or a dishcloth to help her clear up, thought talking to her in the late-night hours might be a better time for a discussion, a proper hello. There's something about kitchens, he's learned, after years of communal living, the excuse to be doing something with your hands that makes them a good place to start talking.

Not that they ever stopped, really.

Which meant he'd thought she'd be happy to see him, at least.

Didn't know how to handle it, when she wasn't.

Still. New day and all. He sits up, pulls some joggers out of his bag, gets dressed. Readjusts his St Christopher medallion, which always twists to the back when he sleeps, then follows the smell of frying sausages, ignoring the family photographs mounted on the walls as he descends the stairs. Pink carpet, soft as moss, then outside the kitchen, he pauses.

He has never known how to talk to her, this mother of his.

Best to keep it brief. Jovial.

Good mooooorning, Mother Hen, he says in the voice of Robin Williams as he walks through the door. She turns and beams at him, her floral apron tied over her dress. Such love in her eyes, for the film he's referenced, perhaps, because he remembered it's one of her favourites; or because it's him, maybe, because he came home. Because she got to hold him at two in the morning in the driveway and didn't shed a single tear or say a single word except his name, like she knew this moment would come, like she'd been patient and rewarded but any emotion around this situation had dried up long ago. A lump, hard and painful, in Bren's own throat, when she'd suggested bed, for the both of them, soon afterwards. Twelve years passed, without seeing each other, but come on now, lights out. Routine was always a vital component of her existence; television until midnight, word searches and warm cocoa until the early hours, sleeping through until six. She only needs four hours, a side effect of the pills or, Bren has long suspected, of never leaving the house. Never tiring herself out enough to require proper rest.

How did you sleep, sweetheart, she asks him.

Like the dead, he says. It's the jet lag.

His mother nods, her pale blue eyes not leaving his face. She's aged considerably since he's been away; her hair is colourless, almost transparent, lines crinkled across her neck.

Always best to soldier through, he says, when she does not ask him anything else.

My seasoned traveller, she says.

Perfectly salt and peppered, he says, which she doesn't understand, at first; takes a beat before she gives her low, bellowing laugh, a sound that has never suited her but he likes, all the same. Good sign. She returns to the frying pan, turns the spitting sausages with a pair of tongs.

I can do that, Bren says, but she says don't be silly, pet. Why don't you go on into the dining room, I'll bring it through.

The dining room, with its patterned carpet and even more family photographs; the window that looks out onto the gravel driveway that Bren does not like to think about.

I'm good, he says, I can help.

I don't need help, sweetheart, she says with her back to him, and it is his turn to nod, at that. At the pointed, pleasant nature of that sentence; you've been away, but I'm fine, he thinks she's implying; see here, just how fine I am.

It is a mild morning, almost March. She's opened the window to let out the sausage smell, and he hauls himself onto the kitchen counter like he used to, the cool air like breath on his back. Finds, as ever, that he can't sit still. He slumps back to the floor, turns to the fridge and pulls out butter and ketchup and milk, all in the same places as before. Only a few changes, he notes. Almond milk, now, in the door. Low-cholesterol margarine.

I couldn't sleep, Josie tells him, out of nowhere. The kettle boils and, thrilled for something to do, Bren pours the hot water into the two teacups she's laid out on saucers.

Oh, no? How come?

I was too excited, she says. Let it steep, for a minute or two, pet, before you add the milk.

Bren pauses in unscrewing the lid, says oh, sure.

I just lay there all night, she goes on. Couldn't wait for morning.

And yet we went to bed ten minutes after my arrival, he thinks, but does not say. Old confusion, like a knot in his stomach.

His mother has turned back to the sausages now. Bren swallows, says ah, that's nice. Thinking, this changes nothing. This sentiment expressed in this kitchen: it'll change nothing.

She butters his bread for him like he's a child. Squirts ketchup on the side of his plate. He finishes making the tea – gets it wrong, probably, too much or not enough milk – and they carry it all through to the dining room, same table, same upholstered chairs. Bren does not look at the one at the head of the table as he sits, takes the napkin his mother hands him and tucks it into his neckline, for jokes. Meat juice, sweet tang of sauce. Josie watching him as he eats, as if awaiting his review.

Delicious, he tells her, and she beams again. You not having one?

Oh, no. I had my porridge, first thing.

Water and salt?

You remember!

Course, he says. She tells him she has it with a drop of almond milk, now, though. Good for her gut health, apparently. Although Freya is aghast because of the air miles, importing all the almonds. It's impossible to get organic ones from Europe, so if she asks, don't tell her, all right? As far as Freya knows, it's just water and salt, like before.

I've not even seen Freya to say hi yet, Bren says, thinking of Nora's mad-haired mother; the way she'd let him spend hours next door, when his own mother was frantic, or else not speaking – existing, as though he didn't. But if and when the topic of almond milk arises? he ventures. Your secret is safe with me.

Josie doesn't chuckle at this, like he'd hoped; just nods, blows on her tea. The clock thunks loudly, a wooden grandfather clock that had, in fact, belonged to his mother's grandfather. Muscle memory of meals spent at this table, scanning for something, anything, to say. She has not asked him about his travels, or his flight, his life or his heart or his reasons for being home, after all this time. Which would've hurt, when he was younger. The lack of questions about school or his friends or his feelings. Not now, though. Nope. Another bite of his sandwich. Thick swallow of bread. Long drink of his hot tea, eyes down on the tablecloth, which is starched. Pristine.

So, Josie says. How was Nora's last night?

Small cough, then, caught in his throat.

Presumably that's what you came back for, she says. Bren drinks another mouthful, then puts down his cup. Gives a one-shouldered shrug, lifts his sandwich to his mouth.

Was she thrilled to see you?

Thrilled, he says, after he's chewed. Not sure I'd say that.

Surprised, then?

Definitely surprised.

Josie watches him eat, something gathering in her face.

You didn't tell her, she says.

I didn't think it would be a big deal, he says, and when his mother raises an eyebrow, he says, well, I knew it would be *some*thing, but thought it would be better, in some ways, to just show up. This was her . . . engagement, after all. I figured if I made it about me coming back, that would steal the limelight. And I didn't want to do that.

Pause, then, his mother's cup in her bony, birdlike hand.

I think, Josie says, coming home like this will have stolen the limelight anyway.

She starts to fiddle with the lace of the tablecloth. Worrying. And Bren eats his sandwich and hates it, the fact that he might have caused her to worry, because worry is where it starts, something small and insignificant and then –

Why don't I take you out, he says to her; leaving the Nora stuff behind. She looks thin and frail and like she needs to eat something hearty, a good steak, maybe. Pie with mash and a load of greens. He's missed pub food, himself, too. Proper gravy, hot chips.

Out, Josie repeats.

Somewhere for dinner, he says, to celebrate my homecoming. Tonight, maybe?

Oh, she says. That's lovely of you, Bren.

The clock ticks between them. Thunk of the pendulum. Teaspoon in her cup, one stir, then two.

We don't have to, he says.

I thought we could have a quiet one, is all, she says.

Didn't you have a quiet one last night?

Not with you, though, darling.

No, he says. Not with me.

He has to recalibrate as he finishes his sandwich. Recalling the pace of life around here, in this house. With that empty chair that never used to be empty; that had someone else sitting in it, who knew how to handle his mother, knew how to care for her, what to say, how to be patient and adoring without going mad, and going mad is in itself a concern, something he's not thought about for god knows how long, sudden zip of heat where his heart is, which he ignores as he drains the rest of his tea.

What d'you want to do, then, he asks her. Shall I cook? We could rent a film or something?

Rent a film, Josie repeats, and laughs, the worry now gone from her face. I do have Netflix, my love. And I have chicken casserole on Sundays. Remember?

And he does, of course. He does.

–

After breakfast, Bren steps outside the front door, swears, and doubles back inside. He forgot how bloody freezing it would be in England this time of year, had been so preoccupied last night he'd barely noticed. Thankfully his old down jacket is still hanging in the understairs cupboard, still bright blue; still fits. He zips it up to his neck and is back out in the cold with the two-pound coin his mother pressed into his hand, again like he's a child, like he's mowed the lawn and got his pocket money and is off to the corner shop to spend it. She's out of milk; there'd been an inhale of panic; he'd said he'd go, don't stress.

There is no shop in their village so he'll have to walk to the next one over, a slightly larger settlement with a farm shop and the cricket club. Its own pub, too, The Nag's Head, famous for its microwaved ready meals, its watery lemonade from the pump, a place he and Nora would go because it was somewhere warm in winter, somewhere away from his mum and her mum and the *lovebird* comments from his –

He exhales, marvels at his breath on the air. Feels slightly spaced out, and is it the surrealism of being home or in a different time zone, he doesn't pause to wonder. Heads down the driveway, unthinking, past the playing field. The swing set where they'd sit and talk as the sun sank below the treeline. Remembering the blood-orange sunsets, the cooking smells drifting from the cottages as darkness fell. This path, right here, veering behind the cottages and through a graffitied alleyway, across the wooden bridge over the river, this walk he did countless times, alone and also with Nora. Clearing his head, giving his mother privacy the way his father taught him to do when things felt too much; when Josie was crying constantly or staring at the wall or chattering at high speed to someone who was not there and he was told he was better off out of it by the person who handled it, who handled her, protected him, and then died.

He walks faster now. Iced puddles cracking underfoot, legs carrying him on autopilot along the mud track that runs parallel to the river. Past the backs of the cottages, the willow leaning into the green water, the oak tree in Freya's garden behind a thicket of brambles.

Flash of iridescent blue, as he walks. A kingfisher, so unbelievably bright but then gone, as if it never was.

He'd had two long-haul flights to prepare himself for this. For coming home. To anticipate how it might feel, decide what he might say to Nora and his mother, and yet he hadn't said any of it to either of them. Hadn't felt the need, hadn't had anything, really, to respond to, or work with. Clearly his leaving wasn't as much of a big deal to them as he'd thought it might have been, keeping him up at night sometimes when he'd had the right amount of alcohol; or if he was wild camping, waking to white peaks above the cloud line that could've been heaven if he believed in such a place, which he doesn't. But a scene like that would prompt him to think big thoughts about the past, all the same. Reach for his phone to touch base, pay for an hour at an internet café, early on, before international sim cards became a thing.

Turns out he needn't have worried. They were fine. Which is a relief, in all honesty, as he rounds the dilapidated old barn, corvids lined like vultures along the roof. Watching him with their black eyes and black feathers, yeah, you better keep walking. Past the farmhouse with the trampoline and swimming pool he'd never seen anybody swim in. Irate dog that often barked at the gate, not there, now, obviously, would've passed away long ago, wonders whether it barked till its dying day, Nora was so determined to befriend it every time they walked past, talked to it in a soothing voice to no effect, kibble-stained teeth, no wagging tail, yeah, you better keep walking. Into the forest, then. The mud wetter and thicker here, as the track ends; he tries not to get it on his boots. Has his mother's carpet to be mindful of, now. Pulls out his phone, remembers it's dead. Walks on until the shop, almost an hour away.

Inside, the bell dings, he buys the milk, pays the woman at the counter. Someone he doesn't recognise, who doesn't know him either. He gets a coffee because he doesn't want to head home yet. Doesn't know what he'll do with his day. Look at flights back, probably. Reach out to some old school friends, if any of them are even around any more. Scattered across the country working office jobs, married or with kids or both, from what he's seen online. Early thirties, now. Most people with lives he doesn't want, never wanted; the coffee is bad, instant and too bitter. He drinks it anyway, the paper cup warm in his palm. A man walks his terrier along the country road. Doesn't say morning, as he passes. No *kia ora* or *buenos días* or bowing of the head. Which suits him, actually, right about now. He finishes his coffee, the backs of his knees cold where he's been sitting on the concrete.

And then he stands, stretches, and makes the mistake of looping around the cricket field to kill time. Stops to look at the village noticeboard with its printouts advertising jumble sales and line dancing and there's the old photograph he never even considered would still be there, of the cricket team that won the county cup in 2005. Faded with age. Barely visible, if you didn't know who you were looking for, but there he is, in the front row, in his white jumper with his orange hair and crooked smile that Bren himself has inherited, sudden, sick roll of heat through him at the sight of it, running cold as he stands and stares and then turns round and heads back to the woods.

–

He walks until sundown. Drops the milk off at his mother's and tells her he's going to meet some friends for lunch. Lovely, his mother says, doesn't ask which friends, which is just as well, because his phone is still dead, so he couldn't message anyone even if he wanted to.

He does go and get lunch, though. Needs to eat, just like he needs to work and live, wherever he is. Walks for miles in a different direction and finds a country café selling scones and sandwiches and ice cream all year round. Optimistic, he likes that. Pays by card, his Velcro wallet in his back pocket. Talks to some strangers out on a bike ride, gorgeous day isn't it, the start of spring, so unusual this time of year.

Unusual, yes. All of it.

He eats his sandwich – second of the day, chicken salad, this time, before he remembers it's chicken for dinner too – drinks his cappuccino and takes his empty plate up to the counter before he leaves. Thanks the owner, says goodbye to the cyclists. Walks some more until the light is lost – too early, because it's still winter, despite the bluebird sky – and is coming up the gravel path home with the horizon hazy, now, lavender soft. Half expecting his mother to be waiting in the window, when instead it is Freya he bumps into as she's getting out of her car. Nora's mother. Looking much as she did before, like a middle-aged hippy who might be found meditating in her greenhouse, which he would take, any day, over the actual madness of his own mother. Hours, he'd spent, in her company, helping her to shell peas with Nora, sampling her terrible, vegan cooking – grimacing, and teasing, and laughing about it.

He had laughed a lot, in Freya's house.

Hello, he says, and Freya jerks at the sound of his voice, drops her bag of shopping on the gravel. Some groceries roll out of it, a tube of Pringles, a few loose apples.

Brenavin? she says, as he hurries forward to pick it all up, grinning at his long-lost nickname. You gave me the fright of my *life*.

Didn't think I'd aged quite so terribly, Bren says, but sure.

Freya does not laugh; seems perturbed, mesmerised even, by his face. She is staring at him as he straightens up with her shopping; he swallows, clears his throat.

Josie said you were back, she says. But I . . . well. It's different, seeing you in person. Like seeing . . .

Don't say it, he thinks, and she doesn't; the silence stretches between them.

A handsome thirty-year-old? Bren suggests, and Freya snorts, but it stops her staring, at least. Gives Bren a chance to nod towards her porch door and say, let's get your shopping inside, shall we?

Years of intrepid travel, Freya says, and all you can think about is getting my yoghurt in the fridge?

I am my mother's son, he says, and she snorts again. Opens the car boot, passes him more bags – these two are for your mum, she says – did you remember the almond milk, he does not ask – then she waves him through her porch door, says he may as well make himself useful, now he's here. Those top cupboards won't reach themselves.

Inside, scent of jasmine, ylang-ylang, just like before. Seashells hanging on strings, densely patterned wallpaper, a new rug, he thinks, in the hall. He puts the bags on the table in the kitchen and it rocks forward onto its bad leg. Satisfying, somehow. And kind of maddening, too, that it still hasn't been fixed.

Freya, it seems, is already over the shock of seeing him. She slings her coat onto a chair and starts bustling around, unpacking the groceries so that Bren can, in turn, take a look at her. Kimono over her dungarees. Hair greying, but only slightly; she's ten years younger than his own mother. Just as lean and wild-haired and nimble as ever, the kitchen still crammed with jam jars. The beckoning cat waves at him from the window sill. There were hundreds of them in Japan, stacked in shop windows, at the entrances of temples. This one is swinging its left paw; inviting friendship, he thinks, if he remembers correctly, and not money and fortune, though it could be the other way around.

Tea, Bren? Your mum's bits are all long-life, so they can wait.

Why not, he says, so she fills the kettle and takes it to the stove, asks him how long he's been back. He glances at the clock on the wall, hot pink, flamingos for hands. About twenty-six hours, he says.

And where'd you come from?

New Zealand, he says, and she says ah, yes, Nora did say.

Her kimono flows behind her, cape-like, as she moves between the cupboards.

You've spoken to her, then, Bren says, as he lowers himself into one of her mismatched wooden chairs.

I speak to her most days. She is my only offspring, after all.

This feels pointed, but Bren doesn't bite. Mostly because it's fair.

So you've spoken to her today? he asks, trying to sound offhand, and Freya throws him a packet of biscuits.

Either open them or put them in that top cupboard, she says. And no, not yet. I'm working the late shift, tonight, so she's not coming for dinner, and I expect she's hideously hungover after . . .

She twirls to face him, her kimono spinning like a flamenco skirt.

You went to her *party*?

Bren opens the biscuits.

You came all the way back from New *Zealand* to go to Nora's *engagement* party?

Well yeah, Bren says, pulling out a digestive. What's wrong with that?

The question, Bren, is what's right with it?

The weight of this reframing creaks between them, like the broken leg of the table. Still there, after all these years.

It just felt like time, he says.

I'll say! Freya says. After twelve years!

Bren takes a bite, then swallows. Freya shakes herself like a disgruntled hen puffing out her feathers, then returns to unpacking her shopping; not, however, about to let it go.

I'd understand you flying home for her actual *wedding*, she goes on. Oh buck and fugger, I already had carrots. But last night was just a little soirée, wasn't it?

There were loads of people there, actually, Bren says. We barely got a chance to talk.

You flew around the world for her party and didn't talk to her once you got there?

She didn't seem to want to, he admits.

At this point, the kettle starts shrieking. Freya tells him to pass her two cups, behind him – but he remembers, needs no instruction, has already pulled two mugs from their wall hooks. She fusses around, pours the water, then hands him his mug with the tea bag still in it. No milk. No offer of any, either, dairy, almond or otherwise.

What're you playing at, Brenavin, Freya asks, when she sits

across from him, pulling her knees into a lotus position atop her chair. Bren says he isn't playing at anything, and she stares him down.

What, he says.

Why would you come back for this party, of all things?

That's the second time someone's asked me that, Bren says. Clearly, I shouldn't have bothered.

Oh, don't be a martyr.

Why weren't *you* there, anyway? Are we not a fan of Robert?

Freya, who is swallowing a mouthful of tea, spits out aha! My point *exactly*! so that half of it spatters down her front.

What point is that, Bren says, as she dabs herself dry, and she says you *know* his name is Robin.

Isn't that what I said?

And I adore the man, as it goes. Intelligent, bold dresser, more of a feminist than Nora, I think, sometimes. I simply don't approve of traditions that force women into societally approved boxes, so an engagement party went against my principles, is all.

Bren lifts his chin at her.

I did wonder about that, he says. I'd never pictured it, for her, either. The whole marriage thing.

Hm, is all Freya says, as she reaches for a biscuit.

I always thought she was a free spirit, like you.

Don't do that, Brenavin. Don't try to get me on side.

What side would that be?

The side that suddenly roots for you, when you show up twelve years too late, Freya says. After abandoning everyone the second things got tricky.

She gives a crunch of her biscuit, in finale. And unlike Nora the night before, Freya does not seem to regret her words. They glare at each other over the table, steam rising from their mugs, until Bren says that actually, Freya? Things had been tricky for a very long time.

Dismissive sound, then, from her.

So how long are you staying, she asks, after another glug of her tea, letting the awkwardness slide on by. Are you planning on seeing Nora again? Spending any time with your mother? Or just vamoosing, when it suits you?

I don't know, Bren says. I've not thought about it.

Course you haven't, Freya says. He sighs, blows his fringe out of his face. He is about to say well, thanks for the biscuits, if nothing else, see you around, when Freya says the past doesn't need digging up, Bren. That's why it's the past.

He tries to meet her gaze, at this, but the steam from her cup has clouded her glasses.

I'm not here to dig anything up, he says. It's just a major moment in her life, isn't it? I couldn't ignore it. Because contrary to what you might think of me, Freya, Nora and I *have* kept in touch. We're still friends. In spite of . . . everything.

She is looking at him with both of her beady, honey-gold eyes. He's always thought she is birdlike, in a very different way to his own mother. Josie is frail and fluttering; Freya, by contrast, is a hawk, sharp and watchful, talons poised.

Digging up the past isn't my style, anyway, he adds. I prefer to leave it behind.

Three ticks of the flamingo clock, then, before Freya gives her high, cackling laugh. Well, she says, raising her cup to him. At least you're self-aware.

She takes another mouthful, says ah, milk! and springs up from her chair, before sloshing some into their mugs. So we're agreed, then, she says. The past stays in the past?

She doesn't look at him as she says this.

Little niggle, which he can't quite place, so he lets it go, says sure.

Welcome home, then, she says, before moving things along, as if the milk has lightened more than just the colour of the brew. She takes another biscuit, asks him about real things, now. About his travels and qualifications. The outdoor pursuits he's taught, the people he's met. When was his darkest hour, where did he get the sickest, did he fall in love with anyone, man or woman or other.

Good questions.

The sort his own mother never asks.

After half an hour – teas finished, biscuits demolished – Freya says he should probably get home. And in the hall beneath the wind chimes, he turns to Freya, who is holding out the shopping she must buy for Josie every week, standing there with her mad hair and her dungarees, something about Nora in the shape of her chin.

I'm not, he says, and stops himself.

Freya waits as he takes the shopping from her, the wind chimes stirring above their heads.

I am not in love with your daughter, he says. In case that needed . . . clarifying.

Freya holds his eyes; her glasses clear now. A hawk, no longer hunting.

I'm over it, he says. What I asked you to tell her, when I left.

Chimes, fading, to silence.

I should hope so, she says, eventually, though she doesn't look him in the eye. Off with you now.

Off with me, he says, stepping out into the cold, and he hears her laughing as she closes the door behind him, his own mother waiting next door.

five

All day, Freya's questions hang over him like spiderwebs. Easy enough to ignore, but still somewhat irritating. He spends the night drifting in and out of sleep, unable to pin it on the jet lag, this time, or the alcohol. When the sun comes up he reaches for his phone and tries to send Nora a text, but who is he kidding; he's never been great with words.

At breakfast – porridge for her, Weetabix for him – he asks his mother where it is that Nora works. She tells him she runs an art café in London, but he knows that, already. Nora has sent him pictures in the past, sometimes tells him about the workshops or pop-up exhibitions she's hosting. Arty stuff he doesn't really understand but sounds right up her street, calligraphy and crocheting and a feminist book club; this one time, some kind of face yoga that reduced wrinkles, which to him felt distinctly *un*feminist; not that he said so, in reply. Sounds cool, was all he said.

But where exactly in London, Bren asks Josie, and she says oh, somewhere in Cricklewood, I think. Lovely name, isn't it? Like a place from a children's book. He nods. Drinks the milk from his bowl then tells her he's off to see a friend; which is true this time, he hopes, as he catches the bus to town and then a slow train into the city. Navigates the underground, which he hasn't done since he was a teenager, feeling lighter now that he's somewhere new, all adverts and escalators. By mid-morning he's striding from Kilburn station towards the place with the lovely name and a few less-than-lovely pubs, a Polish deli, an ice cream parlour. Street after street of Edwardian houses. He googles art cafés in Cricklewood and there is only one, so he follows the blue arrow and by noon, he is standing outside.

And there she is, behind the coffee counter. Making coffee, which he'd not expected; he'd thought she was the programme co-ordinator or events manager or something, that she'd be out the back doing admin, but of course she's here, sleeves rolled up, talking to a customer. Frothing milk and smiling, as she speaks.

No flower crown, this morning. Her hair is tied up in a ponytail, her face make-up free, like it always was when they were young, when the girls at his own school discovered foundation and mascara and something to intensify their eyebrows which always kind of scared him, though he never said so, pretended it was hot, like all the other guys did. Nora was only known in his circles through him; she was at the state school over the road from his grammar school; the girl with the weird eyes and weirder milf, lol, yeah, she's all right though, he'd say, dying inside because that's all he *would* say. Burning with shame at himself, but not her. Never at her.

Now, though, she does not see him and he does not go inside. His excitement at seeing her has faded, and instead he feels hesitant; it hadn't gone as planned, surprising her the first time, so he's not sure what's compelled him to try again. He tries to figure this out as he watches the customer take their coffee, sit at a table in the corner. Small vases on each, dried canary grass. People eating flapjacks, drinking lattes, working on laptops with their earphones in; all women wearing linen or wool or corduroy, and Nora herself is still at the counter, not even aware of his presence. Just being her, with that smile and hair and naked, Nora face, and Christ alive, she's radiant.

But, Bren muses, what he said to Freya still stands.

You can't be in love with someone you've not seen for over a decade.

And because of that, he should either walk straight in or else walk away, and it is while he is trying to decide which that Nora looks up.

Does a double take.

And Bren raises his hand, hi, hello.

She does not seem shocked, like before; remains where she is. Blinks, reaches for a cloth, wipes down the surface. Maybe she didn't realise it was him, Bren thinks. Or worse, she did realise, and he's messed up, again. Should've called.

But then she disappears behind a curtain beside the coffee bar, reappearing with a bag on her shoulder, a padded jacket over her dress. Crosses the threshold of the café – plaster flooring, the colour of unfired clay – opens the door and says hello, and Bren says it back.

You're making a habit of this, she says, as the door closes behind her.

Turning up announced?

I was going to say blindsiding me, Nora says, but that works too.

I hoped you'd have some kind of lunch break, Bren says.

I do, she says. On Mondays I go swimming.

She tilts her shoulder towards him, the one bearing her bulging tote bag. A rolled-up towel pokes out the top, bobbled like it's washed every week, or else never before seen a drop of fabric softener; his mother would be horrified.

So this is a bad time?

Yes, she says, though she doesn't sound flustered like she did at the party. More amused; like she'd half expected this.

Here's a crazy thought, Bren says, as a woman with purple hair emerges from behind the curtain in the café, taking up Nora's place behind the counter; he has a vague memory of her from the party. You skip swimming today, he says, and I'll buy you lunch instead.

Or, Nora says, without a beat, *you* skip lunch, and come swimming.

Skip *lunch*?

Well. I'm playing it fast and loose with the verb *skip*. We'd eat afterwards.

I was gonna say, Bren says. The Nora I know never skips a meal.

The Nora you know has a job and a life and a precious one-hour lunch break, she says, looking at her watch. And it takes twenty minutes to get there, and twenty minutes to get back.

And she swims on Mondays, Bren says.

Right, she says; an actual smile from her, then. Tiny gap in her teeth, as the purple-haired woman watches them through the glass shopfront.

Then let's swim, he says. I'll buy some swim shorts, at the pool.

It's not a pool, Nora says, but she's walking now, which Bren takes to be a good sign. He strides alongside her, has to walk surprisingly fast to keep up.

You mean it's a lido?

No, she says, but you're getting warmer.

She is still smiling, slightly. Pleased, he thinks, that she can be the one to surprise him here, to hold all the cards, and for that reason, he doesn't ask any more questions; lets her guide him onto the tube, then the bus. Loud whoosh of the carriage, voices silenced at points, due to the noise. It's a little awkward but less so, he thinks, than the other night. Just like being in kitchens, Bren has found that walking or moving – not looking at each other over a table – is always a good way to avoid, or on the flip side, even attempt, a hard conversation.

They chat about normal things, at first. What he's been up to since Saturday; not a lot. What she's working on at the café, how great it looked from the outside, she'll show him indoors, when they get back, if he wants. Off the tube, up the escalator, onto the 189 bus. Bren looking out the window, thinking too hard about what to say next.

I still can't get over seeing you like this, Nora says.

They pass another bus on the road; Bren leans back, certain it'll collide with theirs. The London streets are so tight, almost claustrophobic, and he's not used to this kind of traffic. She lets out a little laugh at this, and it sounds like sun sparkling on water.

He has missed that sound.

It stirs something, deep inside him.

Do I seem different, he asks her, and she seems to consider this; says yes, but also no. He knows exactly what she means, and is about to say so, but then she says you're still wearing your St Christopher.

He looks down, where the pendant has dipped into the V-neck of his T-shirt.

Course, he says. Hadn't you noticed that on our calls?

Nora shrugs as a low-hanging tree branch clatters against the bus. I'd noticed you wore a twine necklace, she says, but didn't realise it was the same one.

More branches thwacking the glass.

I've never taken it off, Bren says, and she looks at him sideways; hasn't looked at him properly since she saw him waiting outside her shop. He sees disbelief in her eyes, but also affection, for the first time since he got back.

Well, that's a lie, he reasons. I take it off when I go through security.

Skewed laugh, from her, then.

I doubt stainless steel would set off the alarms, she says.

You mean, Bren says, touching the charm, it isn't pure silver?

It's whatever the hell I could afford off the market at sixteen.

And look at you now, Bren says. Selling ceramic pots for seventy quid, and antique writing sets for three figures.

I sell them, Nora points out, I don't *buy* them.

Still, Bren says.

You looked at our website? she says, after a moment, and he says sure. It's really awesome, Nora, what you've built. What you're doing.

He doesn't quite *know* what she's doing, but it seems the right thing to say. She blushes, looks down at her shoes. And then she says this is our stop and they both struggle to get down the stairs of the moving bus; disembark to an uncrowded street, calmer winds, today. Nora leads him past some green lakes and over a small hill, the air fresh, conversation easier, and then they're joining the back of a short queue, passing a sign that declares it's the Hampstead Mixed Bathing Pond.

A pond? Bren says.

I book my slot every week, Nora says, but there's probably space for you, this time of year. I only do a few lengths, so you can wait here, if you'd prefer.

And let you have all the cold-water fun?

She shrugs, says well, like you said, it's not like you have any swim stuff.

There're ways round that, Bren says. Nora moves forward in the queue, says you can't swim naked, Bren.

She blushes again, even as she says it. At the very idea of him embarrassing her in public, with his nomadic, unashamed attitude, the way he gets on planes, jumps off cliffs, does what Bren does, without a care. Or perhaps she's blushing at the idea of him naked, full stop.

What *do* you take me for, he asks her, in mock outrage.

It's a good question, she says, but then she's showing her phone to the ticket office and he's pulling out his wallet, paying for a slot. She doesn't wait for him but heads straight for the women's changing block, as though set on showing him he's not about to thwart her plans by being here. Which is fine. Again, only fair. Bren ignores the signs for the men's and follows the other guys to the entrance, finds himself by an expanse of open water. Large clouds overhead. Ducks and swans, heads bobbing in the wet green. An unexpected oasis in the city, like a cenote or lagoon.

He takes it all in, then strips down to his boxers.

Folds his clothes beneath a bench, thinking, sure.

He'd hoped to have lunch with her if he was lucky. A sandwich, a hot chocolate, perhaps, bought as a peace offering. But instead Nora has brought him here, to swim in the throes of the English winter in an outdoor pond, where there is sky, and water, and magic in the mundane. Something flits across his heart like a match being struck, as he rubs his elbows to keep warm. Why she stayed behind, he will never know.

And then she is there in her olive-green swimsuit with her hair in a pineapple-like knot on her head, and rather than acknowledge him standing there in his pants she makes her way to the jetty and down the metal steps.

You're not in paradise any more, she calls, her voice unwavering as she pushes back into the water.

It's not like it's balmy waters in New Zealand, Bren says, and to prove his point, he takes a running jump straight off the side and surfaces with his hair plastered to his forehead, saying, fuck me, it's *baltic*, and there it is again, her sparkling, waterfall laugh, and it's the best sound, he remembers now, how on earth did he ever forget.

—

They swim just a few lengths before getting out; all she has time for, but also all she needs, she explains, to get that shiny good feeling, does he feel it? In the summer, Nora tells him, she dries off on the grass afterwards, but seeing as it's the end of February and they can see their breath on the air, they wriggle back into their clothes and buy hot drinks from the coffee roaster by the overground. Now that it's damp, her hair is a deep flaxen gold. It drips onto the shoulder pads of her coat even though she'd towelled it dry, Bren's boxers stuffed, sodden, into his pocket.

That was fun, she says. Like old times.

Affection overt in her voice, now. They used to swim secretly in the river behind their cottages; Josie said that they mustn't, Freya said it was fine. His dad, with a wink, saying listen to your mother, you two.

Do you really have to get back so soon, Bren asks her, as Nora checks her phone. Hiss of the coffee machine, people talking. Warm, honeyed feeling spreading through him, after the cold. And when she says yes, he says but don't you own the place?

Co-own, she says. With Shay.

The purple hair girl?

Nora nods, goes to pay for their drinks, and when Bren intervenes she refuses. It's the least I can do, she says, tapping her card to the reader. After you swam in your underwear.

You didn't think I would?

I'm never sure, with you, she says. She's bought a couple of pastries, too, without comment; passes him one as they head back towards the door, and Bren says well, why not try to be? Sure, I mean. Get to know me better, again.

Nora pauses by the exit, her coffee in hand. Mocha, rather. A shot of espresso, dark chocolate flakes. Uncertainty in the set of her mouth.

You don't think we know each other?

I said *better*, Bren reiterates. After years of emails and video calls, he says, I hear a coffee's a good way to start.

Her mouth twitches, and she says okay. Just a sec. Turns away, lifting her phone to her ear. Bren takes a sip of his cappuccino, watches the people in the café while he waits. They're just like the people in her café, though there are more men in here; a woman with a dachshund in her lap; a barista making drinks the way *he* used to, with clenched-jaw focus in case he boiled instead of frothed the milk.

Shay says it's quiet, Nora says, when she turns back.

Great, Bren says. So shall we . . . sit?

Sure, Nora says, and they do. Peel the lids off their cups, both drink.

Are you leaving, then, she asks him.

What?

Are you leaving the country? Is that why you came to see me today?

No! Bren says. Well, I will be leaving, obviously. But not right now.

Soon, though?

If you want, he says, and it is meant to sound light, but she says no, and it is more forceful than either of them expected; someone at the table next to theirs looks up, just briefly, from their laptop. Nora drops her gaze. Drinks more of her mocha.

Why is this so hard, she says, and Bren looks into his own cup.

I can think of a few reasons, he says.

Nora laughs, then, or at least tries to; tears a piece of pastry from inside the paper bag and puts it in her mouth. Chews, for a long time, so that eventually, Bren is the one to speak.

I'm sorry for showing up without telling you, he says. The other night, I mean.

Nora nods, swallows. Says no; he's already apologised.

She's sorry she wasn't nicer about it. This Danish, by the way, is unbelievable.

She offers him a piece. He takes it.

You're always nice, he tells her.

I'm not, she says. I want to be, but I get it wrong a lot of the time. It's an effort. Whereas I look at some people and think, they are just good to their core. Like your mum. Or like Robin.

Or this pastry, Bren says, while he chews.

It's easy for them, she says, but I have to think about it. I feel like I think too much, sometimes. Or all the time.

Bren doesn't know what to say to this, or indeed what she's getting at. Nora had always been one for these sorts of conversations – earnest, near philosophical – and he was always happy to listen, but not necessarily engage. A personality thing. A boy versus girl thing. Raised by Freya versus Josie, who knows.

You have tattoos, Nora says next, and he drinks more coffee. Says yeah.

A lot of them, she observes.

It became kind of an obsession, he says. Collecting them, each place I went. But I'm a coward, really. I only get them where you can't see them. Unless I'm swimming with my shirt off.

She blushes again; he did not mean this to sound so flirtatious, but he finds it's easy to fall into, around her. Like before. There was always something between them, something magnetic they weren't able to touch, but could both undoubtedly feel – a palpable force between their poles.

What was that scar, Nora asks him. On your leg?

You've really been checking me out, haven't you?

No, she says, and while he was just teasing, he's also aware that they are both unsure of how to be together like this, in person; the conversation swinging between nonchalant and intense; small talk to wildly specific.

It's just a scar, he says, with a shrug.

But how did you get it, she presses. It's a bloody great *massive* scar, Bren.

I've had a few accidents over the years, Bren says. Occupational hazard.

What happened?

Bren slurps more of his coffee. It's near heavenly after the cold water, warms his throat, the soft, numbed part behind his ribs. A few of them broken, in this same accident, from where he threw himself, hard, onto his board.

I got bitten by a shark, he tells her.

Funny, Nora says, breaking off another piece of pastry. What actually happened?

I got bitten by a shark, he repeats.

Bren, she says. Come on.

I know it's something people say, Bren says, like, I was mauled by a bear, or lost a fight with a croc, but seriously. I got. Bitten. By a shark. In Australia, when I was teaching some kids to surf. About four years ago.

Nora stares at him.

It wasn't a big deal, he says, leaning back on his stool. It was pretty small, probably old. It wasn't like a scene from *Jaws*, or anything. I didn't even pass out; I thumped it on the nose, and it swam away. They stitched me up, gave me some painkillers, and I was back on the surfboard a fortnight later. What? Why are you looking at me like that?

Her face looks strange. All affection gone; contorted, now, like she's mad at him, rather than awed.

It was fine, Nora, he says. I'm fine.

Clearly, she says.

Nora, he says. What –

You email me about *chocolate*, Bren. And sunburn. And the nice view out of your window, yet fail to mention you got bitten by a freaking *shark*?

Stir of his coffee, mostly froth, now, at the bottom of the cup.

I knew it would freak you out, he says.

Knew it would freak my mother out. That you'd tell her.

But the ease of the past hour – the acceptance of him showing up, their shared swim, her laughter, the slow, hesitant reaching for some sort of normality between them – has vanished. Nora's pink cheeks are flaming, now.

How are we friends if you never tell me anything real? Anything that actually happens to you?

Like getting engaged, you mean, Bren says, before he realises he's going to. Or, I don't know, moving in with your boyfriend?

I told you those things!

No, Nora, you didn't. I just figured them out, from the new background on your webcam, or because my mum mentioned something on the phone. Or because you sent me an invitation, attached to a blank email.

That again, Nora says.

What, you'd rather circle back to a senseless shark bite?

I'd rather circle back to what the hell happened to us, Nora says, her voice taut. We used to talk about everything.

Her eyes are bright. Shining, in a way he can't handle. But he makes himself look at her the way she is looking at him, straight in the face, coffee cups and a whole lot more between them, fucking hell, and there's him, just trying to be friends.

Life happens, right, is all he can say, because for all his good intentions, all his hopes to make amends after the party, she can't play it like this. Can't play it like she doesn't know, like they can crack on as they were, as if nothing happened. Even though that's exactly how he tries to play it, too. Most of the time.

I've got to go, she says, standing up.

I thought you had some time?

What I *have* is a life, Bren, Nora says. A business, and a job, and a partner who you never ask about, which means I never know how to – what to –

He keeps looking. Her anger, now, morphed into upset.

It might not be shark bite material, she says, as she shoves her stool beneath the table, but I *have* tried to share that stuff with you, Bren. It just felt like you never wanted to hear it.

Bren does not respond to this. Doesn't know how to. She looks as confused as he is, and they hold each other's eyes for a moment in which they see and don't say all that they want to and then she repeats that she has to go, and Bren watches her leave, winding her scarf around her neck and the wet ends of her hair. Wondering how he'd got it so wrong, yet again. Why he can't ever get it right.

–

Nora gets back to her café, hot despite the cold, riled with emotion. Without saying hi to Shay, she dumps her bag and coat in the back room and sits down at the desk with the company laptop, which freezes when she jabs at the touch pad; a spinning wheel suspended on the screen.

Hello to you too, Shay says, sticking her head through the curtain.

Sorry I'm late, Nora says.

You're actually early, Shay says. I thought you were gonna be another hour?

Too busy, Nora says.

Too flustered, more like, Shay says. You look like you ran all the way back from Hampstead.

I'm behind with the chakra workshop, Nora says, double-clicking on the touch pad.

Nora, Shay says. D'you remember what Desmond used to say?

Nora does not answer, clicks once again at the still-frozen screen.

Desmond was their sculpture tutor at Saint Martins; a big, brawny man everyone called Baloo, mostly behind his back. He'd roared with laughter the first time he'd heard it, before humming Robin Hood and Little John for the rest of the lesson, wrong movie, Des, Nora had told him; same animation, though, good catch.

He said that art journalists are the *last* thing a society requires, Shay says. Not artists, even, but the people that *write* about art. Which is the height of sophistication, right? But also the most expendable career on the planet.

Nora does remember this, but does not see why it's relevant. Uh-huh, she says, as she holds down the power button to reboot the machine.

Our chakra workshop is the equivalent of art journalism, Shay tells her. Not exactly the most urgent of projects.

Great, Nora says. I'll be sure to write that on the digital ads. Improve our chances of selling some tickets.

Jeez, you're flinty, today.

You're flinty every day, Nora fires back, and rather than huff, Shay barks out a laugh, says she'll leave her to it: this charming mood of hers.

He got bitten by a shark, Nora says, as the curtain falls.

Background voices, clink of teaspoons. Shay pokes her head back into the room.

Bren got bitten by a shark, Nora tells her. He has this ginormous scar on his leg which was just, like, *staring* at me, in the water. He's been away for twelve years and has at least twelve tattoos to show for it, and he didn't tell me about them, either, and they look ridiculous, Shay, honestly, like a Rorschach test threw up on him, all abstract and ugly and *weird*.

Shay nods, her bottom lip protruding with interest. Nothing, in their eleven years of friendship or six years of business ownership, has ever seemed to rattle her.

This is the redhead, Shay says. Who showed up on Saturday, and then again today, looking all shifty and besotted?

He is not besotted, Nora says.

He is shifty, though.

That's just Bren, Nora says. He's somehow super confident and really awkward, all at once. I don't know how it's even possible, but that's him.

Oh, it's possible, Shay says. Kind of like Jesse Eisenberg. Or Cillian Murphy.

I guess?

Andy Warhol, too. Come to think of it, practically every white male artist who ever made it big. Penis equals god-given confidence, equals the prerogative to be socially awkward aka a demonstrable dick. And yet there they are, getting rich and famous anyhow.

Except Bren isn't rich, or famous. Or an artist.

He is a dick, though?

No, Nora sighs, he's not. Just does some dickish things, maybe.

Like not telling you he got tattoos, Shay says.

Right.

Or turning up at your engagement party, to surprise you. That *douche bag*.

Nora stares at the laptop background, which is a photograph of Horace asleep on the art café floor. Then she walks her feet slowly in a quarter-circle, spinning the desk chair so that she's facing Shay, who's watching her from the doorway. Bangles on her own rose-tattooed wrists, which Nora barely notices, or at least has never asked about.

Am I overreacting, Nora says.

You? Shay flashes her sharp-toothed smile, her nose piercing twinkling like a fleck of glass. Never.

Nora nods, once, and Shay snickers. Looks over her shoulder, tells a customer she'll be there in one sec, then looks back at Nora who is now chewing her thumbnail.

He is fit, Shay says. The redhead.

Bren, Nora says.

The tattoos and the shark scar might just have tipped him from nomadic hipster into dark, dangerous question mark, Shay says.

He's definitely a question mark, Nora says. The laptop has rebooted, is ready for the password now. She types it in but the screen shakes, rejects it.

And he's single? Shay says, and Nora bashes the keys too hard as she retypes. Yes, she says. Or at least, she thinks so.

You don't know?

He's not exactly forthcoming, in that area.

I thought you said you were best friends?

And I thought you were off men, Nora says, still so hot, from rushing back; how is she sweating, like this, when it's February.

Men, yes, Shay says. Question marks, no.

Well with Bren, life would be a series of question marks, Nora says, and Shay says sign her up. When Nora shoots her a look she says hey, no judgement, please! That not everyone gets to be as lucky as her, in full requited love with a nice normal guy who washes up and pays half the mortgage and understands pink tax. Some of us have to scrape the barrel with the Brens of the world, okay? And Nora wants to say that Robin is more than just a nice normal guy, and that to be with Bren would hardly be scraping the barrel, but both seem to imply things she does not want to, should not need to prove, and so she says neither. Tries the password again, her hair still soaking into her scarf.

–

That night, Robin is home before her, and he has called this venue that he loves, doesn't she love it, too? It is *beaut*iful. A white box in the middle of a silver birch forest, glass roof, lots of light. Definitely different. Debatably intimate, but that's on them, and their guest list.

I'll call them tomorrow, if you like it, he says.

Where is it?

Devon, he says, which is random, Nora says.

Or romantic? By the ocean, lots of space. It could be a nice getaway for people. I did a shoot there, once, when it was first built, Robin says, as he flips his laptop closed, clears the dining table of work so that he can make room for dinner. He's wearing felted slippers on his feet, a dark green jumper rolled to his elbows.

I remember thinking it was so peaceful. I'd never seen anything like it. They do yoga retreats and stuff, not just weddings. I still know the guy that runs it, Jed something.

Well, give Jed something a call, Nora says. Why not.

I will, Robin says, but then he says hey. Are you okay?

I'm fine, she says. I'm great.

Everything good with the café, today? How's the chakra series going?

Can I leave you with these onions, she asks him. I really need a shower after my swim, today. I can't warm up.

Course. Have a bath, if you need.

Yeah, maybe I will.

In the bathroom, she opts for speed and stands beneath the showerhead on full blast. Trying to work out her thoughts, separate them into strands. Marrying Robin. Seeing Bren. Feeling one thing and also another. Anger, love; resentment, concern, and something else of a different colour, a shade she can't quite identify, a mix of now and then and what's coming. She goes to shampoo her hair, uses conditioner, by accident. And when she gets out, her skin red raw, she finds she's replaying that stupid fantasy kiss, just kid's stuff, though, like wanting to be a Power Ranger or a pop star when in reality you wouldn't want to be either of those things; she's thinking about Robin, too, and the venue in the woods, so sleek and far away. She'll tell him she's not sure about it. She'll tell him right now. But once she's dried off and in her dressing gown, she glances at her phone on the bed, Robin singing along to the radio in the next room.

Look, Bren's text says, on the screen: *this is not going how I'd hoped.*

New message, then, because he sends them in stilted sentences rather than one long block; like he's talking to her.

It's meant to be a nice thing, being here

Meant to be good to see you

Sorry about the party

Sorry about the shark

Sorry about the nothing-ness that apparently isn't interesting, like the chocolate

I actually brought you some back from the airport

I forgot to bring it, today

But to me, Nora, friendship IS all that stuff. The nothing that makes up your days, or how your life looks, like the Polaroids you printed, or like your Monday swims, or the pastry you bought me at lunch.

Three waving dots as he deletes, and then types, for a prolonged moment.

And they might seem insignificant over email or a video call but they're actually THE significant bits, to me, the real things. Shark bites aren't real, I don't think. They're not representative of my life out there, or who I am. Or what I want to know about you.

Because I do still want to know you.

(Better. I want to know you better.)

Thanks for the swim, and the coffee, and sorry if I ruined your lunch break

and yes

I'll be leaving soon.

Nora holds her breath as she stands in her dressing gown, watching the screen domino down with message after message. Robin still singing next door. Onions caramelising by now, in the pan.

So I know I've screwed up but it would be nice to see you again, if you wanted.

For dinner, maybe.

Three waving dots, for another half a minute, but then nothing else appears. He's done. So Nora picks up the phone just as Robin begins a deep baritone of *I Don't Care* by Ed Sheeran in the kitchen and she replies, before she can decide not to.

Dinner, yes, is all that she types back. *At mine?*

–

Which is how Bren ends up on Nora's doorstep, almost a week after the time before. It's early March, now, the sky an antiseptic, English grey. In the daytime he wastes hours in a Costa Coffee in town, avoiding his mother and that house, that shared driveway he does not think about. Night dark and damp by six in the evening as he rings her doorbell, a bottle of wine under his arm.

It's been six days since the party. Four since the cold swim and noticing how long and pale her legs were; four of wondering, between his meandering walks and mindless chat with his mother and single-line emails to the outdoor centre – back soon, yes, zero-hour contract, still fine – whether her legs had always been so long. Hard to tell, over video call. Over traded emails and unsent texts. Not that he wants to think about her legs. Not that he makes a habit of that.

It is a Friday. He'd showered and put on aftershave, hated how it made him smell of teenage boy and so showered again to get it off. He has a jolt of a moment where he realises the Robin guy might answer, but before he can arrange his face for such a meeting, the door opens and it is just Nora, like last time, and she looks pretty, and nervous.

Here's the chocolate, Bren says, before she can say anything.

He pulls it out of his back pocket, the slab he'd bought as a last-minute thought at the airport. Weighty in its green sleeve and gold foil.

It really is life-changing, he assures her. Even if you don't like coconut, it's like. Really great.

I do like coconut, she says.

Great, Bren says, again. He says, too, that he brought wine – doesn't tell her this was because his mother insisted, you don't go for dinner at a friend's, Bren, without wine (like she'd know) – but Nora ignores this and does something he is not ready for: steps forward and puts her arms around his neck. It is the first time they have hugged since he got home. The first time they have touched, properly, since he left.

The wind lifts his hair, and hers too.

He puts his own hands on the small of her back.

It's just an acknowledgement, he thinks, that he is here, as he said he would be; pre-planned, pre-arranged. Bringing chocolate and wine after a string of apologetic texts; he does wonder when she is going to apologise to him, too, but that dissolves as he breathes her in, scent of clementines, bright, and alive.

Stupid, Nora whispers, and she sounds breathless.

What is, Bren asks, but she steps back, small shake of her head, says to come in, that Robin's in the shower. And then they're in the kitchen and there are crisps and beers on the table but she can open the wine, if he'd prefer.

Beer's fine, he says.

Great, she says; that word again, so limp and lifeless. Like *lovely*, his mother's favourite.

Your flat's really nice, Bren says, as she takes a bottle opener from a drawer. I didn't say that to you, at the party.

I didn't give you a chance to say much of anything, she concedes. And then when I did, I jumped down your throat.

She must mean the upset in the café, post-swim, and Bren realises that they're both on the back foot, here; both apologising without actually saying it. It relaxes him, somewhat. He takes the beer from her. They hear the creak of the shower tray from the next room; a thud and a bounce, as if Robin has dropped the soap.

He was late home from work, Nora says.

It's fine, Bren says.

He's really keen to meet you, she says. Bren drinks some more beer, says yeah. It'll be good to meet him, too.

Great. Lovely. Good.

So what's – Bren says at exactly the same time that Nora says how's – and they break off, saying no you go, no – what were you –

How's your mum, she asks him.

Don't you speak to her, pretty often?

But I mean how are you finding it? Being home, with her.

Which is vague, he thinks, and yet all-encompassing. He puts his beer down on the table, takes a crisp from the bowl. It's fine, he says. Nora is by the kitchen island, uncapping a beer for herself, or for Robin, maybe.

She's the same, Bren answers.

I think she's doing really well, Nora says, for what it's worth. She hasn't had any episodes, or anything. For a long time.

Do we have to talk about this?

Nora looks across the island at him, the beer bottle poised in her hand.

No, she says. Not if you don't want to.

Well I don't want to, if that's cool.

All right. I just thought it was really nice, how happy she was, when you got back.

Was she?

Of *course* she was. She called me, the morning after you got home.

Saying what?

Nora opens her mouth, closes it again. Turns to the sink, fills a jug with water from the tap. She thanked me, she says, over her shoulder, but the tap water drowns it out so that Bren has to check when she approaches, sets the jug down.

Thanked you?

I know, she says. It was sweet, but senseless. I said it wasn't me that brought you home.

Except it kind of was, Bren says.

Well she was beside herself, Nora says, as if breezing past what he'd just said. He is confused by this, by how she wants to talk about real things, but if he tries, it seems she doesn't want to hear it.

Mm, Bren says. Well. We went to bed ten minutes after I arrived, so she didn't seem *that* happy. And day to day, things are pretty muted, I'd say.

That's the medication, Nora says. It . . . mellows things, for her.

I know that, Bren says. I did grow up in that house.

Silence, then. Stretched, for several seconds.

And I know *that*, Nora says. But I've also been here for the last twelve years, Bren. And I'm trying to tell you there's nothing to be scared of, any more.

I'm not *scared*, Bren says, and Nora says you know what I mean, but he does not. Who is she to claim, after a brief weekly phone call, or shared neighbourly dinners with Freya there too, that she has *any* idea what it's like, to grow up like that? To hear your mother wailing through your closed bedroom door, to pray for the soothing sound of your father's voice, to dread the silence more than anything, that deep, still-bodied silence, because that meant shutdown, the person inside lost somewhere, for hours at a time. Days, even. Weeks.

I just, Nora says, and Bren says well don't.

His heart is beating like the grandfather clock back home. A heavy, slow clunking, too loud for the room.

Nora turns away from him, towards the hob, and Bren drinks more beer. Remembers what she said, at the coffee roasters after their swim: *why is this so hard*.

So you missed me, then, he says, forcing his voice into gentle mockery; easier than sitting in the awkwardness of whatever the hell they're tiptoeing around. That's what you're saying, right? That I should come home more often?

She glances round at him, a paring knife in her hand.

Josie would like that, she says. Yeah.

And is she really talking about his mother here, he wonders, and Nora is blushing, now, which perhaps means she is wondering the same thing. Or maybe the flame on the hob is just warm as she's heating the oil, scraping some pre-crushed garlic into the pan, and can he help with anything, no, she says, no thank you.

Silence, again, just the steam from the wok. And Bren is just reaching for his beer and asking if she'll go swimming again on Monday, when she turns to him, her cheeks definitely red, there's no hiding it, and she looks like she's full of emotion, words or regret or something else he half recognises, but then she says Bren. Please don't.

Don't what, says another voice, before Bren can respond, and it is then that Robin walks in.

–

Bren had not paid him much notice at the party. Robin had been a little drunk, surrounded by friends, and Bren himself had got talking to some people who had seemed interesting enough; distracting, at least, when Nora was giving him such a wide berth. But now, freshly showered and with his shirt unbuttoned, Bren sees, for the first time, that Nora's fiancé is real. More than just a photograph, or a line in an email. Which means that Bren can no longer pretend that he's no one.

There he is, standing in the doorway of his own kitchen. Shower-damp, shoulder-length hair, wearing a plum cotton shirt and lounge trousers. And he's tall, far taller than Bren. Not smiling, exactly, but his eyes are warm, chocolatey-dark. Attractive, Bren supposes, in an artsy, asymmetrical sort of way, with his brown-black hair and soft-looking stubble and an air of ease that Bren himself has to force but here, on this guy, seems effortless. Because he's a touch older, maybe. Not by much, but enough to make Bren feel . . . less than, somehow.

But less than what?

This is not a competition; there is no prize. They're just having dinner and hanging out and, as Bren had assured Freya, not digging up their past, which is overgrown now, anyway, with new grass. A ring on Nora's finger. Tattoos – an actual shark bite, for crying out loud – layers of sunburn and old bruises come and gone across Bren's own skin.

What have I missed? Robin asks, as he buttons his shirt.

Casual, like they've all been friends for years. Nora has turned back to the hob, is cutting strips of raw chicken, pearly pink, into the wok.

Not much, she says. We were waiting for you.

Robin glances at Bren with a gentle smile, and Bren swallows – whatever it is that needs swallowing – and stands.

So great to meet you, Robin says, as he clasps his hand with both his own, and Bren notes that his use of the word great, here, seems genuine. His handshake firm, but not threatening. Not threatened.

You too, Bren says. I've heard a lot about you.

Which isn't strictly true, but it's what you say, isn't it; he feels awkward about it for the first time as he sits back down; aware, finally, of how he never bothered to ask after him. Never asked how things were going, between them. What he's like, even. Who he is.

So are you over the jet lag yet? Robin asks, and other questions come, too, flowing like water, is he adjusting to the cold British weather? Sunrise, so late in the day, here. Walking? Walking where? Just around, you know. Getting his bearings.

Nice to see your mum? Robin says, as he uncorks some red wine – not the bottle that Bren brought, but something French, expensive-looking. Nora said that Josie's –

Will you make the guacamole, please, Nora asks, and this was his job when his dad hosted burrito night, so Bren rises from his chair just as Robin says sure – because of course, she was talking to him. The guy in the plum shirt with the suave stubble and shared bank account, the one who proposed, who is on a first-name basis, it seems, with his own mother. Bren pretends he was simply leaning over for more crisps. Sits back down as Robin takes a knife to an avocado, twists the two halves apart.

I wanted to thank you for all the fridge magnets, Robin says, as Bren feels something strange settling in his stomach.

They weren't for you, he wants to say, that settled-something now churning.

Oh, he says, instead. Sure. I knew Nora was bound to have a big fridge, so.

Weird thing to say. Meant to express he knows how much she loves to cook, comes off as implying she's fat, or something, which she isn't. Not skinny, either, not that it matters. He's never looked at her like that. Sized her up, thought about her in a way that ranks her somewhere, in terms of attractiveness. Maybe once, at a party when they were sixteen, when he saw her in this particular red dress, memories he'd buried because there is new grass, remember, *new grass*, and a beer, thank god, that needs drinking.

So tell me! Robin says, as Nora moves her spatula around the wok, and Bren takes a long glug to hide his face. Where's the best place you've been?

Um, Bren says, lowering his bottle.

Hard to choose?

Like choosing a favourite child, Bren says.

My parents would definitely choose my brother, Robin says.

So would mine, Bren says, if I had one.

Unsure laughter, then, from Robin. Nora passes him the coriander; Robin shreds it with his hands; Bren watches them work alongside each other, wordless and practised, in their kitchen. Lemon juiced. Hob turned off. Food scooped into pre-warmed dishes before being brought to the table, Robin offering another drink, Bren? and then they're all seated and Nora is handing Bren a serving spoon, citrus and spices on the air.

Guests first, she says.

Which is an odd word for him, he thinks, out of Nora's mouth. There's a formality about it, he muses, as he takes the spoon from her. Not one he'd have used, if the tables were turned. A *guest* is invited into one's home. Temporarily. Tips easily into intruder, if they outstay their welcome. This, from the girl who used to fall asleep in his games room. Feet in his lap. Drool down her chin. Held him, in the driveway, when his dad –

You're very skinny, Nora observes, as Robin hands him a tortilla.

Am I?

Sinewy, Nora says, and Robin blasts Nora! Leave the poor guy alone! I gained ten pounds when I moved in with her, he says to Bren, in what is seemingly a conspiring tone. She's nothing if not a feeder.

Always has been, Bren says. Flashes, then, of shared popcorn in that same games room; Creme Eggs in her pockets; three ice cream scoops, instead of two, if you're going to do it, Bren, do it *right*. It's not clear whether Robin heard him over the scraping of the spoons, or the faux sound of offence that Nora makes in response. It helps that you're a *sensational* cook, Robin adds, leaning to one side as though squeezing her knee under the table. A fizzing starts up, inside of Bren, at that. Like a can of drink that's been shaken.

Well, it all looks great, Bren manages. Thanks.

And Nora nods, her cheeks still that permanent pink, says of course. It's so nice to have him here.

Lovely. Great. Nice.

Tortillas, lifted to their mouths.

Do they actually eat fajitas, in Mexico? Robin asks, after a generous bite. Or is it like chicken tikka masala – a Britishism you wouldn't actually find in India?

I never saw one, Bren says. But I'm sure they're about, for the tourists. In Cancún, or whatever.

Ah. You weren't in Cancún? Robin says, with a tilt of his head, which Bren takes to mean: you weren't a tourist?

He's heard it before, from plenty of people. Eye rolls. Good for yous. And what will you do, after this? He's wasted enough breath trying to prove the way he moves through the world is more than a *holiday*, more than partying by night and catching rays every day. More than an extended gap year. More than an existence that'll lead him, presumably, nowhere. But so what if it wasn't? So what if flicking between outdoor centres and continents and rental contracts feels dubious to most people, prompts a raised eyebrow and unimpressed *oh*, so what if they don't get why that's as good a life as anything back here, with these dishwasher-safe plates and home insurance and ladders being climbed in an office or an art café or a – wherever it is Robin works? All of that, and for what? An annual respite in a warm country near the ocean, for two weeks, if you're lucky. When Bren's whole *life* is a respite from all that, he thinks, as he takes another bite of his wrap. A rejection, even, of what's expected of everyone in a broken system, where you grow up, pay bills, care for your kids and then your parents, pay off the mortgage you almost didn't get approved in the first place, pay for your own funeral, too, if you're a good sport, then die after never having felt *alive*, never having seen or done anything, no thanks, not for him.

Robin and Nora are waiting for him to respond, and when he doesn't, must assume he didn't hear the question.

How's the work, out in Mexico, Robin tries, instead. Not that you're there, these days, I know. The adventure scene is a tad easier to picture in New Zealand.

Bren spoons more guacamole onto his plate.

I led biking tours for a company in Oaxaca, he says. For a while.

Like mountain biking?

Any kind of biking, Bren says. Mexico had opportunities

all over. City tours. Overnight bike-packing. Whatever I was paid to do.

So you do have to think about money, Robin says, and Bren takes another large mouthful so he's spared answering, for a moment. He's known this guy all of five minutes and already he's being grilled about his mother, his finances, his job. What do *you* do, he wants to ask, but no need, he can tell just from looking at him with his burgundy shirt, his tapered trousers, he's a designer, probably, or an architect. He knows that Nora met him at art school.

I get paid for the legitimate work I do, yes, Bren says, and Nora stops chewing, her own mouth full.

He didn't mean – she tries, just as Robin says I didn't – and they break off, wait for the other to speak; fragmented pause; Robin, turning back to Bren.

I was just curious, he says. Crease of concern between his eyebrows, because he's offended him; and Bren feels bad then. Just slightly.

It's enough money to live on, he says. Not enough to buy a house, or save up for any big purchases, or whatever. I won't be driving a Volvo any time soon.

Robin nods, but Nora frowns. Keeps looking at Bren while she swallows.

Not that there's anything wrong with Volvos, Bren says.

No? Nora says. There's a high, questioning note to her voice as she lays her wrap on her plate. He hears it, that pointed pitch; Robin must too.

Am I missing something? Robin says.

Yes, thinks Bren. No, says Nora: his mum drives a Volvo, that's all.

Although drives is a generous term, Bren says. Pretty sure it just sits in the driveway, these days.

No one has anything to say to that. Dinner happens. Just

the soft folding of wraps, scoop of spoons in the sauce. Nora gets up, brings the wine to the table. Tops up Robin's glass, sits back down.

So what's your – Robin begins, but Nora says sorry, can we just, and Bren pauses with his wrap halfway to his mouth.

Can we just establish, she says, moving her hand in a small circle, that if you're not willing to be critiqued on the way you live *your* life, Bren, why is it that you get to criticise your mother's?

I wasn't critiquing, Robin says, to Bren. I was just asking.

I wasn't criticising her, Bren says, and Nora grabs Robin's wine glass for a drink, her own glass empty except for the foam from her beer.

What did you mean then, she says, and Bren is not sure what she wants him to say; what will make things better, between them. Because this isn't about his mother. This is about how she stayed here, and he didn't. She is, it seems, so angry with him – when really, he should be angry with *her* – and she's using his mother as an excuse to get all self-righteous. He knows it. She knows it. Robin, who doesn't know it, is watching them both, his own tortilla stilled in his hands.

I was just saying it's not so different, doing what I do, Bren says, with his one-shouldered shrug. Making money, holding down a job.

I think you were saying it's entirely different, actually, Nora says.

Bren lowers his wrap to his plate; it slowly unfolds itself, revealing a mush of peppers and chicken.

It was just an observation, he says.

Nora, Robin says, in a tone that Bren can't unhear. Like he understands something Bren does not, when Robin is the one that doesn't understand all the things between the two of them. Long summers. Longer winters. Family barbecues cut short, so they could hang out alone, in his games room or on the village green, trading hoodies and jokes and small, unspoken parts of themselves. And yet Nora responds. Puts his wine glass back down on the table and nods, almost imperceptibly, in Robin's direction.

The Philippines! Robin says, out of nowhere. You've been there too, haven't you?

Yes, Bren says.

Tell me, Robin says, is it true they're obsessed with karaoke?

Er, yeah.

And what, Robin says, and this is a very personal question, Bren, for such an early stage in our friendship.

Okay.

What is your karaoke song of choice? You look like a Ricky Martin man, to me. *She Bangs*.

Nora laughs; Bren doesn't.

Now don't be shy, Robin says, and he has perfect white teeth, the sort Bren has seen advertised inside in-flight magazines; the result of Invisalign, surely, or gallingly good genes. I'm right, aren't I?

Bren would be the *last* person on earth to sing *She Bangs*, Nora says.

Bren would be the last person on earth to sing at all, Bren says.

Come on, man. You actually lived in the Philippines and didn't once partake in their ancient customs?

Karaoke is hardly ancient, Bren says, and Robin says he's a *Purple Rain* fan, himself, quite fancies Prince's white gloves, too, for a special occasion. Circa 1985, The Brits. For the wedding maybe! He hadn't thought of that! And Nora, this dinner is exceptionally good, by the way. As inauthentically Mexican as it is.

Agreed, Bren says, and Nora dips her chin; half in apology,

half appeased, Bren thinks. She offers him a third tortilla, which he takes.

The conversation loosens up, from there. More jokes, fewer questions; they keep eating, talk less about travel and work and home and more about inconsequential things, which are, by Bren's own admission, more significant. Nora still sews for fun. Embroiders poetry and names into napkins for christenings, or birthdays, makes a bit of money on Etsy as well as via her own shop, doesn't charge enough, Robin says, for her talent. Robin is a photographer (I was close, Bren thinks); specialises in antiques; fusses with grids and snoots and chases a lot of unpaid invoices. Freelance, though he prefers the term footloose and fancy free. Favourite city: Paris, or Madrid (Bren's is Rio). Never been outside of Europe apart from when they went to Boston for a wedding; they went to New York for the day, Nora cried at the MOMA. What's MOMA, Bren asks, and Robin thinks he's kidding.

And how do they spend their Friday nights? Bren likes to hike, rock climb, yes, he's bungee jumped and skydived, too, multiple times, but the water is where he likes to be; forget Full Moon Parties and night clubs and local bars, lazing down a creek under a setting sun is the only real high that he craves, while Nora and Robin are jointly obsessed with animated movies, some of them dark as hell. *Watership Down*, *The Last Unicorn*, *The Plague Dogs* –

Do *not*, cries Robin, talk to me about *The Plague Dogs*!

And things are finally normal, like Bren had hoped it might be. Old friends, having dinner, although something is still fizzing inside him as he sits across from her, like this. At her kitchen table as they exchange scraps of each other but are still, he thinks, holding back, somewhat, presumably because Robin is here.

He goes with it, though. As Robin plugs his final wrap with sour cream to soothe the spice, and Nora scatters red chillies inside her own; as Bren does the same, mirroring her movements in a gesture that means nothing, or perhaps, in some buried, awakening part of him, says see, Nora, we shouldn't hold back. Because you and I? We can handle the heat.

–

And so he turns it up, without meaning to. In the living room, as Robin makes coffee in the kitchen, after dinner.

The fairy lights have vanished. Furniture pushed back into the centre of the room, the makeshift dance floor long gone. Bren sits in an armchair as Nora settles opposite, on the sofa.

Third time lucky, Bren says, and she pulls a crocheted cushion onto her lap, waiting for him to explain. We've not been normal since I got back, have we? he says. At the party, or the pond. I was hoping tonight would be the night.

Nora lifts a stray thread off the cushion cover. Says right. That she wishes. Well.

A habit of hers, not finishing her sentences; one that Bren thought she'd have grown out of, by now.

I don't want to argue, Bren says. If you've got something to say, Nora, can you just say it? So we can get back to normal?

I think, she says, and there's a crash from the kitchen so that they both flinch, and Robin calls out, sorry, butterfingers! As you were! And they look back at each other, Nora flushing red again, this time, Bren thinks, because she is marrying someone who has – who *says* – butterfingers.

You think what? Bren prompts.

I think our versions of normal are very different, she says.

Well, obviously, Bren says. Don't take that the wrong way, he adds, holding his palms up. Just because my mum stays home and sees no one –

She sees people!

She sees you and Freya and the postman, Bren says. But just because that's *her* life doesn't mean I'm judging yours, he says, gesturing around the room. It's great, for you, what you have going, here. As much as it pains me to say it.

Nora holds his eyes, then. Mesmerising, as ever, one blue, the other a kind of green-brown; there's a name for it, he knows, a colour he can't recall. Words gone from his brain, when she looks at him like that.

She looks, but says nothing, so he keeps talking. Tries to explain.

It's just not what I pictured, for us, he says, glancing at the rug and the bookcase and the pictures on the walls. Voice level, to show he's not being accusatory; just nostalgic. Remember, Nora, how we said we'd not buy *things*, but acquire stories and sunburn and scars, and I did that, I'm doing that, but look, here, at what's yours.

Reliving this, though he does not say it out loud.

And he thinks he knows what she'll say; thinks she'll ask, what *did* you picture, then, but instead she says: there was no us once you left, Bren.

There is no clock in here. No ticking between them, no sound. Just this thing that they've danced around for years, which hadn't seemed to matter when he was thousands of miles away, but here, now, with those eyes on his and the smell of her so close – body lotion, Christmas, clementines – he finds that he wants to know *why* she didn't come with him. Is burning to know, in fact, why she didn't give him a single reason why not, and yet answered his calls and his emails as if things never needed to be explained, as if he should just get over it, get over her, which he did, didn't he, *he did*.

I've missed you so much, Nora says next.

Her voice, so quiet.

Sometimes I miss you so much I forget what I'm doing, she says. But I'm also *so* furious with you, Bren.

There. She's said it. And it's what he'd expected, in a way, after how she'd acted at the party and the ponds and over dinner, but it's also *not* expected, after twelve years of friendly dispassion. Something new rises between them now that it's out there: a joint, moon-like hurt, impossibly big and full.

I don't think you get to be, Bren tells her.

They keep looking at each other. Are still looking as Robin walks in with a tray declaring that he comes bearing hot drinks, and biscotti – do you like biscotti? Who doesn't like biscotti! Handing Bren a coffee, placing Nora's hot chocolate on the side table. Dark, it looks, at least eighty-five percent; which will be bitter, Bren knows, as she raises it to her mouth. Bitter and, he'd have thought, not at all to her taste. Not the flavour he'd expect her to choose.

–

So, Bren, Robin says, stretching his long legs out on the rug. Please do pepper us with honeymoon ideas.

It's getting late, and Bren thinks he should probably leave. He's uncomfortably full, doesn't want the biscotti, but eats it anyway. Dunks it in his coffee, feels it give beneath his teeth. *Honeymoon*. The term as sickly sweet as the biscuit.

It depends, he says, as he chews; Nora's eyes no longer on him, but on her own cup. Their prior exchange resounding like a bell.

On what you like, he goes on. What you'd want from it, how much time you'd have.

A standard two weeks I think, Robin says, looking at Nora, who dips her chin in a nod. She's wrapped both hands around her mug, seems withdrawn.

You like art, right, Bren says.

And the ocean! Robin says. And dancing! Badly, but it's still dancing.

Art and the ocean and bad dancing, Bren echoes.

It'd be nice to explore outside of Europe, too, Robin says.

Where is the money coming from, for this, Nora asks, and Robin says aha, we have a plan, remember, and she raises her eyebrows as she drinks more hot chocolate but it's loving, that look, and not derisive, and the fizzing in Bren intensifies. It feels so intense, it's a wonder they can't hear it, so he speaks purely to override it, says Latin America, maybe. Somewhere like Cuba or Peru.

Peru? Robin says, as if it's the first time he's heard of the place. Biscotti half eaten in his hand. *Peru*. I like it! Like two Paddington Bears, he says, nudging Nora's rib with his elbow; she laughs, shaking her head because it's dumb, or because she actually finds him funny; Bren can't quite tell.

The more Robin talks, the less Bren feels undermined by his age and height and career. He's a creative with nice teeth and bold – bizarre – fashion sense, whose cultural references thus far have extended to Prince's wardrobe, a string of Pixar movies, and now, an illustrated bear from a kids' book. Clearly, he's not as sophisticated as Bren first thought, but then, in a flicker he decides to ignore, that *does* mean he makes more sense for Nora. A guy with warmth, and soft edges. An ability, it seems, to read the room, lighten the tone. In any other scenario, Bren would really like him.

Why, he thinks, does he not like him.

So what is the plan, then, he asks, and Nora and Robin break eye contact, both look at him across the coffee table.

For the wedding, I presume, he says. You said you have a plan?

Nora's feet are pressed against Robin's thighs; Robin puts his hand on her foot. Bren tries not to notice these things.

Well, Nora says, and Bren raises an eyebrow. Waiting for her to say oh, you know, these things take time. We haven't set a date or even thought about it, because this is what his mother had implied, in passing, and he wants to meet Nora's eyes as she admits this; wants to lift his chin in a small, wordless acknowledgement.

Are you sure this is what you want, that lift will say.

I am not, her eyes would say back.

But instead she looks at Robin who smile-shrugs, then back at Bren as she says actually, we're moving on things quite fast.

Other eyebrow raised, now.

Fast? he repeats.

Or rather, on an expedient schedule, Robin says.

I'm not following, Bren says, and Robin says they're going rogue – another smile, then, at Nora, would they *stop* that already – I know a place, Robin is saying, he did a photo shoot there once, in the woods, it's *extraordinary*, and they offer this cancellation package where you can get married on a fifth of the budget if you're willing to move last minute. You have to sacrifice some things, obviously, like whether all the guests can make it, but they'd prefer a small day, anyway, so yeah, they've put their names down, and are going to see it this month, with the hope that they'll be married by the summer.

They host this planning day, Robin goes on, as Nora puts down her mug, her long hair shielding her face. Where we decide on all the things we want, and pay up in full, so it's all good to go. And then we wait.

But Bren still isn't following. Doesn't want to.

Wait for what, he asks.

Well, Robin says, and it's the first time he looks less than delighted; his voice taking on a note of regret. For someone else's misfortune, really, he says. Whatever might cancel another wedding, last minute.

It's not always a bad thing, Nora says, and her voice, Bren thinks, has changed too; sounds almost wooden. The couple get pregnant, or something, so decide to postpone.

Or their photographer ends up double booking, Robin says, so they reschedule.

People really care that much about photographers? Bren says.

There is a pause, then; Robin's turn, to raise his eyebrows; no, Bren says, sorry, I just mean, people would seriously move their whole wedding just for that?

People go a little crazy with weddings, Robin reasons. But we won't. We want this to be easy, and stress free. Right, Nora?

Right, she says. Still not looking at Bren.

So we'll get our ducks in a row, pronto, Robin says, and then one day get a call that'll say we're getting married in a week or two, or three.

Or we could be waiting till next year, Nora says.

Okay, Bren says. Wow.

The enthusiasm in Robin's face fades, just slightly, at Bren's lack of it. Nora stays focused on the now-empty mug in her hands.

We don't expect everyone to make it, so last minute, Robin says, misreading Bren's expression. Only if they can, and want to. Let me show you the venue, he goes on, putting his own mug down and leaning forward. I've never seen anything like it, he says, tapping on his phone. It's this stunning structure made of pine and recycled glass, look, and it's got these sliding doors that open out to the forest and it's not far from the beach and, and, and, he keeps talking, but Bren is not listening, does not want to hear what makes this venue so special and magic and so very them, and this fizzing inside of him is not settling as he looks at Robin's phone screen, unseeing, a faint ringing in his ears.

Wow, he says again, when Robin has scrolled to the final picture on the website.

He sits back in the armchair, feels a pressure in his feet.

I was going to tell you, Nora says, her voice gentle, more like her own. But Robin only firmed up the details last night.

I wasn't sure she was gonna go for it, Robin says, in the conspiring voice he'd used back in the kitchen; he smiles too much, Bren decides, it's unnerving. But then you asked, Robin says, and, well.

I thought why not, Nora says, and Robin kisses her on the forehead. Bren puts his coffee down, says cool, that's cool for you guys. But it's late. He should probably, you know. Head off.

Stilted pause, then. Robin saying, you don't want another coffee?

I'm good, Bren says. Thanks. For dinner, and everything. It's been great.

That word again.

I'll be in touch, he says, standing up. Before I go.

Go? Robin says, and Nora is trying to catch his eye, now, as if she's trying to say something without words.

Yeah, Bren says. I'm checking flights to get back out there.

You don't want to stay for the wedding?

Robin, Nora says.

What? You were just saying last night – she was just saying last night, he says to Bren – that a fast turnaround might mean you could be here for it. Which was a big tick, for this rogue old plan of mine.

And at this, Bren looks back at her.

Really?

I wouldn't put that on you, Nora says, embarrassed. If you want to go, you should. It might not even happen, anyway.

Those eyes of hers, like whirlpools. Like they could drag him under.

Because of the cancellation thing, she says.

But also, your best friend only gets married once, Robin adds, and she says his name again, *Robin*, but Bren ignores it, says, you said that?

What?

That I'm your best friend?

Well, yeah, Nora says.

Sudden notion inside him, then. Like the base dropping out of something he hadn't known was there. Bren stands still, like that, the coffee table between them. Nora remains seated, the cushion in her lap.

All right, Bren says. I'll be there.

No intake of breath, or sardonic raise of an eyebrow.

Really? she says.

It's you, Nora, he says, as if they're the only two in the room. Of course I'll be there.

There is another long moment of no clock and no breathing and then Robin stands up and says smashing, and Bren and Nora break eye contact. Bren glances at Robin, who is back to delight, so good to finally meet you, Bren; next time, we'll pick your brains on Peru.

Next time, Bren nods, as he leads him to the door. Thanks, again, before he's out into the night air. Drinking it down cold, thinking what is this, what just happened.

What on earth is happening here.

six

That went well, you say, as you wash the mugs in the sink, Nora drying them afterwards with a tea towel. These ones are too precious to run through the dishwasher. Not a mistake you'd make again, after the crack in her beloved yunomi in the autumn of 2016, devastating, RIP; she'd cried.

Yeah, Nora says. After a rocky start.

That's okay, though, you tell her, she'd anticipated that, right. With their history.

You're not entirely clear on that history but she's implied it's difficult, there's a lot of hurt there, they were young, friends that were more than friends, not family but close to it, you've got the gist. And Jon dying was – she doesn't like to talk about it – so painful, in more ways than an ordinary death. She'd told you all about it once, after a lot of wine; she had cried, then, too, then panicked that she'd said too much. You'd told her she'd said just the right amount, and held her, through her tears. Unfazed.

Now you hand her an – uncracked, perfectly washed and preserved – mug; she takes it, dries it carefully. It is late, and you are both tired and quiet.

I told him I'd missed him, she says. When you were out here, making the drinks.

That's very sweet of you, you say, because it is. What did he say?

Not a lot, she says.

He's a man of few words, you say. I got that. Is it, er.

You consider your next sentence; run the hot tap, squirt in some more Fairy Liquid, because the wok needs another go-round. You'd been soaking it since making the coffees, but the sauce is stubborn, still congealed at the sides.

Is it hard, you ask her, hearing him talk about his travels, like that?

Nora makes a small noise, something she keeps back in her mouth. Mm.

It's okay if it is, you say.

Sort of, she says. It's just strange to think about what didn't happen, I guess. Not that I feel regret, or anything. About what I did, instead.

She says this last part in a rush, as if she doesn't want to think about it, and you say Nora, it's normal to have regrets. It's one of the things I love most about you, in fact.

She frowns a little as she dries the last mug, says, what, my capacity for regret?

Your capacity for seeing the wondrous possibilities in everything, you tell her, waving your Marigold-clad hand in an arc. This paint shade, or that paint shade. A wedding, or no wedding! You care, so deeply, Nora. More than most. You're so . . . diligent, about living.

She protests at the praise, but is frowning less, now. Appreciates your attempts at profundity, you think, when it slips out like this. That old art school rhetoric still inside you, somewhere, Adrian Searle, eat your heart out.

Plus I regret a ton of things too, you tell her, *like how I didn't soak this damn wok straight after dinner*.

You do?

Sure. But it doesn't mean I yearn for any of it. I think about what could have been, sometimes. If I'd pursued architecture, like my parents wanted. If I'd taken that Rome residency, after graduation, I mean, who knows where I'd be. But just because I think about them, doesn't mean I *wish* they'd happened.

Nora is putting the mugs away, now. You can't see her face because of the open cupboard door, and you keep scouring at the scum in the wok.

I was so upset with him for going, Nora says, from her place on the floor. But I was so fixated on being upset with him, I'm not sure I realised how . . . upset I was, with myself.

You nod. Just let her talk.

We'd spent so long planning our trip, she says. There were so many things I wanted to see and do, and because I was so mad at him I just retreated into *staying*, as hard as I could. Helping Josie grieve, and managing Freya, and applying to the best art schools as a kind of reaction, for something to *do*, and not ever thinking for a moment that I'd get in. And then I did. And then I met you.

And now here you are, putting mugs in a cupboard with your dreams having died a wingless death, you say, and there is a marked pause before Nora lets out her dazzling laugh, because she hadn't expected that, and she straightens up, closes the cupboard, says yep, pretty much.

You are still at the sink, still battling the wok. She puts her arms around your waist and rests her face in the curve of your back. You start to dance, a little, swaying your hips, and she moves with you. Thanks, she says, her voice muffled, and you slow to a stop. Seeing Bren just brings up a lot, I guess. And he makes me feel . . . unworthy, somehow.

You tell her he shouldn't.

Not least because you don't need anyone else to prove your worth, you say, in a mimicry of her mother, and she snorts. But because – back to your own voice, now – he clearly adores you, Nora.

She stays entwined around your waist.

He came home for our party, you say. The idea that you're unworthy, or dull, by his standards, is all your own reading of this – it's not coming from him. And hey. He's sticking round for the wedding, now. That'll patch things up between you, don't you think?

Another mm from her, then. She lets you go, rootles around for a dishwasher tablet in a drawer; places it inside the cap, clicks it shut.

Speaking of which, you say, as she closes it, and the machine whirs into life. Jed wants a clearer idea of the wedding party.

Jed?

The venue owner? Or manager. Whatever he is, I'm not sure. But he wants to know if you're having bridesmaids, and if I'm having groomsmen. Get a rough idea of a guest list and *all that jazz*.

You belt out the last line, and Nora replies as if you haven't just broken into Broadway song, saying she's not having bridesmaids; you've established this.

Well I'm having Goose as my best man, you say. Predictably.

Can you imagine if you didn't?

Tears, tantrums, cut ties, you say, and all that just from my mother.

No laughter from her at this, just a sincere outbreath, like *right*. You wipe the draining board down, say doesn't she want someone like Shay as her maid of honour, or something?

Nothing with the word maid in it, Nora says. My best woman, maybe? But I also kind of hate that.

You are not surprised; she is her mother's daughter, after all, but you ask her why, all the same, as you drain the water from the sink.

The fact that I have to have a favourite *woman* and you have to have a right-hand *man*, and all this hierarchical nonsense that is *best*, she says, when my mum, or even Josie or Shay or, I don't know, Gill from primary school – they're all really important women, in my life. Nobody's *best*, or more honourable, than the rest. It can really end up hurting people, this stuff.

You have suspected, in the past, that this is why a wedding had been off the table all this time. Not because of her feminist mother. Not because Nora herself had no interest. But because she didn't want to cause any upset to herself or others; preferred to carry on, as they were. In an unrocked boat.

So ask Bren, you say.

What?

Have a best man, too, now he's sticking around. Or a brides-man, maybe. If you don't like the term best.

Umm, Nora says. I don't know how that would . . . land.

Your mother would love it! you say. Defying convention. And it's an olive branch, to Bren, too, isn't it? You said yourself he was your best friend. Although there is, you admit, one stark problem with that plan.

What? Nora says, and she sounds worried, so you scoop her into an embrace, the yellow Marigolds still stretched up your forearms.

The wrath of Shay, you say.

Oh, I don't know, Nora says. She'd probably be fine, if we made Horace the ring bearer, or something.

Now *there's* an idea! A dog-friendly wedding? Maybe *that's* what's different, about our day! Forget plus ones, everyone bring a dog!

We don't even have a dog!

And I still don't understand why, you say, as you pull off the Marigolds and leave them hanging over the kitchen tap to dry. Discuss it, once more, as she puts on her moisturiser, quiet, then, as you each read a chapter of your books. Turn the lights off, bubbling with how thrilled you are. How excited you are for the months – and indeed, the rest of your life – ahead, and you are thinking this as you drift into that flickering film-like lucidity as she lies there beside you, looking up at the ceiling. Too still, as though she is firmly awake, but before you can ask if everything's all right, you're gone, and a dream has taken you under.

seven

Bren missed the last train, is walking home when Nora calls him. He'd spent half an hour on a platform bench while he waited for a cab, who wouldn't take him as far as the middle-of-nowhere village, but *would* take him to the town where he went to school where, from there, he could either call another, or walk the two hours home.

He'd decided on the latter. Felt restless anyway, eager to move. It is two in the morning now, but he still feels wired. Draws his hands into his coat sleeves for warmth as he follows the river back home.

There is something sinister about the water in the dark, he thinks, tar-like, slow-moving. Stars and snowdrops aglow, everything else dark and still. Even the fizzing he had felt, over dinner, has petered out, at last. Whatever that was about.

But then his phone is vibrating in his pocket as he ducks under a willow, and he pulls it out and it's her and he's fizzing all over again, sliding to answer, saying, hello?

Did you mean it, she asks, as Bren keeps walking along the canal. Boots on the hard mud path, vision adjusted to the dark.

Sorry, Nora, he says. Could you be more specific?

Kind of snarky, but, he reasons, also fair.

The path converges into a strip of long grass, wet against

his boots; they're supposed to be waterproof, but already his socks feel damp. He should probably re-proof them, was planning to do so in New Zealand, and yet here he is in England, walking home via the river he used to swim in with his best friend who is calling him, after midnight, making him feel things he was sure he wasn't going to.

Will you stay for the wedding, she asks, and he doesn't answer just yet. Imagines the flush up her neck. Wonders where she is. In bed, maybe, beside that guy. Beside Robin.

I don't want you to be there if you don't want to be, Nora says.

I could say the same to you, he says, and she says what?

He keeps walking through the dark, thinking. The stars keep being stars.

You never wanted to get married, Nora, he says. Last time I checked.

And when was the last time you checked?

She does not sound angry, or even amused. It's a neutral question, and a good one, at that. It's not like they've swapped notes on that stuff, in recent years. In all fairness, he'd never intended to stay abroad for this long, either. But look what happened. Look where time took him. He left. She stayed. Life went on, anyway.

We were kids, she says, as if reading his thoughts, and he senses, now, that she must be alone. I didn't know what I wanted. I didn't know that I'd meet. That I'd feel.

Like marriage material?

Marriage is such an awful word, Nora says. It even *sounds* stale.

I agree, Bren says, which is why I'm confused you've gone for it.

She falls quiet again, but things feel easier this time, not so tense. It's the dark, Bren thinks, as he passes a canal lock, two sleeping swans on the grass. It's the phone, rather than being in-person. It's the beer and the wine and too much dinner, it's the shared musings on stale words, strange lives.

Have you been talking to Freya? she asks.

Just the once, Bren says. But I do have my own thoughts on these things.

Turns out, Nora says, so do I.

The grass thins into a more packed-down path. Dirt, haphazard stones. He passes an old mill, then a concrete bridge that he does not cross. A small gravel-flecked road that he does, before he rejoins the towpath.

So why are you calling, exactly? Bren says. Just to check I'm cool with you getting married, after all?

To ask if you'll really be there, Nora says. Like you said you would be.

Bren moves the phone from one ear to the other, his hands so cold it almost hurts. Thinking that, while his knowledge of psychology is based on *The Sopranos*, and a few friendly chats with a half-girlfriend that was never really a girlfriend – just a fellow redhead taking a break in Bali, ahead of her psychotherapy training – he knows deflection when he hears it. Is quite the master of it, himself.

When I was in New Zealand, he tells her, the first time round? I worked at the bungee centre for a while, on the Kawarau River.

I remember, Nora says.

There'd always be people that would sign up to jump and just stand there, he says, looking over the edge. Psyching themselves up. Counting down, overthinking it. I saw it time and again, Nora; none of them ever jumped. It was the ones who walked straight to the edge who actually bungeed.

Silence, between them, as she listens.

It's what I did, when I left, Bren says; pushing this thing

around, between them, as if it's a leftover bite of something they've shared, but not finished. And I didn't regret it, he tells her, I still don't. I don't regret not hanging around, wearing a black suit and tie, shaking people's hands who I'd never met and would never meet again, eating fucking cheese and pineapple on a stick.

It is the first time he has referenced his dad's funeral, aloud.

Not just to Nora. To anyone.

I didn't overthink it, he says. I just jumped.

Nora stays quiet, aware, it seems, of how raw this is. How new for him, despite the time that has passed.

Is that what you're angry about? Bren asks her, remembering her hushed voice in the living room, only hours before. *So furious with you, Bren.*

One of the things, she says. He has to swap hands, because of the cold; put the other in his pocket. The moon is out, too, amid the stars. A silver-white eyelash in the sky.

Well, for the record, Bren tells her, in case she doesn't remember: I left because I had to. Because if I thought about it, I never would.

He keeps walking, moon-shadows across the path.

But I did miss you, too, he says. So much, that it was easier to pretend that I didn't.

A small sound, down the phone, but it's just her breath. Relief, or confirmation; something thawing between them, as she says yeah. Like a question, or like she knew. She doesn't embellish, or go into her other reasons for being angry, so Bren doesn't go into his.

Nora? he says, and she says yes?

How is it that you're calling me, at this time of night?

With Robin, presumably, close by.

He hears a rustling then, it is loud, disruptive, like she's flipping a mattress on the other end of the bloody line, but she's probably just drawing a blanket around herself, shifting deeper into an armchair.

Because I really *would* like you at my wedding, she says, her voice soft. But before I get attached to the idea, I need to know that you won't get on a plane, Bren, just before the ceremony, or something. Because I want to let all this – weirdness, between us – go, now that you're home, but I don't think I can take you *bungee-ing* out of my life again.

I won't, he says.

You promise?

I'll let you track my location, if you like, he says. As long as I can track you back. Kind of weird, otherwise.

I don't need to track you, Bren.

You sure? It'll be a hoot, I reckon. Watch me go from my mum's garden to the corner shop to my bedroom and back. Wild.

He hears her breathe out again. Feels a lightness in himself, as she does; as she says fine, and they both tap their phones in silence, locations accepted on their screens.

So now we've cleared that up, she says, my next question is a big one.

You're not going to ask for my karaoke song, are you?

Laughing, she says no. She's asking if he'll be her best man.

The canal ends. He's on a country road, now. No cars, or buses. Just them.

Robin suggested it but I don't know why I didn't think of it, she says, and the words spill out, like she wants to say them before she can change her mind. And it's also my way of saying I'm so *happy*, Bren, that you came home. That you're here for this. Which I've not been all that clear about, I don't think. So far.

And when he says nothing, she ploughs on.

Robin's got his brother, Goose, as *his* best man. And

I'm not doing the whole bridesmaid thing, or the maid of honour thing, because the word maid is even worse than marriage.

Bren can no longer feel his hands; his toes, too, are numb with cold. The countryside looks the same, the grass and hedgerows and pylons dull shadows in the night, the signpost saying he's only half a mile now, from home, and yet the night feels unfamiliar, somehow, surreal.

He is staying for Nora's wedding.

She wants him to be her best man.

She is marrying someone, soon. Someone with a brother named –

Goose? he asks.

Yeah, she says, and Bren hears her smile down the phone. It's a family nickname, obviously. Something about his long neck when he was little. Plus his real name is Ryan.

When Bren doesn't respond, she says like the actor, Ryan Gosling? A baby goose?

That's pretty tenuous.

In-jokes always are though, aren't they, Nora says. You'll like him. He's like Robin, but a bit more . . . blunt. And really funny.

I'm sure, Bren says, and Nora exhales, as if satisfied.

I'm so happy, she repeats, and for the first time since the party, she sounds it. That fizzing, inside him, crystallising into something small and hard, like a seed, as he wonders – no, *knows* – that he's the one who's made her so. By coming home. Agreeing to stay.

What about you, then, Nora asks, as he follows the road past the church, the graveyard creepy as hell. Flicker of saying no, we can't bury him, he'd hate that, all that earth, down in the dark, he liked the dawn, the trees, Mum, please.

What about me?

Past the church, now. Nora's voice has changed octave with interest, and it is nearly three in the morning and she is still wanting to talk and the graveyard is behind him and that seed grows a tiny shoot inside him.

Are *you* happy? she asks. You said you don't regret . . . the past. And you seem happy enough, whenever we talk. But I just wanted to . . . check.

I'm good, Bren says.

So was there anyone for you, out there?

Anyone . . .?

You know. Special.

God, Nora, he says. You sound like my mother.

Well, I don't know how to ask these things! Did you . . . date?

Not really.

Take any *lovers*?

Nora, stop, he says, but despite himself, he starts laughing, because that's what she's doing. They're still laughing as the road opens out onto the green, the swing set skeletal on the black grass; lights on in his mother's living room window, even though her bedtime was over an hour ago.

Shit, he says, but Nora says I was just joking. You don't have to tell me if you don't want to.

He's picked up his pace again for home, but at this, he slows down; her prior question weighing between them. A few, is all he says. What do you care, anyway?

I don't, Nora says, as he crosses the green. I was just curious, that's all. You've never talked about it.

You've never asked.

Just as well, she says, because there's no room for any plus ones at this wedding of mine.

This spontaneous sometime wedding, Bren says.

This long-time-coming, maybe-spring, maybe-summer wedding, Nora says.

Wait. If you don't get a cancellation by the summer, do I have to. I mean, would you want me to –

The venue guy thinks we'd likely be married by June, Nora says. July, latest. And if not, we regroup. There are fewer weddings come the autumn, see. Fewer cancellations.

Got it, Bren says, after a pause. So if you're not married by July, you'll relieve me of my best man duties?

He is coming up the driveway now, boots crunching on the gravel.

Yes, is all that she says.

The surrealism continues. He is fine with this; she's fine, too. They are both fine or both figuring out how to be, and isn't that, he thinks, essentially the same thing.

What duties does a best man actually have, he asks her, as he reaches the door.

I don't know, Nora says. Hand out cake, maybe? Tackle Freya if she objects, halfway through the ceremony?

There's another, longer, pause.

Two things I can do, Bren says, and Nora says thanks, well, I better go. Attempt to get at least *some* sleep before this big week.

And when he asks her why, what's this week, he expects her to say just work, my commute, but instead she says she's made a wedding dress appointment for next weekend. Seeing as they're moving fast, now, on this thing.

This thing.

Bren stands on the doorstep, not wanting to go inside. It is cold, and his dad died in this driveway, and he hasn't thought about that properly until this very moment and yet all he wants to do is stay on the phone, talking to Nora; filling himself up with other feelings.

Sure, Bren says, eventually. Are you.

He clears his throat.

Going alone?

Nora laughs again, but it takes on a wooden quality, this time, like her voice earlier that evening. Shay has to watch the café, she says, and it's not really Freya's scene, and beneath the wood there is a sadness which means before he can think he's asking – is it a best man thing?

Quiet, then. Clear of her own throat.

If we're going to do this, Nora, Bren says, let's do it right.

His words hang like the night around him. He wonders if she remembers that this is what she used to say about the ice cream in his mum's freezer, raspberry ripple, always, three scoops not two, and while she doesn't acknowledge the memory, she does say . . . okay. And he doesn't quite know why he said it. Doesn't quite know why it poured out of him, boiling, like kettle water, maybe just because – like he'd thought – they can handle the heat. Nothing's changed. Best friends first, right, even as two grown adults with a history; *because* of it, even, a history that feels far away and yet too close, taking up all of his air.

A goodnight, then, in the dark sea of the driveway. She tells him she'll text him, when she's confirmed her appointment. And after the call ends he stands there for another minute outside his mother's door, thinking. His hands, so numb with the cold by the time he tries, that he can't get his key in the lock.

–

He does not wake with the light, because for that he would have had to have slept. Josie was dozing in her chair when he got in; he'd covered her with a blanket, turned off her reading lamp that, as far as he knew, she never used for books. Word searches, she'd always liked. The ones in true-life magazines like *Take a Break*. They're so *fascinating*, she told him once, when he'd caught a ludicrous headline about falling in love with a Ferris wheel. Stranger than fiction, Bren, you wouldn't believe.

He gets up and showers off his lack of sleep. Towels himself down and untangles the St Christopher Nora gave him for his sixteenth birthday. To protect you when we're travelling, she'd told him, which only brings up more thoughts, the smell of her bedroom, Freya bringing them lemonade while they flipped through travel guides, and he is taking the stairs afterwards, fully dressed, hair damp and mind elsewhere when he stops halfway down, because it is entirely silent.

There is no noise from his mother.

No footsteps or radio, no porridge turning in the microwave. Two more steps and he can see that her bedroom door is still closed.

Rush of heat, then, through his body.

All is fine, he's sure. It had been a late night for her, after all; later than usual. A few more stairs and he makes himself open her door, just so, only to find the bed is made. Maybe she's still asleep in the chair, and hadn't heard him showering; unlikely, when she wakes at the mere suggestion of a sound, but no, she's not downstairs, either. He calls her name, then. Nothing. Checks the kitchen, the downstairs bathroom, runs back up to her bedroom, heart like a train in his chest. Maybe she *does* go to the shop, sometimes. Maybe she's filling the bird feeders in the front garden; back down, front door open, empty but for a blackbird which scarpers over the hedge. Volvo still in the driveway because she doesn't drive; can, of course, but won't; not since he was five.

He closes the door and the recollections sear through him, hot and sudden, like nausea. How things had changed, so slowly. Her willingness to do normal things fading like the colour of her hair. No more driving. No more attending parents' evening. No more part-time job at the florist. Her gradual slip into solitude, but still smiling, still *I'm well, thanks* to the neighbours, when she wasn't; Nora and Freya, the only ones who knew. Who saw and heard things through the wall. His father, handling everything. Counting out her tablets while Bren ate his Cheerios, falling still if he found there were pills missing. Phoning the doctor, then. First-name basis with the receptionist. Prescriptions collected alongside the shopping, kitchen roll, semi-skimmed milk, six milligrams of anti-psychotics, good day, Bren, how was school.

And now two decades later, Bren stands in the hall without him, his train-heart off its tracks as he says okay, out loud: okay.

Next thought, that he could knock for Freya.

Ask if he should call the police, like they did once; she would know.

Wouldn't she? Or is he the only –

And then the back door opens and there is a second where his insides harden then melt with relief, and his mother is walking into the kitchen with a dozen tomatoes cradled in the fold of her apron.

Morning! she says, and she looks tired, but normal enough. Eyes alert. Shoulders straight. Slips off her garden shoes onto the doormat, careful not to spill the red fruit.

Where were you, Bren says, but Josie doesn't catch his tone, which is just as well, he thinks, as it was rich, coming from him.

With Freya, Josie says, brightly. We have tea and toast on Saturdays, and she gave me these beauties. I thought you might want a full English, after your late night.

She moves further into the kitchen and Bren watches her, double-checking for signs. No tear tracks down her face, no slight twitch of her mouth, so he moves forward, relieved, helps her unload the tomatoes onto the side.

You're all right, though, he asks, and she says of course. But what about him? She was so worried, when he wasn't home by midnight. So worried, Bren thinks, that she fell asleep in the chair.

I missed the last train, he tells her. Ended up walking home.

Walking? Bren! You should have texted! I could have . . .

But she tails off, because she couldn't have, and they both know it. That car is as good as dead in the driveway, a hunk of metal and rubber and bad memories.

It's fine, he says. And thanks for the thought, he says, nodding at the tomatoes, rolling like billiard balls across the counter, but I'm heading out.

Again, pet?

Yeah, he says. Fancy a walk.

Even after your long walk home, last night? How was it, at Nora's?

Good. Fine. She's actually asked me to be her . . . best man.

Weird words, in his mouth. Still surreal, but he expects a flutter of delight from Josie, at the news. A beat of misunderstanding at such an oddity, followed by her usual glazed expression, a passing *lovely*. Instead she looks up in alarm, as if he'd just told her he was off to get another tattoo.

You're Robin's best man?

Not Robin's, he says, Nora's. They're defying convention, or whatever.

He can see his mother working hard to process this concept. But she seems to accept it, thanks to years of friendship with Freya, probably, then moves on to her next concern.

Is that a good idea? she asks him, following him out of the kitchen, as he pulls on his boots in the hall. When he asks her why it wouldn't be, she says is it wise for you to make promises like that, Bren? When you'd need to be . . .

She twirls her hand in the air.

More acquainted with a state of permanence, she says.

Heat in Bren's face, then, as he laces up his boots. Caught between amusement and shame. As a rule, they do not discuss his inability to stay in one place. The way you don't draw attention to a facial birthmark, or one's continued mispronunciation of a word; no need to make him feel bad, and in turn, her too.

That's all fine, Bren says, as he straightens up. She's hoping for some kind of cancellation deal, or something, by the summer. So I told her I'd stay.

Josie blinks, her apron hanging loose over her floral dress.

You'll stay?

Until the wedding, yeah.

Oh, *Bren*.

She does not rush at him, like she'd done the night he'd arrived, but she does lift her hand to her mouth.

It's not a big deal, he says, feeling hot for a different reason, now. It's just a couple of months more. If that's okay.

Of *course* it's okay. Oh, Bren, she repeats, and this time, she does move towards him; loops her twiglet arms around his waist with a strength that surprises him. He inhales her; bread flour, magnolia perfume. Hesitates, then pats her on the back.

You'll be here for Easter, then? she says, looking up at him like a child. He may not be tall, but his mother is tiny; seems to be getting smaller by the day.

I guess so?

Your father *loved* Easter, she says, didn't he? And she lays her head against Bren's chest once more as he struggles to respond, then draws back and dabs at her eyes with the tissue she keeps bunched beneath her sleeve. Better than Christmas, he used to say, remember?

And Bren does.

It's not so long away, now, Josie goes on, as she folds the tissue back under the cuff of her cardigan. Middle of April, this year, in fact.

Cool, Bren says.

Maybe it would be nice if we did something for it? All of us, together?

Whatever you want, he says, because he knows it'll just mean a pot of tea in the kitchen, hot cross buns on the lawn, at a push. I'm going to miss the bus, he tells her, even though he has nowhere to be.

And then the *wedding*, Josie says, so soon! Oh, I can't wait, Bren. What *lovely* things to look forward to.

Definitely, Bren says, as he pulls on his coat.

I can't wait, Josie repeats, and he nods, playing along. Like she'll be able to leave the house for it. Like she'll have no problem putting on a cocktail dress and high heels, one of those stupid little net hats. See you later then, he says, ending the conversation. Closing the door, and walking away, the morning cold and clear as glass.

–

What are *you* doing here, Shay demands, when Nora walks into the café the following Saturday. They split weekend shifts and it is not her turn to be here, making coffees, selling ceramics, sweeping the floor of crumbs. Not that Shay is doing much of that, by the looks of things; she's reading a well-thumbed paperback behind the coffee bar, twiddling her purple hair in her fingers.

I've got an appointment in London this afternoon, Nora

tells her, which she'd intentionally kept quiet, all week. So thought I might as well stop by.

That is so sad, Shay says.

Is it?

Yes! Go to a café that you don't *own*, for crying out loud, on your precious Saturday! Or go and wander round a gallery, or a shoe shop! Don't come to work if you don't *have* to work, Nora, Jeez.

Never worked a day in my life here, Nora says, and Shay calls her sad again, while simultaneously seeming happy about what she's just said. Because it's true. It is such a soothing space, Nora thinks, as she crosses the room, with its exposed plaster walls, the handmade objects on the shelves. And for some reason, since the night of the fajitas – before that, even, at her party – Nora has felt the need to be soothed.

Behind the curtain in the back room, she finds Horace lying beside the radiator, his limbs long and grey, a cluster of paws. Nora feeds him a biscuit from the jar on the desk. Strokes his silken ears, looks into his glum, drooping eyes, before she opens the summer events timetable on the laptop and stares at it, without seeing.

So why are you here, again, Shay asks, sticking her head through the curtain. What's the appointment for?

Nora says, without wanting to, that if she must know, she's going to look at wedding dresses. Because they're moving on this plan of Robin's.

Horace groans.

The plan where you get hitched at the drop of a hat?

Nora nods. Says they're telling people to be ready for a quick turnaround. If they can make it, great. If not, it doesn't matter. People have lives, right, and they're not set on a big, fancy day, anyway.

So you keep saying, Shay says. You decided on Devon, then?

Sort of. We're going to see it, soon. To, I don't know. Decide on things.

What things, Shay asks, and Nora twirls her hand in the air.

Everything, she says.

Sounds stressful, Shay says, though it's meant to be the opposite. So, Shay says, a bit like packing a hospital bag ahead of giving birth, I'll need to pack a wedding bag that I can grab at a moment's notice?

Pretty much, Nora says. Robin would love that. He's really taken with this spontaneity thing. His notebook is *filled* with ideas.

Hold the phone, Shay says, Robin has *ideas*? And he's writing them in his *note*book? His notebook that he's carried around like an oxygen tank ever since our first year? What is *up* with that? He's usually so unoriginal. So passive.

I get your point, Nora says.

So you're going dress shopping so you can pack your emergency wedding bag, Shay says, because your fiancé wants to marry the pants off you. And that makes you sad because . . .?

I'm not sad!

You are either sombre or sad and no, I could not tell you the difference, Shay says, but get away from the laptop and come and eat a pastry, why don't you. I could even come with you, if you want. If you can push back the appointment to tonight?

I don't think so, Nora says. They already squeezed me in last minute.

Send me pictures, then. You'll need a second opinion, at least.

I'll have one, Nora says, because she does not need to hide this.

Freya came round, then? Shay says, waving to a customer who's leaving, and Nora says no, she's patched things up with Bren. Sort of. So . . . he's coming.

To the wedding?

Well, yes. But also to my appointment.

Shay removes the portafilter from the coffee machine and bangs it to get rid of the ground beans. Another customer approaches the counter for a scone; Nora serves her, takes payment, looks back at Shay when she's done.

Why, Shay asks her, would you want your non-committal red-headed friend, who has a certain predilection for grubby clothing and terrible tattoos, helping you choose your *wedding* dress?

Because he's going to be my best man, Nora says.

It is the first time she has said it out loud.

That guy who rocked up at your party, she imagines Shay saying, that guy you've never quite got over, yes, I could see it in your eyes that night, all that unspoken history, don't deny it, but instead all Shay says is *I'm* not your best man?

Nora bites at the catch in her thumbnail.

Would you want to be?

Christ, no.

An eye roll, then, Nora's pulse resuming its normal speed.

Good to know he'll be at the wedding, though, Shay says. At least there'll be one other thirty-something singleton there, for dancing or drinking or whatever shenanigans he might be open to.

Nora continues to gnaw at her nail.

Since when do you care about being single, she asks.

Rarely, Shay says, unless I'm at a wedding. That changes things, temporarily. All that love gives me a burning in my loins, the need to celebrate being young and alive in a kickass outfit. I'm thinking my green satin jumpsuit.

Naturally.

Plus you know I've always had a thing for gingers.

Do not say *gingers*, Nora says. We're not fourteen.

D'you think he'd go for an angry, purple-haired dog-mum?

I think he'd be lucky to have you, Nora says, but something is happening inside of her, a clam closing where her heart is, and she says she's got to go, the boutique is a bit of a walk away and she doesn't want to be late or sweaty or whatever, when she gets there.

You look kind of sweaty already.

Thanks, Shay.

Take a croissant, Shay says, taking some tongs to the glass counter, maybe you're having a sugar low.

To which Nora agrees. Because that, surely, is all that's wrong: a dip in her blood sugar. Which is dangerous, she knows, damn near transformative. Robin says she becomes a different person, it's almost frightening, has been known to throw snacks at her from a safe distance until the hungry angst of her recedes, and the Nora he knows and loves returns to the room.

–

She gets to the shop ten minutes early. Brick walls, swirling white stencils up the windows saying *Pre-Loved, Vintage Couture*. She half expects Bren won't show but then he's there too, hands shoved in the pockets of his down jacket, flash of blue nylon against the pavements. Hey, he says, with his half-smile, and she says it back. They hug, which still doesn't feel normal, and when they break apart he tells her she has sugar on her face.

I had an almond croissant before I got here, she explains,

as she touches her chin, brushes it off. I should have brought you one, sorry.

He says it's okay and they stall, rain beading on the sleeves of their coats.

So shall we, Bren says, looking at the glass door of the shop, and that clam of her heart feels stuck now, as if dunked in resin.

I'm kind of nervous, she admits.

What about?

It's meant to be fun, this part, she says, but I think there's a lot of judgement, too, about your budget, and your taste, and I have a low budget and weird taste, as it is. And it's just happening so fast, she says, by which she means the dress, of course, meaning the sudden engagement turning to a sudden wedding to a sudden situation where she is here, with him, outside this door.

So let's sack it off, Bren says, after a moment.

I can't, she says. I booked an appointment.

Then cancel it. We'll go somewhere else for the day.

Oh yeah? Like where?

He lifts his shoulders in a shrug, his hands returned to his pockets.

Paris, he says. We're near St Pancras, aren't we? And you like croissants?

He is teasing, she thinks, but he's looking at her as though he's not, and she feels a flush of heat, despite the cold air.

Let's go, she says, turning to the shop door.

To Paris?

To where we *planned*, she says, as she rings the buzzer. Her words hang there as if they're a pointed reference to the past and she regrets it for a second but pretends not to; stands back, waits. He is silent. Eventually a tall, thin woman opens the door, dressed in every shade of beige possible. Nude lipstick, taupe shoes, camel-coloured jumpsuit.

Ms Harper? she says, and they're ushered inside, told to leave their wet coats, please, on the hooks by the door.

They both do as they're told. Shoes off, too, if you could, the woman says, which is more unexpected, but they remove those as well. Could be in Paris, Bren says to Nora in an undertone as they walk down the ramp to the shop floor, and Nora hits him lightly on the arm, says he's just sore she didn't bring him a croissant. It's funny until the beige woman turns to them with her arms crossed. Like they're whispering schoolchildren, not showing the dresses their due respect.

These are the gowns, she says, and Nora looks past her to the five rails standing atop the polished wood floor, spotlights illuminating the silk and chiffon and lace, suspended like skins.

All pre-loved, but still of the highest quality with no repairs required, the woman says. Please keep in mind that we don't provide alterations or returns.

Nora rather thinks she sounds as if she's reeling off a script she recites several times a day; but there's an edge, too. Not boredom, exactly. Contempt.

Everything you see is labelled up at our very best price, the woman goes on, not making eye contact with either of them. So please don't try to haggle me down further if you find one that you like.

Oh, says Nora. I wouldn't –

They're all old season, of course, all with a unique history behind them, so if you want brand new, or something that can be nipped and tucked to fit your figure – she looks Nora up and down, at this – then I suggest you go elsewhere.

A beat, then. Bren is frowning.

No, Nora says, I want something sustainable, definitely. Second-hand.

We prefer the term Vintage Couture, the woman says, and Bren says what's the difference, and Nora talks over him, says sure, sorry, thank you.

Nod from the woman then, press of her lips. The dressing room's over there; she's got another customer in an hour, so take a look at what you'd like to try; she'd recommend three, four if you're quick. Then pop these on the hangers – she hands Nora a set of wooden pegs – and once you're down to your underwear I'll help you into your choices. Please don't touch the dresses without my assistance.

Wouldn't dare, Bren says, and the woman looks at him properly for the first time.

Are you the groom, she asks, eyeing him the way she'd eyed Nora. The air seems to tighten, somehow, even though Nora had fully expected this question, at some point; she tenses, folds her own arms.

Nope, Bren says. I'm the best man.

The best man? I've had brothers in here, before. Friends. But never the best *man*.

He's *my* best man, Nora says. Not *the* best man.

Depending on your perspective, Bren says.

I see, the woman says, though Nora is not sure that she does. Her lipstick is the exact shade of her skin, she realises now, which is just one shade lighter than her jumpsuit. Everything considered, orderly. No room for blurred lines; best men of brides, or the muddied feelings that might stir up.

I'll give you fifteen minutes to browse, the beige woman says, gesturing to the dresses behind her. I'd suggest starting at the front, here, and working your way through each rail, even if you think you know what you want. Most women do, but then their body shape dictates something entirely different. You're a pear, aren't you, she says, with another glance at Nora's waistline. So I'd suggest a fuller skirt.

Thank you, Nora says, though she's not quite sure what she's thanking her for, and then the woman is clacking away in her beige heels when Bren says wait, sorry what?

Told you, she murmurs, and it's meant to be light, uncaring – remember the judgement I knew was coming – but Bren says no, excuse me, raising his voice so that the beige woman stops walking, turns around.

What just happened, he asks her.

Bren, Nora says.

Why did you just compare her to a pome fruit, he asks, and the woman stares at him. A star, maybe, or the fucking sun, sure, Bren goes on, and there's that warmth again, blazing in Nora's chest. Her clam-heart, broken open.

The beige woman keeps staring at Bren for a long, hard moment, and then at Nora, who says sorry, it's – it's fine. Tilt of the woman's chin, then, before she turns once again and crosses the floor to the glass office in the back. Shuts the door.

Charmed, Bren says, but Nora is rattled now. Because of the dress thing, but also the Bren thing; the melt of her, at what he'd just said.

I think we should go, she says. This doesn't feel right.

Bren turns from the office and looks Nora's way, and his eyes are alight with an outrage she's seen before, when they were young. When some guys from his school woofed at her, in some moronic reference, probably, to her mismatched irises. Calling her Collie Dog, or something, she didn't care.

But Bren did.

He always did, even if, back then, he wouldn't say it.

I think it feels right enough, he says. You wanted to try on wedding dresses, didn't you? And we're in a room full of them.

But I –

Let's find you the best dress in the goddamn room, Bren says, and then *not* buy it, out of principle, and send that woman a crate of mouldy pears to thank her for her services. Unless you legitimately find the best dress on the planet, in which case we can swallow our pride.

He is trailing past the gowns as he speaks, touching the hangers as if they're books on a shelf. These look good, he says, stopping at a colourful section near the back. You don't want to wear white, do you?

She said we should start at –

Oh, live a little, Nora, Bren says. Start wherever the hell you want.

And despite how he had defended her, just then, she senses that he's angry with her, too, and not only the beige woman. Avoiding her eyes as he moves through the rails, and she stands there, with her split-open heart, wondering whether she should leave.

What about this, Bren says, before she can speak, and he pulls out a lace slip with off-the-shoulder straps, in an almost-gold, definitely-not-white. It shimmers under the shop lighting, the fabric reminiscent of sunlight.

He looks at it, then lifts it off the rail.

Strange sensation, then, like a flower opening inside her. Because it is beautiful. And because he knows her. And because he is here, for her, for this, holding out an olive branch made of fabric and dainty, near-invisible stitches, the sort of thing she'd have chosen herself.

So she doesn't leave.

She looks at the dress on the hanger.

Maybe, she says, as if daring herself to say it. Maybe . . . something like that.

Then peg it, Bren says, holding it out towards her.

And she does.

–

Bren taps his foot against the wooden bench outside the dressing room. The beige woman is in there, to begin with, helping Nora into the first dress, and then the telephone rings, sharp and high from behind the glass office door so she retreats, heels clicking. Good riddance.

She put a bag over my face, Nora says through the curtain.

She what?

She put this shower cap-style bag on my face so I wouldn't get make-up on the dress, Nora tells him. Even though I told her I'm not wearing any.

Crazy, he says, weddings make people crazy, and Nora does not respond to that. He keeps tapping his foot, scrolls briefly on his phone. Alone, now, on the shop floor, only the shuffle of clothing audible while he waits.

Mouth dry. He wishes he had water. Weren't they meant to drink champagne or something, at these things, cheap wine at the very least? The adrenaline of the morning – the push-pull of not wanting to be here, but wanting to be here for *her*; his fury at the woman, seeping into a fury with Nora he's not quite managed to let go – is waning. Instead he feels stupidly nervous, like Nora did before they came inside. Surprised by the jitters in his chest as he reminds himself that this is just his friend in an outfit, and he's seen her in plenty of outfits before. Pyjamas. School uniform. That red dress she wore when they were sixteen, some sequined thing she'd found in a charity shop which meant he couldn't look at her, all night, didn't know what to do with the feelings it unleashed.

I don't know, Nora says to him, from behind the curtain.

Don't know what?

I don't know what I think about this. I'm not sure that it feels like me.

Well good, Bren says. Else you'd get married in your rainbow poncho.

. . . you remember my rainbow poncho?

Just come out, Nora. Let me see.

A pause then.

The moment, before it happens.

And then she pulls the curtain back and she's standing there, and despite his prolonged preparation, like a long-haul flight, like a dozen years of talking himself out of this, Bren is not ready for what comes over him, right then. Seeing Nora, in that dress. In this soft, flowing fabric that is also somehow fitted around her hips, sheer and stretchy and almost blush in colour, like the inside of a strawberry; like her cheeks, when she is pleased, or self-conscious, or shy. The lace stops just beneath her shoulders, and he'd never thought about that part of her body before. Never noticed them. She is not an apple, or a pear, or a person from his past. She is here. She is now. She is . . . perfect.

What, Nora says, as Bren stares at her.

It's not right, she says, is it? I'll try the next one.

No, Bren says, and he clears his throat. Leans forward, says it again: no. Come out of the changing room, at least, he says. Walk about in it.

Nora glances back at the mirror, then concedes. No socks as she steps out of the dressing room, towards him, and he isn't tapping his leg any more and he also isn't breathing.

She stops a few feet in front of him, shrugs with her palms up. And even though she is not looking at him, she seems to know he can't stop looking at her, because her strawberry cheeks are back. And he can't believe he is looking at her in a wedding dress when that was never the plan but at the same time, he can't believe that he is not the guy who gets to stand beside her while she wears it for real. He will not get to stand at the end of an aisle with the birds singing and clouds criss-crossing the sun, because they'd get married outside, now that he thinks about it, and she'd walk towards him through the grass, with her bare feet and long hair and her wild heart that should have been his.

She cannot marry Robin.

It is a clear thought that moves through him, as if from elsewhere, like a sudden wind, and he simply accepts it, like all of the choices he's made, all the reactions he's had and not thought about over the last twelve years. Something to live with, and not work against. Something to trust, because you can't trust much in this world, but his gut, his sense of what has to be done; *that* is something he can rely on.

Nora is looking in another mirror now. Smoothing her hands down her waist.

Maybe it's okay, she says to her reflection, and Bren says Nora. It is more than okay.

eight

Jed calls you. He calls you when you are editing at home at the kitchen table, which you promised Nora you wouldn't do, when weekends aren't for working, but she's out shopping for a wedding dress with Bren so what she doesn't know won't hurt her. You'll do other things too, before she's home, things that are still work but of an acceptable Saturday kind: hoover the hallway, wash the bedding, clean the gutters, even, if you have time, after the mulch of winter has you both lamenting how, every time it rains, it ends up flooding the yard.

Robin, it's Jed, he says when you answer, and you say it's nice to hear from him and he says you bet it is; we've had a cancellation, already.

A light goes on, inside you. Already? you repeat, leaning back in your chair then standing up, instead, going to the window.

For the twenty-second of April, Jed says, if you want it.

We want it, you say. Details, then. This, that, yes, you'll pay the deposit right now, and course, you'll firm up the guest list, the bridal party – you'll be in touch! Wow! And you trust, well, you hope everything's okay with the other couple.

Jed pauses, says ah, well. Broken engagement, this one. It happens.

Oh, you say. That's a – a real shame.

Sometimes it's not meant to be, Jed says, and you nod, feel momentarily terrible that your mood isn't dimmed by this news, but then again, maybe he's right; maybe those people, whoever they are, will go on to find what is meant for them, instead; you trust in that, always have.

You thank Jed, promise again to make payment, smiling so much once he ends the call that you feel almost drunk; look it, too, when you catch sight of yourself in the kitchen window. Laughing, then. Scrolling to speed dial. Not for Nora: she'll be in the dress shop, right about now, and you don't want to interrupt.

S'up, your brother says, picking up just before his voicemail kicks in.

S'up, bro, you say back: a greeting the pair of you traded in irony, for years, because you were the last two people on earth who'd say such a thing. We've got a wedding date! you tell him. Write it down, please, before you forget.

Kay, Goose says, and you say are you doing it?

I'm in the middle of a boss fight, Robman, Goose says. I am literal moments away from beating this dude, after weeks of trying. I am not getting up to get a pen.

And yet you answered the phone?

You never call on Saturdays. I figured there was an emergency.

Oddly touched, you tell him to call back, which he does, ten minutes later; ten minutes of jotting things down in your notebook, ideas bouncing around like ping-pong balls. You are just scribbling something else when Goose appears on your phone, a photo of you and him in a bumper car, and then he's saying okay, when is it, what do you need.

Did you beat the boss? Obviously he did, what do you take him for. Take advantage of his good mood, he advises you, and so you do; talk logistics immediately, how you'll get your parents to the venue, your grandma, too, who hates any form of public transport, any food that isn't packet ham, any outfit that isn't her tattered lilac cardigan. Leave it with him. He'll pack the ham. Tempt her out with a sherry, buy her an untattered lilac blazer, perhaps.

He is a good guy, your little brother. Blatantly uninterested in weddings like most men (aside from yourself) and stepping up all the same because he senses it's important. You spend ten minutes rattling through your ideas, the surprises you want to keep under wraps, and then he says so you're not going to tell her the biggest surprise of all?

You go quiet, that light in you fading, for the first time since Jed's call.

I wasn't planning to, you say. Do you think I should?

I don't think anything, Goose says. I'm just covering my bases.

You're such a lawyer, you say, and he says he doesn't want to put his foot in it, that's all. Or maybe he does. Maybe it's good fodder for his speech.

Unease in you, then, but he says I'm kidding, Robin, chill. It might just hurt her ego, a little bit, if it comes out later down the line.

The word ego stirs something in you, and you remember a personality test that did the rounds at art school. Picture a room. In that room is a cube. Describe that cube. Yours, sort of standard sized, like the box you'd use for jump squats at the gym, Nora's small as a sugar cube, Shay's so big it filled the room. That represents the size of your ego, you were told, and you'd all cracked up, amazed at the accuracy.

You reckon? you say, but Goose says hey, you know her better than I do. You're just always straight with her, usually, so why keep it a secret?

Why, indeed. The question hangs heavy in your chest as you hang up and pay the deposit, shoot Jed an email to say it's done, can he confirm receipt as and when, cheers, exciting! Unease transferring to panic, just briefly, as you close your laptop, because maybe you should have checked with Nora first. But you're sure it'll be fine. You'd agreed to be spontaneous, after all. It'll be a surprise. Like when you first asked her out for a coffee and she said make it a croissant and you've got yourself a deal.

Unexpected, you'd thought, and irresistible. The start of something good.

And there have been many more surprises like that, since. Your shared love of animation and show tunes and hot, drinkable Marmite.

The launch of her art café, which left so little in your joint bank account you couldn't afford champagne, to celebrate; instead bought her a bottle of Shloer, astonished at how good it tasted, of pipe dreams turned sparkling success. Because, against the odds, that dream turned a profit two years later: real champagne then, shared with Shay, all three of you drinking it out of plastic cups on the shop floor, thrilled and tipsy and triumphant.

Surprise gifts, too, like oil paintings or embroidered socks. Surprise special dinners simply because it was a Thursday and more recently, you think, as you tidy your laptop cable away, something that surprised *you*, as much as her.

The biggest surprise of all, Goose had called it.

Which worries you, more than this impulsive wedding date you've just booked, as you check your watch, knowing she'll be out of the dress shop by now.

It was innocent, though. This thing you have not told her. Which is not what you'd lead with, if you *did* tell her, because that suggests that it's not, so you'd just have to launch straight in. Tell the whole story.

Tell her you were doing your client a favour one day for his antiques store; Myke with a Y, remember? Anyway, he'd acquired this vintage ring he'd asked you to collect on your lunch break because you'd be passing by the auction house – course, sure thing. Happy to. So you took the paperwork and had a chat with the man at the desk who checked it over then handed it to you in a leather box, which you put in your pocket to take back to the shoot. And you texted Nora because her café was nearby. You bought her a bagel, she bought you one back, and you had a glorious half-hour by the water and the memory is so vivid it's like you're back there as you kiss her goodbye. As she warms her hands in your coat pockets, pulls the ring out and looks at it as though you'd meant it to be hers.

You see it all cross her face, like this memory, now, crossing your mind.

The surprise – that word, again, that feeling, that fork in the road – and her stunned, slow-dawning comprehension.

You see the crease at the bridge of her nose and then you see the joy, the unbroken wash of it as she looks up and says yes when you didn't even ask the question; had agreed you never would, because she didn't want that, and all you wanted was her, ring or no ring, so it had never occurred to you to argue.

But all of a sudden it seemed like she did want it, and who were you to take that away?

Who were you to say, you've got this all wrong, because actually, she'd got it right, as ever. And it seemed so obvious as you stood there with that centuries-old ring that you'd need to buy off your client now, but he'd love the story, would see it as a romantic blunder come good, turned life-changingly charmed, you'd figure it out, somehow, seeing as she'd answered three times, yes yes yes, to a question you'd wanted to ask but hadn't.

So you did not let it go.

You took it, and ran with it, and now you're getting married. Soon, now that there's been a cancellation. Now that the twenty-second of April, your wedding day, is only six weeks from now, which you'll text her, right now, *surprise*.

Mad, how these things happen.

What life throws at you. If you're ready to catch it, and run.

nine

They leave the shop without buying anything. Without speaking to the beige woman, even, who is still on the phone in the back room. And then they're out on the street and it is dusk, and Bren feels warmed through, and spaced-out, like he's knocked back a shot of whiskey.

Thanks for coming, Nora says to him. Which feels formal, he thinks. Like she, too, senses what has passed between them, and is trying to pretend nothing has. A taxi drives past; a runner with a reflective headband, puffing into the early evening air. Bren watches these things moving fast, wonders if he should tell her what is rushing through him, as well. If he should stop her on the street while she is still wedding-dress-less – wedding-*ring*-less – and tell her what just happened. What he's realised.

He is just drawing breath to say her name, when she makes a noise of surprise.

Well, she says, looking at her phone. Looks like we should go back.

Back where?

Twelve years, he thinks. Or even further. The moment I met you, or you gave me my St Christopher; the moment I got on that plane or made that phone call at the airport, whichever moment I could go back to and change this, just tell me, and I'd do it.

To the dress shop, she says, so I can buy something, after all. Seeing as we've now set a date.

It is not raining, but there is white noise all around, traffic and footfall and a roaring in his ears. She doesn't even pause, or soften her words. Just holds her phone up, shows him a blur of messages from Robin.

They had a cancellation, she says. For the end of April.

Insides spinning, blurring, like the reflectors on a bike that goes by.

That's so soon, Bren says, and she says she knows; sounds taken aback, like him. But she is looking back down at her phone, already. Tells him Robin's paid the deposit.

And despite what she'd said before, she begins to walk away from the dress shop, down the street. Bren follows, the movement helping, like it always does, so he can at least form a full sentence.

So, he says, how do you . . . feel, about that?

Great, she says, too quickly, he thinks – that word, again. *Great!* I've not seen the place, obviously. I was hoping we'd have that planning day, before we . . . locked in. It is stunning, though. And Robin loves it.

But is this what you want, he says, and it comes out of him like that kettle water, scalding, but she either doesn't hear it, or doesn't want to. Doesn't answer, as she taps back a message to Robin. And that scald starts to blister, now, all the way down.

We've got to get the legal bit done separately, she says, reading Robin's message aloud. Before, or afterwards. It's not licensed, is the only thing.

The only thing?

Bren stops walking, pulls out his own phone. Starts searching for the nearest tube station. Jabbing the app that won't respond, like it's frozen, got some kind of damn bug.

Hey, Nora says, doubling back. What's wrong?

I'm just trying to find the route home, he says.

I *know* the route home, she says. I was going to stop back at the café, first, though. D'you want to come?

Not now, he says. That damn app. He swipes up, shuts it down, reopens it.

Are you all right, Nora asks, frowning now, and that question dampens the heat and the hurt, inside him, like sand thrown on a fire. Because it's the sort of question his mother would ask, without really caring. Without knowing how to deal with the answer.

I'm fine, he says. Just conscious of the time.

Four thirty? Nora says, glancing at the clock on her own phone.

I said I'd be back for dinner.

All right. Let me just give Robin a ring, and I'll come with you.

No need, Bren says, but she's shaking her head, says she should tell Freya and Josie about April, but Bren says no, he can tell them. Why doesn't she just head home.

Walking again, after he's said it. Along the kerb, past the potholes filled with rain. More cars in the road, another bike. He wishes he had a bike right now. Like he did in Oaxaca. An aluminium frame, two wheels, covering miles without any effort, so much distance, all that space, new views to wipe all other thoughts away.

His feet will have to do, though, but he isn't tall enough to outstrip Nora's stride. She keeps pace easily enough, trotting by his elbow. Bren, she says, then again: what's wrong?

Nothing, he tells her.

It doesn't seem like nothing, she says.

It seems like you should go home to your fiancé, Bren says, rather than getting on the train home with me, don't you think?

She does stop walking, at this. He hears the *what*, in her mouth, even though she does not say it, knows it's what she's thinking as he reaches the end of the street and turns onto the main road. There are more cars here, rainwater sprayed by fast-moving tyres, sundown seeping to the grey-blue of night. City lights, like noise. Like the rushing, cold wind. Things he tries to outstrip, as he strides on, leaving Nora somewhere behind.

–

What happened, some girl asked him once, on a beach in Bali. It was dark, like now, but there were no traffic lights or headlights or gold-lit shopfronts: just the moon, as big as her pupils. There were a few people not far from them, smoking and shouting, enjoying themselves, board shorts, braids in their hair. Bren had got his first tattoo, that day. He was not sure how he felt about it, but he was fine with that; fine with her, this girl; fine with her question that was meant to show an interest and make him feel seen but instead washed over him, like the sea on the sand at their feet.

Life, he replied, because he would not say death, and because her question was so huge, he could make his answer the same.

It comes to him now, like the shuttering billboards above the old car wash he's passing. Her gaze, vacant. Stoned. His father's face looking up at him, almost pleading, as his heart stopped beating in the driveway. His mother's shock. No tears. Nora, holding him afterwards, and he walks faster and gets out his phone, checks the flight scanner app instead of the route that'll take him to the tube station.

Close, balmy air, he craves. So different to the cold, colourless March of right now. Sand soft and white as talcum powder, as the girl on the beach fingered his then-long hair. Asked him, in her breathy voice, if he wanted to talk about it. Like nobody had ever tried to unpeel the layers of him, like this, as if Nora hadn't done that already – didn't even need to, in fact, and so he'd laughed at her, this girl in her bikini and sarong on that beach. Properly. Three years after he'd left. He hadn't laughed in so long, and he told the girl this: I haven't laughed in so long. Like she'd healed him, somehow, not because she'd pried him open with that question, but because he knew the answer to it on some deep, molecular level, no, I do not want to talk about it, that is the last thing I will ever want, to talk about all the things that won't change if I do, and so they did not talk and they did not touch or fuck or trade phone numbers. She left, he thinks, sometime before sunrise, as he fell into an exhausted half-sleep there on the sand, and the next day he felt like a shell, like what made him a real, feeling person had upped and left from the inside. Just like the light in his father's eyes. And right now a car blares its horn at him because he has crossed the road without looking, still fixed on the flight app, so he throws his hands up, sorry, shit, blood racing, everything too bright and too dark and that old sparking wire in his gut, it's this place, it's being home, it's breathing the same air as his mother, even, which does something to him, makes him emotionally unstable, and he's scared he'll end up like her, her stuff is hereditary, after all, but he doesn't need to think about that, he refuses, keeps moving.

–

He finds a burger place, seats himself at a booth. Music playing, wooden forks, the menu laminated and half the size of the tabletop. He lifts it to look, not absorbing any of the options, not sure if he's even hungry. And when he finally lowers it, Nora is sitting across from him; Bren jumps at the sight of her, and swears.

What was *that*, she asks him, thudding her phone onto the table, the screen alight with his tracked location.

You scared me!

No, she says. Before, out there. What's going on with you?

But Bren can't answer. Flips the menu over, looks at the drinks. Nora keeps staring at him, her concern changing to confusion, then anger.

I thought you had to get home?

I changed my mind, he says. Fancied a burger.

Which, now he thinks about it, isn't a lie. He needs carbohydrates and salt. Something solid and grounding, hot chips, some kind of kick back into the present, sriracha mayo, maybe, some sliced jalapeños.

I don't understand, Nora says.

Bren is still scanning the menu. Doesn't understand, himself.

You were the one who offered to come dress shopping with me. You were the one who said you wouldn't up and leave, or bungee jump out of my life again. But you've just pissed off, for no reason.

He is not sure he's ever heard her swear before, and it throws him. He lowers the menu and almost laughs, mainly because pissed off means being angry, to him, it's not a verb, but she's so cross, he knows he shouldn't laugh at her right now. And it's not funny. Not really.

That's not how this works, Nora tells him, gesturing between them.

And what is this, again?

What does *that* mean?

It means, Bren says, that sometimes you're not over something when you think you are, for Christ's sake.

He regrets it as soon as he's said it. Tries to cover himself.

Like the fact that I got on that plane, he says, and you didn't.

Nora's mouth opens, just slightly, at that.

Shall we share some fries, he asks her.

Back up a bit, she says, not looking at the menu he's proffered. You're mad because I didn't come *with* you?

I think I'll get the chilli beef, he says.

Or you're mad that I've set a wedding date?

A side of onion rings, maybe.

How are these things related? Nora asks.

Come on, Nora, they're entirely related! You weren't going to settle down. You were going to see the world, do something different with your life.

No, Nora says, *you* were going to do those things. Just last week you were saying how great I'm doing, when you came over. What changed?

That's my question, Nora, what changed?

I don't need to justify my life to you, Bren.

No, but you need to be able to justify it to yourself.

She opens her mouth to argue but then the waiter appears. Youngish, acne on his chin, biro poised. Bren orders the chilli burger with large fries and a beer, whatever you've got, Corona, fine, and Nora is still looking at him as the waiter turns to her, his pen hovering above his notepad. And for you?

Uh, Nora says. Um.

She skids the menu around on the tabletop.

A lemonade, she says. And . . . the falafel burger. Please.

They don't come with fries, the waiter says.

That's okay, she says.

Order some fries, Nora, Bren tells her.

I don't want fries, she says.

In what world don't you want fries?

In this one, she snaps, as the waiter takes the menu, raises his eyebrows at Bren, as if to wish him luck, then retreats. Nora crosses her arms.

Things change, Bren, she says, and her voice is hard. You left. And I met someone.

It is the first time she has circled close to the subject. He feels it. He's sure she does, too. Something charged, between them, as someone turns up the restaurant music at that exact moment, afternoon turned to dinner service, lights dimmed.

I'm getting married because I want to, Nora tells him, and Bren nods, once. Slow.

Don't do that, she says. Don't act like you don't believe me.

Nora, I literally just nodded my head.

If you must know, I have thought about this *a lot*, she says, because she knows him, knows what he's thinking. Robin is not someone I've *settled* for. My life is not something I've fallen into, because of a *missed opportunity*, or whatever.

So you're happy? Bren asks. It is not meant to be accusatory; it is genuine. He wants to know – now he's seen her, in that dress, and his own heart has flooded with things he'd not wanted to feel – what her answer is.

Yes! she says, but he hears the hesitation in her outbreath, before she rushes on. Happiness isn't only found in adventure, Bren! Which you would know, if you'd spent any real time with anyone, these past twelve years. If you hadn't just.

What?

Disappeared, she says. With only a goodbye to my *mother*.

A goodbye? Bren says. It was hardly a *goodbye*, Nora.

Fire inside of him as he says it, gush of regret, blazing-hot shame. Someone drops a glass by the bar. Smash and scatter, brief silence, and then it is Nora's turn to say what.

Don't be coy, Bren says. Don't pretend you can't remember.

Remember *what*?

The message I left with Freya.

The waiter comes back, then, with their drinks. Eye contact broken as he puts down his beer, her lemonade, says is that all okay for them; yes thanks. And when she looks back at him, he feels like he's turned the same colour as his hair. Red with the memory. The humiliation of all they'd agreed, intuitively, never to speak of. But there is something happening to Nora's face, too, as she studies his own. A stillness settling over her, which means something starts to dawn on Bren, too.

I called your house, from the airport, Bren says, watching her reaction. And Freya answered. I told her where I was going, and that I was going now, but that I didn't want to go without you. That I didn't want to . . . do anything, without you.

It is still mortifying, to him, all these years later.

I made her write it down, he goes on, as Nora stares at him. What town I'd be staying in, what airport you should fly into. And I.

Told her I'd wait for you, he does not say, because he can't bear to repeat it.

Was told she'd pass it on, he finishes. All that anger in him, changing colour, like Nora's face. Her stillness, now, quite unnatural.

She didn't, is all that she says.

They look at each other over their drinks.

Why didn't you . . . she begins, her voice catching. Why didn't you call the house again. Or email me, or something.

It was just too crazy when – and another memory comes at him, his father falling down, in front of him, so he talks faster, to keep it at bay – and you were at school, and I wasn't, because –

My dad's heart had stopped and I was a mess.

And I found a flight leaving that afternoon, he says. With one spare seat. And I didn't think about it, I told my mum I wanted to go and she just said I should, if I needed to, and so I just . . . went. Because I couldn't be there, with her. I couldn't *do* anything, to help.

He wills Nora to move. Just nod, even, but she doesn't.

But we had a plan, Nora, I know, Bren says. And that hadn't changed, for me, just because I left . . . a bit early.

She keeps her eyes on his. The only part of her that seems able to move, searching his own; like she's not sure whether to believe him.

I had to race to the airport to make it, Bren says, reliving the nearly missed train, his sprint through security. But at the gate I stopped to think, for like, two minutes, and I knew I should tell you, before I got on that plane, so I called. It was after school, by then, but Freya picked up, said you were next door with my mum. '*Like you should be*,' she said.

Swallow, then, as he remembers. Knowing that would be the story, always; that he'd left in his mother's hour of need: when that need was in fact endless, and if he stayed, he'd never be able to break free.

But we were boarding, he says, so I just told her, instead. She was fuming with me, Nora, for leaving, but when I asked her if she'd tell you everything, she said she would. And I really thought I'd get on that plane and you'd come join me, at some point. After the funeral, maybe, when you were ready. But you never came. You never even . . . picked up the phone, or sent an email, to say why.

The memory of it like heartburn, as he recalls checking and rechecking his phone, waiting for her response, sort of sick and sort of free but also certain he couldn't have stayed. Calling her house, in the end, a few weeks after he'd touched down in a new place and rented a room and still heard nothing.

Saying hi, when she picked up. Long pause before she said it back. Dredging up the courage to ask, you spoke to your mum, then? and her reply, tight, and quiet: yeah, Bren, I did.

Shame, afterwards. Hot, and thick.

So I guess that's it, he'd said, with a tightness of his own.

Yeah. I guess it is.

And not once, in all this time, had he considered she'd not been given the right message; not once had he conceived of the fact that she might never have known that he'd left, yes, but not left *her*. That he'd wanted her beside him. And like the bubbles in her lemonade, all of his resentment, all his own fury and confusion, rises to the surface, and dissipates. Everything he thought had been her rejection of him, evaporating, because it turns out she must have been thinking the same.

They feel this, in the quiet parts of themselves, as the city sky beyond the window falls to black. Ice melting in her glass. Music thumping overhead.

All this time, Bren says, you thought I'd just gone?

No nod, or noise; Nora's face doesn't look like her own.

God, he says, as the music changes. No wonder you're so mad at me.

–

Nora leaves, but does not head home to her flat. She gets on a train and then a bus to her mother's cottage, watching unseeing through the dark; Bren stays in London, saying he wants to eat, walk, clear his head. Alone, she feels like a set of jangling keys, all nerves and sharp edges, the bus jerking stop-start at every junction, but soon enough, she's letting herself through the porch, only to find the house empty. The greenhouse, too. So she sits at the kitchen table and waits, hardening with every tick of the hot pink clock. Numbers, swirling, in her head.

Twelve years, it's been, since she saw what she saw in the upstairs bathroom; since she pretended not to, and tiptoed away, reeling. Four weeks of silence and shame, avoiding Jon, until she didn't have to, because he was gone. *Gone*. Twelve years since his cardiac arrest, since Nora held Bren as he yelled no, in the driveway, no, Dad, no. Nineteen minutes for the paramedics to arrive, *sixty-two* of trying to restart his heart. Josie, inside. Freya, pacing. Nora, not knowing how to feel about this man she had loved, was livid with – but what did it matter, now, because he was dead. And there was nothing left to do, except quash it all down.

Twelve years of keeping that secret.

Twelve years, too, since Bren had left.

Nine, since she fell for Robin, though there has always been a part of her that felt something was unresolved, something restless inside her, and now she knows why. Because what Bren has told her changes everything. But it shouldn't, because it's less than two months now, until she's married.

Two halves, to make up a heart.

Two people, taking up hers.

And who knows how much time has passed in this kitchen – could be an hour, could be less – but then she hears footfall on gravel and her mother calling her name, Nora? when she sees her shoes by the door. And then she's tramping into the kitchen without removing her own, bright yellow flowers in the crooks of her arms.

Again, with the spontaneity! Freya says. She is wearing a kaftan over her thermals, tonight, and has a few twigs in her hair; she must have been pilfering crops from the local daffodil farm. Not a Sunday, is it?

She lays the daffodils on the side and starts pulling jam jars off the shelves, filling them with water from the tap. Nora, while she does so, finds her voice. Says no.

What's up then, darl?

A complex question; a complex answer. Nora has been trying to find the right words since she'd left Bren in the restaurant, before their food arrived. Unable to eat, unable to think straight. On the train and on the bus and for god knows how long at this wobbling table. Wondering how to lay out all the hurt and assumptions and whys, the room pressing in on her, the lucky cat waving back and forth. Taunting.

Freya glances round, plucking a stem or two from the bouquets.

Has something happened? she asks, but Nora can't answer.

Is it Robin? her mother presses. Or the wedding?

No, Nora says, her anger, dammed behind years of silence, now surging forward. No, it's nothing to do with the *wedding*.

Okay, Freya says, in a suit-yourself kind of voice, turning back to her jam jars once more. I was just asking.

Were you? Or were you implying, yet again, that there's some kind of problem with me wanting to marry the man I love?

It is like she is reminding herself of this.

Like she has to say it out loud.

Is this a chat for the greenh –

I don't want to go near your damn greenhouse! Nora bursts out, and Freya turns, her eyebrows arched into her hair. You pretend you're all wise and stoic, you tell me to *come back to my centre* and breathe out all the bullshit but you know what, Freya? You're the one that's full of it.

Nora's voice is not measured, like she'd wanted. She wants to throw plates and jam jars and lucky cats, but words, it seems, are the easiest choice. Freya looks bewildered. What was that, Nora knows she is thinking. What is this.

We've been over this, Freya says. And I've made my peace with it. Marriage isn't for me, but –

Right, Nora says, her anger a crashing wave now, salt in her wounds as she says *you* just prefer having affairs with men who are already married.

There is no sound, after she's said this.

Not a breath from either of them.

And Nora's adrenaline retreats, now that she cannot take it back, now that she's put it out there, finally, but she forces herself to keep staring at her mother, who stares right back, her face white.

I know, Freya, Nora says. I saw you and Jon, that time. In our bathroom.

Whatever you thought you saw –

Don't do that, Nora says, and her mother sees how serious this is, hears it, in her daughter's voice, and stops talking. But Nora has only begun. All of it finally rushing out, even though this wasn't what brought her here, not what she came to throw out into the room like the plates she still wants to smash, the sea shells, the greenhouse walls, this farce her mother has built for them both, their family friends, all lies.

Don't pretend, Nora says. I know what I saw. I don't know what it was, between you, and actually, I don't *want* to know – don't want to think about it – but you definitely weren't just friends.

And with this, it seems, Freya can't argue.

But I'm not here to get into that, Nora says, because she isn't; she'd made a choice, long ago, to lock all that away, but the lid has been blown off, tonight. Collateral damage. I'm here, she says, to ask you something else.

Nora – but Nora says no, and her mother falls silent again.

Did you answer a call from Bren, the day he left, Nora asks.

A blink. A beat. A wave back and forth from the cat.

I told you –

You told me he called to say good*bye*, Nora says. Sorry and goodbye.

Freya is looking at her, desperate, and for a slice of a second Nora wants, so badly, to be wrong. Would give anything, in fact, for Bren to be the one who had wronged her, the way she'd always thought, because she has tried to ignore the thing with Jon but the call with Bren feels bigger, almost, because it's her, because it's him: because it's *them*.

He says he called here and left me a message, she says, asking me to join him. Did you take that message.

I'm –

Did you take that message, Freya?

I didn't know what to do, her mother says, and her voice is unlike her own: soft, and pleading. Jon had just . . . died, and . . .

A roaring, now, in Nora's ears.

I know it looks bad, Freya says, I know you must have drawn conclusions, but there's more to it – and then he died –

I know he fucking died! *I know!*

Tears, now, in Nora's throat. With grief, or rage.

He died and I *hated* him! Nora says. Bren's *dad*! Our friend! But after I saw you together, I couldn't *look* at him, I felt so – sick, and ashamed – and then his fucking heart gave out and I didn't know what to *do* with that, Freya, so I've kept it quiet all this time for Josie, not for you, d'you understand? Because it would *kill* her. It'd fucking kill her.

No tears, from Freya. No reply.

And then my – my best –

But there is no language, for what Bren was; what he is, still.

– he *left*! Without me! And I was heartbroken! And it turns out *you* caused that, Freya! Why! I want to know why! Are you really so against me being with someone? So sour about being a bitter, lonely spinster that you had to stop *me* being with him, away from here? Away from *you*?

Yes! Freya cries, and her eyes are wild. Yes, Nora! Jon died! Out of nowhere! I was in shock, you have to understand that! I was devastated, but I had to hold it together – I had to be there for –

Don't pretend you're her friend, Nora near-spits. What kind of friend would do that, to someone?

Her mother lets out a winded noise, at this, puts her head in her hands. Nora stays rigid in the chair, and they stay like that, heartbeats like deadened drums, until Freya lowers her palms.

And then Bren phoned the landline, she murmurs, and he said all of these things. How he felt. Where he would wait, for you. And I was grieving, Nora, I was bereft, and I – I couldn't have you leaving me, too.

The silence stretches like time itself, then. Twelve whole years of it.

I didn't mean t –

Didn't mean to what? Sabotage my entire life? Let me think that what I had with Bren was nothing? Watch me meet someone else, get *engaged* to someone else, someone I wouldn't have even *met* if you hadn't hidden that phone call –

But you did meet him! And you're happy!

That is so *not* the point.

Be with Bren, then! He's back, now!

Freya, *listen* to yourself. I am not like you. I am not willing to play with people's *lives* like that. I can't just swap Robin for Bren, Jesus, *nothing* is that simple, and if you thi –

I know it's not! Really, I do! If you would just –

No, Nora says again, and she stands up, shoves the chair back so hard it collides with the kitchen counter; she hears the backboard split. It's a chair they'd painted together when she was little; yellow, like the daffodils, splintered now on the floor.

You were eigh*teen*, Nora, Freya says, following her into the hall. I couldn't have known it would hurt you so badly, for so long. I couldn't have known he'd have stayed in touch, or turned up, like this, out of the blue.

It's not out of the blue, though, is it? We – Bren and I – we –

She is dizzy, with all of it. With what they are, or should have been. Best friends, promised for more; knowing that, without needing to say it, because they felt it, she'd *thought* they'd felt it. Second-guessed it, felt rejected, ever since. Freya keeps talking while Nora tugs on her shoes. Making excuses, defending herself, but she doesn't want to hear it. Flashes of the people she'd cared about – Josie's face, Jon's laugh, Freya touching his arm and him kissing her neck and Nora's world shattering as she glimpsed them, from the stairs – Bren on the swings and in her room and halfway across the world but huge in her heart, across the table, saying he'd wanted her with him – had *always* wanted her, with him – and then she's out the door, the air cutting cold on her face. She needs to move. She has to get away. She understands, truly, for the first time, why Bren walked out the way he did; because things can hurt, for so long, then all at once become too much. And so she walks out, too. Her mother calling behind her, from the porch, Nora, please, I didn't want to lose you, and her saying, well, Freya, twelve years too late? It looks like you just did.

ten

One week has passed since. One week of no messages from Bren, and several from Freya, at first: please, Nora, answer your phone, can we talk about this, before those messages dried up, too. A new strategy, probably, a freezing out from her principled, prickly mother: fine. Nora merely ignored her harder.

You've been quiet, Robin says on the Friday night, as they eat takeaway noodles straight from the foil. Gyoza in a plastic tray, salmon-pink slices of ginger. Miso in a cup, cloudy and hot on the coffee table.

Just tired, she tells him. He's been away on a shoot all week; she'd not had the energy to tell him about Bren and Freya, when she'd got home last weekend. He'd been giddy because of the venue, their newly confirmed wedding date. She hadn't wanted to ruin that. And then by the Sunday he was gone for an antiques roadshow, and she'd been left alone to think and work and catch the train into the city each day, springtime lightening the mornings, prolonging the evenings, like her own understanding of her past and present. Nothing quite normal, any more.

I meant all week, Robin says. Normally you shower me with snapshots of your day. Your breakfast. Funny typos. Strangers wearing excellent hats.

Nora takes a mouthful of noodles, chewing as he says a particular highlight was when she found a pink rhinestone on the floor of the flat, when neither of them owns anything bespeckled with rhinestones. You just wanted to use the word bespeckled, didn't you, she says, after she's swallowed, and Robin laughs. I used the word buffeted, this week, too, he admits. It was a proud moment.

He is being gentle, and not prying; sitting beside her with ease, his shirt unbuttoned. An animated fantasy playing on the television.

I discovered something, this week, she says, because it's the right time to say it. And because if she tells him – the way she tells him everything – she'll surely be able to make sense of it.

Oh yeah?

Yeah. It shouldn't be important, but it feels. I don't know.

Robin mutes the television.

Is it Bren-related, he asks her, and she looks at him quickly, her heart quick too. He puts the cup of miso down on the coffee table. He seems like he's got a lot of . . . baggage, he says. For someone who seems to think he travels light.

That's perfectly put, she says. And very observant.

I am a photographer, Robin says, feigning conceit. Leaning over for another gyoza. But his stuff isn't your stuff, Nora. You know that, right?

Nora nods, prodding around in her noodles with her chopsticks. She can't quite recall how much she's told Robin, in the past, about Bren and his childhood. That they'd roam the farmers' fields together, sure, spend hours climbing trees, talking on the swings. Because that's what teenagers do. Not because Josie was having an episode, and he needed to be kept out of the house. Tears sometimes streaked on his cheeks that she never once acknowledged, because he'd wipe them away when he saw her.

I think it's hard for him, being home, she says. With everything.

Robin nods, a fleck of soy sauce on his chin.

His dad dying, you mean?

Yeah. But that's only one part of it. I glimpsed what it must have been like, growing up with Josie. A mother who was okay one day, then really not, the next. And then when Jon died – his name, she thinks, almost hard to say out loud – so *suddenly*, when he was the one who, in Bren's mind, held everything together . . .

She can't finish. That man's a mirage to her, now. All the good things about him, as dead to her as he is, like his lifeless body the coroner came to take away.

It was pretty tragic, she says. And I think Bren's cut himself off from that tragedy, and everyone else in his life.

Except you, Robin says.

Yeah, Nora says. She eats more noodles, tries to find a way to tell him about the phone call, which with this context, surely, explains why it's so unsettling – it's about Bren's heart, not hers, and it's only bothering her because she cares, and who wouldn't care about a guy like Bren who doesn't even know himself how much he's hurting – but then Robin asks her a question, in an even voice. Do you have feelings for him?

Nora splutters on a nub of wasabi.

What do you *mean!*

I mean the boy next door has returned after a decade away, Robin says. The boy you planned to travel the world with. Who looks at you, by the way, like he wants to eat you.

He does not.

He does, he says, and his expression is neutral, nothing smug or possessive in the line of his mouth. I just wondered if it was messing with you, a bit. That's all.

Nora watches him dig for a prawn in his own noodles. The television flicks to a new scene, and she feels warm and too full and she should just tell him. She should just say yes, she's mixed up. She's confused, because of what she's found out this past week, and wouldn't anyone feel the same, and because it's Robin he'll understand and talk it out and things will be fine and how they're meant to be. But what if they're not. What if this unpeels a layer she can't put back, so instead she says, in a level voice: there was never anything between Bren and me.

Not officially, Robin says.

Not at all, Nora says. He's. I'm.

These prawns are so good, tonight, Robin says. Not as salty as last time.

He keeps eating; Nora blinks, takes a moment. Then he looks up, picks up her train of thought. You said you discovered something, he prompts. This week.

Yes, she says. I found out that he . . . wanted me to go with him. The day he left, and everything, he phoned my house, and spoke to Freya. Told her.

That he didn't want to go, without me.

Didn't want to do anything without me.

That I should join him, like we'd planned, she says. *And* he explained why he had to leave so suddenly. Because of how it was, at home, for him. Which I guess I always knew, on some level, but it hurt so much that he'd never explained himself. I just figured he found it easier to ignore the whole thing. Or pretend I was the one in the wrong, for being so sensitive.

Robin is watching her as she talks. Watching her realise, now she's saying it out loud, that she might start crying.

All this time, I've been mad at him for going, without saying so – and he's been mad at *me*, for ignoring him, and not giving him an answer. When it was Freya, who didn't pass on his message. Got lucky, I guess, when we were both too wounded to talk about it.

Another scene starts up on the television. Nora watches it, and Robin keeps watching her, his chopsticks still poised in his hand.

That's . . . terrible, he says, after a stretch of quiet.

I know, Nora says, her voice quiet, too.

But why would she do that?

She said, Nora tells him, that she couldn't lose me, as well.

Little shrug, then. Just one shoulder, like Bren, rubbing off on her. Because Robin knows about Freya and Jon; is the only person on earth she has told, late one night when they were baring their souls and their secrets, because it's what you do when you're falling in love and want to know every corner of the person you're lying in bed with. Although she has regretted telling him, sometimes. Worried what he thinks of her mother, or of Nora herself, for saying nothing. Because is it cowardly, to stay silent? To not rock the fragile boat that could so easily sink, even when there was nothing wrong, when Josie's son was home and her husband was alive and her friend had not betrayed her, and still she took anti-psychotics, still she stopped driving, still she couldn't cope when the boiler broke or a cat caught a dove in the back garden and she'd cry and cry and cry.

Are you . . . okay, Robin asks her, and Nora lifts her wet eyes to his.

I could barely look at her, she tells him, meaning Freya. And Bren and I . . . we've not spoken, since we realised. I guess neither of us knows what to say. And I just feel, she says, blinking her tears back. A lot of things.

You wouldn't be Nora, if you didn't, Robin says.

And she is grateful for his faith in her. For not questioning her again, about Bren. For understanding the shock of the phone call and the *second* betrayal of her mother and not prying into what that means, what does it mean, she does not know, she wants to finish dinner and watch the film and just carry on as they were.

Robin does not unmute the television, and Nora does not finish her noodles. She does, however, take the last gyoza when he offers it.

I'm guessing we're still okay for the twenty-second of April, he says, after they've eaten. And it is teasing, she thinks, but also a good question, and Nora says yeah, of course, without pausing to wonder whether that is a good answer. It's fine, she says. She's just not sure, now, whether Freya will be there.

Robin has been stacking their empty takeaway dishes, but stops at this, cocks his head. Really? he says. I know what she did was wrong, Nora, but she's your mother.

And a liar, Nora says. Standing up, taking the stacked trays in one hand, the leftover noodles in the other. In the kitchen, she puts the latter in a Tupperware. Wondering if, by not being entirely honest with him – with herself, even, about all this – *all of what* – she is a liar, too.

But the evening goes on. Cutlery dropped in the dishwasher. Plastic bags in the recycling. Robin reminds her, as he rinses the foil trays, that they still haven't seen their wedding venue. For the planning day. He'll book a room one weekend, they'll make a trip of it, maybe the sea air, the distance, will make everything seem better, perhaps, with Freya, but it is not Freya she's even thinking about; her head is with Bren twelve years ago on that phone, saying what he said, wondering what she would have said back. Can you book the registry office, maybe, Robin asks, as she puts the remaining soy sauce sachets in the fridge. So we can get the legal bit locked in? I think doing that first would be nicer, if we can. So we're *married*, once we're married.

Yes, she says, I can do that.

Which is what she'd have said to Bren, she thinks. Yes, I can do that. I can fly out to be with you. Which disturbs something inside of her; stirs the certainty she has felt, for so long, into a swirl of something else. Churning her up as they finish the film. As they brush their teeth, read for a while by their bedside lamps and then, when they are flicked off and she is still abnormally quiet, Robin curls himself around her. Asks, with his face in her hair, if she ever considered telling Bren, about Freya and Jon.

Their blinds are not fully closed, and the street light slats are silver-white on the wall. Cold colour, like the feeling inside her, as she says no. She would never. She couldn't risk his mum finding out, and anyway, what good would it do? Bren can't handle the normal hard things, as it is. One parent dying. Another on meds. If he found out his hero was not a hero at all, not the man who made things okay, embodied something solid, in his life, it would break him. Like it would Josie.

Like it did you, Robin says, into the dark.

Which is meant to be caring, Nora knows. Empathetic. Is meant to remind her that he sees her and still knows, intimately, those dark corners that she showed him, all those years ago. But it is only once he's fallen asleep, still holding her, that she can let her tears fall. She cries silently about all of it, the history, the betrayals, the stirred-up love and regret. Not knowing how she got here, or where she should go; what's haunted her, always, stepping into a new shade of light.

—

And then it's the last week of March and another Sunday rolls around, which is usually the day she'd go to Freya's, if her mum wasn't on shift at the hospice. She'd take ingredients, often, do the cooking, or else be subjected to whatever spread her mother would throw together – tomatoes, of course, sliced cold or stewed with red peppers; hummus, flatbreads, anything she could scrounge from the reduced section. But for the third week in a row, Nora will not be going for lunch. She will not be cooking for or eating with her mother this Sunday, and this feels painful and strange and Robin knows this, too, so on waking nuzzles into her neck, says right. What shall we do with our day?

He smells warm, of tea and toast. She reaches for her phone, checks her weather app.

Glorious sun predicted all morning, before a downpour – the start of another named storm, come the afternoon. An excellent excuse to curl up by the fire with a Pixar movie, Robin says. Proverbially, he says, when she points out they don't have a fireplace.

And while she agrees, she also feels the pull to something more extreme – she is craving the cold water, some alone time. So she pulls on her swimsuit, tells Robin she's going to the lido while the sun's out. Are you okay, he asks her, as she packs her swim bag, and she says she's fine, why?

It's still a novelty that we won't be spending our Sunday being lectured on mussel farming, Robin says. Or misogyny.

I know, Nora says.

It's okay if you're kind of sad as well as pleased about that.

I'm not, she says, throwing spare underwear into her bag. I'm just angry.

Angry is a kind of sad.

Robin, can you stop being so *perceptive* for once, she says. I just want to go for a swim, not a therapy session.

Robin lies back on his pillows, says okay. Sure. She kisses him roughly on the forehead and leaves, walks down the concrete path with her chest tight, that anger ebbing into guilt. She texts him that she's sorry. She loves him. Sorry again.

He replies immediately with three tortoise emojis.

Little snapper turtle, he calls her, sometimes. When she's tired or hungry or hormonal. With relief, she puts her phone away and walks to the pool, feels everything falling through her, like she's an hourglass. Like she's being tipped over, and turned upright, over and over again.

–

An hour later she walks up the steps from the changing room to the edge of the pool. It's not the Hampstead Mixed Pond, but it's still got a certain charm. Cool air, smell of wet grass. She lowers herself in and, alongside the other lone swimmers doing lengths, finds herself musing that everyone, surely, must have someone like Bren. Someone from their past, who would throw a question mark over everything if they showed up at the wrong – or maybe the right – moment.

Surely it is not just her.

And surely it does not mean that things need to change.

Another lap. Another thought.

Because she believed she was someone who knew herself. All that art and sewing, years without a mobile phone and so forced into introspection; has no aversion, she is certain, to her own shortcomings. But what if, she thinks, as she glides through the water, she doesn't know herself at all. What if she is just someone who thinks too hard.

Someone who wouldn't jump.

She swims for an hour, but then lane swimming is over, the sun gone. Nora gets out, dries off, dresses and walks with wet hair towards the high street. Clouds purpling, now, the storm brewing. She buys some bits for lunch, thinking less under the supermarket lighting, then swings by the haberdashery, stocks up on black thread. Buys a new blue she can't resist. Periwinkle. Lovely to say, like pumpernickel. Something Robin will appreciate when she shares that with him, at home. It could be her something blue, stitched into her skirts, she thinks, as she pays. She hasn't been thinking about the wedding nearly enough.

And just as she steps outside, the heavens break and the rain comes and she has to run and shelter beneath a bus stop, wetter than she was in the pool, even, aghast at how sudden it came down.

How the day could turn like that, in a second.

Coat soaked and shoes sopping, she texts Robin to say she'll be late. The weather, crazy. Light that proverbial fire.

She waits, but there are no ticks to register he's read it. He's probably making a playlist for the wedding, or watching flash mob groomsmen dances online, and she gets this feeling, at the thought, the urge to run back into the rain. An urge she ignores as a bus pulls up along the kerb, slow and heaving. Then the doors hiss open and there's a woman descending the steps with a pram, another person helping her lift it, a guy with red hair and a blue coat and Nora jolts; sits upright, and stares.

Bren?

He looks round at her after he's lowered the pram and the mother has bowed forward into the downpour. Nora sees him seeing her, sees the surprise that mirrors her own.

Hi? she says, confusion sluicing between them, like the rain. What are you – doing here?

I came to see you, Bren says. But I didn't expect you to be . . . waiting?

I'm not *waiting*, Nora says. It's raining.

And you . . . hang out here, when it rains?

I was shopping, she says, lifting her tote bag, which is as soaked as her coat. And then world war three started falling.

Insane, isn't it, Bren says. I've seen worse, in monsoon seasons, but this feels extreme, for Britain.

That's climate change for you, Nora says, echoing her mother before she can stop herself, but Bren doesn't appear to notice. He seems ill at ease, less self-assured than usual. Like he doesn't know where to look.

The bus hauls itself away, spraying yet more water, and Bren steps closer, his boots drenched. The wind has picked up, too, flattens his red hair against his face almost comically, like he's standing on a mountain top, being filmed for a cologne advert. He looks like a film star, Nora thinks. So bright and out of place, in his blue coat with his gold earring. Dark patches down his trousers, ruining the image.

I was just stocking up on some staples, she says, because he hasn't said anything more, and she feels skittish. She nods down the road at the haberdashery.

Milk and bread? Bren asks.

Silk and thread, she says, and he grins, because she remembers. It was their stupid in-joke, when they were much younger. Referring to how she could spend hours making art with anything she could find, but Bren, hungry and eventually cold, would pull her towards home before dark. How things have changed, she thinks. How things are always changing.

I probably should have texted, he says. Sorry.

Nora shrugs. Says she's used to it.

I don't know why I don't, he says, shifting on his feet. I suppose I'm just not in the habit of announcing my arrival to anyone. Or my departure.

He rubs his neck.

Is it okay that I came, he asks. We haven't talked, since.

I know, she says.

Did you speak to Freya?

I yelled, Nora says. And now we're not speaking at all.

Ah.

Have you seen her around?

Pretty sure she's avoiding me, Bren says. I see her lights on in the evenings, and my mum pops over there like usual, but I'm not exactly seeking out her company. I've not got much to say to her.

You and me both, Nora says.

Scuff of Bren's boot, then, along the ground. A dustbin lid scoots along the street behind him, where it's been blown off its base.

Did she tell you why she lied, Bren asks her. Not that it matters, now.

Now that you're marrying someone else, he does not say, but she hears it through his silence, and for a half-second, she has another urge – wants to tell him the truth about Freya and Jon, as the bin lid takes to the air. But why would she, she wonders, except for some kind of hard-boiled revenge against her own mother? A staunch belief in the truth, when that truth would do more harm than good? So she crosses her arms, takes a breath, and says no. It was just selfish, I think. She just didn't . . . want me to leave.

Bren scuffs his boot again, those stains on his trousers brown-black. Petrol, she thinks, or ink; blackberry juice from the brambles they'd raid as kids, sour-sharp, the occasional sweet hit when they'd spend hours in the farmers' fields.

He looks so lost, standing there in his stained trousers and wet shoes. So alone and, for the first time since the engagement party, almost sad.

Do you want to . . . come back to mine? she asks him. Robin's there, though.

Why *though*. Why the note of apology in her voice.

I assumed he would be, Bren says. Which is fine. Obviously. And I'm sorry, about the other day, if I made it seem like it wasn't. I really . . . want to like him.

Nora blinks. Bren's half-honesty here has floored her, which must show on her face because he presses on, I'm your best man, right, and I promised to be here, and I've been thinking a lot about what we pieced together, last week, and it doesn't change anything, I don't think.

Those green eyes, locked onto hers. Those words reverberating through her like he's caught her, then let go, as if she's a guitar string.

Doesn't change anything.

So I'm here, Bren says, hands deep in his pockets. If you still want me involved.

I want you involved, she says, with a nod. Bren keeps looking at her, rain on the ends of his hair like dew. Then he nods, too. Sits down beside her on the bus stop bench, removes his hands from his pockets.

Sorry I bolted, after the dress shop, he says. It was a weird day for me. It's been weird since I got back, to be honest. Seeing you with this life.

He breaks off, the wind gushing round them, like the sea.

I guess your life panning out like this, he says, just reminds me that I don't have one, here. I'm still stuck in the past, I think.

His words stain Nora's heart, like the rainwater soaking into her shoes.

But I'm trying, he says. I'm here, aren't I? And I've been fixing up my mum's car, he says, gesturing at the oil spilled down his knees. Because that driveway is a hard place, for me, and I figured I've got to face into the hard things, like a normal person. Which sometimes I think I'm just not.

What? Normal?

Sometimes I think I've got her . . . tendencies, he says. My mum's. She shuts down. I run away. Different reactions to the same issues, maybe.

You don't have her issues, Nora says, and he says maybe not medically. I guess we'd probably know by now.

You don't hear voices, do you?

Only the standard ones, he says, and when she looks alarmed he says he's kidding. Kind of. He just regrets a lot. Has this inner narrative that loops round and round, all of the time, unless he's moving, or a *forced* kind of scared. Which can shake it, for a while. Living somewhere new. Kayaking through ravines. Leaping into canyons.

Whereas fixing the car he was cleaning, when he died, Nora guesses out loud, is actually scarier, and Bren doesn't say anything for a really long time but then he dips his head, says right.

And Nora aches. Wants to tell him that Jon wasn't who he thought he was. Wants him to let go. Wants to hold him, make everything better for him, like she always seemed able to when they were young.

I'm sorry . . . things went the way they did, she says. I wouldn't have ignored you, if I'd got your message.

And I would've spoken to you, about it, Bren says, if I thought you hadn't.

More rain. Mad winds. Raindrops smashing so hard on the ground, it looks like shattering glass. Nora thinks of Robin at home, planning their wedding, probably cleaning, almost certainly singing, but she also thinks of how this yearning, younger part of her wants to stay here beside Bren in this storm, and she thinks about how she can't feel both things, can't *want* both things, and why – that question, yet again – why is this so hard.

I left because of my mum, Bren tells her, still watching the rain. Which was selfish, I know, but also survival. In a lot of ways.

Nora can't bring herself to nod. Can't quite forgive him, for that part.

But I stayed *away*, Bren says, because I thought I'd read us . . . all wrong. And I know I was only seventeen, and I know what I said probably seemed . . . stupid.

That you wanted me with you? she wants to say, but doesn't, because she does not need to clarify. Does not need to remind him of what was. So she just looks at the rain like he's doing and says no, Bren. It wasn't stupid.

Slow breathing. Shoulders touching. *Didn't want to do anything, without you*. And then Bren does something she doesn't expect, and threads one of his hands through hers. It is tender, and his skin is cold. Dotted with old freckles she still knows so well. Then he rests his head on top of hers. Moves to kiss the side of it, just lightly, but the feel of his lips in her hair ripples through her like his words from before, everything trembling and longing and wrong. And he lingers there, with his mouth, and she lets him.

Neither of them pulling away.

eleven

Sunday morning, and you're alone. Wedding emails sent, payments pending, and you're all caught up on edits so think you'll get some other things done while Nora swims. While she clears her head, runs some errands, and you decide to do something that'll cheer her up once she's back. Coffee drunk, Crunchy Nut crunched, then you put on your messy jeans – paint-streaked, frayed at the knees – and head out the back door into the yard.

It can't be called a garden, really, because there is no grass; just a square of land bricked over and sprouting weeds, but it is still yours, nonetheless. Yours and hers. Clovers push through the cracks in the ground, and there's a hole in the fence that backs onto the alleyway, a glimpse of wheelie bins, tarmac, more weeds.

You've made fond memories out here, though, you think, as you manoeuvre the ladders out of the shed. A shed you'd always intended to convert into a studio, but is instead crammed with tools and stacks of old sketchbooks, reels of fabric turned damp from winter. Right there is where you like to drink white wine spritzers, come the summer. Nora in a sunhat, thumbing through the paperbacks Shay has lent her while you twiddle on your laptop, editing to the white noise of trains and traffic. Planes, sometimes, because you live slap bam in the Luton flight path, inhaling all sorts of aircraft fumes, Freya lamented, toxins, aldehydes, you name it. Today, though, there's none of that. No sunhats or pollutants, no laptop or mother-in-law-to-be predicting your untimely death from noxious gases in the air. Just you on an ordinary day cleaning the gutters, as you've promised you would, too many times. Climbing the ladders with garden gloves on and the clouds fast-moving. A storm is coming but you do not remember this, at first. The sky has been clear all morning, and then out of nowhere, it isn't.

It breaks, with the force of a glacier collapsing, as if in slow motion.

And the wind is wild but you're almost there, you don't do things by halves, so you hold on, intent on finishing the job. Wanting to unclog the remaining leaves but then the rain is so heavy you have to give up. The ladder wobbles, you say whoa there, out loud to no one. Laugh at yourself, like you're talking to a horse, down Bessie, and the ladder tilts back again. Safe. On the way down though, classic, you slip because of the rain or the wind or perhaps both and you fall onto the wet brick, not all that far, but the sound is like shock, a hard solid crack, and that shock is felt in your elbow and your head and your ribs and the pain is so extreme you're sure the former has been broken, fuck, fuckit fuck.

You don't say those words, though; just lie there, dumb in the rain.

No laughing at yourself now. But the weather is almost biblical, so you have no choice but to get up, and there's no blood, just a graze, a pulsing in your head. Glad it wasn't worse. Glad that nobody saw. Glad that, while tender, your elbow does actually seem fine, moves the way it's supposed to, shot of sharp pain again as you flex your wrist, but the rain only gets worse so you hurry to put the ladders away. Chuck the dirt you've unclogged into a bucket before it pools into a soup of more mulch and then you're inside and changing into dry clothes and feeling agitated that this sacred free Sunday, of all the duty-bound Sundays spent at Freya's, is now a washout. And that Nora still isn't home; she's been longer than you'd thought. Your elbow smarts with pain, and you are not one for bad moods but it looks like you're in one; you make an angry noise through your nose.

You check your elbow in the bathroom mirror as your head pulses. It's red, looks tender, that's all. You want a hug. You want to lie down. You want to be hugged while you lie down, and you are going to tell Nora what happened, in passing, as part of your low-key, fake-firelit afternoon, a movie, maybe some wine, but then she comes through the door with someone else. With Bren.

And that agitation in you sparks again at the sight of him, when he's never bothered you before, via anecdote or in person, because he's just Bren, Nora's old pal, Nora's slightly sloppy, kind of aloof, short-arse childhood sweetheart who was never actually her sweetheart. These thoughts surprise you, flying through your mind like darts.

It's still raining, hard, when they both bundle into your flat.

The pair of them soaked to the bone.

Hi, Nora says, sounding breathless. Look who I found, outside.

Brief silence, while the pair of them drip onto the carpet. Not that you likely look any better, with your wet hair and swollen arm; there is a moment when your gaze meets Nora's and a current passes between you, a look without words, but you try to keep things relaxed. Robin-like. Good swim? you ask her, ignoring, for a moment, the fact that Bren is here.

Two swims, in the end, she says. In the lido and this crazy rain.

Storm Beatrix, you say, going to the airing cupboard and pulling out two towels. Good to see you, you say to Bren, though you don't look him in the eye.

Are you . . . okay, Nora asks, as you help peel off her jacket. And you say sure; that she'll want a bath, presumably?

A bath? Bren says, as he tousles his hair with the towel you'd passed him. At one o'clock in the afternoon?

Do not underestimate the wrath of a cold Nora, you tell him – or rather, you tell the coat hooks near his head, because it's still an affront to have him here on your

Sunday, your private afternoon with the wine and the cleaned gutters and therefore potential sofa sex if you were lucky, so you don't *feel* like looking at him, this gate-crashing friend of hers whose gate-crashing is wearing a little thin, now, if you're honest.

Nora is nodding, says it's true. She gets mean when she's cold.

I find that hard to believe, Bren says, and you both say no you wouldn't, and you think you see Nora cringe, a little, as you speak in unison. At how married you are, already.

Would you like a hot drink, you ask Bren, thinking that you definitely need one, yourself; a soothing herbal something, camomile or passion flower, to ease these darts of agitation inside you. You work hard to keep your voice jovial, though, uncaring. And you see Nora noticing. See her realise that you do care that he's here, ever so slightly, but aren't about to show it.

Maybe just some dry clothes? she suggests.

I don't need – Bren begins, but you speak over him, say sure, you'll find him something. Mi casa es tu casa.

Apparently.

In the bedroom, the rain thrashes at the windows like a pressure washer. You get on your knees and start hunting through your drawers for some clothes that might fit him, but they'll all drown him, who are you kidding.

Surprised at yourself once again for these mean thoughts. Kind of like Nora when she's too cold, or hungry. And then she's in the room with you, closing the door, sitting on the bed with her sockless feet, saying I didn't plan this, Robin. I swear.

Okay.

We've not spoken since . . .

The missed phone call that would've changed the trajectory of your lives?

I never said that, Nora says.

I know; I'm saying it. But it's fine. It's . . . great that he's here.

You put two hands on the carpet, steadying yourself, then return to rifling through your drawer. You can feel her watching, and this bothers you as well. Elbow aching, you pull out some joggers and an old jumper that you think, maddeningly, will probably complement Bren's eyes, and then she asks you why you're in a different shirt to earlier, and why your hair's all wet.

I cleaned the gutters, you tell her, and she says really?

Finally, you say. And instead of being rewarded with *Ratatouille* and a little afternoon delight on our sofa –

You did *not* just say afternoon delight.

And you can't help it, you're half smiling now, because you know which phrases bother her, especially in a sexual context – the word *panties*, the term *hanky-panky*, just call it sex, Robin, you total weirdo – laughing, because it's funny, because you love her laugh – and your agitation lifts, just like that, your bad mood gone. Nora is smiling too, though it's tentative, you think. You go over to her. Sit beside her on the bed.

Are you okay, she asks you, again. You seem distracted.

Funny, you tell her. I was going to ask you the same thing.

Just cold, she says. So you run the taps for her in your small, windowless en-suite, the gush of the water like the rain in the yard, not knowing what she is thinking, not knowing what you are thinking, just that she seems jittery and you feel unsettled as to why that might be. Hot water, rising, in the tub.

Does he make you nervous? you ask her, as you squeeze in some bubble bath, swirl it around.

Bren? she says. Of course not. Why would you say that?

Because I think you make *him* nervous.

Internal disturbance, then, that you can't explain. Something opening. Like you're falling, or floating, not unpleasant but not normal, either, as it is dawning on you that maybe there is something *not* normal about this situation, about how he shows up unannounced, about how she lets him, then seems flustered, not quite herself. Which could be why you're not yourself, either. An engagement party is one thing. Your Sunday afternoon quite another.

Just the thought of you in the bath did something to his face, you tell her, and she says no it didn't.

Were you looking at his face?

No – I –

You let out a low, teasing laugh, and move in to kiss her, slow and deep, a little tongue. The opening inside you widening, so vast, now, it's like you could swallow her whole. She seems taken aback but then she's kissing you too, and you undress her, the steam from the bath clouding the mirror, tap water covering the sound of your breath in her mouth. You have not kissed her like this in a while. Everything pulsing between you, at the idea that you are not alone, that Bren is in the next room, that *you* are here, that *you* are hers, slight bite of her neck in your teeth, catch of her voice in her throat.

So we're okay? you murmur, moving your mouth downwards.

Rain on the window. Steam up the glass.

Just cold, she repeats, and she really is breathless now. You kiss her once more, open her up and she is wet not just due to the rain and she lets you touch her like that, the way she likes, but then she says your name, Robin, and you come back to yourself; lift your hands off in surrender.

Just checking, you say. That we're okay.

Yes, she says. Still breathless.

Dizzy with desire, still hard, you say all right, then. Enjoy your bath. That you'll get him a drink and make nice.

twelve

Nora rushes what would usually be a long soak. Pulls the plug so that the bathwater drains, still hot. Because something feels wrong about them being in a room without her, after what's happened. The brush of Bren's lips on her hair, the rush and the guilt of it, even though it was nothing. And Robin's own kiss, soon afterwards. Like he'd sensed a change.

The storm roars on as she steps out of the tub; the radiators pumping out heat. She dries off, winds her hair into a towel and pulls on an oversized jumper dress from her wardrobe. She's always hated putting clothes onto just-wet skin, has spent years sourcing – even making, when she has time – clothes that feel like air or water to the touch; like the wedding dress that Bren had picked out.

A flicker of it, then, as she pulls this dress over her head.

Of Bren's face when he saw her in it.

Robin's face, too, when he'd proposed by the river. Just now, when he'd kissed her like he had, like he wanted to drink her down. She'd not seen that in him before. Not tasted that sort of urgency, even when they were first together and free-falling into love, sky-high moods and a shared toothbrush and eyeing each other instead of the art at the galleries they wandered round; hours talking; tremoring orgasms; the smell of him left on her pillow.

These memories are what make her open her bedroom door, now, near silently. That see her moving down the hall towards their voices and hovering, without saying anything. Hoping this thing that's brewing is all in her head, but she can't help it, there's some kind of gnawing in her gut that she can't ignore and it's leading her by the hand, causing her to act like an animal version of the good adult self she has always tried to be.

And it gets more technical, Robin is saying, beyond the half-closed door of the living room. Give anyone the worst subject in good light, and they're golden.

Pun intended? Bren says, and she imagines Robin's smile, at this, his good teeth. Wine glass lifted in acknowledgement.

Why antiques, then, Bren asks, and this is good, Nora thinks. A reasonable question. An effort being made.

I just fell into it, Robin tells him. Kind of like you with your adventure stuff? I actually dabbled in three degrees, before landing on photography. And after graduating I was mostly shooting artworks in museums and archives, items for luxury retailers, that sort of thing. Antiques just kind of rolled my way, after that.

Silence, then; Bren nodding, she suspects, from behind the wall. And things seem fine, she thinks, after all. She'll go fetch herself some wine; they'll talk about Peru and Bren will stay for the planned evening movie, maybe. They'll order takeaway, the Japanese place does a deal on Sundays, and this strange feeling inside her will settle while Robin, too, is put at ease, and Bren learns that her home, like his mother's driveway, can be a safe space, somewhere where old feelings can just . . . fade away.

I do like the history of it all, Robin is saying. Every object has a story, just like a person. If you look beyond how they present themselves.

A pause, then. Nora decides to stay where she is.

It's why I never liked portraiture, Robin says. People can be unpredictable, which I don't like, so much.

Bren, it seems, does not quite catch the pointed nature of Robin's words, but Nora hears how strange they are, coming out of her partner's mouth. How deliberate, like his work; capturing an angle that someone else, someone less observant or emotionally in tune, might not.

So those portraits in the hall, Bren says. They're not yours?

Robin laughs at this – not unkindly – and says ah, no. They're Nora's favourite.

Another pause, then. This time, Nora thinks, because Bren does not like being laughed at.

You're not Nora's favourite?

And *that* pointedness is not missed. She hears Robin's voice change; a note of hardness, like he's unimpressed.

They're by Robert Mapplethorpe, Robin says. But it's the subject she's into, rather than the photographer. Nora loves Patti Smith.

I know, Bren says. I was there when she bought a copy of *Woolgathering* from a jumble sale, when we were kids.

Small noise, from Robin, in understanding. Nora waits for him to see the pun, make the joke: *Just Kids*? but he doesn't. The only noise another blast of wind against the front door, causing a slight draught in the hall.

Look, Bren, he says, eventually. I can tell you're not a fan.

I don't know anything about Robert Mapplethorpe, mate, Bren says.

I meant of me, Robin says, and Nora's heart stalls.

I'm not *not* a fan, Bren says.

Well, the feeling's mutual, Robin says. You seem like a cool guy, Bren. You've got to be, to be such a close friend of Nora's. But I'm starting to feel a bit uneasy, to be frank. About how you mess with her feelings.

Nora's breath stalls now, too; where, she wonders, is *this* coming from.

I've never once messed with her feelings, Bren says, after a tight pause. That whole thing was a misunderstanding.

I'm not talking about Freya's phone call, Robin says, and Nora can almost see Bren's face, his chin lifted in defence.

Or even how you travelled the world without her. I'm talking about all the stuff that came afterwards. All the times you'd arrange a video call but wouldn't show, because you forgot. Then calling her up out of nowhere, without asking if it was a good time to talk.

She could've said if it wasn't.

But she wouldn't, would she? Robin says. And I think on some level, you must know that, Bren. I'm not having a go, he says, and Nora imagines him holding his palms up, I'm just telling you how it is. How you light her up, when you deign to make an appearance, but also how . . . unworthy you make her feel, too.

That is not how I make her feel.

Except it is, Robin says. She told me so.

Nora's heart, no longer stalled, cuts out completely. *Shit*.

And look, Bren: I just want the wedding to go right for her. It'll make her day, you being home for it. That's all she wants. But I'm just asking, after all I've witnessed, if you could not let her down, this time. If you could do the right thing, for once.

Inside, the silence, stretching; outside, ongoing pelt of rain. Nora thinking fast and slow, but just as she's about to speak Bren says well that's up for discussion, isn't it? What the right thing is, here? Because there's a hell of a lot more to what Nora wants, I think. And historically, I don't tend to do the *right thing*.

Which is when the silence breaks. Clunk of a glass being

put down on a table as Nora snaps into action, swings the bedroom door back on its hinges, calls hi, she's out, and can someone pour her a glass of red wine, please? and her stalled heart revs back into gear.

–

In the kitchen, she strips the lid off some shop-bought tzatziki and rustles in the cupboard for some pitta bread. Robin asks if she had a nice bath, not looking at her as he pours her a glass of Merlot.

Is everything all right, she asks, nodding towards the living room, where Bren is now sitting alone, the door pulled closed.

Sure, is all that Robin says. He swirls the wine, but does not taste it, which is a game they play in front of waiters – tastes like wine, very wine-like, thank you, please proceed. Now though, he simply puts it down, too hard. Like he's drunk, or angry, even.

Robin, she says. Come on. I overheard you both, in there.

So why are you asking?

I appreciate what you were saying to him, she says. But you didn't need to. He's been through a lot. He doesn't –

You are not defending *him*, here, surely?

I wasn't aware I needed to *defend* anybody, she says, and Robin says look, Nora, I gave him the benefit of the doubt before I met him. I thought it was some show of latent loyalty, showing up at our party, but it's never exactly been a healthy friendship, has it? And did you hear what he just said to me, in there?

He was just – joking around!

Well it wasn't funny, Robin says, and Nora says, no, and she'll talk to him, too, but –

Talk to him? Hey, Bren, just a heads-up: when in England, best *not* to imply you'll try to steal the bride from the groom.

That is not what he was saying.

I think it was, actually. But just because his dad died twelve years ago, we have to tiptoe around him? Even though he just said to me, plain as day, that he doesn't do the right thing. I mean, what *was* that?

I think it was just the truth! Nora says, though she's aware she's clutching at straws, here, as confused by Bren's words as Robin is. I think he carries a lot of guilt, you know?

And so he should, after he walked out on Josie, like that.

She mouths at him, like a carp in a tank. She's never seen him so churlish.

Robin, she says. This is crazy. You're acting – she wants to say crazy, again, wants to deny all he's implying, she loves him, she's marrying *him* – but to say so feels ridiculous, makes it real; it surely doesn't need to be said.

Let's just have some pitta, she says, instead. But Robin is rubbing his elbow, looking pained, says he doesn't want to eat pitta right now.

You always want to eat pitta, Nora says.

Can't you just tell him to leave? Robin says, ignoring her attempt at humour. Defiance in his face. Their lives around them as they stare at each other, the kettle plugged in, cookbooks thumbed and splattered, their favourite pages folded down.

You want me to tell him to leave, Nora says. When I've spent the last four weeks hoping he'll stay, for our wedding?

At that moment, the weather flings something sharp – a small branch or stone – at the kitchen window. They both flinch, but the glass holds, and when they look back at each other, Robin seems to have softened. At the word wedding, maybe. Or the waver in Nora's voice. Like he's stepped back into his own shoes – or rather, the socks that Nora had knitted him one Christmas, warm and steadied on their tiled floor.

Long pause. His anger, ebbing.

No, he says, and he's quiet; still rubbing his arm. No, you're right.

Relief washes over her, then. Like the sun that is due the next morning, after the storm blows through overnight. And she's about to go over to him, but then Bren is in the doorway, saying can he help with anything, and there is a moment where both men look at each other; Robin, listless now, rather than angry; Bren looking awkward, swamped in the clothes that aren't his.

I'll just, Robin says, and he gestures at nothing. Says sorry, slides past Bren into the hall, and closes the bedroom door behind him.

Is everything . . . okay? Bren asks.

Why did you have to say that, Nora says, rounding on him, and Bren doesn't ask what she means. He must've overheard their row, or assumed that Robin would have shared what he'd said; known there's no point denying it.

In my defence, Bren says, he started in on *me*.

He did not start *in* on you, Nora says. Robin isn't like that.

She picks up her wine, doesn't drink it, as Bren says, right, okay. He seemed pretty riled up to me, but –

Please don't, Bren, she says. I can't do this.

And before he can reply, she steams on, reaches for something that would make sense; something she thinks he'll understand. Something she, too, can make sense of.

I don't have many people I can count on, in my life, okay? But what I do have is the both of *you*. When it suits you.

Bren tilts his head. His St Christopher watching her, like a third eye.

You're my two favourite people, Nora says, unable to keep

the emotion out of her voice. But ever since you got back, you're making me feel like I have to . . . choose.

Stillness, in the kitchen. The wind, outside, finally dying down.

You really think that, Bren says, in a low voice. And she says after the way they talked to each other, in there? Yes. But he says no, not that.

You think I'm only in your life . . . when it suits me?

Nora says nothing. Drinks her wine.

It's true then, he says. What Robin said? That I make you feel worthless?

Unworthy, Nora reasons, and she's already apologetic, hating the shutters that'll come down, how he'll retreat from her, now she's confirmed it. But I was angry with you when I said that, she says. It was before we knew about the phone call.

Tannins, from the wine, on her tongue.

But I did make you feel that way? Bren asks.

And Nora looks at him, standing there in Robin's too-large clothes. At the pendant she bought him, the patron saint of travel, but also protection. And she wants to say yes, but he also said you light me up, remember. But she stays quiet, because sharing such a thing won't do anything good, for anyone.

I never . . . intended to do that, Bren says.

And *I* didn't intend for Robin to share that with you, Nora says. I'm sorry, I don't know what's got into him. I'm a big girl, Bren. I don't need him . . . managing my relationship with you.

Relationship, Bren echoes, and she says yes. He nods, seems sad, but she doesn't know what he wants from her; there is no definition for what he is, what they have, and he must know that. Outside, the gutters, newly cleaned, drip rainwater onto the ground.

I think I should go, Bren says. The storm's eased up, a bit.

Yeah, Nora says.

They stand there for one more moment and then she follows him to the front door; refuses his offer to return Robin's clothes; he can keep them, okay, thanks, of course.

I'm sorry for . . . whatever happened here, he says, once he's stepped outside. Me too, she is going to say, but he turns to her before she can, saying for the record, Nora? You weren't someone I checked in with when it *suited me*, or just when I wanted to.

He is standing where he did four weeks before, when she first saw him at her party.

It's fine, she says. Really.

No, Nora, he says, just let me say this. Because I *wanted* to reach out every day. I thought about you all the time, if I let myself. So I got really good at *not* letting myself. Trying to detach from . . . everything, back home.

Nora is aware that this is important, what he's saying. Aware, also, that Robin is only metres away, behind their bedroom door.

And I always thought home was complicated, for me, Bren says. But maybe it's not. Maybe now I'm here, it's easier than I thought.

Everything *can* be easy, she says, nodding. I'll talk to Robin, and it'll be fine.

And Bren's nodding back, and there's a second where she thinks things *will* be fine, just like she's said, but then he stops. Shakes his head slightly, instead, and says sorry, Nora. But what is it you'll talk to him about?

Us, she says, after a protracted pause, rain glistening on the parked cars in the street. I'll make him see there's nothing to worry about, here. That we're like family.

Right. Except you were never just family to me, Nora.

Everything in high contrast, as he says it. Soaked ground, red hair. Feelings she cannot name.

I'm probably way out of line, saying this now, Bren says, but I got it wrong once, when I left, and I didn't put it right, or even talk to you, about any of it, so this is me . . . talking, this time.

Nora is staring at him.

And maybe we missed our chance, Bren says, and maybe I don't get what you've got here, with Robin, but I see you looking uneasy, Nora, every time the wedding comes up, and I'm just saying, if there's a part of you that feels like this whole thing is – not what you want? Then you can walk away, like I did. With me.

That's ludicrous, Nora wants to say. *You* are ludicrous. But her brain isn't working, her mind is not connecting the synapses that fire between thought and language, and she doesn't imagine him kissing her, this time, doesn't feel much of anything except a stunned blank dumbness as he says just give it some thought, okay? Before he heads down the path into the blurred, storm-wrecked day; a day where everything has changed.

–

Almost every hiker – and in fact, most thrill-seeking tourists – Bren has crossed paths with in recent years has seen *127 hours*. A film about Aron Ralston who went walking alone in a canyon in Utah, only to get trapped under a boulder for five days. Five days of waiting, with no communication, his mind *primed* for any glimmer of rescue. Five days of wishing he'd told someone where he was going. Five days of self-reflection, extreme regret and agonising possibility. Five days of hell, essentially, ending only because he cut off his own arm and willed himself towards freedom.

Bren thinks a lot about that movie in the five days after the storm. His own five days of no contact. Of regret, and possibility. Five days of priming himself for any message from Nora, which does not come, and he can't be sore about that after Robin's point because yes, *he* has been known to disappear for months at a time, but in all fairness there wasn't a question to answer, wasn't a wedding three weeks from now; wasn't a situation where, while not his actual arm, it does feel like he's cut off a part of himself and held it out, is waiting to see if she'll take it.

He's aware the comparison ends there; he's bleeding out hope, not blood, with three meals a day and a bed to sleep in and innumerable cups of coffee; checking his flight app to stay occupied between his walks and his mind-numbing conversations with his mother. But Bren can feel something clotting inside of him as he begins to check flights more frequently. An itch, almost, that is becoming hard to ignore. He does odd jobs for his mother to pass the time. Checks his bank account, baulks, does some handyman jobs for the next few days around the village until someone says he looks *so much like Jon* and he decides he's earned enough cash for now, enough to put towards his ticket back to the outdoor centre; emails traded; yep, the next season's contract is still his; does he want to do his NZOIA Rock 2 assessment, sure, yeah, sign him up.

Long days like this. Longer nights. And then, on the fifth evening, Bren watches another movie, in the company of his mother this time. No amputated limbs in this one as she sits with her herbal tea and he sits scrolling for routes back to Auckland, cheapest via Singapore or Shanghai, but in spite of himself he ends up lowering his phone and watching the film properly. The protagonist needs to *find herself*, but to do that she needs time alone, she's going to walk some distance with a giant rucksack; there's a comic scene where she can't pack it properly and Josie laughs her bellowing laugh and asks if it's ever like that for him, he grins back at her, says he packs much lighter than that; snaps his toothbrush in half, even, stuffs his socks in his shoes. It's kind of nice, they are laughing together, and then the woman in the film comes to realise what the viewer has known the whole way and something happens, inside Bren, as the credits roll.

Because what if Nora is just getting some distance, he wonders, before she gives him her answer? This feeling in his gut, this feeling that has steered him right his entire life, can't be wrong – and is telling him, too, that *she* knows what's right. That she just needs time, unlike him, who has no attachments or commitments – to sort things out.

He thinks about the perceived mistakes he's made, as monochrome photographs appear on the TV screen. How people judge him for his actions. Which he'd admitted as much to Robin, not as a threat but in self-deprecation, almost: he doesn't do the right thing, historically, not when it comes to life's milestones. Gap years. Weddings. Funerals. Which hadn't gone down so well, judging by the look on Robin's face, the way he put his drink down, hard. But it wasn't *Bren's* job to reassure him, especially when he doesn't really care what Robin thinks of him; when the only one he cares about here is Nora, and there's that itch, inside him, again. A certainty he's not felt, before. The credits end, the screen fades to black, and he amends his search on the flight app to two tickets – two seats – instead of one.

Well, Josie says. I really enjoyed that.

Yeah, Bren says, unmoved. She *really enjoys* everything she watches. He's never heard her express anything else, negative or impassioned or otherwise.

D'you want a hot cocoa, pet, before bed?

She asks him this every night, and every night he says no thanks, because he isn't eleven, not that he says this last part. He doesn't head to bed just yet, though; bookmarks the cheapest double flight, first. Singles, not returns. Then puts his phone down, only to see his mother looking straight at him from her armchair. Mug of tea on her side table. The painting that Nora had given her for her birthday, one year, propped beside her reading lamp.

What's up? he asks her.

I was going to ask you the same thing.

How come?

You seem particularly distracted, this week, Josie says. Watching that film is the first time you've sat still for more than two minutes.

I rarely sit still for more than two minutes, he reasons.

Well, Josie says, I suppose that's true. You're still staying for Easter, aren't you?

Classic, he thinks. Concern for him, eclipsed by the more pressing preoccupation with this vague get-together of hers. He says yes, though, and she says good. And for Nora's wedding, too?

Something must show on his face at this, because his mother actually points at him and says *there*, Bren. There's that distracted look I keep seeing – and this surprises him, not only because she's noticed, but because he's not able to hide it, after years of managing his emotions. He tries to rearrange his face. Tries to look unruffled, nonchalant. But then –

You're leaving, Josie says to him. Aren't you?

More surprise, at her, but also because ordinarily, that *would* be his plan.

I'm actually not, he says. Not anytime soon.

And whether it's this new certainty he's felt since the film, or whether it's just apparent in his tone, his mother seems to believe him. Appraises him from her chair, her slippered feet propped on a pink, wooden-legged pouf.

I'm making cocoa, she says.

I don't want –

I'm going to have some, she says, before she leaves the room. Bren checks his phone once more then stands and stretches, deciding to go up to bed while she potters in the kitchen. But something stops him. Catches his eye. He goes over to his mother's table and picks up the painting he'd noticed, earlier. Nora had been experimenting with oils at the time, smudging it with her young fingers. *Cy Twombly style*, she'd told Josie, as his mother unwrapped her gift, let out a coo of faux interest. His real name was actually Edwin, Nora said, and he had a love affair with Robert Rauschenberg and moved to *Italy* because he didn't like New York, *and* he refused to climb up ladders in case he fell. Which is why all his mark-making happened at the bottom of his huge paintings, like this.

Is that so, Josie had said, while twelve-year-old Nora caught her breath.

Although this is a really small painting, Nora had realised, embarrassed. Good things come in small packages, Josie had told her, squeezing her hand. Unless you're entering a marrow-growing competition, Nora replied, and his dad, who was folding up wrapping paper, had laughed, said now *that*, Nora, is your mother talking.

The memory dims, like the standby light on the TV. Bren puts the painting down and looks over at the other armchair by the bookcase. There's a stack of mountain guides on that side table; his dad loved Wainwrights and Corbetts and Munros, wanted to bag all of the latter, before he. Well. Bren lingers, but then goes over to those, too. Wants, partly, to leaf through one; finds it's enough just to look without feeling like he might cave in, and then he sees the black vase on the bookshelf and realises, for the first time, that it's an urn.

Sick jolt of shock, then, and he's up the stairs, trembling, like an animal that needs to shake out trauma, like a human that needs a cold shower, maybe, a midnight walk. But first he shoves open his window for the slap of night air and throws himself onto his bed; is scrolling through his emails when his mother knocks on the door, five minutes later.

One cup of cocoa, she declares.

I said I didn't –

I thought we could share a cup together, Bren. Before bed.

It isn't a request. Bren sees a flicker in her, then, the mother behind the medication and relapses and crying fits and drifting, distant niceties that make up the majority of their relationship. But beneath all that, there is her laugh, his jokes, her telling him how to bake this, that he can't drink that, nor swim there, or climb this. He sits up, slowly, takes the cup.

I miss you, Josie tells him, and Bren coughs as he sips his drink. It's tepid, too lumpy. Grit of powder on the back of his tongue.

I'm right here, he says, after he's cleared his throat.

But I feel like I don't know you, Josie says, and she says it gently, as though she doesn't want to spook him. Even though you're home now.

Bren, rash-hot after what he'd seen downstairs, feels a shiver through his conscience, that quiet, stifled part of himself he doesn't like to listen to.

To be fair, he says – because he does try to be fair, when his conscience pipes up – you don't really ask me much.

Or you don't really tell me anything, Josie says, with a twist of her small mouth; playful, it could be, or deflective; he isn't sure. It's like you're scared to be in a room with me, she says.

I'm not scared.

But you don't want to be in a room with me?

Another mouthful of cocoa, after she's spoken. Bren knows he needs to tread carefully, here. That they're in an emotional danger zone, even though he's been so intent on keeping things light since he got back. Eaten dinner with her, filled her bird feeders, shared TV time and morning coffee and –

I haven't heard voices in a long time, Bren, she says, and his blood jolts the way it had when he'd seen the urn. I haven't been confused, Josie goes on, or frightened, and I'm ticking along, pet, quite happily. Or as happily as I can, without my boys around.

Resignation in her features, then, and Bren feels his guilt morphing into curiosity, almost.

We've never talked about the past, have we, she says, blowing on her cocoa even though it's lukewarm; for something to do, he suspects, as he looks up at her from the bed. How it was for you, she says, growing up, with me . . . the way I am. And your dad dying, like that. When he was our only constant. Your only . . . normal parent. I do understand that, Bren.

But Bren cannot respond. Cannot get his head round how articulate she's being, how emotionally astute, and she seems to get that, too, comes to sit beside him on the bed.

I understand, she repeats. Why you had to leave, because you couldn't be here, without him. But also because you *knew* I'd be fine. I know you wouldn't have gone if you could've done . . . anything more, for me, my love.

He lets her take his hand, wondering if this is true. Whether she just prefers to forgive him, or genuinely believes it, blinkered by her medication, perhaps, or a mother's love.

The girls seemed to think it was such a tragedy, you leaving, like you did, Josie says, nodding to the wall shared with next door. But I like to think it was a sign of faith from you,

Bren. Faith in me. In knowing that I'd be okay, when so many people think I won't be. And, she says, squeezing his hand, in knowing there was more for you, out there, too. Which makes me so proud.

The room is too warm, too close. Even with the window wide open.

I see him in you, you know, Josie says. The way you forge ahead, no matter what life throws at you. And life threw a lot at us, your dad and me.

But Bren does not want to do this. Does not want to go there. For so long he'd wished she would talk to him, properly – about anything that wasn't the garden, or the weather – but they are past that now, it is too much and also too little too late, so he frees his hand and puts his mug down on the floor and manages to say one small word in reply. Thanks.

And does that help, she asks. Does that put him at ease? Or is there something else . . . that's bothering him? And for years he has wanted her to notice, to care, for years he had hoped she would look at him and really see his hurting heart or scraped knees or gather him to her and comfort him, instead of ironing the bed sheets or watching koalas on the television or staring at the wall while his dad advised him to go outside, and she's sitting here in his bedroom doing just that, looking and seeing, and he does not want this from her, and yet he blurts out that it's harder than he thought. Being home.

Josie does not recoil when he says this. Simply nods and drinks more cocoa, says this is bad, isn't it, I can't've stirred it properly.

Light breeze through the window. Another light sip. And he thinks that's it; thinks she's already lost interest, but then she says, hard, being home? Because of? and gestures towards the driveway, to downstairs, with all its ghosts, and he could give in and say more but there's that wall he's spent thirty years building so instead he says because he found out, recently, that Freya didn't pass his message on to Nora, when he left. And it's been kind of rough. Being here for her wedding, when things could have been . . . different.

Oh, Josie says.

Yeah.

Freya did mention that. I'm sure it was an accident, Bren. Slipped her mind, maybe.

Well, whatever, he says. It happened.

The night air is mild; a fox calls from afar. They sit there, mother and son, Josie drinking, Bren not drinking, wishing she would leave, or stay; an ache, in his chest, at the strain of not knowing how he feels or what he wants and how it can so often be both.

You know they're not speaking? he says, and Josie says yes, it's *aw*ful. It's breaking Freya's heart, not that she'd admit it. She's working long shifts at the hospice, pretending she's not bothered by it. But they're not like us, Bren. They talk every day, usually, and I'm worried about them. Especially with the wedding so close.

Sting inside of him, at this last part.

Even after everything he's just said.

I'm hoping, if I get them together at Eas –

You don't need to be worried about *them*, he says, because it's been two minutes, two minutes of his mother seeming to see him and hear him and already she's flittered on, concerned with other people, not absorbing a word of what he's shared when *she* said she felt like she didn't know him, and he *tried*, goddamn it, he was trying. You should be worried, he says, about the wedding *itself*.

And he thinks this assertiveness will finally be too much for her, thinks she'll take their cups, say goodnight, but instead she asks what he means.

I mean I think Nora's just wandered into this life, Bren says. One she wouldn't have chosen, if she'd had the right information. And I want to be her friend, I do, but I also want to be . . . what she needs.

Josie raises one translucent, barely-there eyebrow.

And what's that? she asks him.

An alternative, Bren says. Someone to show her there are options, here.

Are you saying you're an option, for her?

I'm saying I think she wants more than this, Bren says. More than a life in a one-bed flat with a mortgage to pay and Friday-night films.

Josie sniffs. And he thinks this is the moment where he might have truly upset her – unable to stop himself sounding superior – but there's more to it than superiority, it's the doubt he sees. Nora's hesitation, whenever the wedding comes up; the free spirit who's tied herself down, the artist who sells the art of other *people*, the world open and waiting for her, still, if only she would jump.

But then Josie says: I do wonder, Bren, if it might be the other way around.

Silence, in the room. He frowns.

What if it's not about Nora not going, his mother says. But the fact that you didn't stay?

Her voice is not angry, or sad, or affectionate. It is neutral, as if she's merely asking whether he wants another cup of cocoa.

It's not that, he says, and Josie sighs. Stands up, holds her hand out for his mug. And she's at the door when he feels the need to prove his point, says something's just not right with Nora. I can feel it. The wedding's less than a month away, and they've not even sent out invites. Or visited the venue.

But they're going, tomorrow.

What?

Nora texted me to say they're heading to the venue this weekend. For a planning day, or something, and his mother is still talking but Bren is not listening and he shakes his head because it's all wrong, he knows it's all wrong.

Sweetheart, his mother says, but he says no, it's fine, she'll see. Because he's seen something in Nora, ever since he's been home. Felt how she'd held herself when he'd kissed her head at the bus stop, heard her laughter at their in-jokes and her fury at his bad habits and how she couldn't say no, couldn't tell him he was crazy, five days before, when he said she could come away with him. Because he is not crazy. He is not. He does not stay indoors and nurse old scars, he gets out there, he forges forward, he tastes real life and reaches for more and does not think before he jumps and he knows, in this stifled, hopeful heart he's carried, for all these years, that it's time for Nora to do the same.

thirteen

First weekend of April, and the storm's long gone. Buds of blossom, push of crocuses through the soil. They book train tickets and get up early and go, pull into a station backed by a red-brick building, mounds of green beyond the tracks. On the platform Nora takes a photograph on her phone and sends it to Josie, ignoring the unopened messages from Freya. Ignoring the fact that there are none from Bren. That there hasn't been, since the weekend before, with the rain and her bath and –

So this is Devon, she says, as she and Robin roll their suitcases to the taxi rank. Seagulls circling. Smell of salt and tarmac and chips.

Nice, huh, Robin says, as he waves at a cab driver leaning against his car door, and she repeats the word back at him. Nice. Because it is. Because she has nothing more to say. She feels both excited and confused about being here when they'd promised each other a small, affordable wedding and yet it's cost them over two hundred pounds just to travel here, to wander round the venue they've already paid a deposit for to be cajoled into spending more on the 'extras'. Robin was sharing these *extras* with her on the train down; additional charges for the fairy lights in the trees and the linen napkins which cost more than the cotton napkins and the florist that can wrap ivy garlands around the wooden beams which really elevates the space when they'd said they wouldn't have flowers at all. Ivy isn't a flower, though, is it, Robin reasoned. It's just greenery. And then he'd promptly leant his head against the train window and napped for the rest of the journey.

Through winding back roads, the taxi takes them to their cabin in someone's garden, miles from anything except a country pub, several large houses and their wedding venue, a two-mile walk away. They pay the driver, struggle with the lock box and stumble in, before heading straight to the pub for lunch. Their venue visit is later in the afternoon; best to see it at golden hour, they'd been told. As if the shade of light would romanticise them into spending more money, wanting things they were sure they would not.

Prickling thoughts like this, in Nora's mind, as she asks Robin for a rum and Coke. He goes to the bar, she looks at the paper menu. Then her phone. Please, Nora, Josie has replied to her photograph. Will you just call your mother?

She turns the phone over and Robin comes back. He is drinking a Guinness, when he never drinks Guinness, which she says to him. Feel a bit ropey after the train, he says. Need the iron. Winks, as he lifts it to his lips, and she doesn't tell him that was Jon's drink, doesn't tell him the thick black of it makes her feel sick, that it seems like a sign, him drinking that, right now. Instead she sits back and looks out the window at the square of pub garden and Robin has to ask her what's wrong.

Nothing, she says.

Everything.

Bren, her best man. Best friend. Who had said she could walk away with him, and what does that actually mean, she wonders, for the hundredth time, as she raises her glass to her lips, ice clinking softly against the lime. Does it mean he wants to *be* with her, or that he just wants to recapture their youth, see the world together? And isn't that maddening, in itself? Refuels some kind of rage in her that she's misdirected at him, for so long, after what Freya did. More fury, then, at her mother, as she puts her glass down. Fury that feels like shame because Jon and Josie were married, in love, like her and Robin are right here in this pub with his thumb stroking hers, saying what a menu, but Freya messed *that* up too, those vows, and what if that is in Nora, as well? This propensity to ruin things?

Something's not right, Robin says, once they've ordered the burrata, and she looks up at him, flushed, but he's still reading the starters. Figs aren't in season, he says; maybe they should've just ordered the focaccia. What, he asks, seeing her face.

Nothing, she says, again.

You've been saying nothing a lot, lately.

Same as you, she says, because he has also been unusually quiet since Bren's unprompted visit, the weekend prior. They are not themselves, she thinks, but then she says it out loud. Robin drinks some of his stout, wipes the foam from his lip.

No, he agrees, rubbing his elbow. Maybe you'd feel more *your*self, he says, if you cleared the air with Freya.

Nora bristles.

I've seen all the messages you're ignoring, he says. And I see you messaging Josie, instead, because you know she'll pass things along. It's okay to miss her, Nora.

I don't *miss* her, Nora says. I'm too angry.

But the wedding is so soon, he says. Don't you want –

I want to stop talking about this, please, she says, and she is surprised at herself; sees Robin's own surprise reflected back at her. He stops stroking her hand. They drink their drinks. A dog barks loudly from the bar. *Wonton*, the owner barks back.

Their eyes meet again across the table; small smiles, not showing their teeth.

Wonton?

Add it, Nora says, because they keep track of pets they've met who are named after foods. Cookie, and Crumble, sure. Rolo. But also a cat called Crème Fraiche. Dogs named Brie, and Bagel, and Toast, and – Nora's personal favourite – Aubie, short for Aubergine.

Not sure we'd go for Wonton, Robin says, reaching for Nora's phone to tap it into her notes app. But after he's added it to the list, he keeps looking at the phone, then says sorry, Nora. I can't let this go.

He turns the phone back to her, shows her the thirty-six notifications next to Freya's name. She's your mum, he says.

Appeasing note in his voice, which makes Nora push back her chair because she's tired, she wishes *she* could let this go but she can't, and how does he not get how painful this is when he knows about the affair, knows about the phone call, knows –

You're being a child, avoiding her like this, Robin tells her, in a voice that sounds like he's tired, too. Done with whatever is happening, here. It won't just go away, he calls after her as she makes her way to the bathroom; as the door to the ladies' swings shut, behind her.

–

They call another cab even though the venue is only a short walk away, Robin saying he's shattered, and anyway, he wore the wrong shoes. So they pay the obscene fare for a ten-minute journey and the driver drops them at the edge of the woods next to a gold-stencilled sign and Devonshire all around them, clouds above, trees ahead, the ocean somewhere they can't see.

This way, then? Nora says, and Robin nods down the treeline. Everything smells of pine and sea salt, like one of the soy candles she sells at the café. And then the long path opens out into a clearing and there's the building she'd seen in pictures, made of wood and recycled glass, sleek but also self-important, somehow. Like it belongs in the grounds of a sculpture park.

What d'you think, Robin asks.

It's, Nora says, and doesn't finish, but then the manager meets them at the entrance – something they would not have been able to locate themselves as the handle is non-existent, the door blending with the grain of the wood. Jed claps Robin on the back, clasps Nora's hands in his own and bows, slightly. He is wearing white linens and Birkenstocks. Enunciates slowly.

My friends, he says. Come, look around. Familiarise yourself with the space.

And what a space it is, Robin says, and he sounds sincere, even though Nora thought he might look at her in jest, a raised eyebrow, please, earthlings, charge your chakras before crossing the threshold. He does take Nora's hand, though. Leads her inside, where the early evening drenches the circular, empty room. Wooden beams, exposed brick; a floor-to-ceiling glass wall that overlooks more of the forest. A young woman dressed all in black appears, offers them iced water, prosecco? then flutes appear on a silver tray. Nora takes one, wanting to feel relaxed, giddy, something other than the leaching of oxygen from her brain as she trails behind Jed in his white linens and Robin with his prosecco glass, because this is where they are getting married and this is not how it should feel, being here, feeling none of the things she is supposed to.

We usually have the ceremony in here, Jed is saying, opening his arms as if welcoming an aura into the room. We line the chairs all along the back there, so you can say your vows in front of the trees.

Incredible, says Robin.

It is, Jed says, it really is. If it's a nice day we can open out the doors, of course – they slide back, let me show you. Or you could even have the ceremony on the veranda itself, though we don't have acoustics out there. You remember we're not formally licensed?

Yes, Robin says, we've booked a registry office, haven't we, and he looks at Nora and she nods, because she did do that, as promised. Sips the prosecco she does not like, lets it effervesce on her tongue. More staff pass around them like sprites, one of them raking leaves, another carrying a yoga mat across the veranda and out of sight.

And, Jed says, as he slides back the glass doors in one smooth motion, the harpist can go here, in this corner. Great for photos, see where the light casts through the silver birch, and while Robin nods, Nora says sorry, what harpist?

If you decide to use her, Jed says. She's part of the Gold Package we spoke about, on the phone.

Gold Package? Nora says, and Robin says he showed her on the train, and she says she doesn't want a harpist. No offence, she says to Jed, then to Robin, we don't like harpists, do we?

All harpists? he says, but she does not laugh. Feels hot. Asks if there's a bathroom she can use, and Jed points her to another near-invisible door at the back.

Once alone, she leaves her prosecco glass on the quartz sink, locks herself in the pine-wood cubicle and tries to breathe herself back. This really is a greenhouse moment, and out of habit, she pulls out her phone to call Freya; hits another number instead, at the last second.

Again, with work on a Saturday! Shay blasts. I'm totally capable of running this café without you, for a day, pal.

Nora looks at herself in the huge mirror. Aēsop hand soap, rolled towels in a basket. Floor tiles that cost more, she reckons, than what she'd hoped to spend on this wedding.

Nora? Shay says.

Yes.

Why are you calling? If it's to check on the invoicing, I already –

It's not that, she says. I just. I'm at the venue, and it's.

Shay says hang on, and Nora hears a shuffling, the din of the café quieting as she presumably steps behind the curtain into the back room.

It's? Shay prompts.

Beautiful, Nora says.

Sweet!

But not in the right way, Nora says, a little panicked now. It's kind of – too beautiful?

How is that even possible?

I don't know! Nora says. But Robin's so excited, Shay, and I've gone along with this, and it's so soon, and it all just feels so . . . soon, she says, again.

She keeps looking in the mirror, as she talks.

Needing her friend to hear her.

Needing her to say, Nora, if this isn't right, then you need to listen to that. But instead Shay says that nine years with Robin is the opposite of soon, isn't it? It's about time, in fact. And if the venue's a bit fancy, so what? It's what weddings are. You can't fight it. No matter what your mum might say, or how much shit I've been giving you for it. Playful, loving shit, mind you.

Yeah, Nora says, and the word is uncertain in her mouth, like a question. Like Shay still has to convince her this is right. Like she's convinced her of so many things in the past; to open their café, for one thing, to increase the price of her embroidery prints, to try the softshell crab at their favourite sushi spot even though she loves the sea and all its creatures and felt like it was wrong to eat such a – holy *hell* this is good, how have I not ordered this before.

Because Shay knows her.

Really knows her.

But what she doesn't know is what Bren said to her, last week. *Walk away.* That he'd wanted her with him, then, that she could join him abroad, now, and in this kaleidoscope of confusion Nora also keeps seeing the unwanted image of Jon kissing Freya's neck in an unlocked bathroom, not unlike the one she's standing in, right now. It keeps coming to her, unwanted, like when you're told not to think of a pink elephant and all you can think of is pink elephants, don't think about marriage when you're about to get married because he *was* married, to Josie, and look what married people do to each other, look what *almost-married* people are already doing because there's another elephant here, too, Bren with his red hair and green eyes, why are there no windows in this stupidly chic bathroom, *if there's a part of you that feels like this is not what you want, then you can walk away.*

It's going to be great, Shay says, as Nora keeps staring in the mirror.

I'm still not speaking to Freya, she says.

So that's what this is about?

No, Nora thinks. Maybe, she says.

Then just show up at her door tomorrow! Shay says. Freya'll just make you embroider your row on a piece of rawhide and burn it in some ceremony of forgiveness, or whatever, and all will be right with the world.

Exhalation, through Nora's nose, because she can't quite bring herself to laugh.

Sorry, Shay says, on a piece of *paper*. Forgot she's vegan.

Apparently, Nora says.

That doesn't mean it's going to be vegan food, does it, at the wedding? I'm expecting some kind of hog roast, please.

Or a pizza van. Wait, it's you guys. Of course it's a pizza van. As long as it's not too fancy for that?

I'm sure it's in Robin's notebook, Nora says, and Shay says well then! Get back out there, lock in all the details and be done with it. Married, fancily or non-fancily, and full of pizza by the end of the night.

Yeah.

It's going to be great, Nora. Squeeze Robin for me, won't you.

I will.

Just a hug, obviously. Not his arse or anything. Although he does have a very nice one, to be fair.

Bye, Shay.

Send pictures! Shay says, before she ends the call, then follows up with a text: *of the venue, obvs, not his arse*.

Nora breathes out. Turns on the tap, splashes her face. Dries her hands with one of the gorgeously soft towels – it'd get Josie's approval, for sure – and collects herself for one more moment before she re-enters the main room.

All okay? Robin says, once she's crossed the floor. He and Jed are standing on the veranda just beyond the open glass doors. Nora herself stays inside, but nods in reply. Tries hard, for the rest of the visit. Listens about the videographer and photographer package that Jed *highly* recommends, the brass band, actually, we thought we'd just make a playlist – but with such weak Wi-Fi, here, that's a risk – and we *could* have a band, Nora, if you wanted, we've saved enough money with the cancellation, and as numbers might be small, last minute, it might fill the space a bit better.

Speaking of which, have they got their final guest list yet?

Soon, they'll confirm soon.

And will they be needing hotel recommendations? Best that they block-book rooms, to save disappointment, especially as you're not local and everyone will be travelling, any elderly relatives, to think about? Wheelchair users? And onto the fun parts, now, taking seats at a table with a thick book of laminated pages listing added costs and suggestions, though none of it is compulsory, there's this stone staircase out the back, here, do you see, we have a lot of brides entering the ceremony from that angle because it's quite an entrance, and then you, Robin, you could stand here if you wanted a first look, very popular with couples nowadays, for the photos, have a moment together before you stand up in front of everyone.

Everyone, Nora thinks.

The word echoing, in her head.

And I think it lends a kind of gravitas, as well, Jed says, especially if you adjust your ceremony to later in the day. Golden hour, maybe. Or dusk? We even had a midnight wedding, once. By candlelight. Everyone stood around the fire pit, the best man was Irish, he sang this hauntingly beautif –

And *her* best man comes to Nora's mind, being in front of *everyone* comes to mind, parades through her head like the pink elephants she is not thinking about and she says, out loud, without meaning to: no.

Robin and Jed both look at her. Jed's smile is salesman vague. Robin himself looks distracted, almost dazed – floating on a cloud, Nora thinks, when she has both feet hard on the ground.

You don't *have* to have a midnight ceremony, Jed says, waving his hand. Nor do you have to use the staircase, if you'd rather just enter through the door, there? Robin mentioned you're having your own best man, Nora, he could even walk you down the –

No, Nora says again, as Robin keeps looking at her. I'm never going to walk down an aisle, she'd told Bren once as they sat in the oak tree, legs swinging, and he'd said me neither and she thought she'd changed her mind but now Bren has said walk away with me and –

I don't think this feels right, Nora says. There is a silence then, broken only by the soft sound of bubbles in Robin's glass.

That's . . . fine, Jed says, as Robin turns to face Nora fully from his chair. That's what this planning day is for! To find your version of what *does* feel right.

Could you give us a moment, Jed, Robin asks, without looking at him, though his voice is calm. Jed's smile falters, just slightly. He stands and bows again, says he'll scout out more bubbly, even though Nora's glass is still standing atop the bathroom sink, golden and expensive and undrunk.

Robin doesn't speak, once they're left alone. He's holding himself strangely, like he's in pain. Cradling his elbow.

Can we please go, Nora whispers. Afraid the staff will hear her. Afraid, too, that her voice might crack, if she says it any louder.

She doesn't need to say anything more. Robin does not get angry, or make her feel bad, or ungrateful or dramatic. He dips his chin, says nothing for a few stretched seconds, then he says okay. That he'll talk to Jed, and join her out front.

And she takes his hand and squeezes it, just like Shay had asked her to, but he doesn't squeeze hers back. Instead he pulls away and walks through the circular room, Nora skirting the building so she doesn't need to face Jed, or the staff, or Robin's deep disappointment. She can hear all of it, though, from where she stands by the invisible front door. Snatches drifting through the gaps in the wood. The deposit, non-refundable, but he's here until seven, they need to pay in full to secure the date they'd reserved, policy, and yes, he understands, thank you, we truly hope, yes, him too.

–

They walk back through the birch trees in silence. Nora could brush his shoulder with her own if she angled just half an inch to the left, could lean into him, thread her hand through his. She doesn't dare.

The road is deserted. Their taxi, gone. There are no other cars, no cyclists, nobody else to distract them from what has just happened. And what has happened, Nora wonders, as they stand side by side, with no clear path or next steps.

Shall we talk here, Robin asks, or do you want to go back to the . . .

He gestures in the direction of their cabin with its seascape paintings and quilted double bed, their suitcases left unpacked.

Here's good, she says, so they cross to the grassy bank and a large wooden gate – it's stiff, Robin struggles, she says can I help – but he finally tugs it free. They startle a rabbit into the hedge, but are otherwise alone, and they walk for a while and then sit when they find a fallen tree stump. Close, but not touching. Unsure. Robin lets out one long breath as Nora holds in her own.

Are you . . . sure you want to do this, he asks.

Two heartbeats. A chirr, from a bird.

Actually, he says, before she can answer, that's not fair of me.

Course it is, Nora says, her voice strained. I *want* to tell you what I want. But it's like I don't know. I don't have the words, to . . .

Explain, she thinks, how her life has been shaken like a Magic 8 Ball. Different answers held in her hands.

But it's not fair suggesting this is all on you, Robin says. You're distracted, Nora, I see that, but I've been pretending I can pin it on other things. Freya, being so off, about the engagement. Bren showing up, and that phone call you found out about, and all your hang-ups because of that affair you saw –

Nora puts her head in her hands, because he knows about that; knows her, too, better than anyone.

– and I've been pretending it's one or all of those things, Nora, when really, there's something on me here, too. Something I've not told you.

New feeling, then, inside of her.

A slow-motion spread, like time itself is decelerating. Robin rubs his face, then cups one side of his head as he stares out at the unploughed fields.

I knew you never wanted to get married, he says. You'd always made that clear. Although I'd have married you after our first date, if you'd've let me.

A smile then, which soon fades.

And here we are almost ten years later, he goes on, after we've formally given notice, and seen our wedding venue that seemed perfect, to me, and I just have this sense, Nora, that you feel . . . backed into a corner. Which is understandable. Because why would you be all in, all of a sudden, after years of being . . . well . . . not.

Nora's thoughts – snared, in her head – start to uncoil, as he says this last part. With gratitude. Because he is not mad at her. He is not even questioning her, not storming or crying or even demanding answers, and his mildness, his reasoning, his calm, even Robin-ness, is something she has always been drawn to, but she will not take advantage of that, she wants to keep talking, but to do so, she has to meet him on his level.

I guess it did throw me, Nora says. You buying a ring and all.

There is a pause, then. A stopgap, where she thinks he might laugh, pull her into him with one of his long arms. But instead he goes very still, looking out at the empty fields as he says that's the thing, Nora. I didn't.

A car drives along the road behind them, leaves a whoosh of silence in its wake.

Didn't what?

I didn't buy a ring.

And Nora thinks he's teasing. Thinks he's joking, *April fool's*, but then he makes a pained kind of noise before turning to look at her, his mouth set. And he says he wants her to know, before he goes into it, that the reason he hadn't told her before now is just that it felt so right, when it happened. And he didn't want to take it back.

Take what back, Nora asks, and Robin breathes out.

I didn't mean to propose, he says.

She hears him say it. Doesn't understand.

It was a ring I'd picked up for a photo shoot, Robin says. You just found it in my pocket, at lunch.

But, Nora says, you asked me to marry you.

I actually didn't.

I'm sure you did.

Trust me on this, Nora. I didn't say anything. You found the ring, and said yes.

Sinking realisation, then. *Oh god*.

But the thing is, Robin says, shifting sideways to look at her straight, his eyes pleading, I had to make a choice, Nora. In those three seconds, I had to decide something.

Nora tries to stay with him; tries to focus.

And I decided there was no reason *not* to run with it. We weren't going to do the wedding thing because you said you didn't want to. Which was really your mother saying *she* didn't want you to, I think. And we figured we didn't need it, which we don't, Nora, we don't *need* to get married. It's expensive, and we love each other anyway, but I saw the . . . excitement, in you. Just for a second, when you thought I'd asked.

Nora makes a small noise, deep in her throat.

Because the truth is, Robin ploughs on, I've always wanted to marry you. And I could live with you not wanting to marry me, if that's how you felt, but then you said yes. And it was happening.

Several crows take off from the far edge of the field, black wings against the sunset.

I'm so . . . embarrassed, Nora says eventually, after the crows are long gone.

Please don't be, Robin says. I should have told you.

I can't believe you went along with it, like that.

I'm *ecstatic* I went along with it, Robin says, and his voice shifts to its usual, Robin-like cheer, and it is like the sun, if the sun had a sound, and it thaws the dread she hadn't realised she'd been carrying, for weeks. Truly, Nora, he says. It was the best thing I never did. Thank you, misunderstanding. Thank you, universe. Thank you, three unprecedented yeses!

He yells this last part to the sky, trying to make her laugh, and it's sort of working but she also feels like crying; thinks she is, in fact, as he cups his head again, like his own shouting has hurt his ears.

But if you're not ecstatic, Nora? Robin says, lowering his voice once more. Then we can talk about that. Like we talk about everything.

He takes both her hands in his, and Nora can tell from his tone that he thinks he's done it. Thinks he's softened what was hard, cleared the clouds of what has felt heavy, between them.

Except we don't, Nora says. Talk about everything.

Robin blinks.

You wanted to marry me, from day one?

Well, technically day two, Robin says, because I asked you out for a drink first, but you said you'd prefer a croissant, so it was the next morning, when we got pastries and hot chocolate. You ordered the eighty-five percent. Which surprised me. And you started talking about the magical properties of cacao beans and then, smooth as anything, moved on to the theoretical difference between writing and drawing, and I knew, right then, that I wanted to marry you.

But, Nora says, not sure what is bothering her so deeply, here – why did you never say so?

A pause then. Like Robin doesn't understand the question, or thinks he's already answered it.

Because you didn't want to, he says.

But this has to be two-way, she says, taking her hand out of his so she can gesture between them. This has to be about what we both want. We've been together for *nine years*, Robin. Nine years, and you never once told me you wanted to get married.

Does that matter?

It does, yes! It really matters!

Because how can they start something she has no idea how to be in, wrapped in white lace and harpist music and served with a hog roast for a family she barely has, when the ones she *does* have – Robin, looking at her, now, Bren, on her doorstep, then – aren't even their full, honest selves with her? Nor she, with them?

I want to be with you, Nora, Robin asserts. Wedding or no wedding.

But to the detriment of what you actually *want*? Nora says. I can't be that person, Robin! I can't let you go along with a life that isn't what you'd choose.

She thinks of Josie, boxed up at home.

Jon, straying, because life with her was not what he'd hoped.

But what I *choose* is to be with you, Robin repeats, and he seems angry now, just like he was the other night as she says but how can I trust that, now?

Because it's us! We're Robin and Nora, aren't we? Or is this not even *about* a wedding, he says, and she hears something else in his voice, a shift from anger to fear as he says it's starting to feel like you're looking for a reason to get out of this. And like an idiot, I've just given you one.

You're not an idiot, Nora says, reaching for him.

What am I, then? Your fiancé, or just some guy you were killing time with, until the guy you actually wanted came home?

She gasps at this, because she had feared this might get thrown out there but still it gives her whiplash; had he *heard* what Bren had asked her, last weekend, has he been sitting on that, all this time? Or just piecing together what he can't have missed? Sudden inkling, then, that there is more he's not telling her, but she doesn't ask, it is instinct to defend, to say instead that that's not what this is – she loves *him*, she does, but he was the one person she thought was straight with her, the one person she could always trust, and suddenly she's not sure who he is or what he wants and he, too, is looking at her like he feels the same way.

They stare at each other, on the felled tree. Their breathing, out of time.

You said yes, he murmurs.

But you didn't ask, she says, did you.

Which is the truth that grows between them, as they sit there with the day ending, all around them. Nightfall, now. Their hands growing cold.

fourteen

Bren is in a chain café in town, on a hot date with his laptop. Shooting out emails to different adventure centres, enquiring for the winter season, keeping his leads warm, his options open. He never usually queries this far in advance, just shows up and banks on availability, but he needs to do something. Busy his bouncing brain, his bouncing knee. Fighting what could be some kind of encroaching psychosis, surely, when he can't sit still, can't hear his own thoughts through the noise. He scrolls on the flight app again, between emails; prices have gone up, because he keeps checking, probably. Damn algorithms.

Define stir crazy, he googles, when he closes the app and sees that Nora has still not texted him back.

Define the brain disorder that he thinks about, but never names out loud. Ninety-nine percent hereditary, apparently.

He gets up for his second coffee and isn't thinking about all that when a girl he used to know – a vague connection from secondary school – joins the queue behind him. Although vague is probably inaccurate, seeing as he'd lost his virginity to her after a school hockey match one night. He remembers the pastel curtains in her bedroom. The soft cotton of her bra. How she'd tasted of spearmint Polos and how, the next day, she'd told her friends he was bad in bed. Cruel, and humiliating, though he no longer cares. Does care, though, about how red Nora had turned, when she'd found out. How she'd gone and lost her own virginity, not long afterwards.

Bren? the girl – now woman – says, from behind him. Brennie Fergs?

Hi, Lisa, Bren says, arranging his face as though he's pleased to see her.

I *thought* it was you! God, it's been *so* long! I thought you were off nomad-ing, or whatever?

She is wearing a lot of make-up; looks pristine, if you like that kind of thing. Bren has the fleeting thought that she will be thanking herself for putting so much effort in, that morning, in front of the mirror. Her lips are peach-pink and glossy, Julia-Roberts-wide.

I am, Bren says, then, without thinking: I'm just back for Nora's wedding.

The wedding, he's sure, that won't be going ahead.

Nora? Lisa frowns. The girl with the – wiggling her fingers in front of her eyes, and Bren remembers, beyond the bad in bed rumour, why it was they did not stay friends.

You mean her heterochromia?

Oh! Lisa says, her manicured nails fluttering to her mouth. Is that what it was? I'm so sorry. That's terrible.

They move forward in the queue, one person closer to the till.

Why is it terrible, Bren asks.

She's not, like, dying, or anything?

What? No! It's just like, a birthmark, or something. Or having red hair. Jesus.

Red hair *is* quite the curse, though, Lisa says, regressing to some old banter that was never that funny in the first place. She touches his arm as she says it, and Bren steps away from her, pretending he's merely keeping pace with the queue.

You hear these things though, don't you, Lisa goes on, when he doesn't respond, now that we're this age? D'you remember Kady Hall? She's got some auto-immune thing now, bless her. And my cousin Simon, he got cancer, *and* divorced, all within the space of like, a year.

Bren does not know this person, but pretends to care. Brutal, he says.

So brutal, Lisa agrees, as another person orders their coffee, and Bren squints at the menu, as if trying to decide what he wants. So you're just back for the wedding? And you're not the one marrying her?

What?

A laugh, then, from Lisa. She sweeps her fringe to the side.

We all had bets, Lisa says, that you'd get hitched on a beach somewhere, on that world trip of yours. It's all coming back to me now.

Right, Bren says.

But you're single?

Why would you assume that, he asks, but rather than deadpan, he realises it might sound as though he's flirting back. He orders his coffee, taps his card.

I'm going out on a limb here, Brennie, Lisa says, and nobody else has ever called him that but her, this girl who called him *bad in bed* fifteen years ago, who doesn't know him at all but is touching his arm again as his cappuccino gets made behind the counter, milk frothing, steam hissing, someone else's name being called, Elaina? for an oat latte which is sitting, uncollected, on the side.

Or do you have someone already, Lisa asks, as Bren pockets his bank card. Doesn't look at her when he says yes.

Ah, well. Can't blame a girl for trying, she says, unfazed. In our thirties, now, aren't we? Need to settle down, if I can.

Then I'm definitely not your guy, Bren tells her, and she

laughs again, orders her own chai latte. Does he fancy a catch up, anyway?

I can't, Bren says. I've got to get back to – he gestures beyond the window – my mum. For lunch.

Sure, she says, clearly choosing not to comment on how he'd just ordered his cappuccino to drink in, rather than take away. How's she doing?

Odd question, Bren thinks, when she doesn't know his mother. Does she. Prickle of discomfort, then. Old fear, about what people know, what they've heard. Visions of her traipsing in her slippers around Sainsbury's; talking to nobody on the street; crying in the police station, mouth twitching. She's fine, he says.

Because I never got the chance to say I was sorry, Lisa says, and Bren assumes she's referring to the bad in bed thing, but then she says when your dad died, and all.

Bren stiffens. Looks back at the drinks menu on the wall.

Filter.

Espresso.

Macchiato.

We all felt so bad for you, when we heard, Lisa says. And then you didn't come back for upper sixth, so none of us could say anything, or even . . . check you were all right.

Someone calls his name. Someone says Bren, or at least, is calling out Ben, and that's close enough, he'll take it, he reaches out for the white cup on its saucer, shudder of bone china in his hand.

So are you? Lisa asks him. All right?

And he says course, it was a long time ago, still not looking at her as he says it was nice to see her, and she says you too. There is a pause between both her words like she is taken aback by his response which is entirely normal, he thinks, he's sure, and he puts his coffee down on the table he was sitting at and leaves, without drinking it. Laptop shoved in his bag. Cold sunlight outside. Long strides taking him out of town and into the countryside, too much caffeine in his veins, already.

–

Hitched on a *beach*, he scoffs, once he's miles away. Along the riverbank, with its reeds and its swans, the underpass with the old graffiti that used to be green but has faded to white. Ali Cat Is A Ledge. JM LUVS BP. He has a flash of bubble writing back at school, the smell pens Nora loved to use at her kitchen table, the apple flavour, the blueberry, in what *world*, Freya asked, does this smell like blueberries? Their world, Frey, his father had said, as he watered her plants through the open back door.

Bren walks so fast he could be running. Pulls out his phone to check the flights yet again, and they're still there, the two tickets to New Zealand that he could buy right now, if he dared. He lets his mind wander as he opts for the long way home. Picturing where they might stay, in Queenstown; Kelvin Heights, maybe. Or closer to Arrowtown. Good brunch there. Plenty of trees, Nora would love the colours in autumn. The way people sieve for gold in the river. Or maybe they could go somewhere else entirely? Visit the markets in Delhi or Marrakesh for all the bright fabrics, the fresh oranges, the loose-leaf teas. Detox, from everything. Maybe she'd want to open her own stall, or shop, or art café, sell her own wares. Paint or draw again. He could take groups out biking or hiking or rock climbing, help her close up at night. And they wouldn't head home afterwards but to the beach, or the local bar. To the secret spot on the shore they'd make their own. Skimming stones. Leaning in, her mouth on his, and they'd taste of each other, he is lost and daydreaming and so far gone he walks past the signpost for home and makes it to the next village before he realises, has to double back like a moron.

Bren? his mother calls, when he finally makes it home.

Hi, he says. He has brought her things from the village shop, to make up for the detour. A bunch of tulips, a bag of hot cross buns, little gifts that show he is a good person, a thoughtful person, not someone who wants to wreck a home or a promise that's been made that, to be fair, he was not part of. A person who loves his mother, who loves his best friend, and doesn't love make you do hard, questionable things, sometimes the hard things are the right things, the things you're told not to do.

His mother fusses over the gifts he's bought.

Tells him they're lovely. That tulips are her favourite, he's so sweet for remembering; which he hadn't, but says that he did.

–

Next morning: Wednesday. He has a hot shower, two boiled eggs and an entire cup of coffee before he checks his phone. Still no reply from Nora, and she's been back from Devon for a few days now. He throws himself into his mother's garden because she has an endless list of jobs that don't need doing, in his opinion, but which he can do for her anyway. He gets hot while he's weeding, takes his T-shirt off, realises Josie might see his tattoos so puts it back on again. Gets out the mower, cuts her already neat grass. Freya's lawn next door is unruly, brimming with wildflowers, but his mother prefers to keep hers respectable. Pays a professional to maintain it, maybe, seeing as he's never seen her in her gardening gloves, or in the straw hat that hangs by the back door.

The sun is strong for early April. Sweat beads on his

hairline, and memories rise like the tiny moths in the grass as he mows. Family barbecues on bank holidays. His dad flipping burgers. Both mothers in deckchairs while he and Nora swung their legs in the oak tree, talking around packet ice lollies, laughing. They'd laughed a lot, back then. He wonders if laughing less is an adult thing, or just a them thing. A not-sure-where-you-stand-with-each-other thing.

Sweat in his eyes, now, as he cuts the mower. And then a swear word explodes over the fence, followed by a small crash from next door. And while Bren has not seen her, since all they'd found out – has avoided her in the driveway, not popped over for more tea – it's a reflex for him to call out, all right, Freya?

There is a short pause before she calls back, Brenavin? Could you come over here, please? I've dropped the Tomorite.

The what?

Just get over here, will you?

He considers it, then drops the handles of the lawn mower, curiosity winning out over pride. Unlatches the gate his father built between their fences and finds Freya scrabbling on her knees on the decking, in a pool of broth-like liquid.

What a mess, he says as Freya scoops the spillage towards her, her hair tufting so high out of her head she looks like a leafy vegetable herself.

So observant of you, Bren, she says.

Her audacity is kind of outrageous to him, but also unsurprising. She's always been thick-skinned. He's guessing she'll just blast by the whole intercepted phone call thing. The whole, lied-to-them-both-for-no-good-reason thing. Then she snaps at him to *do* something, to go and get a Tupperware, man, from the log store!

Shaking his head, Bren does as she says, retrieves two and hands one over. Freya snatches it and starts scooping the fluid over its rim with her hands, her kaftan now stained with it too.

What is this stuff, anyway, Bren asks, crouching at the other end of the decking, trying not to get it on his shoes.

Tomorite, Freya repeats. Tomato feed, for my cordons.

Expensive stuff, then?

Not in the slightest, she says. But waste not, Brenavin.

And he can't help it; he laughs. Finds himself easing up, a little, as she rootles around on all fours with her mad hair and grubby hands; wondering, not for the first time, why this woman, of all people, would have kept his message from Nora. Would have stopped her from boarding that plane.

It's the last thing he'd have expected, from her.

Freya was always badgering them to be unencumbered by societal norms. Let them stay up late. Bought Nora her first packet of condoms and told her to get lucky, but not unlucky, like she had – not that she regretted it, of course, she rather liked having a pal she could paint with, and read to, and teach to cook so *she* could make dinner for *her* one day. And they'd laughed about all that, him and his parents, with affection. Sometimes awe. His dad had delighted in her. His mother, even more so. Freya marched for women's rights and animal rights and the rights of the planet that was burning up and freezing over and dying, day by day, didn't they know, didn't they *care*? She had opened his mind in ways that his own mother had not, and for that reason, Bren thinks, as he watches her scurrying about, it is hard to remain fully angry with her.

What's it do, then, he asks, as he joins her in her rescue attempt.

Tomato feed? Funnily enough, Bren, it feeds my tomatoes.

She wipes her forehead, leaves a brownish streak on her eyebrow.

Such promise, you had, as a boy, she tells him. All that heat abroad must've addled your brain.

And the disapproval in her tone throws him right back – *Nora's with your mother, like you should be* – and that's it: he snaps.

I don't think you're in a place to tease me here, Freya. After what you did.

She looks up at him, then, over her Tupperware, and their eyes meet. Wild and gold on his steady green.

Well, she says, and she stands, her knees cracking. Give me a minute, will you, before we get into all this.

Why, he says. Is it a greenhouse moment?

A snort, then, because he's remembered, but she says no, Bren, not quite. But it is a moment for alcohol, I reckon, don't you?

–

Freya cleans herself up inside while Bren decants the tomato feed back into the bottle. She reappears after a short while wearing fresh dungarees, two glasses of tomato juice clutched in her hands.

Bit early for a cocktail, isn't it? he asks, as he takes one from her.

Not when it's a breakfast cocktail, she says. Home-made, of course. My little labour of *Love Apples*. That's what they were called, back in the day, due to their aphrodisiacal qualities. Probably why I can't get enough of them.

Bren chokes, just slightly, on his drink.

Don't be a prude! Freya crows, settling on the decking beside him. We all need some spice in our lives! And my punters seem to agree.

Your punters?!

Not *those* kind of punters! she says, seeing his face. I sell *Love Apple Juice* at farmers' markets and things. Slap labels on them, charge a fiver a bottle.

That's terrible.

That's capitalism.

Not the price, Bren says, the name. Surely people just think they're buying apple juice?

Exactly, Bren! It's a crying shame that oranges and apples get all the attention, don't you think? Imagine opening someone's mind to the possibilities of a tangy, sweet-as-earth tomato, grown on our very own island, no less. More vitamins, fewer air miles. It's all part of the plan, Brenavin. Cajole the apple juice bores into expanding their horizons.

Bren decides not to engage on this, knowing she's playing for time. He takes another sip, mouth tingling. Waits her out.

I suppose we should talk about the elephant in the garden, Freya says, after a swig of her own. And I don't mean my statue of Ganesha.

How long have you been waiting to say *that* sentence?

Oh, a good twenty years.

Traded smiles, then, as they both drink again. Soft clink of ice on their teeth.

Nora isn't speaking to me, Freya says, when she lowers her glass.

I know, Bren says.

So she's speaking to you?

Why wouldn't she be?

Josie implied you've been somewhat . . . solitary, for a while. I wondered if something had happened, between you two.

You mean after we clocked that you'd lied to us both?

Maybe Bren is imagining it, but after he's said this, Freya looks almost relieved. She cocks her head at him, then tucks her legs into a lotus position. Puts her glass down.

Lied is a bit strong, she says. You need to communicate, for that, and you and I barely spoke, Bren.

Unbelievable, he says.

Am I?

It's not *our* relationship that matters here, Bren says, and you know it. You feel bad about Nora, and frankly, Freya, you should. You had no right to withhold that message from her. No right to rob her of that chance.

And what chance is that?

To see the *world*! Get out of here! Do – more.

Chase some crush across the globe, you mean? Freya shoots. It seems, Bren, that I'm the one who wanted *more* for her, here.

Some *crush*?!

Yes, Bren! I'm sorry, but what would you rather coin yourself? What have you proven yourself to be, to her, over the years?

Bren's mouth hangs open, astounded at how assertive she's being. At how he, in spite of everything, is the one on the back foot here.

We're, he says. She's my.

Freya raises one eyebrow.

My best friend, Bren says, and it sounds infantile as soon as it's left his mouth. The wind blows then, sweeps their hair over their heads. Freya's glass, left on the decking, tips over. And it's because of how he's been feeling, because of how agitated she's made him, because he can't get on a plane this second or bungee off a bridge that he has to take a risk some other way so he says, without holding back: maybe more than that.

He thinks this will stun her. Provoke a staggered silence, at least. But Freya simply scoffs as she picks up her glass, takes another swig and says come *on*, Bren. When have you ever been more than that, except in your own head?

It is harsh, and she does not apologise for it. But Bren has nothing to apologise for here, either. So instead he asks her a question: the one he's been asking himself, ever since he got home.

You think she's happy, marrying Robin?

I really do. She loves him. She loves her home, and her business. Loves her *life* here, even if it's a life you wouldn't touch with a barge pole.

But it's a life she might not have touched either, Bren says, if you'd given her my message!

And not doing that was a selfish, impulsive move I can't take back, Freya says, and I hold my hands up, there, I do. I've been waiting for you to piece it together, for years, but it turns out I needn't have worried, because the pair of you never talk properly. Which only proves my point.

Which is?

That you don't *know* her, Bren. Just because she was there for you, on the other side of that wall, when you were kids, or at the end of a webcam, when you called? That does not make her yours. She's moved on, Bren.

But I don't think she has, Bren says, and he feels as childish as he sounds, now. Stands up, wants to pace back and forth. Settles for shoving his hands in his pockets.

This thing, between Nora and me, he says, it's two-way. She replied to my emails. She called *me*, too. She was there, because she wanted to be, and I –

Came home, thought she'd take one look at you, and you'd run off into the sunset?

No! Bren says. That's not what this was. But then I . . . spent some time with her, Frey, and there's something between us. I can feel it.

You can feel regret. You can feel nostalgia. You can feel vaguely drunk, because I've put a drop too much vodka in this juice.

And she's been so quiet recently, Bren says, like she's scared to talk, or something, but I'm supposed to be her *best man*, for Christ's sake. If everything was fine she'd be in touch, wouldn't she? So I think it means she's doubting things, Freya. About this wedding.

I'm sure she is! Freya says. Because doubting is what it is to be human! Are you telling me you never feel even slightly bad about leaving, before your father's funeral? And do you think *I* never once looked back on my choice to cut loose from my parents? D'you think your mother looks around her house, swallows her pills and thinks she's lived her best, brightest life?

Freya grabs a twig by her foot and starts shoving it through the gaps in the wood, dislodging bits of moss and dried mud as she talks.

You left when you did, Bren, and that's your cross to bear. None of us will ever fully understand it, unless you get yourself to a therapist, or some kind of spiritual leader, which I would fully recommend, at some point. And we all wonder about it, but we don't force you to go over and over it. We don't bash the moral hell out of you for it.

She flecks more mud, more wet leaves, onto the decking.

So the real question you have to ask here, Freya says, is not about Nora's choices, but your own. Do you really think she would be happier with you, abroad? Flitting between places, instead of living her life here?

I guess we'll find out, Bren says. Seeing as I've asked her to come with me, when I leave.

And it is this, finally, that stuns Freya into stillness. She abandons her twig, for a moment, and stares up at him. The moon is out, still, even though it is mid-morning. Sharing the sky with the sun.

You told her how you feel? she says, and Bren shrugs. Says it was . . . implied.

Oh, yes, because *implying* your feelings has really worked out, in the past. See, Bren – she goes back to her twig – it's all hot air, between you two. You might think that Nora is the key to solving something, for you, but the truth is you need to solve your own problems for yourself.

So you're saying, Bren says, I should spell it out, when I see her next? How I feel about her?

Not at all. I'm saying you should let her get on with her life.

Which is kind of hypocritical, he thinks, but there is something else dawning on him, as he watches her scratching at the dirt with her twig. Because she may be a hypocrite, but she is also right, in a way. He has not been clear. He has not told Nora that he . . . loves her. That he *fell* in love with her, long ago, but now he wants to *be* in love with her, share a life somewhere, which is the part that comes, surely, after you've made sense of your own feelings. Faced into them, instead of running away.

I made a mistake, Freya says, because she seems to think he's absorbing her advice. I put myself first, when I didn't pass your message on, and it backfired. So I suggest you don't interfere, like I did. I suggest you leave her heart alone, Brenavin, and in the same breath, protect your own.

Her harshness has softened, now, so much so that Bren feels something like pity as he looks down at her. Because what she did with his phone call, twelve years back, cannot be changed. Some things, though, he thinks, as the wind picks up again.

Some things are still to play for.

Okay, he says. Thanks.

Yes, Freya says. Good talk. Might make things less awkward, at least, over this Easter lunch your mother's planning.

That's really happening?

Apparently. I think she's hoping Nora and I will make amends over a slice of simnel cake, or what have you.

She stands then, too, brushes down the backs of her knees. And Bren turns, ready to head back through the garden gate, only to find that something is still bothering him.

Freya? he says, and she straightens up, their empty glasses in her hands. Did you really only hide my message because you didn't want her to . . . follow me? Was I truly that bad a choice, for her?

Freya is quiet for a while. Wind tousling her hair. He can't read her expression from where he's standing; it is like she's looking past him into his own mother's garden. A place they'd eaten burgers, played Twister. Been friends, through all the seasons.

But all she says is she'll offer to host it here, now that she's thought about it. The Easter lunch. There's more shade, with the oak tree, and she's got a bigger tablecloth, too.

You're not going to answer my question?

I'm not going to divulge the sad, pitiable things from the very depths of my soul, Brenavin, no, Freya says. But thank you for giving me the opportunity.

Bren looks at her. Nora's mother, in her dungarees, with her lonely edge and unusual lifestyle. Realising, as they stand there, how similar they are. A shared superpower, almost, this inability to hold the hard things, the things he was never taught how to handle; the things she, clearly, won't ever want to share.

Easter, then, is all he says, by way of response.

Easter, Freya says back, with a nod.

fifteen

You cancel some things. Things you'd organised for her, because she is always organising things for others, birthday teas for Josie and Sunday lunches for Freya, home-made gifts via air mail for Bren, hand-knitted hats for Horace, even, Shay's dog. And you'd thought it would be special to make plans centred around her, for a change. Her, instead of her strong-willed mother and old neighbours that cause chaos without meaning to. Her, with her good, solid heart that seems lost, right now. Like your own.

You make the calls, craft the emails. Can't ask Nora to help because she didn't know about all the bookings you'd made. But you do ask her what she wants to do about the registry office, the legal bit she herself had secured.

Should we cancel the registrar, you ask her, a few days after you get home from Devon.

Which is really you asking: should we cancel this entire thing.

And Nora is quiet as she eats her dinner. Chewing slowly, like she's got toothache. As if her mouth is bruised, like your arm, which is feeling less tender but everything else is off, now, including her face, which looks different to you, somehow, as she does not say yes or no or what do you mean.

In the end, she suggests you postpone.

I think we need time, she says, taking your hand. Which is her saying *she* needs time, but if nine years wasn't enough, then how much longer will she need?

Small nod of your head, though. Yeah. Because what else is there to say. What more is there to do, when you won't walk away. Want her, and this, and the life you have built, and this is not a movie with the nice guy giving an empowered speech on a tabletop or tipping her backwards and kissing her in the rain, sometimes things have no structure, no narrative arc, but just are, just continue as they should. You are you, and she is her, and life goes on like it always has and you find you don't have the energy, the headspace, the gumption, to demand any more while everything feels so wrong and at the same time, nothing has changed.

So you go to work. You have dinner, you go to bed, you do it again the next day and the next. Things are subdued and there is less laughing and she lies close to you at night still, but even with her head on your pillow, her toothpaste breath mingled with yours, you can feel yourself pulling away. Not meeting her eye. And you notice her, too, staring into space. Spending long hours at her café, staying late when she's usually home.

She is here, but not with you. You are here, but not yourself.

It's like we're two branches floating on the surface of a river, you would say to Goose, if you felt able to talk to him about this. Like we're both caught on the same current, but she is either ahead or behind and there's nothing you can do to keep pace. All you can do is keep afloat. Trust that you'll wash up on the same bank downstream, which means saying nothing. Which means not having the big animated movie moment that demands an answer, *the* answer, because what is the question, when she'd already answered it, but in fact you hadn't asked? It hurts your head to think about it. When you think about explaining to your friends, your family – your parents, god help you – so you don't.

You have dinner, go to bed, get up, do it again.

Hurt. Hope. Endure tension headaches as you edit your photographs, cancel the plans, don't send out the invites she'd made. Hug her back when she hugs you goodbye before work, which she does, long and loving, her face not looking like hers but it *is* her, it is Nora, in your bed, in your hallway, walking down the road to catch her train as you stand at the window and cancel more plans and wonder what the hell's going on.

sixteen

Nora is in the back room at the art café when Josie calls her. She puts down what she's been working on and answers, worried because it's a Thursday and they don't usually speak on Thursdays; Josie always calls her on the first Wednesday of the month.

Nora? Josie says when she answers, as if to check she's called the right number, and Nora asks her if everything's all right. Tilts her head so her phone is balanced between her ear and shoulder, picks up her sewing again.

Fine, sweetheart, fine, Josie says. I'm just calling to tell you I'm throwing a little Easter lunch next Sunday, and I'd really like you to be there. With Robin, too, of course.

Nora goes back to her embroidery.

Pulls the thread through, without speaking.

It is early evening, and Shay is locking up for the night. The laptop screen is whistling with how hot it is in this back room, no window and no air.

Nora has been spending a lot of time in here lately. Thinking. Working. Pulling parts of herself out of her own head with a needle and thread; feeling something she hasn't felt in a long while, the need to create art that means something. Maybe everything.

This is important to me, Nora, Josie is saying. It's *my* invite, but it will be hosted at your mum's – and she says it breezily, like this is of no consequence – because she has more shade in her garden, you see, and more chairs.

Nora's needle darts back through the fabric, fish-like, flash of silver.

I'm not speaking to Freya at the moment, Josie, she says.

I know that, pet, and that's why I thought you could work it ou –

We will, Nora says. Another time.

But you *won't*, Josie says, and Nora hears the desperation in her voice, a manic pitch that's been absent for a long time. I *hate* that you aren't speaking! Life's too short to fight like this, with the people you love most!

It really is so hot in this room. Nora looks down at the work on her knees, thinking, if only you knew the half of it, Jose.

Life might be short but it's also your own, Nora says. And Freya needs to know that, Josie. She can't just puppeteer my life when it suits her.

But your wedding! Josie says, not prying into Nora's words – or else knowing, Nora suspects, whatever Freya has deigned to tell her. You'll have to be talking by *then,* surely? And Bren said it was the twenty-second of April, which is only a couple of weeks away. That's –

No, Nora says.

But it is. Today's the sixth, and –

No, that's not the date, Nora says. We didn't book the venue, in the end.

Josie is silent.

Oh, she says.

Another stitch, with Nora's needle.

Are you, Josie starts. Is everything.

Nora swallows, but finds she cannot answer. She is still

wearing her engagement ring; nothing has ended, officially. But Robin has been distant ever since they got home from Devon, and she has been spending extra time in here, planning and thinking and working. Giving him space, too, which she thought he might need, while still wrapping herself around him at night. Saying she loves him. And he's saying it back, but he's also looking at her strangely when she walks through the door, as if he's not sure who she is, any more.

But she'll show him.

We'll get back on track, Nora says, in the end, because she doesn't want to give Josie another thing to worry about.

So you're not on track, right now?

Nora sighs, puts down her needle. She can hear Shay stacking chairs, clearing space for the lino print class they're running after hours.

I just feel so . . . daunted, by it all, Nora confesses, because she knows Josie won't let her go without an admission. Marriage is so big and formal.

It doesn't have to be, Josie tells her.

No, Nora says. Thinking of Jon, kissing Josie's cheek and Freya's neck, all in one afternoon. The glint of Josie's wedding ring as she clung on to Freya's arm, at his funeral.

I have to go, she says.

Sweetheart –

I don't think we can come for Easter, Nora says. It's too . . . I don't . . .

She thinks of Bren. How they need to talk, sooner rather than later; how she's been avoiding him, and what she has to tell him. How Robin can barely be in the same room as *her*, right now, let alone in a garden with her mother and neighbours pretending all is fine, all is sunny and chirpy like the birdsong that'll drift from the hedgerows. Hot cross buns shared, chocolate eggs traded; whatever it is that Josie has planned. But what Nora has come to realise is that you cannot boil certainty down to a single day, or destination – a wedding or funeral or accidental proposal. An Easter lunch, to make nice. Life, she thinks, as she sits on the phone, needle in hand, is more than the finished piece; it includes all of the untied threads, all of the loose knots torn off with your teeth, all the callouses on your fingers where you stabbed yourself trying, got it wrong, tried again; kept on.

But it's not just dinner, Josie says, and she still sounds desperate. I was hoping to make it a really special day. And it won't be special without you, Nora.

Shay is singing now, as she finishes stacking chairs.

Mangled lyrics to a rock song, *today could be the last day of your life*.

And a part of it, Josie goes on, is that there's something I'd like to share with you, Nora. Something that might make all of this easier on you.

It is a strange thing for her to say. A strange thing to be so earnest about, Nora thinks, when Josie can have no idea about the complexities that are weighing on her, here. What she's been safekeeping, all these years, to protect her.

But even as she thinks this, even as she lays her needle down beside the laptop and lifts the fabric off her knees, she feels she is being unfair. Because Josie's mind is not any less than her own, or Bren's, or Robin's, just because her neurology is different. She should not be so callous, so condescending – so Bren. So she re-evaluates, breathes out, and says okay. What time.

And Josie brightens, instantly. As if they'd only been talking about the weather forecast: sunshine, predicted, for the bank holiday.

Oh, Nora, she says, I'm so glad.

I'll have to check with Robin, first, Nora says. He's been working a lot lately.

He can spare a day, surely, Josie says. Especially on a weekend! Tell him I'm making a cake, and your mum's cooking. Not tofu, though – she promised.

Billow of Josie's laughter then; Nora thinking of her mother's wild eyes, the last time she saw her; the way she's not replied to any of her texts since.

Could you wear a nice dress, for the occasion? Josie says. Maybe that linen one with the puffy sleeves, and the stitched sunflowers?

Sure, Nora says. Oddly specific, she thinks, but sure.

And Nora?

Yes?

It's all going to be okay. I know you don't believe me, pet. But all being together, like old times? And airing our truths? That's the only way to make things lighter, I think. Going forward.

Nora stares at the blank laptop screen, unsure of how to respond. But then Josie hangs up and she is left with her questions in her throat, Shay's off-key singing on the shop floor, and a sense that something, in the ether, is changing.

–

Although a change had occurred, already, after Devon. As soon as she'd returned to work, things between her and Robin fragile – cracked – but not broken. Because she didn't want them broken, did she? Did *he*? After she'd said no, to the venue, but after *he'd* – not lied, exactly – but hadn't shared the whole truth?

Questions plaguing her, like a tangle of dead ends as she rode the train into London, trying to unpick the yarn of her life. Bren, now home. Robin, her home. Confusion where, surely, there should've been clarity.

She had walked into the café and Shay had taken one look at her and told her to go home, saying she couldn't interact with customers with a face like that, and Nora had crumbled; told her all about the venue weekend. How she couldn't be at home right now, but couldn't go anywhere else, either, not to Freya's, not to Josie's, and Shay had listened to every word then said take personal leave here, then, with an endless supply of mochas and Great Dane therapy and my moral support shrouded in tough love.

Nora had hugged her, for that. Misty-eyed.

And Shay had held her. Her purple hair smelling of papaya shampoo and ground coffee, as she told her that things would be fine – she'd figure it out – and did she want a pain au raisin, they were stale, from yesterday, needed eating.

Nora had said no to the pastry, but taken Shay's advice. Dried her eyes and gone home early. Promised to come back with a clearer head.

She thinks about that now, as she leans her head against the glass of the train window, the lino workshop now over. Thinks about how she arrived back at the flat to take a few hours for herself. Let herself in only to hear Robin's voice, when he'd told her he'd be on a photo shoot that day; how she'd frozen, with her key in the lock, and listened; yes, no, I know, keep the deposit, it's fine.

She slipped off her shoes. Lingered with her guilt in the hall and felt sad that she had to, when she had never held back from him before. Though they had, it seemed, hidden parts of themselves from one another, and that was a part of her confusion, here; that fog that had crept in, and wasn't lifting.

More words, from Robin, as she waited. Sorry, thank you, okay.

But can anyone be one hundred percent themselves, with someone, she wondered, as she stood there in the hallway painted the colour she had chosen, and doubted; sometimes liked in the right light. Their shoes by the door. His brogues, her boots. Converse embroidered with tiny stars that she'd been wearing when they first met at a house party, when they'd talked about Cy Twombly and *Fantasia* and he'd asked her out for a drink which turned into a croissant and a walk by the canal and a romance she hadn't seen coming.

But that, she thought – as she stood listening to Robin saying yeah, I'll be in touch – is what it is to be human.

Not entirely sure.

Shedding skins, growing new ones. Not always knowing but working it out. Wondering about two things – two lives, two decisions – all at once, while at the same time? Not wanting to be anywhere else.

This landed, for her, as she heard Robin say goodbye. Heard him slam his laptop shut, make some kind of wounded, un-Robin-like noise, and leave via the back door.

And now her train slows to the stop before her own and she watches strangers getting off, without really seeing, her mind elsewhere. Remembering how she moved through to the kitchen, after he'd left, and saw his notepad lying open on the table. The one he usually carried everywhere. The one he'd filled with names, two months ago, for their engagement party. All the people they knew and loved, before things got so fraught and confused. And she was going to turn away, respect his privacy, but then she caught sight of something she couldn't unsee.

The name of an a cappella group they had both loved, at art school.

Which was something you weren't meant to admit. Loving a cappella. At art school.

And beneath that, there was another name of a pizza van they'd queued for once, at a music festival. The best pizza of her life, she'd declared, and he'd said that was quite a statement, and she'd said this is quite a pizza.

Tears rising, now, as the train starts to move again and she thinks back to the notes that had gone on and on, like the guest list he'd written at the start of it all. Ideas he'd scrawled down. Things about her that she didn't know he'd noticed. Scraps for his speech or their vows, things she'd said or photographs he'd taken that could play a part in the day he'd always wanted, bare feet, pink rhinestones, quotes from their favourite films, *take me with you, for laughs, for luck, for the unknown*.

Tears back then, too, as she read that line. The specific, earnest, not-wanting-to-forget-ness of it, as she sat down to read the rest. Their lives distilled in Robin's handwriting, moments that had happened, were still happening, on that paper, in their house. Pages and pages and pages of it. She alights from the train as she relives it all, stories about their velvet sofa and disused garden shed. The galleries they went to for late-night openings. Henry's bakery down the road – could he make their butter cake, he'd wondered, Nora's favourite, three tiers, four? – and Bren, he had written his name too, followed by three question marks. Best man, he'd written in a new colour, as if adding it after it had been made official. Best person, he'd written as well, ask him to speak, ask Freya to speak, too, a surprise!

Nora read these words penned by Robin's hand. She felt them, deep in her heart. Does, still, as she gets off the train at her station, and wipes the tears from her eyes.

Because it would've been reasonable to want to avoid Bren Ferguson, after everything. To resent Freya for her disapproval, pity Nora for her sad, sorry show of a family that Robin, instead, wanted to bring into the light.

She'd turned another page, in the kitchen. On and on it

went. Nine years of a life shared. Not simply imagined or wondered about, occurring over a screen or in an inbox, somewhere in her head or teenage past, holding on to something that never was. She'd put her hand on the page, touched the dried ink, and felt that clarity – not appearing, as such, but simply emerging through the fog. Knowing, as if she didn't already, what she had to do. What she was going to show him, without words; with the heartfelt effort he'd always wanted to show her. Moon out, now, as she walks home up the hill. Holding on to her own secret, for a while longer. Saving it for the right time. For laughs, for luck.

For the unknown.

–

Easter weekend rises gold and clear, the light like set honey. Come Sunday, Nora puts on the dress that Josie requested, something linen she'd adorned with yellow sequins along the neckline. Robin is quiet as he dresses in a white shirt and chinos, something far subtler than he'd usually choose. He hasn't shaved for a week, or more. Still won't look her in the eye.

I love you, she tells him, as they lock up the house.

You too, he says.

They get on a train and then the bus, a reduced service because it is Easter Sunday, and as they travel, Nora feels like she's blinking in the light of the real world after being shut in the back room of the café for two weeks. Working on her plan, with Shay's encouragement – urge, then, to reach for Robin's hand – but he folds his arms, turns away.

She has the desire to tell him everything, right then, but has to stop herself.

Not today.

Today is the day she has to face her mother for the first time in weeks. The day she'll see Josie, too, for the first time since her son came home. The day she'll be seeing Bren after he asked her to come away with him.

And she's aware, as the bus pulls them towards the village, that she's not yet given him an answer on that.

Aware she's avoided him, while she sorted through her own thoughts and prioritised Robin's feelings; aware, too, that today won't be the day to talk things through with Bren, either. Not with their mothers around, she thinks, as she walks up the driveway with Robin by her side, not at this awkward half-family gathering, not on this day that's – she realises, as she passes the old parked Volvo – the first time they've all been together since Jon died, right there.

Hot shiver, at this.

Blur of emotions as they push open the porch door.

Not knowing – never knowing – what to do with her memories of that man.

She must be in the garden, she says to Robin, when they aren't greeted by her mother in the hall. No whirling kimono or squawk of delight; just the wind chimes above their heads. They move through her childhood home as a pair, bracing themselves for awkwardness. For tension at the table. Forced camaraderie, full plates and polite conversation as the wine flows and the gravy pours but the laughter, surely, finds its way out, because they are family, at the end of the day; Robin's notes had reminded her of that.

And so – in spite of Jon and Freya's secret affair, and Bren's big question she still needs to answer, and Robin's growing distance even though he is standing right beside her – Nora compartmentalises.

Walks through the kitchen onto the sun-patched decking and puts the pudding she's brought down on the table.

Because they are all separate entities, these things. Separate problems, like the gate that divides – or adjoins – their gardens, and she has no idea that they are all about to come to a head. Three hearts. Six, even. Split open, like atoms, before dessert.

–

Bren goes for a walk before lunch. He can feel in his feet that today is a big day. Pins and needles, an itch to move, to shake out what has been clenched tight inside him all night – or indeed, for the nineteen nights since he saw Nora last. His mother told him Robin was invited, today, so it's not like there'll be a big scene, he wouldn't want that, but surely there will be *some*thing, eye contact, shared words, touch of her hand to his beneath the table. Small beats, instead, that tell him yes. I've felt it too, this electricity between us, and I have to sort things out, first, but then? I'm coming with you.

A thrill, then, as Bren imagines it. The conversation he's been imagining for days now, mostly because his mother had also told him something else, in passing.

That Nora had not booked her wedding venue.

Which meant his sense that something was brewing, here, solidified.

They'll be fine, his mother told him, misreading his expression as concern. And they would be, Bren knew. Maybe not immediately – he knows it won't be easy for Nora, dismantling the life she's built, especially as there is no bad guy, here, no one person in the wrong. But not being wrong does not make you *right* together. That's what he'll say to her, when it's time.

When she admits things are ending, with Robin.

This is what he thinks about, as he prepares to see her again. As he walks through the fields to the village with the bad coffee, and heads for the photograph of the old cricket team, which he actually looks at, for a period of time, without having to turn away. That red hair, lighter than his. Kind eyes that he didn't inherit, he doesn't think. And then he finds a bench and decides to jump, like he'd told Nora to, weeks ago, he is sick of waiting around and he always trusts his gut, he wants to trust in *them*. Him and Nora. The way she looked at him when he showed up at her door. Leaned into his kiss at the bus stop, didn't buy a dress or book her venue because she feels, surely, what he feels – so he clicks into his flight app and he hits the button to pay now, to give her something she can trust in, too: him, ready and waiting for her, instead of a missed opportunity long ago. Two tickets, for the pair of them, for a month's time. Spinning wheel, payment processed.

Euphoria.

He looks back at the photo of his dad.

Smiling, like he knows something his son doesn't as Bren puts his phone away and walks back, as calm as the wide green river he follows home.

–

Freya has dragged her kitchen table outside and pushed it next to Josie's garden furniture – passed over the fence by Bren, presumably – so that it can comfortably seat five. There are three types of tomato salad, a basket of crusty bread. A pitcher of Pimm's swimming with chopped fruit, the apple chunks already browning.

Friends! Freya says, when she sees them. She has never called them this before, and the peculiarity of it is not lost on them. Nora swallows. Robin touches her elbow, guides her forward; Freya outpours about the lamb she's prepared, something from the butcher because it's a special occasion, all of them getting together, she can't remember the last time they did it, not that you would've been here, Robin, you're new, well, new*er*, Josie's idea, this whole thing, you know what she's like, when she gets an idea in her head.

Nora tenses up, seeing her mother so nervous, like this.

Hearing her mention Josie, like that.

How's veganism working out for you, Freya, Robin asks, with a gentle attempt at humour that Nora hasn't heard since they'd left Devon.

Oh please, Freya says, we all know I'm about as vegan as a beefburger. Robin laughs, and it is such a good sound, and that sound thaws something in Nora as she stands there by the wobbling table, paper napkins fluttering in the breeze. She sees the relief in Freya, too, at his warmth. Thinks of his notebook, the details, the bigger picture.

I can check on it, if you like, Nora says. The lamb.

She says it to the cutlery, but still. It's an offering, an attempt to be ordinary. Small seeds from the trees flecked on the plates as Robin seats himself at the table, and her mother looks at her for the first time; Nora feels it, but can't yet look back.

Oh, Freya says. Could you, darl?

Tentative, like she's not sure how to play this; not sure she can use this term of endearment, yet. But Nora nods, and Freya jumps on it like a lifeboat, says it's probably raw, you know me, can't cook for toffee apples; I did what the butcher said, but if you could check that would save the day, I'd imagine, and Nora looks up at her as she says this last part, knowing that in this compliment, there's an apology, without words. Which Nora should, but can't quite, acknowledge. So what's new, Freya says, turning to Robin. How's your brother. Still defending evil corporations, for a living?

In the kitchen, Nora finds that her palms are sweating. Underarms, too. Great. She checks the lamb shoulder, takes it out, rubs it with oil and mustard powder, studs it with garlic. She hears Freya laughing from outside, somehow; it feels like Nora hasn't laughed in weeks; but then she is back outdoors and the laughing stops and Robin and Freya both look at her as she lowers herself into a chair, like someone has died, or is about to.

Looks good, is all that she says.

A miracle! Freya says. D'you want a Pimm's?

I'm okay, thanks, Nora says, so that Freya stops, mid-pour. Puts the jug down, loosens the knot in her neck scarf. Half a minute passes. Throats cleared, a greenfly on the butter knife. But her mother, it seems, can't help herself.

Are *we* okay, she says, and Nora says let's not do this now. This is for Josie, today. I'm here for her.

Robin busies himself with separating the knives from the forks, which have been bundled into the centre of the table. He makes unnecessary noise, pairing them beside the bowls and salad tongs and clay candle holders bought at car boot sales or artist collectives, some made by Nora in primary school.

Things *aren't* okay between us, Nora says, but we just have to get through this meal, then –

Robin drops a fork, sorry, he says, waving a hand; Nora sees him wince. A cloud moves over the sun just as she decides not to finish her sentence, because then what, she does not know. Which her mother seems to accept. Simply sits there with the Pimm's and the fresh tomatoes sliced on a plate, Robin counting the number of cake forks left on the table, they're one short, someone will have to have a normal fork for dessert, he'll take the hit, he doesn't like small forks as it is, nor big bowls with the giant rims in fancy restaurants, you know the ones, he is mumbling, he is riffing, he rubs his head like it's hurting him, the conflict is hurting him.

But then comes a coo-ee from over the fence and Josie appears in a summer dress and pink drawstring coat, carrying a large bowl covered in cling film. Happy Easter! she calls as she opens the gate, and all three of them rise from the table.

I brought my pasta salad! she declares. Jon's *favourite*.

Nora stiffens, Freya sighs; Josie props it on the table, and beams. Freya – this is all so *pretty*. I love this tablecloth. And this, here!

She gestures at the strawberries, mint and cucumber floating in the Pimm's with such joy, it's like Freya has made a wedding cake, instead of sliced up some fruit. And Nora, you look *lovely*, pet. I like your dress. And your hair.

Good journey? Robin asks, after he's kissed her cheek.

Oh, I only live next door, dear, Josie says.

Yeah, Robin says, I was just. Yeah.

He sits back down and Josie does too, tucking her pink dress beneath her.

It's so lovely to see you all, she says, almost breathless.

Don't start sobbing over the tomatoes, Josephine, Freya says, pouring her a Pimm's, though Nora thinks, with a wave of hot regret, that her mother, too, looks mournful. Get this down your neck, first.

I thought I might have a cup of t –

Nope, Freya says. Just sit and enjoy the booze like anyone else, on a day like today. Bit of Dutch courage. Robin, tell Josie about your antiques, will you. Nora, could you help me with the condiments?

Why would you need Dutch courage for an Easter lunch, Robin asks.

Josie coughs on her Pimm's, and Freya breezes on, says to stomach my cooking, Robin! Although it's not *all* bad. I do make a mean panzanella. Nora, she repeats, the condiments?

And because something seems off, because she doesn't want to upset Josie who is watching, and because Freya – hard-nosed, unemotional Freya – actually seems rattled, Nora follows her into the kitchen, leaving the back door propped open, the breeze stirring the wind chimes in the hall.

What's going on, Nora asks, once they're inside. Why are you and Josie acting so – but Freya talks over her, says they just wanted to have a nice meal together, after everything. She opens the fridge as she speaks, so that Nora can't see her face.

I was sure I had some mint sauce. Aha! Oh, no. That's pesto. With a best before date of . . . three years ago. Is that edible, d'you think?

About as edible as your mushrooms, I'd imagine, Nora says.

Well, we're still alive, aren't we? Here, take the butter, and the mayonnaise. Apparently Bren likes it on his potatoes.

So Bren is coming, Nora says.

So Josie says. And I just wanted to tell you, Nora, before he arrives, that he and I had a little talk, the other day. Smoothed things over.

Freya still has her head in the fridge. Nora folds her arms, blood beating in her ears, says, eventually, how nice for you.

Don't be so sassy.

You *raised* me to be sassy.

I am not going to argue with you on a day like this, Freya says. You said yourself, we're here for Josie. Take the coleslaw, will you?

She shoves a tub, without looking, into her hands, and Nora puts it down on the side.

But I just want you to know that Bren won't be bothering you, any more, Freya says, extracting two kinds of mustard from the shelf, and passing her those, too. I know you think I meddled in your affairs, Nora –

Poor choice of word, Nora says.

– but I made him see that it was the wrong thing, to ask you to go away with him. Not on that damn phone call, before you say it! But with whatever he said to you, the other week! So we can just put that aside, and focus on what's important, today. Without any added drama.

Nora stares at the back of her mother's head.

He . . . told you, that he asked me that?

And I told *him* to let you live your life.

Nora scoffs at this. Like you did, you mean?

Are we still on that?

What, you thought I'd be over it?

I *thought* it was an excuse to be angry with me about Jon, Freya says, and she says his name, just like that, not lowering her voice or shouldering any blame and Nora almost storms back to the garden, almost grabs Robin's arm and says actually, let's go home, but then Freya withdraws from the fridge and says that's not for right now, either, is it. Let's get through this meal, and then we can talk about all that.

Except I don't want to, Nora says.

Freya lets out a hollow laugh, and Nora can't believe she has the audacity to act so righteous, here.

So we won't talk, she says, ever again? Even after our family gathering?

But we're not a *family*, Nora says, slamming the jars she'd been holding onto the side – so hard, it's surprising they don't smash. We never have been! And what you *did*, how you pretend it's nothing, that's not *normal*, Freya.

Who ever said any of this was normal?! I've wanted to explain myself for weeks, but you wouldn't let me, and now,

Nora, it'll have to wait. Can you reach the gravy boat up there? It seems I've shrunk a few inches, since our fight.

Nora glares at her, reeling. But before she can retort, Bren walks in through the kitchen door. She hadn't heard the porch open, or the wind chimes jangling in the hall. She sees him, and he sees her. Sees his crooked half-smile as he says Nora's never been able to reach the gravy boat, Freya. I don't know why you keep it on the top shelf.

You get it down, then, Freya says, without greeting him.

You're hardly taller than me, is all Nora says, when he turns away.

Just about, he says, stretching for the jug – T-shirt rising, showing the hint of a tattoo – and passing it to Freya who has finally closed the fridge door.

All righty, she says, with a sigh. Let's – wait, Bren. Is that what you're wearing?

Bren glances down at his usual white T-shirt, a little less stained, now, presumably because Josie has washed it; his cargo trousers, though, flecked with dried mud.

Didn't Josie ask you to dress smart? Freya asks him. Drag a brush through that barmy hair of yours?

I don't own anything smart, Bren reasons. And my hair is my hair.

My condolences, Freya says, but neaten up, please, before you join us.

Why?

Just do it, won't you? Honestly, you two, it's like trying to talk to a pair of teenagers.

And with that, she bustles from the room with some chutneys, leaving Bren and Nora alone.

Barmy . . . hair? Bren repeats, watching her go.

Your hair's fine, Nora says. He looks back at her then, and something passes between them. Or maybe nothing does.

Nora can never tell, with him. Can never see through the emotions that rush through her when he walks in, the tides in her turning like they always do in his presence. Cresting waves, a swell of feeling.

Knowing what she needs to say to him, when it's time.

D'you think I actually need to get changed? Bren asks.

I guess so?

They both stand there, not moving.

Want to come? he says. Not to see me get changed, obviously. Just to help me choose a shirt, or something.

I should probably, Nora says, nodding to the back door. Because Robin is out there, and she should get back. She should not put herself in a bedroom with Bren, right now, with Josie's special, strange day laid out before them, like the good plates and paired cutlery. When they should just get through this meal, just be polite, and maybe after pudding she could take a moment, tell Robin that she needs to –

My mum said you didn't book the venue, Bren says. So the twenty-second of April's not happening.

Stillness, between them. Just the lucky cat, waving, from the window sill.

No, Nora says, her throat dry. It's not.

Were you going to tell me that, at some point? Am I no longer your best man?

He doesn't seem standoffish, about this; it's more like he's teasing. His usually shuttered face wide open. Which breaks her, a little. Flicker of dread. She says they shouldn't discuss this now.

Then when?

When we've not got Robin and our mothers sitting outside, she says. As if everything's not weird enough, as it is.

What's weird about it, Bren says, and she opens her mouth with a jilt of panic, because she forgets sometimes – for dangerous, blinding split seconds – that he does not know about Freya and Jon. That she has kept it from him.

Just being together, like this, she says, to cover herself. For the first time since your dad died.

And at this, his wide, open gaze retracts. Like she's yelled. Like he's shielding himself. The things they have not said hanging heavy in the room, like the smell of cooked meat and hot oil, her resolve melting, when she sees him melting, too.

I can help you choose a shirt, if you want, she relents, after seeing his face. Because he's hurting. Because she needs to put things straight. Needs to jump, because she always thinks too much, acts too little, and Bren, who usually acts first but says nothing, looks straight at her as he says yeah, he'd like that. Yes please.

–

They choose something black. The shirt he wore on his sixteenth birthday that Nora finds shunted next to his school uniform. Very Jeff Goldblum, she says when she hands it to him, turning away as he pulls off his T-shirt.

His tattoos are less shocking to her, now. But still she averts her eyes, looking around this room she has not set foot in since he left. It is familiar and yet so affronting, the way it's still exactly how she remembers it. The world map pinned to his ceiling. A drawing she made him, on the wall. Framed photographs on the window sill, faded from years of sun: one of him and her with Jon at a barbecue; Bren on the hockey pitch, another with school friends, his parents, in their garden. More of her and him; two others, in fact, three total. At the beach, when they were twelve, and in a photo booth, a few weeks before he left.

There are six pictures here, and she makes up a half.

Small pain, in her heart, at that.

How's this, Bren says, and she glances round at him, says good.

Good, Bren echoes, and she can tell they are both playing for time, both waiting for the other to talk first. She turns back to the window while he searches for a comb. They can't hear their mothers from this side of the house, nor Robin, whom she'd messaged, said she wouldn't be long. He hasn't replied, though he's read it. Two blue ticks. And that photograph of Jon, looking out at her. Which is what pushes her to stop resisting; spill the truth.

So we didn't book the venue, she confirms.

Bren is adjusting stray locks of hair in the mirror.

Slows his movements.

It didn't feel right, Nora says. She can feel him looking at her in the reflection of the glass; can see his reflection in the window. And as their eyes meet, that heart pain turns into a hairline crack, because they've always been dancing around something, but it's a dance she's never quite known the steps to.

I don't want to walk away, she tells him.

She turns to face him. He keeps his back to her.

I am going to marry Robin, she says, if he'll have me. Just not on the twenty-second of April, and not in that fancy venue in the woods.

A leaf blower starts up, somewhere, from the green.

I don't want a big wedding, Nora goes on, I never did. I hate all the fuss and expectation, the drama and . . . insincerity of it all.

She thinks of Jon saying his vows to Josie in a church somewhere. Thinks of Freya, teaching her that marriage was a box, instead of something you could step into with someone, a place you were excited to go.

It's one of the reasons I never wanted to do it, she says, because Bren isn't responding; still shaping his hair. When we got engaged we said we'd keep it small, but Robin got excited. He does that. Gets an idea, and runs with it. And I really love that about him, so I didn't want to . . . rein that in. But I've had to interrogate why it felt wrong, which was hard, when everything was so . . . accelerated.

Her voice is wavering, slightly, as she says this. Desperate for Bren to say something – anything – back.

And then you came home, she says, when he remains silent. And we found out what really happened, when you left, just as my wedding morphed into this huge thing with a best man and a discounted package deal if we rushed it through and I just felt so . . . mixed up.

She thinks about the accidental proposal. About the list of surprises she'd found in Robin's notebook that meant he knew her, saw her, that what they have is real, as palpable as the ink on the page. That it wasn't the wedding itself that felt wrong, not the union or the person, just the circumstances, the confusion of it all, and she knows Bren had asked her to come away with him, she knows he'd sensed something was off, and she loves him, for that – can she say that, out loud – because *he* knows her, too, and she is so grateful. So lucky to have him holding up a mirror, like that, forcing her to think, slow down, recalibrate. So she knows what's wrong, now. What's right.

Though something is not right, she can see, in the set of Bren's mouth.

I was going to tell you, she murmurs, but it's all been so strange, at home. After we didn't secure the venue. I've been taking some space, sorting out my next steps. So I'm not . . . coming with you, Bren, when you leave. But I really appreciate that you offered. I know that was . . . major, for you.

She swallows, her mouth dry, her heartbeat slow. Slower than she thought it would be, now that she's said what she'd meant to. And she'd known it might be painful, telling him this, after what he'd revealed – that she was *more than family*, to him, but he is, too, to her; that can't ever be taken away. So she moves towards him, arms out for a hug – but then he speaks, and his voice is cold, and hard.

So that's it then, he says.

Which splits open that hairline crack inside her. Because she had hoped – she'd pretended – he wouldn't care. Because this is *Bren*. He gets on planes, he bails on funerals. He doesn't talk to her for months at a time, and he'll shoot off again, when it suits him, he'll get bored, he might already have been doubting his offer, can't have thought, truly, she'd have said yes, I'll come with you, because how could she.

Well, yeah, she says. I'm sorry if . . . you thought . . .

I thought nothing, he says, still in that iron voice. Seriously. Don't look at me like that, Nora. It doesn't matter, and you know what, I'm hardly surprised.

He has taken his eyes from hers, now.

Of course you were gonna stay home, he says. He is holding his body unusually still, and Nora does not react. Doesn't bite back. He is hurting; she has hurt him.

I know you said we'd missed our chance, she says, but –

To get out of here, Bren says. That's all. I was giving you a way out, if you needed one. But you've said you don't, so that's fine. I can get my flight out whenever I want to, now, right.

Right, Nora says.

Because I can *do* that, Bren says. I can do what I want, when I want, I can be free as a fucking bird and it's a good thing, he says, and his voice has gone unnaturally high, if heat had a sound, it would be his voice right now, hot and hurting and alight, and again he says don't *look* at me like that, Nora, don't you dare feel fucking sorry for me.

I'm not!

It's not like I'm in love with you, for Christ's sake. You've always hung on to me like some kind of lovesick schoolgirl, but I was just being a friend, all right? I just wanted to give you a way out of this boring-arse life in the suburbs. That's all. Don't kid yourself.

Bren, Nora says, her voice breaking, because his has, too.

Photographs, framed.

A world map pinned to his ceiling.

His hurt leaching into hers, or hers into his, as they stand there in a room cluttered with their past, airless despite the open window.

Shall we get to this lunch, then, Bren asks, and he leaves without waiting for her so that Nora is left alone, staring at herself, now, in the mirror. His white shirt, crumpled, on the floor.

–

You're back, Robin says, when Nora comes through the garden gate. He is sandwiched between both mothers at the table, and seems drained; has probably spent the last ten minutes being insulted by Freya, or fawned over by Josie; most likely both.

We're back, Nora nods, forcing a smile.

Bren, who'd beaten her to the table, says nothing. Pours himself a glass of Pimm's, then lifts one of the chairs and points it towards the sun so it's not facing the rest of them. Sits down, takes a drink. Nora lowers herself into the only empty seat, warm despite the spring breeze lifting her hair.

You look very dapper, pet, Josie says to Bren. New shirt?

Very old shirt, Bren says.

I like it, Robin says. Rather Jeff Goldblum.

Bren scoffs into his glass and Nora reddens; leans over for some bread, to hide it. Freya, who is dishing out tomato salad with a serving spoon, says really, Bren? You're going to sulk like you used to at Christmas, when your father made you wear a tie?

And despite all that's just happened in Bren's bedroom, despite how terrible and guilty and muddled she feels, Nora feels a zap of panic shoot through her. At how wrong it is that Freya would use Jon's name like that, in front of everyone. Bren seems to tense up, too. Downs the rest of his drink.

So why, Robin asks the table at large, is a smart shirt necessary for eating roast lamb?

His words sound forced, like he knows something is happening here, but is trying to keep things cordial. Nora feels a rush of affection for him; showing up as himself, no matter what's going on at home. She'll show him, soon enough. Another zap through her, at the thought: this time a thrill.

It's a very nice roast lamb, is all, Freya says.

Now that Nora's seen to it, Josie says, and Freya makes a faux noise of outrage, says was that a joke, Josephine? Very good, very sly! See, all you needed was a bit of grog in you and you're blimmin' Lucille Ball! Well, cheers, everyone. Here's to all of us getting together, like this. Making an effort, she adds, in Bren's direction.

They all clink glasses, aside from Bren, who raises his above his head. Nora leans across the table to touch Robin's, who is searching her face due to Bren's mood. She wants to tell him to ignore it, she'll explain later. To just get through the meal. To avoid the pesto, which is inedible; they'll laugh about that, later, she's sure.

So, Robin, Bren says, raising his voice. How're the wedding plans coming along?

Nora drops her knife. Robin, who had just started talking to Josie, turns his head.

Not long till the twenty-second, is it, Bren says. Invites need to go out soon, don't they?

Bren, Josie says, before Nora can find her tongue.

Ignore him, Freya tells Robin, as she passes him the coleslaw. He's just out of the loop, as usual.

Clearly, Bren says. Seeing as I put my life on hold for a wedding I've now found out isn't happening.

Nora puts her fork down, hard.

It's happening, she says, hoping that Robin hears this, and believes her. And you didn't *have* to put your life on hold.

Except you asked me to be best man, Bren says, so it was kind of implied, wasn't it? And now you're what, rescheduling? Eloping?

Eloping! Josie says, with a clap of her hands. Oh, that would be lovely!

Maybe, Robin says, maintaining his easy demeanour. He dishes some coleslaw onto Josie's plate, his movements deliberate, like his words. The world's our oyster, I suppose, he says, but he does not look at Nora as he says it.

Have you ever eaten an oyster, Bren asks, and Robin blinks. Freya says Nora, d'you want some pine nuts on your salad?

Contentious, aren't they, Bren says. Either dodgy as hell, or the height of sophistication. Two extremes, really.

Nora is not sure where he's going with this. She pours herself more Pimm's, finds that she's shaking, slightly.

Everyone says they taste like the sea, Bren goes on, but that's kind of unoriginal. To me, they taste like risk. They taste like life. They taste like doing something in the moment, shucked straight from a fisherman's bucket in Phuket or a shack on a Tasmanian beach, just because you *can*. Because you can't not.

Pine nuts, Bren? Freya asks.

I've had oysters before, yes, Robin says. He has stopped smiling, now, is passing the bread basket to Josie who shakes her head, says she's still got half a roll left, thanks, and Freya says Bren, your salad's getting cold, and nobody laughs.

Quiet, for a moment. The tablecloth fluttering in the wind. Josie says well, this looks, and Freya says do *not* say lovely, Jose, and the two mothers begin to eat. Nora is looking at Robin, trying to communicate without words. Robin looks down at his napkin. Bren looks up at the sky, as if wishing he were on a plane, and Nora finds, for the first time since he got home, that she's wishing the same thing.

I thought about grilling peaches, Freya says, to put in the salad.

Small sounds of cutlery on the side plates.

Why didn't you, Robin asks, and Freya says oh, she's not cleaned the barbecue in a decade, it's congealed in this burnt-black carcinogenic matter, so.

Jon used to clean it for her, Josie adds.

He was the barbecue king, Freya nods. And Bren swears, then, under his breath, but loud enough that everyone hears. Freya cracks some black pepper, loudly. Josie glances over at her son.

Tasmania, she says, to change the subject. I didn't know you'd been there, pet.

Yes you did, Bren says. I lived there for four months, a few years back.

Really? Josie picks at her lettuce with her fork. You've been so many places, darling. It's hard to keep track.

I know nothing about that place, Robin says, when Bren hasn't responded. My sole knowledge of it comes from that kids' cartoon.

Which cartoon? Josie asks.

Ta-Ta-Taz-Mania? With Bushwhacker Bob? Constance and Thickley?

You've lost me, Josie says. Freya winks at Robin, whose returned smile seems to take quite an effort. Nora wants to reach out, touch his hand. Tell him everything's fine. She promises. He'll see.

You're missing out on some great tommies here, Bren, Freya prompts. Bren stays seated for a moment but then gets up and comes over to the table. Picks up his plate to start serving himself. Sets it back down.

We had several long calls when I lived there, he says to Josie. When I was walking the Three Capes track, with a hiking group.

Ah, says Josie, yes.

You don't remember, he says. Don't pretend that you do.

Bren, Nora says, but Josie says he's right, pet. I do have trouble remembering things.

Don't we all, Robin says. I've been forgetting little details, recently. Where I've put my notebook. Which equipment is mine, even, on a photo shoot.

Details, Bren echoes, going back for his chair. Setting it down at the head of the table, while Josie pats Robin's hand.

I'd say where your son lives is more than just a *detail*, he says. It's not like you've got much else to keep track of.

Josie pauses as she lifts a piece of bread to her mouth. Freya says Brenavin, at the same time that Robin says hey, now.

I just don't get it, Bren says, more to his plate than his mother. Living like this.

Get what? Freya blusters. That you're not the centre of the universe? That there are other things that occupy the minds of the people you love?

Nora's conscience stutters, at this last part; she feels as if she'd been on a ship heading for an iceberg, hoping it would turn, come on, turn, but then her mother had to say *that* and she is hurting, at Robin's sad eyes; hurting, that Bren is hurting, too; hurting that she has done nothing wrong, on paper, and yet the two people she cares about most are at this table, unable to look at her, while her mother is citing *love* in front of Josie, when Nora knows – she *knows* –

People you love? Bren repeats. Or people, he says, looking at Nora, who just happen to be here?

Brenavin, get off your high –

No, seriously, Bren says. I've been gone twelve years, this summer, right? And I'd like you to make a list, for me, all of you – he swivels to Freya and Josie – about what it is that you *love*, around here. Not what's easy, or convenient. What takes your breath away, or sets your world on fire. Doesn't have to be a person, even. Tell me what it is that's winning for you, here, in this garden with your damn salad plates and your banged-up cars in the driveway and magnets from places you've never even *seen*, stuck to the fridge, while you're too scared to do anything else?

And Nora has opened her mouth to argue, but it is Robin who gets there first.

I think you should take a breath, my friend, he says.

Bren looks at him over the Pimm's jug. There is a measured moment where Robin looks back, unruffled. The three women, looking at them look.

Sweetheart, Josie says, in the end, but Bren says he just – needs a minute – gets up and goes inside, leaving the four of them at the table. A bee drifts near to the dipping oil, then away again. Josie presses her napkin to her mouth.

I'm so sorry, she says.

What are *you* sorry for, Freya demands. We've not even told him what we're here for and already he's all riled up.

He's right to be upset, Josie says. I am appalling at remembering certain things. It must be the pills.

Or the menopause, Freya says.

I can never keep up with where he is, Josie goes on. I don't *really* understand what he does for a living, either. He uses all these words, all these terms that I can't . . . quite keep in my brain. I do try.

Course you do, Freya says.

He's always been so passionate, Josie says. That's his dad in him. Not me.

Not all passion has to be fire and fantasy, Freya says, standing to scrape the remaining salad onto Robin's plate. Something to *take your breath away*, did he say? We're not any less interesting because we're not scaling glaciers or naked camping with strangers.

Naked camping? Josie says, startled.

You know, without toilets or electricity.

Wild camping, Nora corrects her.

She rather hopes this might prompt some humour from Robin, but he is picking at his salad leaves, not looking at any of them.

Freya's right, he says. About passion.

Still not glancing up from his plate.

It was Elliott Erwitt, he says, who said that photography is about finding something interesting in an ordinary place. That it's little to do with the things you see, and everything to do with how you see them.

Oh, Josie says. That's beautiful.

I always thought so, Robin says. But it doesn't have to relate to photography. Or travelling the world. It just has to relate to that little bit of life you've made for yourself.

He lifts his eyes to Nora's when he says this.

So tell me about seabirds, he says to Josie, already looking back down at his food. I couldn't tell the difference between a goose and a gull, personally.

Josie chuckles, and it is that interaction, more than anything that has come before, that swells a lump in Nora's throat. Makes her want to help Josie, here, and be more Robin; lead with generosity, and kindness. So she steadies herself. Knowing, despite her own anger at the scene he'd just made – anger at herself, too, for triggering it – she is the only one who can appease things, here, and bring Bren back to the table.

I'll check on the lamb, she says, as Josie starts telling Robin about guillemots. Freya passes her the cleared plates, and Nora heads back to the kitchen, half expecting the room to be empty but no, there he is, bent double, black shirt and red hair and breathing out with both hands on the countertop.

She thinks, for a horrid jolt of a second, that he's crying, but his eyes, when he looks up at her, are as cold and clear as before.

What was that, she asks him.

A mistake, he says. Which throws her.

Okay, she says. Then go and make up for it.

I can't, he says, as she puts the plates down on the side. I can't do this, Nora. It's why I left. She drives me insane. I love her, I do, but I can't sit here talking about cartoons and grilled peaches that aren't even in the fucking salad.

Your mum didn't say that, Nora says. Mine did.

Because she barely says *anything*! She doesn't ask or know anything, or *want* to know anything about me! Ever! She never did, even when I was a kid! All her energy goes into taking her pills, doing the laundry, having her toast on Saturdays and her casserole on Sundays and being bored of her own little *life* that's killing me, Nora, with every second that I stay.

Do you *hear* yourself?

But that's how it feels! Being here, it's like there's no air! It's why I can't talk to my own *mother*, Nora, because I've tried! I've really fucking tried! But all the things I've done, all the things I do, to live the life he – the one he *said* I should – I've done it! And she doesn't even care! Just like *you*, Nora. You used to care. You used to want more, as well. But you're the same, you're all the same, and I'm alone, again, I'm alone because you chose him.

And Nora is the one crying, now, but it isn't her, she realises, who has caused this; something has dawned on her, as he raves. Because whatever they had is broken, she broke it, or he broke it, long ago, she's not sure; but actually, that isn't what truly hurts. What's causing him this deep-rooted pain.

Do you really think that's what's wrong here, Bren, she asks, through her tears. What I *don't* want? Have you ever thought that maybe, it's what you're missing?

He looks at her, uncomprehending, emotion in his eyes, too, at the sight of hers, but she keeps going.

I think you move constantly, reaching for this idea of *more*, she says, new places and experiences, hoping *some*thing will fill this hole inside you, Bren. And I can't fill it, either, even though you think, right now, that I can. Simply because – and you said it yourself – I just happen to be here.

Don't do this, Bren says. Don't make this about him, when it's about us, Nora.

But you can't even say his name! Nora says. You can't even say Dad!

That has nothing to *do* with this, he blasts. I bought us two fucking tickets to New Zealand, okay?

What?

I bought us two tickets because we should be together, Nora! We've just been waiting, for too long, and wondering what could have been!

But that's the thing, Bren! Nora cries, and she actually stamps her foot – that's the point of it all! Making decisions and seeing them through, means there will *always* be should-haves, or might-have-beens, but that's *okay*. That's just human. *That's* the real stuff of living. It doesn't mean anything is wrong, and her tears are rolling out of her now, desperate for him to hear her, to see it.

Nora, he says, reaching a hand out, towards her tears.

No, Nora says, stepping back. *I* am okay, here, Bren! *You're* the one who's lost. You're more lost than any of us.

Bren lowers his hand to his side. Watching her.

This isn't about me, he says, is it.

The cat waves. The oven whirs.

Oh, Bren, Nora murmurs. It's always about you.

And right as she says it there is another noise, footsteps broaching from outside, and Robin walks in carrying the empty bread basket, his mouth set as he looks at them, and the pair of them look right back.

Always about him, is it, he says. Placing the basket on the kitchen side.

A beat of confusion. Of quiet.

Not like that, Nora says.

No? Robin says. Seems I've interrupted quite the moment between you two.

There was no moment, Nora says. We were just –

She breaks off, but her hesitation only seems to exacerbate what Robin thinks is happening, here.

I'll leave you to it, he says. To . . . whatever this is.

It isn't anything, Nora says, and she looks at Bren for backup, but he just folds his arms, says no?

No! says Nora, but Robin is already pushing past Bren who makes no effort to block his way. Nora follows him, her tears halted, wind chimes clanging as he pulls open the porch door;

he struggles with it, again, like he can't work out where the handle is.

I just meant he's *selfish*, Robin, Nora says. I meant he makes everything about him. Not that *my* everything, is about him.

But he ignores her. They can see the bus pulling up beside the green through the porch windows; good timing, he says, and she says Robin, this is ridiculous.

I agree, he says. This whole thing.

What d'you –

This! he explodes, with a force that frightens her. Him! Showing up, the night of our engagement party! You, insisting it's fine, just friendship, but *retreating* from me! No venue. No date. No explanation.

Robin –

Disappearing, for hours on end. Not telling me what's on your mind. And we don't *do* that, Nora. That's not us.

I've been working! she says. I've been –

And I've been giving you space, he says, but it seems that was a really bad idea.

It wasn't, Nora says. Robin, please, listen to me.

Why should I? When nine years of that hasn't got us anywhere? I thought we were *it*, Nora. But even wanting more turned out to be some kind of giant conspiracy, against you, when all I wanted was to give us a wedding that made you feel as special as you – as you make –

He is talking over her as she tries to talk back. That anger she saw in him, that Sunday with the storm, descending again, taking hold.

I've spent years, Robin rants, thinking it's fine. No wedding, no ring, no problem! Telling Goose I'm not worried when Bren rocks up, because that's who I am, Nora! Good old, jovial Robin! The well-meaning, laughable nice guy! Fine to string him along, no harm done!

There's no *stringing* along –

Isn't there? Because I'm a patient guy and I may not be a sad, solitary nomad with a damaged soul but I do *see* things, Nora. I see the way he looks at you. And I see you stalling, because of it.

But I'm not, Nora says. I'll show you. Please, Robin, she says, as he pulls open the porch door. Don't make this a thing.

But it is a thing, Robin says, as he steps outside. I'm not the one who doesn't know what I want and isn't brave enough to admit it.

I do know, though!

I've got a blinding headache, Robin says. I've got to go.

Then I'll come with you. I'll –

No, Nora. I need some space.

She reaches for his sleeve, but he says no again, in a voice so angry, so unlike him, she backs off. I've got to go, he repeats. I don't *recognise* you, Nora.

And this breaks her right open, and she has to go after him, has to ask him something, her stupid, surprise plan be damned, but as she steps out of the porch three things happen at once: Bren grabs *her* sleeve, this time, saying Nora, don't; she spins round so fast that her elbow cracks hard into his nose; and a song they both know, both avoid, begins to float through from the garden, and it is confusing, it is a blur of three, four, five seconds, but when she turns to look back, Robin is gone; the bus already pulling away.

seventeen

Nora stands in the driveway near the porch door, breathing hard. The mothers are still in the garden, that song is still playing, and Bren is behind her, his nose bleeding. Asking her if she's okay.

Don't, Bren. Don't pretend you care.

Of course I care.

You were no help back there, she says, rounding on him. Why didn't you tell him there was nothing going on between us?

And without waiting for an answer, I need to go, she says, I need to go after him.

But the song has been turned up loud on Freya's radio, and she can't think straight. In confusion, she looks past Bren, his top lip glistening red, eyes unreadable, into the house. And then Freya's voice carries towards them, what are you all doing, out here? Her own eyes widening as she comes through the hall.

Fudge on a *cup*cake, she says, when she sees that Bren is bleeding, and Robin is gone. Nora says it's not what it looks like.

Nora decked me, Bren says, and without missing a beat, Freya says she's sure he deserved it. Come inside, she says, as the song ends, and begins again; playing, it seems, on repeat.

Nora looks back at the empty green, the bus-less road, wondering once more what is going on, here. Why they're playing the song from Jon's funeral.

Don't get blood on my rug, Bren, Freya is saying as Nora, in spite of herself, follows them inside. I came in for more Pimm's, she says, steering Bren into the kitchen, his nose tipped upwards. But I think at this point I'll crack out the whiskey.

I'm leaving, Nora says, in the doorway. I need to go after Robin.

He's a big boy, Nora, Bren says, just as Josie – who is indoors now too, has carried the stereo with her – says you can't leave! Freya is pulling old tea towels out of a drawer, passing them to Bren, and that song is playing too loudly; Nora wishes they would turn it down. What *happened*? Josie asks, seeing Bren's blood, and Freya says never mind that, Jose. Just tell them what we're here to do. It's time.

But, Josie says, I was going to explain over lunch.

Explain what? Bren says.

And maybe now isn't the right time, after all, Josie says, as if she's not heard his question. She is speaking to Freya, wide-eyed and worried. I think, she whispers, emotions are running a little too high.

Which is what you want, for an occasion like this, Freya says. All four of us in a room, at last. Everyone ready and raw.

I think it's too soon, Josie says, but Freya says twelve years too *late*, more like.

What's going on, Nora asks, feeling torn. She wants to leave, to go after Robin; wants to not be in a room with these two women and Bren and that song, stirring up something inside of her, but at the same time, she can't not know. Josie glances at her, says nothing, pet, with a fluttering hand. That they'll do it some other time.

When? Freya says. In another decade, when Bren's home again, and Nora's still not speaking to me?

Oh, don't! Josie says, wringing her hands. Bren is pale, frowning at his mother over the tea towel pressed to his nose.

Josie, Nora says. What's going on?

And it's saying her name, rather than repeating the question, that does it. That seems to root Josie in place, stop the twisting of her hands. She exhales, puts the stereo on the kitchen side, says okay. Well. As you know, this is a . . . special day, for me.

The song ends. Fades out, comes back in.

I'd planned it for a reason, Josie says, as Freya turns down the volume slightly. I'd had this idea, ever since Bren got home. Because your father *loved* Easter weekend, didn't he, she says, glancing at Bren, who is still watching his mother over his blood-soaked towel.

Better than Christmas, he used to say, didn't he? Less pressure. More sunshine.

Just as much chocolate, Freya adds.

And I thought it would be poignant, Josie says, to come together today, and put a few things . . . to rest. In his memory.

Nora is not following. Her mind is half on the bus with Robin, and not in this room. But Bren shifts in the corner, something flickering across his face as he lowers the tea towel, his nose smeared red with his own blood.

No, he says. Then repeats himself: no.

Nora sees him looking at Josie, then down at his own smart shirt; his mother's shining, patent shoes in place of her slippers. That song is still playing and Nora's brain tries hard to catch up.

It's okay, Josie tells him. It's all right, pet.

Your father died, Bren, Freya says, in the voice Nora's heard her use when talking to her tomatoes. It's time you acknowledged that, don't you think?

And then Nora understands, too. Her desire to go home – to chase after Robin – wanes slightly. As if what is happening here is weighing her down, like stones in her pockets, making it too hard to move.

I know he died, Bren says.

Do you, though, Josie says. Because you seem unable to talk about him.

Rush of air, as the wind blows. Back door banging against the wall.

I thought this could be, Josie says, gesturing at the four of them, a chance to scatter his ashes, together. Finally.

A memorial, Freya suggests.

No, Bren says again.

Sweetheart –

I didn't sign up for this, he says. It's not what I came home for.

He looks panicked; Nora sees it, the look she saw so often in childhood when they'd get out of the house, roam the fields, put time and distance between him and whatever was happening back home. A look she'd not yet seen in him, in adulthood.

But you never grieved properly, Josie pleads.

I grieved just fine, he says.

I'm with him on this, Nora says, and the other three look over at her, surprised. It's not right, she says. It's – inappropriate, she adds, in Freya's direction, but her mother holds her gaze, unashamed, as Josie says Nora, you need to –

We don't *need* to do any of this, Nora says. We had the funeral. We paid our respects.

Bren didn't, Freya says, and at this, something snaps; something Nora knows was already pulled taut, being stretched and stressed, all day, maybe ever since he got back, or for twelve years, before that, with his mum's condition and his father's death and his own suppressed, fearful young heart.

You think I *didn't*? he says. You think I don't think about him, every single day? You think I need to be *here* to know he fucking died? I was there! I was fucking *there*, in that driveway, when it happened!

Bren –

None of you were! None of you saw it! None of you have to play it over and over, how he fell down and puked, all over himself, the way he looked at me like he wanted me to – to help him!

Oh, Bren, Josie says, her face crumpling, but he goes on, he is ranting now, has stopped bleeding from the nose and it's like the words are outpouring, instead, hot and red and gushing.

I had to catch him, *I* had to turn him over, and *I* couldn't make it okay, Bren says, because *he* was the one that made things okay! When things never were! You were too sick! Too scared, too fucking scary! But *he* was there, he said he would *always* be there, and then he wasn't, and I – and I –

Nora watches him, as he melts down. Like she'd always thought he might, one day, half expecting a choked phone call or heartfelt email, except years had gone by and no such thing had arrived and now it is happening in front of her.

Josie has moved towards him, her hand outstretched. *Don't*, Bren says, backing away. Don't touch me. And don't tell me I didn't grieve, just because I didn't wear a suit and tie and sing a fucking hymn. Don't tell me I didn't know how it felt, to lose him.

His tears, now. Nora hears them, through her own.

Bren –

But then he's throwing the bloodied towel on the floor and

brushing past her into the hall, out the porch doors. Footsteps receding. Wind chimes colliding and the Bruce Springsteen song still playing from the speakers, from the funeral, from all the good times in Jon's life, comin' to an end.

The three women are left stunned and staring. And Nora looks at the two mothers, not knowing what to do, and can think only: what would Robin do, here.

I'll go, she says. And Josie nods, and Freya does, too, and Nora doesn't know what she'll do or say but she knows she has to do it, as she crunches down the driveway after his red hair and black shirt and fast-moving feet, and it is him she follows past the parked cars, past the spot where his dad's heart gave out, him she grabs by the sleeve because in this moment he needs her, and she cannot feel what is happening, elsewhere, even though something is, the one thing you aren't worried about is the one thing that matters most and this will haunt her, for the rest of her days, but for now she is catching up to Bren and she is saying his name, and he's saying no, he is saying no no no.

It's okay, she says, shushing him; it's okay.

And she does all she can think to and folds herself around him. She thinks he might pull away but instead he puts his head on her shoulder and it feels heavy and fragile, like a paperweight, and she cradles it in her hands.

They cling to each other on the green, like that. Like yin and yang. And it is so tragic and so sad and so late for this, and it is one of those moments in life that feels like it's not actually happening and yet here they are, here is the grief she knew would come for him, in the end; and here she is, holding him the way she knew she would want to, when it did.

eighteen

The gannets are the ones you want to watch, Josie told you, over the tomato salad and the bread, after the argument that wasn't quite an argument that felt too bright, like the sunlight through the cloud, neon-white, hard to look at.

The way they dive like silver arrows into the water, she said. It's mesmerising.

She looked like she enjoyed saying that word. Used her hands, to show the movement. You'd not brought your camera to the Easter lunch, but you'd wished you had, in that moment.

I've seen them, once, in real life, Josie said.

In real life, you repeated, which was a gentle joke she did not get, because when else is life not real?

And you are thinking about this on the train home, after the bus, which was a blur, a hot shady discoloured blur before the railway station, a non-place, a term you'd discussed with Nora on your fifth or sixth date but was it a date when you were in each other's pockets, by then, sharing a toothbrush holder, a bedside water glass, spending hours in bed when you should've been in the studio or the darkroom or the lectures you missed by accident because you lose all sense of time and duty and daylight when you are with her, when you were with her, which you're not any more, you don't think.

A non-place. You remember the term, vaguely, from an art seminar, as you get off the carriage. Somewhere that is not your own, shared by others before and after you, rush of the trains and white noise and thunder of metal on tracks. Generic places like bus depots and hospital rooms and airports which remain faceless, alienating, no matter who you are, what you've done, *what have you done*, you wonder, as you move through the motions, the memories, streets and alleyways and dead ends with graffiti on the pavement until you're home with the wrong keys in your hands

you ring Goose

you tell him

something's not

nineteen

They sit on the swings before the rain comes in. It is forecast for later that evening, but for now it is fresh and bright, their shoes scuffing on the asphalt. Nora in sandals, Bren in the only shoes that aren't his hiking boots: approach shoes, he'd called them. And this, she thinks, is what they've been approaching this whole time.

I don't want to do it, Bren says.

She stays quiet, at first, a swallow flying over their heads. Then she tells him he doesn't have to. But you think I should? he asks her.

I think it should have been talked about, first, rather than thrust upon you like that, she says. I also think that conversation should stay private, between you and your mum. Or a therapist, even. When you're ready.

She thinks of Freya, muscling in on this whole thing. The shame of it, the gall. And she thinks of herself, too, resenting Jon. Half hating him. Unable to lay him to rest, properly, because he is not the man she had known.

Well I'm not ready, Bren says. And it's pathetic.

It's not, Nora says.

He leans back on the swing like he used to, so far his head nearly touches the ground. You can really *see* the world is a sphere, Nora, he told her once, if you do this, tip way back until you can't see anything else, no houses or pylons or pavements, just the sky, do you see? And Nora had thought, not for the first time, that he was a poet, inside; or at least might be, one day. If he could only understand what he felt, and not just say what he saw.

I can't believe he died, he says, and his voice is so hoarse, so barely there, it could be the wind.

I know, she says, and he rights himself again and says he knows she knows, that she was there, that she went to the funeral, helped with the aftermath he couldn't face and still doesn't want to because it fucking hurts, still, after all this time, nothing helps; why does it still fucking *hurt*.

Nora just looks at him, his hoop earring catching the light.

How do you know, though, she asks. That nothing helps? That talking to someone, maybe, won't help?

I just know, he says. It won't work.

I think you're just afraid that it won't, she says, and Bren says obviously, Nora! It completely terrifies me, that this is it, for me! That I'll be running towards just wanting to feel *better*, all the time, and not crazy – I feel crazy, when I think for a *single* second, so it's better not to! It's better to try and find some goddamn relief that isn't a pill or a psychiatrist, for fuck's sake! I choose *living*. I don't want to waste my life here, I don't want to *die* in a driveway, or cooped up in a cottage because I can't go out –

You are not your mother, Nora cuts in, and Bren hits his forehead, repeatedly, with one fist. Hey, she says, and she gets off the swing, takes his hand in her left; lifts his chin with her right.

You told me that most people overthink things, she says. When it's better to just jump.

That's different, he says, and when she asks why, he says because that's about something that is going to happen. But this has happened, already. It's done.

But everything is always happening, Nora says. How you *feel* is happening. How you want to be, in this life that you're so desperate to live, Bren, that's happening.

That's just art school talk, he says, but he doesn't pull away. Keeps his chin in her hand, regret, she thinks, in his eyes; an apology, even. Love. As real as his jaw in her palm, which she feels for him, too, and which no longer frightens her.

The past matters, she says, thinking back to Robin's notebook. The things he'd paid attention to that she'd lost sight of, when things got hazy. And she's going to go on to say that you can't deal with the present – or the future – unless you let the past in, but Bren speaks first, says he knows she loved him too. His dad.

And at this, Nora takes her hands back. She'd not been thinking of Jon.

I know he was a . . . great dad, to you, she says, all the same. Looking up at the swallows on the telegraph wire. Three of them, preening, with their long-split tails.

But he wasn't a hero, she goes on. He was just human. You don't need him, Bren, for the world to keep turning. And *you're* just human, too. You couldn't have done anything to help him.

You don't know that, Bren says.

Well, either way, you can't change it, Nora says, or how you feel about it. And you can't just force it away, either. You can try and avoid it for another twelve years, if you want. But I'm not sure that ever works out.

Bren pushes the air out of his nose, like he still doesn't agree.

You said you choose living, she says, and he looks away from her now, towards the farmers' fields. But being afraid is a part of being alive, Bren.

She waits for him to say that she's right. To stand and hug her, the way she'd hugged him, not half an hour ago, to be the person she knows is inside, the one she's always defended and cared about in spite of his sporadic contact and questionable decisions.

Baby steps, she says. Talk to someone. Or just talk about *him*. Use his name.

I can't, is all he says.

And Nora nods. All the windows and trapdoors of her flung wide open, letting something in, while something else rushes out.

–

Josie is waiting for her when she crunches up the driveway. Is he all right, she asks, shivering, the light lost now, blue shadows spread on the lawn. Her anorak is wrapped around her like a dressing gown, her face drawn with worry.

He's . . . emotional, Nora says. He's gone for a walk.

Josie nods, and Nora stands with her, not knowing what to say. *Why spring it on him, like that. Surely you could see he's not ready.* But she doesn't want to make Josie feel worse than she already does, so she pulls out her phone to text Robin, as a reflex, only to find – strange – three missed calls from his brother.

He's going to leave again, isn't he, Josie says, and Nora looks up at her. She's staring at the green, at the swing set standing empty.

I think so, Nora nods. I'm sorry.

Don't be, Josie says. I knew he would. Once you were married, or we'd . . . done what I'd planned.

You'd really planned it, all this time?

Well, yes. As soon as I realised how resistant he was, still. I thought it might help . . . dislodge some things, for him. For all of us.

Josie takes her eyes from the green and instead rests them on Nora.

Clearly Bren isn't ready for that, she says. But you are, I think.

Except Nora cannot bear the thought of scattering Jon's ashes, now, after everything, and she has her phone in her hand with the missed calls from Goose, so she says I actually need to get back to Robin, now, Jose. I was just going to call him, and as she says it, her phone actually rings, and it is Goose again, so she turns her back on Josie to answer.

Nora? he says, and his voice crackles with the sparse signal. Yes, she says, and he asks her, straight out, what the hell is wrong with my brother?

Panic, again, just like when Robin left. Heart jacked up, nausea. She wants to go and lie down, or run a mile. Either, she thinks, would be better than feeling so jammed.

He's a wreck, Goose is saying, without waiting for her answer. He turned up at my flat an hour ago and shut himself in the guest room.

Can I speak to him?

He's out cold, Nora! Like he's sleeping off a hangover! What the hell happened at that lunch? Where are you?

At Freya's, still, she says, fraught. He said he was going home.

Well, he came here, instead.

I'll get on the next bus over.

I don't know if that's a good idea, Goose says. He clearly wants some space.

Then how do I *fix* it, Nora cries, desperate now, and she can feel through the phone that Goose can't deal with this; his distress softens, at the sound of her own.

Look, he says. Let him sleep on it. I'm sure it's recoverable.

Nora clutches the phone to her ear, hoping he's right.

Will you tell him I love him, please? That this was all just a – really big – misunderstanding?

Goose is quiet, then. Bad line, bad feeling.

Was it, though, he asks. He told me about the venue.

I know, but –

I think he's sick with stress, Nora. I've never seen him like this.

Then let me talk to him!

I'll keep him here overnight, he says, but send him home for breakfast. If he'll listen to me. I hate saying this, man, he says, and Nora is crying now, silently, as he says but if you love him like you say you do? I think you need to do some serious damage control, here.

I know that, Nora thinks. That's the *plan*. But she can't explain it to Goose, first, before she can explain it to Robin himself.

Just tell him I'll be waiting, Nora says. First thing, at our flat?

But the line is crackling again, and he's saying more things when the call cuts out and Josie is left saying her name.

Is everything all right, she asks, tentative, and then it is Nora's turn to break in this driveway, with Josie's twig-like arms around her as she rocks her back and forth before ushering her inside, saying what a *day*, Nora, good grief. What a day.

–

She checks her phone while Josie makes tea. Sends a text to Robin, tries to call him, leaves a voicemail. *I love you, I'm sorry, I'll set everything straight, I promise.* The rain has started to fall now, taps on the window while Josie slices cake, carries it to the dining room on two patterned plates.

It's not the roast lamb we were hoping for, I'm afraid, she says, still in her anorak. She leaves the room to hang it up, comes back again. Nora sits, watching it all, her world spinning slowly. Her phone, blank. Cake forks, two teacups. The black urn of Jon on the bookshelf, watching her back.

I texted your mother, Josie says, as she pours the tea, but she wanted to be with her tomatoes.

Her hands are shaking, slightly, as she says it.

Nora says fine. Eats a corner of cake. Says it's good, thank you, and Josie says please don't thank me, Nora, not today. Nothing has gone as I'd hoped.

I know the feeling, Nora says.

Josie looks at her with sympathy, her blue eyes like live wires, but Nora doesn't want it. She just wants to get herself home; thinks about calling a taxi, now the buses have stopped running. But Josie's hand is still shaking as she pours the milk, so Nora tries to focus: asks if she's all right.

Oh, yes, pet. I've been all right for a long time now. No scares, with the tablets. No episodes.

But I mean right now, Nora says. You seem.

She nods at Josie's tremor, as she drops a sugar cube into her cup.

Ah, Josie says, well. I suppose I am a little nervous.

Okay, Nora says.

I've been wanting to talk to you, Nora, for a while. See, today wasn't just a day to lay Jon to rest, physically. But in other ways too.

The grandfather clock thunks from side to side. The rain patters on the window. Nora tells her this is all very cryptic.

It is, isn't it, Josie says, as she stirs her tea. I hoped your mother would be here, to help, but she . . . decided against it, in the end. She'd never shy away from confrontation, our Freya, but sentimentality? She'd rather scoop out her ovaries with a spoon, I believe, was the phrasing she used.

This lands, but neither of them laugh. Josie sighs.

I hate to see you hurting, Nora, she says. Just like I hate to see my Bren hurting.

Nora takes a sugar cube for her own cup.

You're the only one he'd come back for, Josie says. I always knew that. You were such a pair. Full of fun and adventure and *spirit*. It was nice to see, after he'd always been so reserved, always so . . . lonesome. It brought me a lot of joy. You and your mother both did, when we moved here.

Tea spinning, heady, in her teacup.

But I always knew he'd leave, Josie says. I knew he'd have to spread his wings, away from me, and my . . . limitations. And his dad encouraged it, bought him an atlas before he even knew the alphabet. I'm proud of him, Nora, for being so brave. I'm proud that his less-than-ideal childhood made him bolder, if anything, and not a mouse, like me.

Nora does not respond, because she thinks she knows what Josie is getting at. That Bren was always going to come home to her. Because Nora is his home. That she thinks Nora knows it, too, deep down.

But instead she says, I know it's not conventional, having a son who spends his life elsewhere, like he does. But I'm not saddened by it, or resentful. I'm just happy I get to love him, wherever he is.

Josie looks out of the window, at the rain.

And anyway, she says, I rather think convention is overrated.

Nora forks off another corner of cake.

Freya's rubbed off on you there, she says, and Josie looks at her over the table and says ah, no. See, that's the thing, my love. That's what I wanted to talk to you about. If anything, I think I rubbed off on her.

Josie rests her hands on the polished wood table, then. A table where Nora learned to crochet, has drunk tea and dunked biscuits, talked about sparrows and storms, fruit crumble and funerals, spilled milk and psychosis and paint colours. It all seems to weigh between them, the years, the minutes, the knowledge of what is and what isn't, and the moment is long and loaded. Clunk of the grandfather clock, smatter of rain.

I know, you know, Josie says.

You know what, says Nora.

I know about Freya and Jon.

Another moment, then. Shorter than before. A moment where Nora thinks she must have misheard, so she reddens, clears her throat.

I actually suggested it, Josie says, and Nora coughs on some cake crumbs so that Josie has to stand up, pour her a glass of water from the crystal jug on the side. Flush of pink up her own throat.

Don't say anything yet, Josie says, handing her the glass. Please, pet, just listen.

But Nora couldn't speak, even if she wanted to.

You know I'm on a lot of medication, Josie begins, after she sits back down in her chair. A very high dose, for a lot of things I won't go into. Embarrassing, really.

Nora shakes her head, still wordless.

And one of the side effects, when they upped my dose after Bren was born, was a lack of, shall we say . . . enthusiasm.

Josie lowers her eyes to the doily beneath her teacup. Smooths it down with her hands.

For a lot of things, she goes on. A lot of my old interests. Wanting to go places, hike up hills, run the charity bake sales, all of it. I became a hermit, as Jon affectionately coined it, but a happy one. The voices quietened. The crying did, too. Mostly. And being content at home was easier than leaving the house, because if I did, that's when things got hard. But I also struggled to. Um.

Josie is fiddling now with a button on her cardigan.

Show any interest in the romantic dealings one might have with one's husband, she says, colour patching on her neck. Even if one loved that husband very much. And he loved her back, till his dying day. A day that, as you know, came too soon.

Nora stares at her.

Josie touches her collar, as if too hot.

We tried a few things, but it was no use. After it had been a very long time, with no signs of improvement – Bren was young, but not so young that we didn't have any opportunity to . . . well. I'd been reading up about this new medication they'd put me on, you see. And I saw something on daytime television. One of these chat shows with all the shouting and the drama but it's all very human, really, when you get to the root of the thing.

She waits for a response, here, but Nora's face has gone numb.

I thought about it. A lot. And then I suggested he get his needs met, elsewhere. It really was fine with me. I worried our marriage might not survive, otherwise. We were both so young, still. It might have, of course. Jon said he didn't need to . . . well. But I would rather it was out in the open, than he be driven to . . . betrayal.

Nora can't help it. She is blushing more deeply now, mainly because Josie is, and there is not enough cake or water to busy herself with, so she has to simply sit and let the pieces slot into place in her mind; has to look at Josie touching her neck again, her wedding ring still on her left hand.

We said nothing more about it for years, Josie says. He left the military and we moved here, as you know. Bren was at his new school, and Jon was scratching around in that shed of his, doing odd jobs for the neighbours, laying down Freya's decking, and the two of them just . . . hit it off, I suppose. Hard not to, when she is who she is. So bright, and brilliant. And *funny*. Gosh, she made him laugh. Made us both laugh, in fact. So we . . . revisited the situation.

Nora's numbness is receding. Now it feels as if the walls

might close in, like in the video game Bren used to play in the next room, crushing the cartoon on screen unless you could figure out the right set of moves.

You . . . planned it? she manages.

Planned is a strong term, Josie says, with a small smile. There wasn't any organisation involved. No guidebooks, or Post-it notes.

Nora blinks, and Josie smiles wider, says remember? You and Bren were so into your Post-it notes, when you were planning your trip. Orange for him, green for you. Blue for maybes. You had a lot of maybes.

Then she says sorry, she's getting off topic. And she has wondered whether she should've explained, over the years. When the best time might have been, to do that.

Freya and I have talked about it, of course, Josie says, shrugging her birdlike shoulders, but it always felt a bit irrelevant, pet. It wouldn't have been right, when you were young. You and Bren were such good friends, too. We didn't want to make anything . . .

Weird, Nora says.

I see the irony, Josie admits. I know it's messy, Nora. Except it didn't really feel that way, to us. Freya was so . . . Freya. We assumed she'd be open to something . . . unusual.

If Nora could snort right now, she would, but instead she just sits there, red-faced. Cake abandoned on her plate.

This is uncomfortable, Josie says, isn't it.

No, Nora says. Well, yes. But I'm more. Just. Baffled.

Josie laughs at this, and there is a flicker, in Nora's mind, at how Robin would have laughed at that adjective, too.

I would've been, as well, Josie admits. If it hadn't been my idea.

So Freya agreed? Nora says. To this . . . set-up?

Not at first, Josie says, and she picks up her fork, finally eats some of her own cake. There was chemistry there, and so once we'd decided as a couple, Jon went to her, one day. In her greenhouse. She wanted to talk to me separately, afterwards, to be sure it was all legitimate. It was, to this day, the strangest conversation I've ever had.

Stranger than this? Nora says, and Josie nods.

And then things happened, Josie says. Organically, after that. I didn't want to know the details, so they were always discreet, but it was all above board, shall we say. It was an uncommon but remarkable thing, Nora. What it brought us, as a three. Such closeness. Such an understanding, between friends.

Nora swallows, can't even imagine.

But she tries. Her mind opening, a little. Letting in a sliver of light.

Freya and I became even closer after Jon died, Josie says. Because of this private history between us, I suspect, which we never planned to share with anyone. Until we found out you already knew.

Josie sits up straighter in her chair.

I wanted to intervene weeks ago, she says, when you told Freya what you'd seen. That you'd been carrying that, all these years! Oh, Nora, we wanted to sit you down right then, but you were so determined to stay away from her – and I didn't know how I'd broach it, alone, with Bren in the house. This isn't something he could stomach, I don't think. Not with everything else still so – raw, for him.

No, Nora says.

Maybe I'll tell him someday, Josie muses. When he's more settled, or made his peace with his past. Though I have wondered, over the last few weeks, if you'd told him yourself.

But Nora shakes her head.

Never. I was so . . . ashamed, she says, and her voice sounds strange to her own ears; muffled, like she's underwater. I didn't know what to do. And I was so sure that something like that would make things worse for you, Josie, and I knew you were – she is going to say fragile, or unstable, but she knows it is wrong to say such things, so instead she says I didn't want to break your heart. Or Bren's. And I was trying to figure out what to do, confront Freya, or him, and then soon after I saw them together, like that, he died.

Josie looks bereft.

I never raised it with Freya because I just wanted to forget it. The whole thing. But I was so *angry* with them, Nora whispers, and he *died*, like that, with me angry at him –

And her voice catches, and splits. The full revelation crashing over her, like a wave.

I've been *so* angry with him, Nora says, for so long. I sat through his funeral and thought about karma and couldn't say a nice word about him, and I was glad, in a way, that Bren was gone, because I couldn't face him, I – I didn't know how to be around him, with this huge, awful *thing* –

And there are not tears, now, just dry sobs through the shock of it as Josie reaches over and takes both her hands and does not say another word. Just squeezes Nora's palms in her own. So tiny, but with such assuredness. Such control Nora had never conceived of.

They hold hands across the table, like that; as the wave settles, retreats.

And when Josie lets go, it is like Nora can breathe again. Like she can float, if not quite swim; just lie back, and look at the vast open sky. Josie somehow pours more tea, they somehow finish their cake, and then they talk because Nora has questions, and Josie, it seems, wants to provide answers. She talks with a fervour Nora has only seen in her when she's talking about koala bears or seabirds or the settings on her bread machine. About the past, their shared barbecues, Christmas dinner, Easter weekend. Jon's love of bobble hats and Guinness and gravy, and his laugh, so hoarse when it first came on, he sounded like Muttley the dog; Josie asks who; Nora shows her a clip from *Wacky Races* on her phone; none of this is normal, Nora muses, and yet when did life ever promise normality; when did she ever want that, even, or expect it, being raised by a woman like Freya.

She feels calmer as the hours wear on.

On the wall, clear evening light, like water. Like she could drink it down.

She could have tried harder to tell me, Nora says, when they have drained the teapot. Freya, I mean. These last few weeks.

I'm not sure she really wanted to, Josie says. Think of it from her side. All those years of strong, independent womanhood. Warning you against weddings and rom-coms, banning you from watching Disney, and then she went and fell in love with a man, in spite of herself. Or at least, she thinks she did. And pride is a prickly thing, pet. For all of us. Her softer side is not one she is used to sharing.

Nora nods. Knowing, too, that on some level, if Freya had told her – broken down her door, forced her to listen – she wouldn't have believed her, anyway. It had to be like this; had to come from Josie.

And, she asks her, you really won't tell Bren?

For the same reason you didn't, Josie says. I'd hoped to find a quiet moment to tell you all this, without him, and Nora nods; understands.

But something is sticking to her, like a burr. What do you mean, she says, Freya only *thinks* she was in love with Jon?

Josie, who was reaching for Nora's teacup, shrugs with one slender shoulder. Like Bren. Because she wasn't, she says.

How do you –

I just know, she says, and for the first time, there is an edge to her voice, but maybe Nora imagined it, because she is as softly spoken as ever when she goes on. Now, I'm hardly going to correct her on that, pet. She was devastated when he died. Shocked at herself, I think, by how attached she'd become. But Jon and I?

Josie looks towards the urn, as if he's sitting in his armchair, listening.

We were *partners*. We said vows. We shared a bed, we had a child, we stuck by each other in my sickness and his health and made it work, because we talked, and adapted, made it through what might have seemed, to so many, like dead ends. I know I'm not the brightest button, Nora. I'm not smart or savvy or brave. But I am wise when it comes to this. Being married to someone is something I understand. It's sharing the good and the bad, your innermost doubts, as well as your certainties. It's not just lust, or passion.

That last word seems deliberate. Lands, like the first flake of snow.

It's microwaving a curry when one of you is too tired to cook, Josie says, her voice earnest. It's folding their underpants, or doing the shopping, getting their favourite pasta sauce, even if you don't like it. It's stacking the dishwasher together at night, and emptying it in the morning. It's being bored by, and besotted with, the person you chose. And it is a choice, Nora, not just a *feeling*. It's hundreds of tiny choices that say yes, we are in something, together. Even when it's hard, or unglamorous. But, my god, it's yours. Ours.

Nora looks at Josie across the table.

Her mother's best friend. Her best friend's mother.

I didn't want to tell you all this just so you'll forgive Freya and Jon, Josie says. But so you can see that your *own* life should be shared with the one you are most yourself with,

Nora. The one you can talk to about uncomfortable things. The one who stands by you. Who doesn't question who you are, or the tiny choices you make.

Nora holds herself completely still, at these words.

Says she knows.

But do you? Josie says. Because I've watched you wavering, these past few months – and she sounds sheepish, like she doesn't want to overstep, but really, Nora thinks, there are no lines left to cross between them. Not sending out wedding invites? Not buying a dress, Bren said? Rethinking what it is that you want?

Thud of Nora's heart, in time with the grandfather clock.

Ideas of what you want, though, Josie goes on, are often just that. Ideas. Notions. Freya *thinks* she fell in love with my Jon. But sharing a life with someone, Nora; that's what's real. Do you see?

And Nora does. Did, already. To prove it, she takes her phone from the table, opens up what she has not yet shown to anyone and hands it over. And Josie looks down and frowns, and for a moment Nora worries she's got this all wrong, that in fact Josie was pleading with her to choose her son, but then she looks up and smiles, and it is steady and relieved and understanding. Because this woman, Nora knows now, understands more than she'd ever given her credit for.

Oh, Nora, she says.

And Nora is going to respond but then there is the sound of a key in a lock, and Bren is calling out to his mother and the smell of recent rain is flooding in, fresh, from the open front door.

–

Mum, he calls, from the hallway, which is a name he has not said out loud for at least twelve years. His black shirt is soaked through. The shower came on suddenly, would've left him cold if he'd not been walking so fast, and then the downpour cleared and the sunset was luminous, blasting away all the dark. Which is what often happens, after a storm abroad. Everything shifting so suddenly, you get a glimpse of something through the weather you'd thought had set in.

But you don't decide these things, he thought, as he walked around in the lifting rain. You are who you are, you can't change that, just like you can't control bad weather. But then, he figured, as the sun set, that doesn't mean the view is not there, behind the cloud – something to see, or to reach for. And what if he *wanted* to be someone who reached for the good things, instead of running from the bad? What if he *could* decide to do things another way?

What if he jumped?

Home, then, his wet shoes on the carpet as he calls her name; as he hears his mother rise from her chair. Making her way to the hall, where he is standing beside the photograph of his father that she never took down. And why would she, when feeling – remembering – is a part of keeping him close; means, he's realised, you don't have to let go.

Josie stops, like the rain, when she sees him. She looks worn out, and Bren is cold now he's stopped moving but also burning with resolve, and he can't take another moment to peer over the edge and he is sweating and breathless and then he sees Nora, too, with her wide eyes and flushed cheeks and something softer about her jaw.

His mother goes to speak, but he gets there first.

Why didn't you do it before, he asks her. Scatter his ashes, after the funeral?

He tips his head in the direction of the urn on the bookshelf; the urn he's pretended not to see for weeks. And Josie tugs down her cardigan a little, as if in preparation for something.

Still in her summer dress and beige tights, her velvet slippers, the brooch his father bought her twinkling from her chest.

Nora is looking at him too, a few steps behind, but for once he is not looking at her as his mother lifts her chin and stares straight at him with her clear blue eyes.

Oh, Bren, she says, isn't it obvious? I was waiting for you.

–

The garden at sunset is quiet and cast in shadow. Light touching the tops of the trees that line the river as it flows, as it always has, behind the old oak. Its trunk in the back of Freya's; branches swung low into Josie's. Jon's shed. Freya's greenhouse. Long grass, rose bushes, thorns and trellis and overgrown nettles.

Nora stands on the lawn with Bren while Josie unlatches the gate, goes next door and brings Freya through. She has changed into her artist's smock – something oversized she wears to bed – and this is the first time Nora sees her, since she's learned the truth. Feet in her gardening shoes. Wild hair curly-wet, post-shower. She feels an onrush of something that moves her even more than what they're about to do, but she holds back, knowing that now is not the moment to reach out to her mother. To say she understands.

Josie goes back inside for her husband and the three others stand in silence while they wait. New buds on the trees. Sweet smell, after rain. Nora lets it all fill her. The relief of it, how she can mourn without the shame and the secret that had tainted her family and the man they'd all loved. A man who was Bren's father, Josie's husband, Freya's lover, everything to all of them – even though, as she's learned, nobody can ever be one person's entirely.

And then Josie is there with the urn in her hands and the

four of them move towards the base of the oak, and the soil is dark and damp from the rainfall and it reminds Bren of the ocean, spreading on sand; he will tell her that later. Not now, though.

For this moment is not about them.

Josie lifts the lid – or at least, tries to, but it is screwed too tight, so Bren does it for her. Nora sees him keep the lid in his hand.

I feel like we should say something, Josie says. I don't know what, though. Everything we said at the funeral was so . . .

Macabre, Freya nods.

And I feel like this isn't, Josie says. I feel like this is how it was meant to be.

She glances at Bren, who is focused on the roots in the earth.

No words could do him justice anyway, he says.

It is dusk, now, the sunset gone. Stratus cloud, fade of blue. No headstone. No music. Just them, in the place that Jon was, and is, with the grass and the river and the trees as they each take fistfuls of the man who was theirs and scatter him onto the soil and there is so much of him, so much more than they expected, it is sort of funny, after a while; eventually they pour the sand of him into the grass, Jesus, Bren says, he wasn't even a big guy, how is this possible.

And despite the humour and the sweet smell of spring, Josie weeps. Freya puts an arm around her, and Nora, in a leap of love and truth clasps her mother's hand and lets her tears fall, too; Freya looks at her, astonished, but clasps it back. Bren, though, does not cry, or reach for a hand. All he does is touch his elbow, lightly, to Nora's.

Tilts his head back, looks at the sky.

twenty

Bren stares at the stars that are out. The ones he can see, at least.

It is a hazy night, for near-May; summer come early, before it recedes again, not quite ready. He is aware this is the first time in years that he has stood completely still. That stillness, while difficult for him, probably is for most people.

It's why Nora sews, he thinks, and crochets, and draws, and cooks. Why his mother bakes and cleans and waters her plants, why Freya forages for mushrooms and changes the sheets of dying people and why his dad had a tool shed and a never-ending list of odd jobs, fixing fences, playing cricket and bagging Munros and it is not just him, it is everyone, everyone needs to keep busy and moving to fill up their days, or rather, the emptiest parts of themselves.

He can hear the water running through the household pipes as someone – Freya, or his mother, maybe – brushes their teeth. Then the upstairs lights flick off and the garden is plunged into the starlit dark. Slight glow from indoors, haze of light pollution above the treeline. One more look at the stars, stitched into the sky like the sequins in Nora's dress, before he goes inside.

She has not left yet. Freya returned next door and his mother has retired to bed, so it is just the two of them in the lamplit kitchen. She says she'll make tea but then – screw it – gets his dad's whiskey from under the sink. Something decent, a fifteen-year-old smoky something that his mother stirs into her baking, apparently, which is sort of heinous, Nora says, when it should be drunk neat. The way his dad used to drink it.

Bren does not go near the stuff for this very reason, but tonight, he concedes. Watches her pour it into two crystal tumblers before he takes them through to his old games room. And while Nora does follow, she lingers in the doorway. Says she'll stay for one, but then she should.

Go, she does not say. Does not need to.

Which is her way, Bren thinks, of letting him know she has a life to get back to, outside of all this. That she needs to get back to Robin, which deep down, he knows.

Please stay, he says, all the same.

And the buses have stopped running and the taxi would cost a bomb and she seems to mull that over, and perhaps because of this – or because he has asked her for something, straight out – or simply because of the day they have had, she doesn't argue. Sits beside him, takes her whiskey. Folds her legs beneath her.

Mad day, she says, taking a mouthful. Bren sips his too, and winces; it's like drinking lighter fluid. He forces it down. Absorbs the moment. There is a painting on the wall that Nora made him, years ago. Abstract reds and yellows, which make him think of smashed fruit, the tunnels of a heart.

D'you remember that poem, he says to her, as he looks at it. The one you read to me once, on the school bus, about figs?

Sylvia Plath, Nora nods. But it wasn't a poem.

I thought Plath was a poet?

She was. But she wrote a novel, too; *The Bell Jar.* The figs are from that.

Well, whatever it was, Bren says, it stayed with me. That idea of life, branching out, all of the fruit hanging there for the taking. But when you picked one fig, all the others would wither and die.

Nora nods again. Says yeah.

Bren feels the warmth of her, beside him. The heat. After all this time, still. After everything, today. Which is why he needs to go there.

I was going to tell you something, earlier, he says, still looking at her painting. They are not touching. And what would she do if they were; if he tilted her chin in his hand, like she did with him on the swings, a lifetime ago.

I'm not going to say it, now, he tells her, when he feels her tense at his words. But, and he clears his throat, drinks more whiskey, likes it better, this time round. All that I said, in my bedroom? That was . . . wrong of me. You never *hung on to* me. Or if you did, I . . . wanted you to. So I didn't mean it, and I'm sorry, Nora. I lashed out.

Nora makes a small, acknowledging noise. Sinks lower into the sofa bed, which is so comfortable, Bren thinks; like it's still moulded to their bodies, him here, her there; chocolate stains on the cushions from their many shared packets of Minstrels.

I really did buy you a plane ticket, he says. I wasn't joking, about that.

Seriously?

Yeah. For the both of us, back to Queenstown.

She thinks she'll tell him he's deluded; laugh at him, or worse, look like she feels sorry for him, all over again. But instead she sips more whiskey, keeps it in her mouth, before swallowing, then says, did you ever do that personality test? With the cube and the horse and the ladder? And when Bren shakes his head, she says okay, and shifts on the sofa to face him.

Picture a room, she says, any room.

This room?

Any room. Don't be difficult.

I'm not!

Inside that room is a cube, Nora says. Can you describe that cube to me, please? Whatever comes to mind.

So Bren does, after a moment. Sort of fish-tank sized, the kind you might get in the middle of a Chinese restaurant. And it's opaque, made of concrete. Nora nods. Small, approving lift of her lip.

Next, she says, picture a ladder. Where is it, in the room, what does it look like?

He tells her.

And then a horse, she says, and once again he obliges. There's more, Nora says, the weather outside, and something about a storm, but I don't remember what those bits mean. We'd have to google it.

What do the first bits mean, then?

The size of the cube is your ego, Nora says, breaking into a proper smile as she taps into her phone anyway, to check. And the cube's colour shows your true nature. Concrete? Impenetrable, I'd say. Hard to understand, or get through to.

I hate this game, Bren says, and Nora laughs, and it is his favourite sound, still, he realises. Drinks more whiskey.

The ladder represents your ambition, Nora goes on. You said yours was tall, and also far away, on the back wall, which I think means your goals are . . . lofty. Unattainable, maybe, or at least kind of hard to pin down.

I'm sensing a theme, Bren says.

But the important thing, here, Nora says, is the horse.

Okay?

The horse embodies your ideal partner, Nora says, and she

keeps her voice serene, even though she begins to blush, as ever. Scrolls on her phone, not looking at him.

My horse is dark brown, she says. And it's usually lying down in the room, kind of grazing, even though there's no grass.

Which means you're attracted to lazy gluttons?

Which *means*, she says, reading from her phone: I prize comfort and reliability above all else, and my ideal partner is calm and fully committed.

Silence, then.

Burn, Bren says.

No arguing with that, is there, Nora says, and she is keeping things light, as usual, they have always played and teased and jibed and not gone there with any real sincerity even though she is the most sincere of things to him, the only permanent fixture he has held on to and he never realised it or told her so he says, without dithering, that doesn't change things, for me.

Nora lowers her phone then. Looking sad but certain, and for once, not scared.

And I hear what you're saying, Nora, I do, Bren says. But sometimes I think, if we'd dated, you and me? Then we'd never have stopped.

He feels as if he has taken his heart from behind his ribcage and rolled it towards her.

Whether we're an ideal match or not, he says, we'd have gone all the way. Wouldn't we.

Another roll, of his marble heart.

And Nora breathes out. A sigh that travels through her.

I don't know, she says. But then: I'd have liked to.

Her voice, so quiet.

But we didn't, she says. Even if I'd got your message, and joined you out there, Bren, I never wanted to travel the world forever. I'm a home body. I like to be rooted. You like to be . . . free.

I wonder if you can be both, Bren says, and Nora says she wonders that, too. They face each other for a long moment, after this. Motionless. Bren, for once, not wanting to move. Then he says, for the record, Nora? He's a really good guy. Robin, I mean. I . . . want to be happy, for you both.

I don't need you to be, she says, as she tips the whiskey side to side in her glass. I thought I did, but I don't. You're. We're – small shrug, palm out – what we are. Whatever that is; it's hard to define. But I actually think that's okay. After all I've learned, recently.

Bren doesn't know what she means exactly, but he's so tired, so drained, so sort-of-not-drunk-but-wanting-to-be, he doesn't ask. Forces himself to sit with the pulsing in his hands and feet. They have scattered his father's ashes today, and with it, he has decided to accept more than one thing: he knows Nora is going to marry Robin. And yet, there is still something he needs to make clear.

Nora, he says.

Bren, she says back, half serious.

He peers over the edge. Thinks about the years below them. This day, between them, like his father between his fingers. The ash of him but also the matter, and atoms, the straw of his hair, paler than Bren's, his voice he can hear if he tries to, calling him and Nora inside after dark, come on, you two, it's time.

What I wanted to tell you is not right to tell you, now, he reiterates. And he feels like he's bungee-ing off a bridge as he says it – body falling in slow motion, like he's not really doing it, because why would you, why throw yourself off a ledge when it goes against all your instincts but you do, people do.

But I want you to know, he says, even if I don't say it. Because how you *think* I might feel, about you, Nora? I do.

Beat of his heart, in his chest.

Slower, steadier, than he'd expected.

I was just . . . scared, I think. Of feeling that way. Because that's when things hurt the most, so I guess I figured it was better not to. And I'm not asking for it back, I know you've made a choice, you've got your life. But I do. Feel that way. And I just . . . thought you should know.

He expects Nora will blush harder, or chastise him for his terrible timing; elbow him in the nose on purpose, this time. But instead, she sighs again.

You're an idiot, Bren Ferguson.

Your idiot? he says, and she smacks him on the arm, and they laugh, and they're still them; everything light and heady like the whiskey in their blood or the wind rushing past as he sails through the air on the bungee cord that did not break. And when they've been quiet for a long while, Nora no longer laughing but resting against his shoulder, he says her name, in a low voice. Nora.

Hm?

Won't you always . . . wonder about us?

Stillness, between them. No sound.

I think, she says, slowly, we're far past wondering, Bren. Don't you?

And it seems she has nothing else to say to him, about that. Falls asleep, eventually, in an upright position, as the night lightens to dawn and Bren sits there and listens to her grinding her teeth, feels her flinch, as if she's dreaming, her face pressed against his arm.

Without waking her, he takes his phone and amends his flight as the sun comes up. Feels his world opening again, because it does that, when you have no ties, when you can react, when you make a choice to keep moving, and he gets up and heads to the bottom of the garden with the oak and his dad and the morning chorus is a din, by sunrise. He emails the Queenstown adventure centre; tells them his arrival date. Thinks, as he looks up, about how he helped him make this bird feeder, right here. Casting back to that day, the radio drifting through the kitchen window, the sandwiches they'd stopped to eat in the shade, and it all wells up inside him, love and pain both, strange, to him, how they go hand in hand. His dad. His heart. Gone, broken; still beating. And when Nora is awake he goes back inside and makes her a coffee because he hasn't noted she doesn't drink the stuff and she takes it from him and smiles, at his mum, too, in her slippers, coming downstairs. And it is over, whatever it was, whatever it never nearly became; it is done, and now he can go.

twenty-one

Nora leaves Josie's cottage to iron out her own life; hers and Robin's. To get back to him, put things right. Her mother is still asleep next door when she steps onto the driveway at six thirty, the curtains drawn. There was no right moment to say anything the night prior when it was all about Jon, and then Bren, so she tries to communicate with her now, via text, on the train home.

Josie told me, is all she can manage. And then, *I love you*, which is something they do not say. And she can see that Freya has read it due to the double ticks and must not know how to respond because there is no reply, no three waving dots, but then she sends her a single photograph, of the tomatoes in her greenhouse, red and shining.

Survived the Spotted Wilt, she tells her. *I'll make you my tomato jam*.

Which is enough for now.

Because there is time, Nora decides. An entire lifetime to say what needs saying to her mother, but for now she has something to say to someone else. Something to ask. Something to finalise, once and for all, as the train pulls into the station and terminates and her life feels like a drum roll, steady and quick-paced and building towards this next part, all change, please, all change.

—

She gets home early, like she'd promised. She'd tried to reach him that morning but his phone was still off. Out of charge, maybe, rather than because he still won't speak to her. She left him messages to explain all that had happened last night, while he'd been with Goose. And despite everything, she feels calm. Knows – hopes – that right now, the morning after, she'll be able to resolve everything.

The front door is not double locked, which surprises her; he's beaten her home. Inside, though, she is met with a distinct quiet. No radio, or sound of the shower. Slither of a morning moon as she hangs up her keys. Says Robin? to no reply.

But there he is, sleeping on the sofa, with his laptop shut on his stomach. She crosses the threshold and sits down beside him; puts her hand over his.

It's me, she says, and he stirs. I thought you were with Goose.

His eyes are still closed, and he sounds half asleep, still, like he's struggling to rouse himself. She pushes his fringe back from his forehead. Tender, and gentle.

Came home after midnight, he says. Strange dreams.

Nora nods, though he can't see her. Her thumb, calloused from her needle, caressing his own.

I'm so sorry, Robin, she says. About everything.

And at this, he opens one eye.

I'm not pulling back, she promises. I know there has been stuff . . . to explain. But it's good stuff. Not bad, secret stuff.

The silence between them is soft, like the velvet sofa beneath them. The sofa they took so long to pick out. A day in Ikea, to no avail, then the British Heart Foundation. In the end, an old furniture store closing down with *Reduced!* posters in its windows, this one, it's the one, how do you know, I just *know*, Nora, don't you?

Robin laces his long fingers through hers, in response. And it is this that tells her there will be no more fighting, this morning, which she was afraid there might have been. Would have faced into, if needed.

I promise, she says, when he has still not said anything.

How was, Robin asks, and fails, because there isn't a verb for what happened; he must have read her messages, after all, listened to her voicemails.

Scattering the ashes of my long-dead neighbour who had an affair with my mother? Nora says, and Robin, bemused, says yes; he's closed his eye again.

Revealing, she says. I've got a lot to tell you.

Robin makes a noise as if to say he's listening, but she says not now. That she has something to show him, first.

She feels her mood lift as she says it. Feels the moment she'd been putting off – because she'd wanted to savour it, make it right – gradually arrive, like the sun rising after a long night. But Robin does not move. Seems close to sleep again.

Robin, she says, and he says mm? And she's going to say what's the matter. But she knows, already; can't expect him to feel fine, after the last few weeks. The unexpected proposal, the planning and cancelling of a wedding, the adrenaline and the stress and the hurt on top of all the work and travel he's always doing, shooting on location, editing back home, new clients, old ones. Devon. Easter. Their fight in Freya's porch, after what he'd overheard. Which she can make right, if he'll let her, this minute.

So she stands up, tugs on his hand.

Robin, she says, gently. Come on.

My head, he says.

She stares down at him, at their linked hands. His shirt is unbuttoned and she can see the snail trail of dark hair from his belly button, disappearing beneath the band of his jeans. You've still got a headache?

Really bad, he says.

Have you taken some painkillers, she says, to which he says yes, and before she can ask, he's been eating dry toast, too, and sipping water. Which is what they do when they feel unwell; pop some pills, eat some toast, and it has always worked for them.

What I've got to show you will perk you up, she says, and he hears the promise in her voice, then; finally opens both eyes.

Should we talk, he says, after they have looked steadily at one another for several seconds. About what happened yesterday, with Bren?

Yes, Nora says. But afterwards. Please.

So he agrees, wordlessly. Lets her keep his hand in hers, lets her pull him up from the sofa and lead him out of the living room and through the kitchen out the back door, up the concrete steps into the yard. Towards the shed which was meant to be his makeshift darkroom or her sewing studio which they never got around to converting; just sits there, spiderwebbed, rotting with rain. Apple crates piled by the door, which they'd pilfered from supermarkets when they'd first moved in. Some women have a lot of shoes, Robin said, as they carted her stuff from the moving van. You, Nora Harper, have a lot of yarn.

And now, she pushes open the door, ducks inside, and Robin follows. He is so tall he has to stoop, which disorientates him, says he must be dehydr –

But then he sees what she has brought him here to see, what is suspended in the centre of the shed on a wire hanger, covered in a sheet.

What is this, Robin asks her.

It's my wedding dress, Nora says.

Your . . .?

I couldn't find one that felt quite right, before, she says. None of it, really, felt right. But you did, Robin. You do.

She doesn't say anything more, just yet. Instead she lifts the bed sheet – has to stand on her tiptoes – and then steps back with it bundled in her arms, the dress left spinning, slightly, like a ballerina in a music box.

I've been working on it since we got back from Devon, she says. It's something I tried on and liked, mostly, at that vintage place, but it needed some . . . tweaking. I let it out a bit, because I'll want to eat a lot of cake, on the day, obviously, and I talked with some textile artists about how to embroider into this particular fabric, which wasn't easy, like I'd thought it would be.

Note of worry in her voice, as she talks; longing for him to see what this means.

I broke a load of needles, she goes on. The material's so much thicker than it looks, but at the same time, I wanted it to feel lightweight, like I was wearing pyjamas, you know? And I've managed that, I think. I removed some of the underskirt, see, here. Then I started the embroidery, which is what took the time, really, because I got a bit carried away, but I couldn't tell you about it because I didn't want you to know until it was done.

Robin is still staring at the dress, as if he can't hear what she's saying.

I saw all those surprises you were planning, Nora tells him, in your notebook. And I just . . . wanted to do the same, for you. I didn't want you to think I'd marry you out of, I don't know, pity, or to smooth things over. Or in any sort of gung-ho, *why not*, reaction. I want to marry you because I really *want* to marry you, Robin.

She feels like she's botching this. Stumbling through it. Saying the word marry, too much.

That's what you were doing? he says. All those hours you've been working late?

Nora nods; skims the skirt with her fingertips. She would like him to touch it, too, or better yet, touch her. She wants to look into his face and watch him realise that she was not pulling back from him, before. On printed invites, maybe, and a shiny venue, deposits and harpists and fanfare and fuss. But not this. Not all the things that they share, which she has embroidered into the gown, by hand.

Do you like it, she asks him as it twirls, slowly, on the ceiling hook. Or is it . . . too much, do you think?

She had only meant to embroider one line, from their favourite film, along the inseam. Had then darned another into the hem, and had planned to stop there, but there was so much more that kept coming to her, like the lines in his notebook that must have kept coming to him. So she kept going. Adding in-jokes about bare feet and croissants and musicals, the phone number to their local takeaway, co-ordinates of the bench where he'd proposed with a ring that was not his but became hers. It was all there. On and on she had sewed, in the back room of her art café, for three weeks, instead of finalising her events timetable, instead of serving customers coffee or hosting workshops, because *this*, Nora, is more important, Shay had said, and she was right.

Is that . . . your yunomi mug, Robin asks.

Broken, but forever in our hearts, Nora jokes. Or on this dress, at least.

She thinks this moment of lightness might coax a smile out of him, but it only leads to more silence. Some kind of struggle, in his face. The dress hanging heavy between them.

I'm so sorry, Robin, she says again. I'm sorry if I've been

vague, instead of clear. But I've been thinking and planning and wanting so badly to make it perfect, wanting this thing we're doing to feel like *us*. And stuff with Freya and Josie and Bren got tangled up in the rush of it all, and I didn't know *how* I felt, until we slowed down, and I could catch my breath.

Robin looks at her, now. At last.

I want to do this, Robin, Nora tells him. But I don't want to do it with people judging, or questioning our decisions. I don't want to spend money we don't have on things we don't need, or catch my mother rolling her eyes, or pose for pictures when we *know* you could be taking better ones.

She pauses, still hoping for his smile.

I know you got so excited about an all-singing, all-dancing wedding day, she says. But I also know this proposal . . . this whole . . . *decision*, to spend our lives together, wasn't ever a decision, for me. It just happened. Which is something that scared me, before, but now I think that's the way it should be. Life happens, and you don't wait for it. And we haven't been waiting. We've been doing it, haven't we? And I want to *keep* doing it, just the same. I want to hang art on our walls and cook great meals and come home to you, every night, so we can go to bed early and stay up late talking and then complain we're tired because we stayed up late talking, and do it all again, and again, until we're old. I want this to be about me and *you*, Robin, not a big fussy day that gets away from us.

Her words are pouring out of her, and she'll keep going if she has to, but Robin steps towards her, presses his thumb to her mouth.

I know what you're going to say, he murmurs, and his pupils are huge, Nora thinks, dark and dilated. You're going to say we don't need to get married, after all, aren't you? That you can wear this dress, on a Friday night, or at birthday parties, and we can just go on being us, as we are. That we don't need to get married, to do that.

Nora tilts her head, so she can speak round his thumb.

No, she says. The opposite, actually. I think we should do it tomorrow. Just us.

Silence, again. Sunlight. Silk of the spiderwebs on the ceiling.

I never cancelled the registry office, Nora tells him. The legal bit we had to do, before the twenty-second? It's still happening. Our slot's at half past ten. And we'll need two witnesses, but I figured we could ask Goose and Shay, maybe, or just pull strangers off the street, like they do in the movies.

Robin steps back, looking stupefied, and it is funny, it is adorable, he is funny and adorable and too tall for this shed and too perfectly hers like he always has been, in his unbuttoned shirt with his uncombed hair, as if she'd woken him in the middle of the night.

You're asking me if I'll marry you?

I'm asking you if you'll marry me, Robin.

And there it is, finally. That big Robin smile. As he says well, he'll have to think about it. And she laughs, and throws her arms round his neck and he holds her close with her wedding dress beside them on its hanger, black thread and ivory lining and words and poems and the stuff of real love stories darned into this one picture-perfect moment that she has pulled off, in spite of everything, a moment that leaves no room for doubt, or stalling, or anyone else: for anything that's not in their arms, right now.

twenty-two

And it should end there, your story. In an ideal, animated movie-style ending, with an inciting incident, stated moral and arc, a feeling of satisfied contentment, credits rolling.

But it is the things you don't actually think about, *the things you don't see coming*, when you are worrying about deadlines or overexposure or the wrong shade of paint in the hall or the clogged gutters you never clean or the way she won't look you in the eye or how a stranger tells you, historically, he does not do the right thing – the *wrong* things – the actual, real-time, threatening things, are what take you down.

On your wedding day, of all days.

Crazy, that; how heartbreaking, how tragic, is what they'll say.

Because that low-level, long-term pain in your head? Turns orchestral, overnight.

You tried to tell Nora about it. Tried to call her as you stumbled back home but your phone was dead and then you were on your laptop searching for answers before sleep and then she was there, *proposing*. In the most glorious pressure point of your entire luck-filled life, of all the moments that do not flash before you like they say they will, but play out as a film that nobody else will see, flickering and then falling away.

Falling, still, as you get up and dress in your favourite shirt. Find your best shoes – are they your shoes – kiss your soon-to-be-wife on the forehead and tell her you'll see her at half ten and she stirs out of sleep, says good luck, because you'd promised to corral witnesses, most likely Goose and his flatmate whose name you forget. The flatmate who forced you to leave because he was playing his music so loud and you couldn't sleep for the pain and the drum and the bass but first, on this day, out your door, you'll make a stop. See a pharmacist or a doctor or one of the two you tell yourself as you leave her alone and the paint is rolling off the walls and you're on the bus into town to find your brother or the doctor and what is the difference what day is it where are you as the trees slip by and the buses drive on and the houses blur, early morning, tricks of the light, you were thinking about Peru and you both loved Paris, walls of pointillist paintings made out of needle-tipped pressure and pin-pricks and pain, so much pain.

Something wrong even as things are, finally, right.

Your last memory of the bus, not of Nora now or back then, but a tear in the film reel, a sentence, when you get

to the counter – you say it, and someone is saying things back, and you try to say more

but find that

you can't

twenty-three

Bren calls Nora, and she does not pick up. It is eight in the morning on a Tuesday, and he'd assumed she'd be on the train to work.

He looks out the window at the birds. Two wood pigeons. Starlings in the gutter, he can hear them, the scrape of clawed feet and kicked moss as it rings out.

He tries three times, then gives up. Turns to look at his rucksack, packed and bulging once more. Socks washed and ironed by his mother. Who irons socks, he said to her, last night. I do, pet, she said. It's my love language. Leave me be.

He'd wanted to speak to Nora this time. Not leave a message that might never get shared, or, now she has her own phone, send a hollow, impassive text. But he has to go. His flight is at one, he wants to be at the airport for half ten, he can hear his mother in the bedroom below, preparing to say goodbye. A drawer rolling open. Fresh tissue folded beneath her sleeve.

He'll try again once he's through security. *Call me*, he texts her. And then he's downstairs, his rucksack lugged behind him, and his mother is offering him breakfast like it is an ordinary day even though she knows that it isn't, because he had told her last night about his plan and his ticket and how he didn't want a fuss made, and he saw her glaze over as he showed her the adventure centre he was returning to, saw her mouth say lovely, even though it wasn't, to her.

So, Josie asks, after he's eaten a slice of toast to keep her happy, after he's checked he has his passport, one last time. Is this it, then?

This is what Nora had asked him, thereabouts, when he'd left her engagement party. And this provokes something in him. Déjà vu; a slow, upward swell of emotion. So much has happened in so short a time, he thinks. When for twelve years, he's scaled mountains and crossed ravines and skimmed atop the darkest, deepest waters, so he could avoid the real landscape of his life.

I guess I've got time for a coffee, he says.

And Josie beams with delight.

–

They take their coffees to the bottom of the garden. His mother has pulled two plastic chairs under the shade of the oak, and there is dew on the grass. Misty morning. Feels like summer; she says this; he agrees.

They sit, the steam rising off their cups.

I'll come home more often, he says to her. For Christmas, and stuff.

You don't have to, darling.

I know I don't.

Both of them, he thinks, reflecting on all the holidays he's missed. All the birthdays. His thirtieth. Her sixtieth. All the phone calls cut short, because there was nothing to say; when in fact there is so much to say, he can feel it like the earth under his feet, the ash he'd let sift through his hands. He thinks of New Zealand and how clean the air is there. How much there is to do and see, how distracted and entertained and exhausted he is, so much of the time, and then his mother says I love you, you know, and he looks up.

It's not that she doesn't say it. She says it often, at the end of phone calls, love you, by way of goodbye. But this feels different. Intentional.

Not just because you're my son, she says. And not just because I see your father in you, which I do.

Bren waits for the flare in his blood, at this, but it remains calm, like the river.

I love you because you saw me at my worst, Josie says. And I know that must have been terrible, growing up, Bren. I know you had to learn to care for yourself, too young. Or to rely on your dad instead of me. But despite that, and I know I've said it before, you knew I didn't need to be babied. You knew you could go and live your life, and leave me to live mine. And that fills me with strength, Bren, that has sustained me, more than anything, since he died.

They can hear the starlings from back here.

Scrabbling, still, in the gutter.

It brings me peace, in fact, his mother goes on, knowing that you're not hovering over me, but doing what makes you happy.

Bren looks past his mother, now, to the branches of the tree curving low over the roof of the garden shed. He thinks about how he and Nora used to jump off at this lowest point, career back to the house for snacks or else force their way through the gap in the hedge to get to the river behind. They swam in it, a few times, against Josie's wishes; Freya encouraged it; Jon pretended not to know.

I'm not sure I am happy, he says, and Josie's face drops, so he hastens to say it's all right. Really. Because surely knowing that, means he can try and do something about it.

He looks down at the soil packed hard around the roots.

His father there, now. A part of the world, down here, which is the same as the world out there, really, wherever he goes. It's all the same land, the same air.

I want to find someone, he says. Someone I can let in, or . . . open myself up to, I guess.

Someone that's not Nora? Josie asks, and he looks at her, then, lets out a breath that's part-laugh.

I don't know that I even let her in, half the time, he says. I think that's the problem, Mum. Even the person I'm closest to has always felt . . . far away.

And it is not what he's admitted, but what he's called her in that admission, which is not lost on either of them. Mum. There is a moment where they feel that, like the dew damp on their shoes, and then Josie says she's getting married today, Bren.

He doesn't quite understand.

She called Freya, first thing, she says. Who called me.

Bren tries to keep still. Fights the urge to stand, or to run.

You two, he says, in the end. You really share everything, don't you?

And Josie smiles. Says oh, you have no idea.

Bren pours his coffee dregs onto the grass. Wants to leave, now. Thinks of Nora, and this thing he is not a part of – how she is bungee jumping, like he'd told her to – how he doesn't get to care. But he does. And that caring, in itself, is not losing. Not a failure, like he'd always thought.

Well, the best man won, he says. Or lost. Depending on my job title, in absentia.

Josie laughs. Little, lovely sound.

Lovely.

It's catching, see.

You'll always be *my* best man, she says, as she puts her hand on his arm. And it is this simple, meaningless compliment that does it. That unleashes something that for so long, he's tamped down. He puts his hand on top of hers, and tells her he's sorry. I know you get why I left, when I did, he says. But I am sorry . . . that I never came back.

If you didn't come back, Josie says, then who am I talking to?

He is not sure he deserves to be let off the hook, like this, but then she says don't hold on to any guilt, here, Bren. There are other emotions that take priority.

Bren had thought, after his meltdown on the green, that he wouldn't be able to cry for at least another twelve years. But it's only been thirty-six hours and he feels a rise of internal colour and heat, presses his empty coffee cup, cool now, to the side of his face.

You're quite wise, really, aren't you, he says.

It's all this alone time, Josie says. Makes you reflective, and opinionated.

Or maybe that's just living next to Freya, he says, and she laughs again, and he recognises that laughter, from his childhood, because it *had* been there. Often enough. Between all the things he'd worked so hard to leave behind.

–

At ten o'clock, Nora is waiting in her wedding dress outside the registry office.

She got ready in her flat, called a cab, arrived on time. Half an hour early, even, but she'd been told in the email from the registrar that this was advisable.

Robin's shoes and shirt had been gone when she woke that morning. No note, just a vague, half-sleeping memory of him saying he'd see her later. Left to garner their witnesses; his brother, and his brother's flatmate, he'd suggested, last night, which doesn't surprise her; Shay would've kicked up a fuss, had to travel in from London; ease and spontaneity here was key, and she'd agreed. What *does* surprise her, though, is that her watch now reads five past the hour, and still, Robin is not here.

She looks up and down the street.

Strangers everywhere, traffic lights changing.

A flicker, then, of doubt. Worrying he is not quite over what they have not quite talked about; Bren, and the fight they had, and all the things she thought she'd resolved with her dress. This thing she'd made and is wearing, for this appointment she'd never cancelled – so lucky, so serendipitous, thank you universe, as Robin would say, thank you fortune and luck and aligning stars.

She'd thought that was, surely, enough.

That they'd hold hands and sign the papers and get lunch for two afterwards, walk along the river feeling happier than they'd ever done, the same as before but different, because they were a family now, officially, as if sharing some open secret with the world, he hers and she his, and yet he is nowhere to be seen.

–

She'd texted Shay a selfie that morning. After she'd slipped into her dress, her hair left loose over her ears. No ranunculi. No jewellery. And just as she was going to leave the house, Shay sent ten exclamation marks and then phoned her, said, mate, you're beautiful.

Nora couldn't help thinking how Freya would've scoffed at Shay's choice of word. Brides, only ever reduced to beauty, no matter what they do or stand for, make or say or care about, but she thanked her friend, all the same, not just for the compliment but because Shay had stopped teasing her about Bren, as soon as Nora had explained her plan. Who was chuffed, the night prior, when she texted her to tell her *he said yes*.

Go get married, already, Shay said. And give Robin a kiss from me.

Thanks, Shay. I will.

After they'd hung up, Shay sent her a stream of emojis, for luck; horseshoes interspersed with clovers, to which Nora replied: *no luck needed*. Three yellow stars. Then she'd grabbed her key and slid her phone into her pocket because of course, she wasn't going to spend weeks altering the wedding dress of her dreams, labouring over the memories and composition and the symbolism of the thing, and not give it pockets, in what world.

–

But maybe she *did* need the luck, because now it is quarter past and still, she's alone. She calls Robin for the fifth time, sixth, but he does not pick up. Goose doesn't answer, either. She tries to sign herself in at reception to save time, keep her panic at bay, but they say they can't move forward without the second attendee present so she steps back for another couple who are both there, both attendees, presumably, both committed and on time, a guy in a leather jacket and a woman with piano-playing hands who get to go ahead of her at the time she is supposed to be signing the marriage certificate, a piece of paper, everyone says, but a piece of paper, it turns out, that she'd really wanted to sign.

At half past ten, instead of signing that paper, Nora is standing outside again, still in her wedding dress and still waiting for the man she wanted to marry, who she'd thought had wanted to marry her.

Cars pass.

The traffic lights turn red.

Drivers glance at her through wound-down windows, a woman with a pram walks by and stares, just like the woman with the pianist hands back inside marrying her person, maybe, signing the paper that changes nothing and yet everything, else why would people do it, why would they want it, why does *she* want it, she has tried not to but she does.

She fiddles with a thread on her bodice while she waits, checks her phone.

Her worries began to ripple, some time ago. Expanding outwards.

And in a flourish of fear she pulls up Robin's name on the screen once again to text, this time, ask him what's happening, is everything okay, everything's *fine*, she thinks, she plans to say, and I thought this would prove that to you, she is thinking this as she types when her phone rings in her hand and it is not Robin or Goose or even Bren but an unknown number, no name.

A stranger.

A hospital.

She is told to come, quickly.

twenty-four

They say something about a bleed on his brain.

twenty-five

She goes where she is told to; the larger hospital three towns over. Flags down a cab and gets in with her embellished dress so showy, so ludicrous. Sun, so bright through the windows. She doesn't see it. Didn't. Looks ahead, the whole of her frozen and on fire as she counts down the thirty-seven-minute drive.

How, goes the thump of her heart. When.

His tiredness. Headaches.

Flashes of anger, so appropriate, so reasonable, that it had felt reflective of her own mind twisting to figure things out, in recent weeks.

The cab parks, and she pays. Sliding doors, green signs to a specialist unit where she heads for the woman at the desk. A woman who looks at her in her wedding dress, and Nora sees her face change, puzzled to pitying. Ironic, how this dress was meant to call for no fanfare and no fuss and yet it is the fussiest thing she could be wearing in a place like this, a place neither of them should be, not today, not ever.

The woman takes a long time looking at her computer after Nora gives her Robin's name. So long that Nora has to say look, she was called, she was told to come here, her partner had a headache, as if by saying this and not the words that had then been used, that that's all there is to worry about.

If you could sit down, the receptionist says, I'll let them know you're here.

Okay, Nora says, thank you. But, she says again, like I said, they called *me*. So maybe I could just go through?

The woman looks at her for a moment longer, as if bracing herself – bracing Nora – for what she's about to share.

He went to A and E this morning, she says. And had to have a CT scan, for severe head pain.

Nora cannot absorb this. Says okay?

Then they brought him straight here, the woman says, for emergency surgery.

Nora stares at her.

Surgery, she repeats, the word alien in her mouth, and the woman nods. Says when she has any further information, she will pass it along. That Nora should sit down, for now. And somehow, Nora does. Somehow, there is a slow motion that takes over what she is hearing, and she has heard a lot, these past two days, Josie revealing a big secret and Bren breaking down and she should not have cared, she should have been here, facing what matters, because what matters is what she'd never seen coming.

A bleed on the brain.

Emergency surgery.

Those hard truths, pressing against her own skull.

–

Milk, salt, rennet. The name of an art show they saw in Paris, the dates they'd met, moved in, bought their sofa. A joke he'd told about his own socks that she can't even recall but they refer to, daily, the relevance of it now lost but it doesn't matter, it's in their lore, *I look at you and I'm home*.

She reads all of these things she's embroidered into her

dress. Reads them until her vision blurs, and has to blink, look up. There is one other woman in the waiting room, with a baby on her knee. The mother is talking to the infant about the colours on the walls. Pointing out the specks on the floor, dots and triangles, which blur as well when Nora tries to focus, as she feels herself frozen or fading. Like time has stopped, like time won't finish, like she will forever be in this waiting room and that's why they're called what they are, because she will be waiting like this for the rest of time, as punishment for making *him* wait, maybe; she is sickness, she is fear, how is there Easter bunting taped to the wall and foiled chocolate eggs in a basket beneath posters that outline FAST and MHA, and then her phone rings, and it is Bren. It keeps on ringing, and the mother with the baby looks at her. And because she is trying to stay calm, because she is alone, because she doesn't know what else to do and she thinks she might die of fear but she can't think about the word die or what she is most afraid of, Nora slides to accept the call.

You picked up, Bren says, and he sounds as surprised as she is. I thought I'd be leaving you a voicemail.

She has no words to respond with. No concept of what she would say.

I'm at the airport, Bren tells her, and when she still doesn't say a word, he goes on: I'm flying back to Queenstown. Thought I'd phone you directly, this time. Just in case.

There's a lightness to his voice, but it's not funny. Has anything ever been? She can hear airport noises in the background, echoes and wheels and a hum of voices; her own still lost in her throat.

Mum said you were getting married today, Bren says.

Blurred eyes, blurred thoughts; blurred triangles on the hospital floor.

So . . . Bren says, and it's awkward; all so far away. I wanted to say congratulations, he says, as well as goodbye.

Nora opens her mouth, but what can she say.

What if saying it would make it more real.

Nora? Bren tries, and there's a tension to his voice, now, a note of impatience. Are you married now, then? Or are you –

But she hangs up, because she can't answer, can't say no, we're not, because *this*, so she stands up and goes back to the desk and before she can ask the receptionist assures her that she's been in touch with the doctors, that they know she is here.

If they know I'm here then why am I still waiting, Nora asks, and it's rude of her but she can't help it, the panic is sucking from her like a leech and they called *me*, she tells her, again.

The surgeon will come through when he's done, she is told. I'm sorry, Miss Harper, I know it's difficult, but try to wait. Can you call someone to come sit with you?

But the person she would call is in surgery – *emergency brain surgery* – so Nora just nods, turns away.

Back in the chair, she takes long, steadying breaths and tries to think. She will have to cancel their pizza reservation, for lunch. Make him something soothing, instead. Soup. He has always loved soup, the simplicity and the comfort of it, she will make a fresh soup for him every day of his life.

His life.

Hers.

She sits and waits, thinks she might die – no, can't think about dying – gets some water from the dispenser, hand shaking, sits back down.

The baby squawks.

The mother squints at her dress.

And when too much or no time at all has crawled by she

goes back to the receptionist who has nothing new to say. *How*, when it has been an hour, a year. She is wearing a locket and a lot of mascara and Nora is looking at it clagged on her lashes and trying to think of the right thing to say that is assertive but not rude like before and it is because of this, this mental dance she is doing between white-hot dread and social restraint taking up every cell of her whole self, that she does not feel him approach.

Nora, he says, but it is not the right voice. It is not Robin's.

And she turns to see that Bren is there, in the hospital lobby. Wearing his expedition rucksack, his face serious. Everything slows for her, then, even more than before.

Bren is here. Not on a plane, but here.

But not only does she not care, now she is openly panicking. How did you, she begins, and he holds up his phone, says he tracked her location. And he's not here to cause trouble – he sees her, in her dress, she's in her *dress* – he's here because she's his best friend, always has been, and when she didn't say a word earlier he knew that something was wrong, and when he looked and saw where she was he didn't think about it, really – he just left the airport, he just . . . came.

The baby is crying now. The mother stands to shush him, walks in back-patting circles around the room but this only makes him cry louder, and Bren glances at them, then at the signs on the wall, the double doors to the specialist unit before he looks back at Nora.

Why, uh, he says. Why are we here?

Robin had a headache, Nora tells him.

Bren frowns.

He's had a headache for a few days and he was going to meet me at the registry office, Nora says, and her voice is measured, somehow, robotic, but then they called me here.

Is he . . . all right?

I don't know, she says. And then she says it again, less measured, this time: I don't know.

Bren's frown deepens. Please go, she is about to say, *please*, Robin cannot see you here, today of all days – but it is as she is about to say this that a doctor comes down the hall and her heart is in her mouth with her stomach, because his eyes are not the eyes of a person who has something good to share.

She floats out of her body as she decides this.

Out of her embroidered wedding dress.

There is a slow, illuminated moment as realisation dawns, as it had on Robin yesterday in their garden shed. As he saw, finally, what she'd wanted him to see – but with eyes that have not been his own, these past few weeks, now that she thinks about it. The way they'd look at her, sometimes, like he did not know her. *I don't recognise you, Nora.* Angry outbursts, *you're being a child*, extreme exhaustion, *he's out cold.* But things have seemed hard and strange of late, weddings are hard, relationships are hard, and he is stressed and tired and she's both these things too, and that's normal, isn't it, that's life. This is a *blip*. A story they will tell on their anniversaries, remember when you got a headache and it turned out to be a brain bleed, madness, total madness, I love you, d'you want the last dumpling, and the doctor looks at her as she thinks all of this and confirms her name, are you Nora, and then he clarifies Robin's name, too.

He looks at her, this doctor. As he stands there in his surgical scrubs.

Looks at her and says that after the scans they took him straight into surgery, but there were complications, that the bleed on the brain was more significant than they had anticipated, and he is so very sorry, but that despite their best efforts, Robin has died.

There is a moment where nobody moves.

The baby cries. The mother soothes.

Bren touches her, on the elbow.

No, says Nora, shrugging him off. It was just a headache. He said he had a headache.

I am so very sorry, the doctor repeats.

No, she says, he was fine.

I understand this is a tremendous shock, the doctor says. Do you have someone I can call, or is your friend here – he glances at Bren – are you able to see her home? We can –

But we're getting married, Nora tells the doctor.

She turns to Bren, who is white, and she says it to him, too, as if he needs reminding: we're getting married.

There was a trauma, the doctor is saying, a trauma that must have occurred days, maybe even weeks ago? It caused a chronic subdural haematoma. And they could have drained the bleed, they did try, it's so rare, with a bleed that severe, that he was able to walk himself into A and E like he did, and do you know anything about that, Nora? What might have caused it?

No, Nora is saying, there was nothing, but the truth is she wasn't paying attention when it mattered. None of us do, she will realise later, when her world is not falling into the black hole of itself, and this all runs through her head, the reality of what could and might occur because while the small dramas unfold – the family arguments and passing comments and daily pressures of not-dones and what-ifs and maybe-tomorrows – while that all plays out, the big things, the unnamed storms, the unexpected rolling darkness could be hurtling your way and you wouldn't even know it, wouldn't ever – until that frozen, light-switch moment standing in a hospital, wearing your wedding dress beside the wrong person – see it coming.

twenty-six

This is what Nora imagines.

What she sees happening, as if on film, as she floats out of her body, time paused but also on fast forward as the doctor comes down the hall.

In reality, he stops in front of her, this doctor in his scrubs who confirms her name and then Robin's. He says what he says about the brain bleed. He says what he says about the trauma occurring, several weeks ago, and she sees Bren's staggered white face, she sees that he is hearing what she is hearing, but not imagining what she is imagining, that's all owed to her deep-set, private panic that does not actually come to pass, time frozen, worst-case scenario, flooding like a burst bank in her head.

What he actually says is that the procedure went well.

That it is a waiting game, now, to see how he recovers, that the anaesthesia will wear off soon, and then Robin will be awake.

Alive.

Are you all right, Miss Harper. Do you need to sit down. Do you understand what I'm saying, here; this really is the best we could have hoped for, at this point, he's so lucky he got here when he did, a marvel, really, that he was still walking and talking with that build-up of fluid in his brain. It's so rare, in a man his age, quite something – if he'd been a year or two younger, even, it could have been a different story, something to do with the space between the skull and the brain, widening with age – it's lucky, again, so lucky.

Lucky.

The only word that makes sense in her head.

She will sew it into her dress. Carry it, always, as if it's stitched into her heart.

The doctor says some more things, mostly to Bren because Nora can't follow, says he'll be back soon with more information, that they should take a seat, call loved ones, if they need to, and Bren finds his voice, Bren is the one to talk first, Bren is the one who asks if she can see him, who says they are meant to be getting married, today, and the doctor says yes, but only her; only family; and Bren says he'll wait, tells her to go.

–

How did this happen, Goose asks Nora an hour later, both of them beside the hospital bed. Machines bleeping. Shadows striped through the blinds. Robin is out of it, heavy from the anaesthetic, the near-death brain injury that he survived because he is lucky, got himself to A and E just in time, wandered to a pharmacist that morning for extra-strength painkillers and that pharmacist sent him straight to the hospital.

Nora will bake this pharmacist a cake, every year, for the rest of her life. She'll offer to make her wedding dress, too, when she sees the small diamond ring on her left hand the day that she goes to thank her, holds her, cries, tells her thank you, over and over.

For now, though, she is sitting in her own dress with Robin's brother by his bedside, and Bren has missed his flight and left the hospital to make calls, gather supplies, because that is what being there for her, right now, has to look like, and there's nothing like a near tragedy, a near miss, to show someone what kind of person they are: what kind of person they want to be.

–

You know what I like about hospitals, Goose says. Nora raises her eyes from Robin's face, unable to conceive of an answer.

The vending machines, he says. They always have the really retro stuff you don't ever see anywhere else.

Like what, asks Bren, who is sitting by the window. He's pretended to be Robin's brother, too, to be allowed in; has not left Nora's side, other than to make the calls that she can't. Brought her water, tea and a packet sandwich she hasn't been able to eat, which Goose has devoured instead.

Caramacs, Goose says. For one.

Yes, Bren says. I forgot about those.

Right? And Pom-Bears.

My god.

And Nik Naks, Goose says, but the really weird flavour. Scampi and lemon, I mean, what is that.

Something that shouldn't be in a crisp packet, Bren agrees.

And yet still tempts me, Goose says, every time.

Nora is looking at Robin's face again, only half listening. He could be sleeping; *is* sleeping. The machine steady, bleeping. His brain bled out, but drained clean.

Bren says he needs them in his life. Like now.

Goose asks him to get two packets. Three, if Nora wants some.

I don't want any Nik Naks! she says, because she is astounded at the pair of them, at how they are talking about such things.

I didn't have you down as one of those brides that wouldn't eat anything on her wedding day, Goose says.

Stop, Nora says, her voice thin. Please.

Bridezillas, man, Goose says, to Bren. Could you get me a Lucozade, too?

–

While Bren does that, Goose takes a call from his parents, who do not live nearby, who are making their way here. Robin's mum calls every half an hour, in case of change, and then that change comes. While Nora is alone with him, not moving. Her hand on his. The afternoon light, fading, like their supposed wedding day, when he stirs, and opens his eyes.

They are both still for a moment as Robin adjusts. Nora afraid that if she moves, she will break it, this thing that is happening, this real-life miracle, this paramount, perfect vision of him waking from sleep to look at her, the way he has done every morning for the last nine years, and will do, for years to come, and then he smiles and says hey, don't cry.

–

He – what?

He almost *died*?

I think so, says Bren, in his mother's kitchen. It was touch and go.

Why didn't you say so, on the phone?!

Nora didn't want anyone to panic.

Panic! Too right I'd have panicked! My son-in-law, dressed to the nines for his wedding day, ends up having brain surgery, instead?! Panic ensues! Panic is appropriate! Panic is the only plausible reaction!

Freya, calm down.

Stop panicking, you mean?

It is late. There are two plates on the table where the mothers have shared dinner without him; presuming he was on a plane somewhere over South-East Asia, by now. Bren has collected things that Nora might need, from next door: a toothbrush, a change of clothes from the selection she leaves at her mother's, and he's just downing a glass of water, the sound of the dishwasher normalising the otherwise surreal set of circumstances that have brought him back home.

It was you, wasn't it, Bren, Freya says, as Bren puts his glass down. You poisoned him, as a part of your master plan, to make Nora yours?

But Bren cannot even laugh.

Something has happened to him, since that moment in the waiting room. Since he saw everything he had wondered about, crystallised into a real possibility. Nora, without Robin. Nora, with her own world collapsing. And everything has slowed for him, since.

Everything has clarified.

Freya stands up, then, and pats down the pockets of her dungarees. Bren is leaning on the kitchen counter, his rucksack abandoned somewhere. At the hospital, he thinks. In the waiting room where he'd left it. He realises, with detached interest, that this doesn't matter to him.

Where are my car keys, Freya asks.

In the bamboo bowl, Josie guesses, in your hall?

I think the two of them might need some space, actually, Bren says.

Jackson Pollocks to that, Freya says. You give people space when they're grieving, or heartbroken. Not when they don't die and you need to tell them how glad you are about that.

The surgeon said he needs rest, Bren insists.

We can be restful company, can't we? I'd like to see him, this son-in-law of mine! And my daughter, in her wedding dress.

They didn't actually get married, Bren says.

But for all intents and purposes, Freya says, today is their wedding day. D'you know, she says to Josie, I never realised how *okay* I would feel about Nora marrying Robin, until it transpired she might not.

Same, Bren thinks. But does not say.

Shall we take grapes? Josie asks, after a short silence.

Nobody wants grapes, Josephine, Freya says. A stiff drink, maybe. Champagne? What is it one gifts, at a wedding, where nobody got married but nobody died, either?

There is a longer silence then, as the reality of this lands for all of them. That lucky cat, being lucky. Waving its left-hand paw.

–

Goose says he'll come back tomorrow, with their parents, first thing. Please don't, Robin groans, but it is tentative, his heart not in it, because the realisation of all that has happened – or nearly happened – is setting in. At Nora's request, Bren has staved off a visit from Freya and Josie, too, so once Goose is gone the two of them are left alone. To try to sleep. To hold each other, knowing that sleep won't come.

You couldn't write this, Nora says, curled onto the bed beside him. She is still in her wedding dress, too tired to get changed into the clothes Bren had dropped off.

You could stitch it, though, Robin says. Maybe along that bit, there.

He points to a swathe of fabric where there is space for something more. A new date. A new line. A new part of their story. She likes the negative space between the black thread:

could've kept stitching, forever, but she'd had to draw a line somewhere, show him the work when it felt done. Except they aren't done. Won't ever be. That's the point of a shared story, she's realised.

Life advice, Robin poses, tracing the blank space at her waist. Never clean the gutters, unsupervised.

Or be extremely careful on ladders, Nora suggests.

Will I have seven years' bad luck, now?

That's broken mirrors, Nora says. It's walking under a ladder that's bad.

Falling off one doesn't seem the best plan, either.

Not when you ignore the blinding head pain that comes afterwards.

It wasn't blinding, Robin reasons. My elbow hurt more, at the time, and the headache was sort of manageable, until yesterday. I just thought it was approaching forty, maybe. Or the wedding, or work. The whole Bren debacle, adding a bit of undue stress.

A bit of undue subdural haematoma, Nora says.

Those are big words for an implausibly big day, Robin says, and she agrees. He strokes her hair as if she is the one who needs soothing, here. She lies in his arms and thinks he will soon slip into sleep, waits for his breathing to change.

Speaking of ladders, she whispers, and Robin says mm?

Do you remember that personality test, she says, with the ladder and the cube and the – horse, they say, in unison, yeah, Robin says, of course.

What was your ladder like, again?

Robin tilts his head on the pillow. He's not even bandaged with gauze; looks normal, apart from the shaved patch on his skull.

It was a rope ladder, he says. Hanging through a hole in the ceiling.

Nora makes a light noise, an ah, yes.

What do you think that means?

That I'm a humble sort of chap, Robin says. Rickety, a bit bungling, maybe, on first meeting. But sturdier than I look.

Small laugh from her, then. Swell of love.

But I think the hole in the ceiling's important, Robin says. It's a ladder that reaches into another room. Beyond what we can see.

He keeps combing through her hair with his hand. Soft, repetitive. Like he's hoping it might send her to sleep.

What's in the other room, she asks him.

Guess we'll find out, he says, his body warm and solid against hers. They drift off, soon after, dreams flickering to the bleep of machines. It is not how they'd envisioned spending their wedding night, although it is not really their wedding night, not yet, a ceremony has not happened, after all, but when they stir at four in the morning, Robin murmurs hey, Nora.

And he proposes something, right then. It is simple and they are alone and filled up with the heady sudden rightness of it and there is a hospital chapel down the hall and they are both dressed for the occasion, or at least, he is after she helps button his shirt.

Are you okay to walk, she asks him, and he says absolutely. That the doctor said motor function should be normal. See?

So they walk to the door. Their passports, which she'd had with her for the registry office, still stowed in her dress pockets. Out the door, down the hall, Robin holding on to her arm. Something old, she says, nodding at his brogues, which of course he had thought to put on the previous morning, even though he'd been in incomparable pain. Something new?

Your dress?

Great. And something borrowed, and blue?

You have your blue eye, Robin says, as they follow the signs for the chapel. Daybreak through the window, burnt orange staining the cloud. They turn a corner and pass a small waiting room, and the colour of the dawn is matched by the red of someone's hair, a guy in a white T-shirt, cargo trousers and hiking boots, sitting on his phone at half four in the morning, a coffee cup, lidless, by his foot.

Robin sees him before Nora does. Stops walking, so that she glances up at him with concern, only for him to nod in Bren's direction. And as she looks over, Bren looks up, too, and then he says oh. Hi.

I thought you went home, Nora says.

I came back, Bren says, with a shrug. In case you needed anything.

Oh, Nora says.

Bren puts his phone down on the chair beside him. He is looking at them both, not just Nora; acknowledging Robin, as well. His face is drawn with tiredness, his hair mussed from where he has tried and failed, presumably, to sleep on the foam leather chair.

Have you been discharged? he asks, and Nora looks at Robin, who tilts his head.

Not quite, Robin says. In fact. Could we borrow you, Bren?

–

And so Bren Ferguson is the sole witness as Nora and Robin are wed – or blessed – by the hospital chaplain. He stands in the front pew in his hiking boots with his sleepless eyes and missed flight, his heart half numbed. He only moves when the chaplain asks if they have rings, which they do not. They were going to buy them afterwards, Nora says. And then. Well.

And then, Robin says, gesturing to his head.

And for a second Bren thinks about taking out his hoop earring and asking if that'll do, for now, for the symbolism, or whatever, but it feels a step too far and this is far enough so instead he scratches his arm, swallows, hard, as Nora says who needs rings when you don't have a marriage licence, and the chaplain seems enchanted by their good humour. Most hospital blessings are probably for different, more devastating reasons, Bren muses, as he watches him false-marry them both. Bedside ceremonies. Out of time. But this morning it's just two people, deciding to share their life, because they can. Because they were always going to.

The chaplain riffs a little, says some things about love and commitment and faith. There is a small stained-glass window behind them, a wooden cross on the wall, in the weirdest, most un-Nora-like scene he could imagine, which is why it works, in fact. That and her patchwork dress, Robin in his silk shirt and smart shoes, a shaved patch on his head. Bren has always known, in a part buried inside himself, that Nora – cold-swimming, tree-climbing, art-making Nora – was too special for normal, and this ceremony is anything but.

It is strangely brief. Bren thinks, as he watches them saying their vows, that he'll feel something significant when it happens. Like he's been expecting to for months, each time he's turned it over in his mind. But just as he'd felt when summiting a mountain or landing somewhere new; just as when he's walked a shore at twilight, pitched a tent above the cloud or paddled into a fjord; just as one thing has never brought him that full gratification, that wholeness he's been looking for – he feels something merely evolve. It is not nothing, but nor is it momentous. Just the sense of one moment in his life sliding into another. Ashes scattered. Feelings shared. I loved you, I loved you too. On we go.

And we're done, the chaplain says, before he claps.

There is a pause in which Bren is slow to start clapping, too, makes a crowing noise like a lost boy because this moment seems to deserve more than four pat-a-cake palms, and Nora and Robin walk past him down the aisle, holding hands, bashful and cry-laughing and Bren gives them a minute alone, still clapping, before he follows behind.

–

Well, Nora says, back in the hospital hallway. Let's get you to bed.

Nora! Robin says. Don't be so *forward* in front of our wedding guests.

Guest, singular, Bren says.

Just the low-key wedding I wanted, Nora jokes, and they all stand there for a second, not knowing quite what to say. Thank yous. Touch of an arm, squeezed hands. And when Nora turns to walk Robin back to his room, Bren wonders whether he should go, too, but instead, he sits back down on the chair from before.

Pulls his phone out, puts it away again. Taps his foot.

A nurse walks past, a doctor, and then when a second doctor passes he says excuse me and stands up.

She is middle-aged, has red hair, like his. Stern eyes.

Sorry, he says. D'you mind if I ask you something?

And the doctor doesn't say yes or no but doesn't keep walking, either, so he says years ago, my dad had this heart attack. And, he. He died.

The doctor's eyes soften, somewhat, but before she can speak, Bren says I was there with him. I saw it happen. And I feel like.

He has to swallow, several times.

I've always felt like I could've done something, he says. When I turned him over, he was looking up at me, and I should've helped. But I didn't know what to do, I just yelled, and freaked out, and stayed with him. And when the medics came, they performed CPR for like . . . over an hour. Just in front of me, and my mum, for so long. And I can't help but think if I'd done that, then maybe . . . he wouldn't have died. But he did. He died.

The doctor clears her throat and asks some questions. How old was he, had he had a history of heart problems, no. Had he vomited, yes. The doctor, nodding. Bren answering as if he's far away, looking down at himself from elsewhere.

Sounds like a myocardial infarction, the doctor tells him. Sadly it's more common than you'd think, in men in their fifties who seem otherwise healthy: sudden death caused by MI. Cardiac arrest.

Bren nods; this much he knew.

But *sudden* death is key, here, she says. The medics are trained to deliver CPR for a really long time in an otherwise young, healthy-seeming person, but in reality? There was nothing they – or you – could have done.

Bren looks at her like she's the sun.

Sometimes, she says, these things just happen. And it's nobody's fault.

Yeah, he says. Thanks. Thank you.

She nods, again. And then she walks down the corridor without another word and he sits back down. Feels his world moving into a new version of itself, just like it had in the chapel, before, and then not long afterwards Nora is back in front of him, looking as dishevelled and exhausted as Bren feels.

I've never been so shattered, she says as she sits down beside him. And at the same time, so unbel*iev*ably awake.

How's he doing, Bren asks, and Nora says amazingly. The doctor says he can't work for a while, he'll need to take six to eight weeks to rest, but most people make a full recovery. And he seems himself, I think. More himself than he's seemed in weeks.

Bren says that's great. They sit in silence for a while, Bren thinking of the doctor, and the long-ago past; Nora thinking of the present or the more recent past, presumably, because of what she says next.

It's crazy, isn't it? she says. That we were all so caught up in other things that we didn't see what was so . . . obvious.

It wasn't that obvious, though, Bren says. I've been googling it. So many people do the same thing, with this. Fall while they're skiing, or on a night out, drunk, then pin the symptoms on other stuff. Heatstroke. Bad colds. Being new parents, not getting enough sleep.

Worrying your wife is gonna leave you before the wedding, Nora says.

Yeah, Bren says, and they sit in more silence with that word, *wife*, as the hospital wakes up around them. A telephone rings. Doors are pushed open, swing closed.

Thank you for not getting on that plane, Nora says.

It wasn't a big deal, Bren says, but she says that it was. And he can't take it, this gratitude of hers. Looking at him with such understanding and love, as she so often does; as he so often hasn't deserved.

I dated this psychologist once, he tells her. A beat, between them.

I thought you didn't date?

Took her as a lover, then, he says, and they both snort, as another nurse walks by with a clipboard. She told me about this thing, he says, called Counterfactual Curiosity. Which I've been thinking about a lot, lately. Like how your life could've gone a different way, if you'd boarded a different boat.

Nora does not move. Just looks at him.

I would've married you, Nora, Bren tells her. If I'd boarded a different boat.

Long look, between them, then. A long, indefinable something like relief; but a relief that also hurts, if pain can be sweet, somehow, a comfort. And Nora stands up, her dress rustling around her and then around him because she drops herself into his lap, wraps her arms around his neck and leaves a hard kiss on the top of his head. She smells of hospitals and linen and citrus. Says his name, and he can't see her face but he can feel her warmth, feel the solid soft Nora of her, pressing him close.

I love you, she says. You'll always be. Well. We'll always be us.

Yeah, he says.

Which is something nobody else could come close to, she says. I chose my boat. But it doesn't mean I unchose you. You know?

And he does.

For so long, I wanted to be the person that could take your pain away, she says, into his hair, or give you what you wanted. But I didn't know what that looked like.

How could you, Bren says, when I didn't, either.

This shared truth binds them, like a rope; or something stronger, more invisible, like spider silk. Then she kisses his head again and gets up. Stands there, looking at him, in her wedding dress. Covered in stories he does not know.

I know it's waiting for you, she tells him. Whatever it is. A person, or a calling, that'll make you feel most like yourself. And then you won't need to keep looking.

He nods. Once. And she does, too, in the direction of Robin's room.

I'm gonna, she says, and he says yeah.

Changes, he calls after her. By 2Pac.

She turns, as she's pushing open the swing door.

My karaoke song, he says. Tell Robin for me?

Her smile, then, over her shoulder, that perfect shoulder he'd not noticed years before, and she's gone. And it is as he's leaving the hospital, typing a message to his mother to say he'll be back for breakfast, that Nora's text comes through in reply, and for once he isn't hoping for anything, isn't hoping for a change of heart or an answer to a question as she says: *Historically, Bren?*

Looks like you do the right thing.

twenty-seven

Six weeks, you have to spend at home. A recovery period which you repurpose as an indoor honeymoon, hibernating in the house. Breakfast in bed and shared bathwater and twisted sheets. Soup, because you love soup. Croissants, of course, seeing as Henry who runs the bakery down the road hears what happened and plies you with pastry because you are his best customers and karma is a freshly baked pain au chocolat handed over, warm, in a brown paper bag.

Get-well cards and bouquets of flowers pour through the door. Niche animated movies play on repeat except when you're sitting in the May-June sunlight in the yard; the day you sign the official marriage paperwork you watch *Song of the Sea* with takeaway noodles and fall asleep by nine, wake to your wife, still sleeping, beside you, in one of your old T-shirts she's stolen without asking.

And throughout this period, you print photographs, because it's you: and you itch to work, to preserve, to capture what's occurred. Task your brother with finding a leather-bound album with the perfect page thickness.

Tack in the engagement party invite which Nora inked at her craft desk, three months ago. Photographs of the pair of you at various parties and on nights out and nights in, at graduation, when she opened her café with Shay, when she first met Horace who looks like a baby horse, not a dog, when you went to God's Own Junkyard with Freya. And amid the photos, Nora also Sellotapes in two receipts. One for the pizza order from the party, and one for the bagels the day you did not propose but she said yes yes yes, by the river.

You remember all of that, before the fall. Before the long, low-level headaches and fatigue. Before you stopped recognising familiar things, your keys, her face – a symptom, you've since learned, of the fluid that built against your brain – before you lost the *you* in your emotions – became forthright or argumentative or else disorientated, unable to fathom what was wrong.

Things had blurred, for a while, but are now, thank the universe, the luckiest stars, back in focus.

You turn a page while she makes lunch. While Motown music plays from the speaker. Your hospital bracelets are here, too, tacked in beside a selfie taken outside the hospital chapel. No flowers. No bow tie. No champagne flutes or big hats but a shaved head and a walking miracle and Nora's eyes, half closed in a smile. A redhead behind the camera, taking the picture. Say subdural haematoma, he'd said. And you'd both laughed.

Like the first time you saw her. She was laughing at something someone had said, and you did not know what she was laughing at; did not know what was coming.

Just as you do not, now.

Which leaves space for a new photograph, in the album.

Which is lucky, again. Or miraculous. Synonyms, really, for the same thing, and if you were a songwriter or a poet you'd write something down about that, but you're just a photographer, just a normal guy, just a husband with a brain that didn't bleed out and a heart that wouldn't give up on what it knew, and that certainty alongside all the unknowns is the real luck, you think. The real lasting miracle, here.

twenty-eight

Nora is in her living room when she sees the email in her inbox. It's been there for days but she'd not noticed it; there have been things to do, people to tell, he nearly died, we got married, I know, it's mad, but it's life.

It is weeks after they made it home. Weeks after they signed the paperwork at the registry office so that everything is formalised and finished. Though is anything ever formal or finished when you're human, she wonders aloud, to Shay and Robin and Freya, which prompts different answers, different conversations. She wonders the same thing again, as she works from the sofa, tonight. Robin is making dinner after insisting he was fine to do so; he feels right as rain, although when does rain ever feel right, right as sunlight, right as rainbows, he has decided to repurpose the phrase and she has decided to let him.

She is darning something into a sock; one of the many pairs she will soon stock in her art café that'll sell like warm buttered croissants. Items of clothing she will end up selling into gallery gift shops, which will turn into private commissions alongside her day job, though she does not know this yet. So she puts down her needle and checks her emails and sees his name beside the subject line: LIFE CHANGED (AGAIN), and opens it, to read.

He has attached a photograph of some shortbread he's sampled in Scotland.

There were mountains to climb much closer to home, he told her, the day that he left. Munros to bag in honour of his dad, and this shortbread, he tells her now, is *incredible*, a family recipe that's been handed down through generations and he's going to send her some so she'll be able to recreate it, preferably for Christmas, when he's next home.

It'll be nice to see you, he's typed. Both of you.

Meaning her and Robin, or her and Josie; she is not sure; it does not matter.

She replies alongside the clang of saucepans in the kitchen, Robin singing to the song on the radio. Says yes, us too. Can't wait. Then she updates him on Robin's progress, says Freya comes over almost daily, brings fresh tomatoes and big attitude and Josie sends bread and cake and handwritten notes and between them they're saying we love you, we're glad you're alive, and that, she thinks, is the best thing, really; that being married is not the tragedy her mother had feared; that there are – were – far worse things out there.

I've been thinking a lot about our mothers, she types back to Bren. How remarkable it is that they're still friends.

She knows he will not fully understand this, because some things are meant to stay secret. Some things won't be conceivable to someone who took twelve years to process his grief, or to forgive himself; he's unlikely to comprehend the layers and shades of what love might look like between two people.

Between three.

But she sends it anyway. Ends the email with a kiss because he did, and thinks about him, and his stupid gold earring, and his red hair and green eyes and sits on the sofa with a warmth inside her when Robin calls out, ready?

And she is. Leaves her phone face-down on the cushions,

wine poured, napkins out. Hope you're hungry, says her husband, as he lifts the pasta out of the pan, saying he added some of Freya's peacevines, for pizzazz. Smiling at her, mostly, Nora thinks, because he found a reason to use the word pizzazz at the dinner table. And they sit down and they eat, and talk. Another evening as the sun sinks behind the shed in the yard, weeds growing between the brick. Gutters cleaned. Windows open, to let in the summer breeze. Life happening, in this kitchen, and beyond.

Acknowledgements

Firstly, my gratitude must go to my excellent editors, all of whom I have been so lucky to work with on this novel. To my first reader and dear friend Clio Cornish, who bookended this process, and never ceases to amaze me with how she can read between the lines, balancing (unhinged) enthusiasm with such professional integrity. To my fellow perfectionist Lily Cooper, whose keen eye, emotional acumen and unparalleled work ethic continue to stagger me, but mostly for her understanding of what this book wanted to be – and for never once wavering in her passion for this project. To Jeramie Orton for her honesty, vision and, most crucially, for granting me the time and space to (re)write, and also to Stella Newing, who gave me the lift and insight I needed after an early draft. Thank you, so much, to all of you.

My appreciation, as ever, must go to my excellent agent Ariella Feiner, for maintaining her stellar belief in my writing, and to Amber Garvey, Gemma Craig, Nikhil Harikrishnan, Amy Mitchell, Lily Down and Melissa Tombere, for all their hard work behind the scenes.

To my fellow writers Katie Bishop and Georgia Leighton, who understand this process better than anyone; thank you for being there at the end of the phone. To the ones who understand *me* better than anyone: Tom Davis, Emma Green, Jessica Lockyer-Palmer, Hannah Cresswell, Helen Moon and my parents, for sitting outside my door, asking all the right questions, and sometimes no questions at all.

I also want to thank Liesel Thomas and Katy Loftus

for their ongoing creative counsel, Harriet Evans for her (much-needed) insight, and Rachel Harris for her pertinent reflections during such a pivotal period: you were – are – all such solid sounding boards.

My heartfelt thanks to those I've worked with at various stages of the publishing process: Natalie Grant, for her admin support and organisation; Shan Morley-Jones, for her thorough and patient copyedits; Riana Dixon, for always being so clear and brilliant; and to the rest of the team at Michael Joseph: Kelly Samler, Frankie Banks, Lily Evans, Courtney Bright and Rachel Myers. You're marvels.

A book, of course, is not complete without a cover, and I'm indebted to the three talented artists who worked on this one. Lee Motley, I loved your early designs, and Lauren Wakefield, your vision for this new route was simply perfect. Thank you, as well, to Maud Saint-Arroman, for giving us permission to adapt your beautiful painting, which not only looks but *feels*, to me, like the inside of this novel.

As for the details: thanks to Mia Hilborn and Neil Turpin, who answered my many questions about marriage certificates, blessings and legal ceremonies. Thank you once again to Flic Box, this time for her notes on the Hampstead Ponds (and the non-negotiable cake stop that comes afterwards). Thank you as well to the ever-inspiring Maria Coffey, who introduced me to the concept of counterfactual curiosity, and to Gavin, for sowing the early seeds of this idea.

A huge thank you to the medical professionals, too: Dr Tom Stewart, for answering my continual questions on the human heart, and for putting me in touch with the neurosurgeon Mr Amar Saxena, to whom I extend my greatest respect and gratitude for talking to me about the brain, and the rarity – but possibility – of certain events that play out in this book. Thank you as well to Susan Smillie, who told me her own story over a cup of tea by the sea, and all the others who shared their accounts online, which backed up all she told me. Any medical errors are down to dramatic licence in the writing of fiction, although I tried my best to keep it closely aligned to the experiences I'd read about.

Once more, I'm sending love and appreciation to Kate for sitting with me from the start, and for her many luminous suggestions while I wrote. My deepest thanks to Helen, as well, for supporting me through the changing seasons of this book, and for being there, unquestioningly, when I most needed her.

And finally, to my husband Clive, again. Always. For all of it; the long drives, the fresh bread, the problem-solving and for the life inside and outside of this book. Thank you doesn't quite cover it.